Catherine Cookson was born in Tyne Dock, the illegitimate daughter of a poverty-stricken woman, Kate, whom she believed to be her older sister. She began work in service but eventually moved south to Hastings where she met and married Tom Cookson, a local grammar-school master. At the age of forty she began writing about the lives of the working-class people with whom she had grown up, using the place of her birth as the background to many of her novels.

Although originally acclaimed as a regional writer – her novel *The Round Tower* won the Winifred Holtby award for the best regional novel of 1968 – her readership soon began to spread throughout the world. Her novels have been translated into more than a dozen languages and more than 50,000,000 copies of her books have been sold in Corgi alone. Fifteen of her novels have been made into successful television dramas, and more are planned.

Catherine Cookson's many bestselling novels established her as one of the most popular of contemporary women novelists. After receiving an OBE in 1985, Catherine Cookson was created a Dame of the British Empire in 1993. She was appointed an Honorary Fellow of St Hilda's College, Oxford in 1997. She was appointed an Honorary Fellow of St Hilda's College, Oxford in 1997. For many years she lived near Newcastle-upon-Tyne. She died shortly before her ninety-second birthday in June 1998.

'Catherine Cookson's novels are about hardship, the intractability of life and of individuals, the struggle first to survive and next to make sense of one's survival. Humour, toughness, resolution and generosity are Cookson virtues, in a world which she often depicts as cold and violent. Her novels are weighted and driven by her own early experiences of illegitimacy and poverty. This is what gives them power. In the specialised world of women's popular fiction, Cookson has created her own territory'

BOOKS BY CATHERINE COOKSON

NOVELS

Kate Hannigan
The Fifteen Streets
Colour Blind
Maggie Rowan
Rooney
The Menagerie
Slinky Jane
Fanny McBride
Fenwick Houses
Heritage of Folly
The Garment
The Fen Tiger
The Blind Miller
House of Men
Hannah Massey
The Long Corridor
The Unbaited Trap
Katie Mulholland
The Round Tower
The Nice Bloke
The Glass Virgin
The Invitation
The Dwelling Place
Feathers in the Fire
Pure as the Lily
The Mallen Streak
The Mallen Girl
The Mallen Litter
The Invisible Cord
The Gambling Man
The Tide of Life
The Slow Awakening
The Iron Façade
The Girl
The Cinder Path
Miss Martha Mary Crawford
The Man Who Cried
Tilly Trotter
Tilly Trotter Wed

Tilly Trotter Widowed
The Whip
Hamilton
The Black Velvet Gown
Goodbye Hamilton
A Dinner of Herbs
Harold
The Moth
Bill Bailey
The Parson's Daughter
Bill Bailey's Lot
The Cultured Handmaiden
Bill Bailey's Daughter
The Harrogate Secret
The Black Candle
The Wingless Bird
The Gillyvors
My Beloved Son
The Rag Nymph
The House of Women
The Maltese Angel
The Year of the Virgins
The Golden Straw
Justice is a Woman
The Tinker's Girl
A Ruthless Need
The Obsession
The Upstart
The Branded Man
The Bonny Dawn
The Bondage of Love
The Desert Crop
The Lady on My Left
The Solace of Sin
Riley
The Blind Years
The Thursday Friend
A House Divided

THE MARY ANN STORIES

A Grand Man
The Lord and Mary Ann
The Devil and Mary Ann
Love and Mary Ann

Life and Mary Ann
Marriage and Mary Ann
Mary Ann's Angels
Mary Ann and Bill

FOR CHILDREN

Matty Doolin
Joe and the Gladiator
The Nipper
Rory's Fortune
Our John Willie

Mrs Flannagan's Trumpet
Go Tell It To Mrs Golightly
Lanky Jones
Nancy Nuttall and the Mongrel
Bill and the Mary Ann Shaughnessy

AUTOBIOGRAPHY

Our Kate
Catherine Cookson Country

Let Me Make Myself Plain
Plainer Still

CATHERINE COOKSON

THE HARROGATE SECRET

CORGI BOOKS

THE HARROGATE SECRET
A CORGI BOOK : 0 552 14787 7

Originally published in Great Britain by Bantam Press,
a division of Transworld Publishers

PRINTING HISTORY
Bantam Press edition published 1989
Corgi edition published 1990

9 10

This book is set in Linotron 11/12pt Century Schoolbook by
Goodfellow & Egan Cambridge Ltd.

Corgi Books are published by Transworld Publishers,
61–63 Uxbridge Road, London W5 5SA,
a division of The Random House Group Ltd,
in Australia by Random House Australia (Pty) Ltd,
20 Alfred Street, Milsons Point, Sydney, NSW 2061, Australia,
in New Zealand by Random House New Zealand Ltd,
18 Poland Road, Glenfield, Auckland 10, New Zealand
and in South Africa by Random House (Pty) Ltd,
Endulini, 5a Jubilee Road, Parktown 2193, South Africa.

Reproduced, printed and bound in Great Britain by
Cox & Wyman Ltd, Reading, Berkshire.

To Dr. David Harle,
to whom I am grateful not only for
his unstinting attention to me
over the past twelve years,
but also for the interest he has
shown in my work.

PART ONE

*As it Happened
When I Was Ten*

1

Robert Musgrave eased himself off the low platform bed set in the alcove and, using his arms, propelled himself backwards across the stone-flagged floor towards the door of the cottage. In doing so he had to pass between the open-hearth fire, and the two small children playing on the mat in front of it, and the back of his wife who was standing at the table in the middle of the room. When he reached the door he lifted up one arm and pushed the sneck; then with a practised fling he swung his two useless legs to the side in order to allow himself to reach the top step, and there he sat for a moment, looking out.

In the fading light he could still make out other cottages dotted here and there on the steep hillside down to the row of dwellings that bordered the shore.

But as clustered as the cottages were on this part of the hillside, Robert often thanked God that he was housed here and not further along the hill in the main town where the principal winding street on the bank of the river ran from Low Lights to the Bull Ring, and from which led numerous sets of steps, some counting up to a hundred, and these giving onto the houses on the hill.

Situated as the cottages were here, the wind coming from the river and the German Ocean did sweep away the stink; but along there it was so congested with the muck and the human offal lying in the streets that in parts they had to wait for the pigs to swarm in in the mornings to clear it for them.

Something should be done. He had said this for many a year. Cats buried their mess and the scorned pigs chose their places to empty themselves, but human beings seemed to wallow in their own excrement; yet the fine ladies and gentlemen could emerge from their big houses on the top of the hill and step daintily over muck without blinking an eyelid.

'Sitting on your bare backside on a cold step is not going to bring him any quicker; he'll come when he's ready.'

He looked back into the room towards his wife. She wasn't looking at him but concentrating on the coarse flour and water dough she was kneading on the table.

'He isn't runnin' the night,' he said; 'he saw the faggot man the day and got no word.'

'He could have sculled across the river to South Shields, the tide's low.'

'Aye, but for only another half-hour or so. That's what's worryin' me.'

'Well, it shouldn't. He's been caught afore by it an' he's gone to his gran's. What's different the night? What's the matter with you?'

She turned from the table, dusted her hands on her coarse apron, then went towards the door. She was a big woman, all of five foot eight and broad with it, but her width was made up of bone and muscle. Providing for her family since the day, ten years past, they had carried her man in, his legs bloody and dangling, had kept the flesh stripped from her. At times, even now, she could still hear him screaming, not with pain, but at the doctor who had wanted to cut his legs off.

He'd always had a dread of having no feet. In bed on their wedding night he had laughingly told her he

10

had one fear in his life, that he would lose his feet. And on that occasion, such was their enjoyment of each other she had tickled his soles and caused him to squeal.

The bone man from along the coast had pushed the bones back into the torn flesh, the while she held him down and Jimmy Harper from next door poured rum down his gullet. So he had kept his feet and the bones had knitted, but not quite as nature intended: his feet were splayed and his legs useless from the knees down.

As if tending a child, her hand went to his head and stroked the straggling hair from his brow, and he put his own up and laid it on top of hers for a moment, pressing it tight, and his voice quiet as he asked, 'Why do you never seem to worry about our Freddie?'

'Because I know nothin' will ever happen to him.'

'Because he's small and slippery?'

'No, no, not that. And he'll grow: he's nearin' the time for growin', they sprout after ten. No, it's because he's got things in his head. He's somehow like me dad used to be, sees things that are comin', and I feel that this'll always help him to keep clear.'

Still gazing ahead, Robert smiled quietly to himself. He wanted to answer her: 'It didn't stop your dad from being picked up by the press gang,' for then she would have likely come back, saying, 'No; and it didn't stop him from escaping them, although it took him two years.' And she was right about Freddie. He was a lucky lad, picking up a tanner here and there and more at times. And then there was his job at the butcher's from where he often brought home a pile of chitterlings; and he was lucky an' all in that his mother wouldn't let him go down the pit. Aye. Aye; not like John. John was down there now in the dark. My God! if ever there was a hell it was down that pit.

11

John was twelve now. He had been down since he was eight. But on that first night down he wasn't the only one who had cried, for he himself had lain wide-eyed following every move that would take his lad into the depths. He himself had gone down as a lad of seven, clinging to a man's waist, the man himself clinging to a rope and being lowered into the black hell. When he was fifteen he realised that a man could become depraved doing such work. He hadn't put it under the heading of that word then, he only knew something in himself protested against his body being used so and his mind being sullied.

Then when he was twenty he got his eye on a lass, just caught glimpses of her now and again, a big strapping lass. It was her hips he noticed first. They swung her thick serge skirt from side to side as she walked. She was only fifteen or so but already a woman, and from her hair to the toes of her steel-capped boots she was strong. She was working in the salt-pans at the time, but her people were fisher folk from across the water in South Shields. Her name was Jinny Williams. He had courted her and married her and loved her, and she had loved him, and she still did. Strange that, him a useless cripple; yet not quite useless, for hadn't he made all the furniture in this cottage, and wasn't it the best and cleanest comfortable cottage at this end of the hill?

It was she who had got him to leave the pit and go into the shipbuilding. They were turning out ships by the dozen on both sides of the river then, and within ten years he had become as good a carpenter as any man who had been apprenticed to it from a bairn. It was during this time he had built the little sculler for John, no bigger than a coracle it was, and it would hold two at a pinch. But it was odd, John never took to it; he didn't care for the river, would rather walk the countryside. No; it was Freddie who, from when he was able to toddle, would tumble into it; and he was sculling like the best of them when he was four, and seemed never to have been out of it since. And it had stood him in good stead. By! it had.

So when he had woken up to the fact that he would be helpless for the rest of his life and that he couldn't walk or move from the house unless he was lifted into the bogie and wheeled down to the town, he realised he still had a trade of sorts, he could make things out of wood. But then it didn't take long for him also to realise that there were carpenters in the town, and it was their living, and that they resented a chippie from the boats muzzling in. So he had concentrated his skill on replacing the cheap stuff with which they had first set up house.

What was more, he had fathered ten children. Nell his first born was sixteen now and married these two months. They had lost Mary, Joe and Harry with the smallpox. Then had followed John. John was the steady one. Then Nancy had come. Nancy, beautiful, big, dark-haired Nancy, like her mother in every-thing but her eyes, for she had been stone blind from birth. Yet strangely Nancy had more light about her than any of his brood, and was indeed the happiest of the lot of them. Next came Freddie, Freddie who now at ten years old could be taken for seven or eight, in fact it was his smallness and babyish look that denied all that was in his head and which had saved him so far from the customs men, and the chimney-sweeps and such.

Billy had followed Freddie, but he too had died, again with the smallpox. There hadn't been another until Jessie came. He turned his head slightly to the side and looked at his four-year-old fair-haired daughter with a face as plain as a pikestaff. She was

13

playing with his latest effort Lily who, at two years old, was making up for Jessie's plainness, being pretty and curly-haired.

'That's Nancy.' Jinny nudged his shoulder with her knee, and they both listened; then they looked towards the steps that led downwards just beyond the adjoining cottage, and slowly through the deepening twilight there emerged onto the rough cinder path that fronted the cottages an eleven-year-old girl.

'You're late, lass.'

'I got talkin', Ma.'

Robert gave a small laugh now as he said, 'You spend your life talkin'.'

'And listenin', Da. An' listenin'.'

'Aye; aye, you're right there. You've got a pair of ears on you like a cuddy's lugs. I've said it afore and I'll say it again, you should hire them out.'

Jinny now backed from the door, saying, 'Come on in, both of you; Freddie will be here when he comes, not afore an' not after.'

'He hasn't come back yet, Ma?'

'No. And I suppose you haven't seen anything of him the night?'

It didn't seem odd to them that they should ask a blind girl if she had seen anything of her brother for her ears were her eyes and she seemed to observe through them things that escaped the sighted.

'I knew he had gone across the water earlier the day, an' when I got to Nell's she and Joe had just got in and Joe said when he was loading salt on a ship he saw him goin' over . . . Ma.'

'Yes, pet?'

'Nell made me laugh although she was very tired. She'd been wheeling coal all day and feeding the fires. But she told me there'd been a fight atween

14

two women: one was after the other's man, she said, and they rolled into the river. She said, it must have taken some of the steam out of them . . . Ma' – her voice changed – 'she doesn't seem to like workin' there in all that steam.'

'No; but who does, pet? There's one good thing about it, though, lass, them that work on the salt rarely get the plague. It's been proved again an' again, so she's lucky in that way. And so's Joe.' And now Jinny added on a yell, 'You! Jessie; leave Nancy alone; let her get settled. All right. All right, take her stick and put it in the corner, an' mind the ram's head doesn't bite you.'

The small child laughed, saying now, 'Can't bite, Ma, 'tis wood.'

'Oh, 'tis amazin' what wood can do. Which reminds me, it's about time we had a light on the subject. Bring a candle, Jessie, and give it to your da.'

The child dutifully went to a square painted tin that stood on the end of a piece of furniture doing duty both as a long chest of drawers and as a sideboard and, taking from it a tallow candle, brought it to her father and he, sitting now on the mat to the side of the fireplace, took a spill from the hearth and, handing it to her, said, 'Light it an' give it to the candle.' And when the child had done this she said, 'You want your pipe lit up an' all, Da?'

'No; not the night, lass, not the night.'

Not tonight because he had no baccy. Perhaps come the weekend one of his friends would drop in a twist or a small bag of snuff; not that he liked snuff, that usually went across the water to Jinny's mother. But there had been no hand-outs for the last two or three weeks, the customs blokes were on the watch. What must it be like to be hated as that Mr Taggart was. To look at him he seemed a decent

15

enough fella; but he was out to get you, get anybody, one an' all, even the occupant of Storey's Hall over at Low Lights wasn't above suspicion. Wasn't there hell to pay when Taggart appeared at that front door and asked questions.

He turned now and looked at his wife who was saying to Nancy, 'Could you eat a griddle?' And his daughter answered with a smile, 'Oh, aye, Ma, anytime I could eat a griddle,' which prompted him to ask her, 'Didn't you get a bite along at Nell's?'

'No, Da, no. 'Cos they were both harassed and had to clean up, and Nell was dead on her feet, she sounded it.'

'Can I have a griddle, Ma?'

'No, you can't, our Jessie; you had your supper not an hour gone. Now get off to bed, and take Lily with you. Take her clothes off, all but her last petticoat. An' you do the same. If you get into bed with them on I'll come in there an' pull the lot off you, mind.' Jessie laughed with her mother, then went over to her father and, her face almost on a level with his as he sat with his back against the wall, she kissed his stubbly cheek, saying, 'Good-night, Da.'

'Good-night, pet. Sleep tight, an' mind the bugs don't bite.'

The two small children gone from the room, Robert now asked, 'Did you hear any crack the day, Nancy?'

'Odds and ends, Da, odds and ends.' She cocked her head to the side and added, 'Oh, here's John.'

Within a few seconds the door opened and there stood her twelve-year-old brother, nothing distinguishing him from a black boy except his eyes and the red gap of his mouth as he opened it, saying wearily, 'Hello there.'

'Hello, lad,' said his father.

16

'Tired, lad?' asked Jinny.

'Same as usual. It's a nice night though, stars out an' a nip in the air. It's lovely an' cool, the air.'

The daily sadness descended on Jinny as she made her way to the fire and lifted from a chain hanging there a round iron pot full of boiling water which she then carried out through a side door into a small lean-to, saying over her shoulder, 'Will you have an all-over-one?'

'Aye, Ma; I want it off me back.' He now turned and looked down at his father and asked, 'What d'you think, Da? It's balderdash, isn't it, them saying it weakens your back to wash it?'

'I agree with you, lad, it's balderdash.'

As the young boy passed his sister he asked quietly, 'All right, Nancy?'

'Aye, John, fine. You know somethin', John?'

'No, Nancy; what's that?' He was divesting himself of his coat and muffler as he looked down at her, and she said, 'Mrs Twaite is gettin' up a concert and it's gona be held at The George. She asked me to go and sing.'

There were gasps now from her mother and father, both exclaiming together, 'You never told us!'

'Well, I've just got in, Ma.' She was laughing. 'And I was keepin' it until Freddie came in to tell you all together.'

'What'll they pay you?'

'A shilling at least, Ma.'

'My! My!' Her father screwed himself round from the wall and grabbed her hand, saying, 'Could be a start, hinny. Could be a real start.'

John was now in the scullery where his mother was cooling down the boiled water with a bucket of sea water she had brought in from outside the front door, and as he unloosened his short leather trousers

17

he said to her, 'I hear there's a man in Newcastle who trains voices.'

'Trains voices! She doesn't need her voice trained; it's as clear as a bell.'

'Aye, Ma; but there's different ways of singin' like.'

'How d'you know? Who've you been talkin' to?'

'Oh, different ones. We get on talkin' at bait time. You know Mr Knight, Billy Knight, he's in the Methodist Chapel choir, he sings, but he said you can't get anywhere, not proper, unless you're trained. He took lessons when he was a lad, that's of course when his people had a shop in Newcastle. They've come down since that.'

'Aye; how the mighty have fallen! Well, get your wash. And there's mutton soup an' some griddles. Then the best thing you can do is to get yourself to bed; no walkin' along the quays or the hills the night.'

He turned his back on her and his voice was soft as he said, 'It's the only time I see the sky, Ma, 'cept Sunday.'

Her head slightly lowered, she went back into the kitchen. What she would give if she could get that lad out of that pit. She would do anything, anything . . . except whoring.

She had just finished laying five plates around the table when the door opened and there entered a ten-year-old boy. His fair hair was sticking out from both sides of a black greasy peaked cap. He was wearing boots and his legs were bare to the ragged bottom of his calf-length trousers; his short jacket at one time must have been grey, and was so long in the sleeves the cuffs were rolled back.

'As usual, you've turned up like the bad penny.' His mother's look was soft, belying the harshness of her words. And he responded brightly, saying, 'Aye, like a bad penny, Ma. I passed one the day, foreign it was. Wait till Pratt looks in his till the night.'

'Where did you get a bad penny, lad?'

'I found it on the sands just as I got to yon side, Da. I looked down and there it was sticking up. It had a funny head on it. I didn't only find one, I found a bunch of 'em together. Look.' He thrust his hand into his trouser pocket and brought out about ten coins, saying, 'I'll just have to pass them now and again else somebody'll twig.'

In the light from the fire and the tallow candle, Robert squinted down at the coin he was holding up before his face and after a moment he said, 'Bad pennies? These could be Roman coins, lad. It could be a find.'

'Oh, well, Da, that makes the offence worse in passing 'em. Anything you find like that you've got to hand over to the authorities in Newcastle. They said so last year when that fella found that mug.'

'He's right.' Jinny nodded at her husband, thinking, How that boy remembers things, then saying, 'Best not traffic with those; put them back where you found them, I'd say.'

'I can't do that, Ma, 'cos the tide'll be up by now.'

He laughed, then said, 'Hello there, Nancy;' and even as she was answering, 'Hello Freddie,' he was already addressing his mother again: 'John in?'

'Aye, he's having his wash.'

The small figure now darted to the lean-to scullery and, putting his head round the door, he said in a surprisingly deep voice for one of such slight form and years, 'Wotcher, big fella. How ya feelin'?'

'As well as can be expected in my condition until I see the doctor, 'cos I've washed me back.'

Freddie laughed, and like his voice, the sound didn't match his size or age; and turning again to his

19

father, he said, but softly now, 'Did you hear that? He made a joke.'

'Aye, I heard.' His father grinned back at him, then asked, 'What's your news?'

'Aw! Things are movin'. I'll tell you when I've had me supper 'cos me belly thinks me throat's cut.'

'Had nothing today, lad?'

'Well, I called at me granny's an' she gave me some broth, but it was so weak I had to help it out of the basin; an' she didn't offer me a bit of bread with it. Eeh! she's a mean scrub. Sorry! Ma. Sorry, Ma.'

'You might be ten and consider yourself a very important individual,' Jinny said to him, 'but to me you're still in knickerbockers and your ears are askin' for it, understand?'

'As clear as Christchurch bell, Ma. But you must admit your ma's niggly an' more than a bit on the . . .'

'I've told you mind!'

Robert was laughing, Nancy was laughing, Freddie was laughing; it was a happy atmosphere, and Jinny, ladling out the mutton stew, thought as she often did, I've got a lot to thank the Almighty for . . .

The meal over, the plates washed in another bucket of heated sea water, they were gathered round the fire: Robert in his usual position with his back against the wall, Jinny on a low cracket next to him – she always sat on a low cracket so her breadth and height wouldn't emphasize his position and condition – John sat next to his mother, Nancy next to him, and Freddie at the other side of the fireplace. Impatient for news, Jinny looked towards Freddie, saying, 'Well, let's have it. What's happened the day?'

'Well' – Freddie drew in a long breath, paused, as a true story-teller would be apt to do, then addressing his father, said, 'There's one thing sure, you won't get any baccy this weekend nor snuff nor a drop of the hard stuff either.'

'They're not runnin'?'

'No, they're not runnin'. But Taggart thinks they are. Somebody's split.'

'Any idea who?' John asked.

'Could be one, two, or three, only time'll tell,' he said. 'You see, Mr Blaze, Mr Johnson, and Alec Crighton were to take a sculler out and pick up some kegs that was dumped on the last run. And also Mr smarty keelman' – Freddie thumbed towards the wall to the side of him – 'He and his mate and their Mick were to make the run down from Newcastle on the full ·tide later the night. 'Twas all set. Then I was on the quay and I saw the faggot man. I was expectin' him. An' I followed him to the tavern. He always goes in the best end and stays at least half an hour. But he was out within a few minutes again. He must have just had one drink, an' as he passed me he tossed me the usual penny. "Faggot-face, you here again?" he said. "Well, that's the last you'll get for some time. You've got me broke with your beggin'. If you don't work you don't eat." It was that last bit, if you don't work you don't eat, that told me. And then he laughed and cuffed me ear an' nearly knocked me on me back. And there was Mr Johnson the cobbler and Ned Tiller from the brewery, they laughed as I went away holdin' me ear. It didn't really hurt but I made on.'

'Then what did you do, I mean just from that, what did you learn?'

'Well, that the trip was off and I had to let them know, that was, our lot, I mean those down in the shore cottages. He'd likely got word to t'others.'

'What about the fella across the river, the one that comes on horseback to the Shields front that you

21

meet at times? They store stuff there, don't they? You've been to his house.'

'Oh, they'd never be on to him; he's a big pot, Mr Gallagher, an' he would get to know in some way. If he'd been expecting a run the night he'd have come along through the market an' down to the shore. Anyway, I went over on spec and he wasn't there. If there's anything on he times it for slack tide so I can skip across.'

'Skip across?' Jinny shook her head. 'One of these days you'll be too late in your skipping in that little shell; you'll be caught.'

'Well, Ma, if I do, there'll be lots of others caught at the same time.'

'They're not as foolhardy as you leavin' it till the last minute.'

'Well, if the tide came on me, Ma, unknowingst like, I'd just use me wings an' fly.'

'Don't be too clever, boy.'

'I'm not, Ma.' Then his tone becoming deep and serious now he said, 'I'm never too clever. I work things out, more so now since that day Mr Taggart thought he was bein' funny an' took me down into the cellar of his house an' showed me the neck manacles they tie smugglers to. Then he started to pump me about one an' another and I played dumb, daft like. No, Ma, I never act too clever. But I can be funny in me own home, can't I?'

His mother didn't answer, and a silence seemed to build up until his father said quietly, 'Aye lad, you can be funny in your own home. If you can't be funny here where can you be funny?'

'I heard something funny today, Ma. I couldn't understand it.'

'What did you hear, hinny?' They were all looking at Nancy now.

22

'Well, I saw two men. It was just after Mrs Twaite had spoken to me about the singing. They were coming out of the inn. They weren't from around here . . . well, not the usual ones that are on the main street.'

'How d'you know that?' John had turned to her.

'Well, by their smell, John . . . you know, I know everybody by their smell.'

'Well, you know lots of people by their smell, but you can't really know everybody by their smell.'

'Well, I know if I haven't smelt anything like them afore, John.'

'What did they smell like?'

'Different: not sweaty, not fishy, not from the salt-pans, nor from the brewery, nor did they smell of the ships or from the top houses in the town. One smelt of snuff like we take to Grandma, but different, a stronger smell; the other one, he smelt of –' She paused, then went on, 'It wasn't scent; like onions, but not onions. Anyway, they were both different from what I had smelt afore except that time when the carriage stopped. Do you remember, Ma, when we walked to the high road that day after we had been through the fields and that carriage stopped and you pulled me back to let the ladies out and pass us? That was a beautiful smell. I liked their smell better than I liked their voices?'

'But what did you hear, Nancy? Go on, tell us what you heard?'

She turned her head towards Freddie now and said, 'Well, it's to do with a tower, an' strangely, they were talkin' about smells and about scent, and one said to the other, "They're on the wrong scent, and we're only here to put them off." They were quite some distance away and I could only catch bits, but it was their smell that caught my fancy, an' that's why

23

I listened. And then one told the other when he had got his order and who had given it to him. He said somethin' about just two hours ago, and he had come pell-mell from the city. And then they said somethin' about the business would be all happenin' across the water in the tower . . . or at the tower. First of all I thought they must be meaning the priory at Tynemouth, but when they said across the water I wondered where the tower was. They moved away then and I just heard one say to the other, "I could never stand him 'cos he imagines he's a clever . . ." He used that word, Ma, you know . . .b. "But he's in for the shock of his life," he said. Is there a tower across the water, Da?'

'What is it?'

Freddie had jumped to his feet. Looking down on his father, he said, 'It must be The Towers she was hearin', Da. That's where he lives. That's where I went, I told you, the big house. I go there with the little parcels. They're special like. But he takes in the big stuff an' all. I'll have to go.'

'*Freddie!* Now you can't, not at this time of night.'

'I will, Ma, I will. I'll have to get across the river afore the tide turns 'cos remember over a year gone, when things were bad, we were glad of him. He helped me, he started me on the running when there was trouble on the Sunderland side and they couldn't get things through. We would have had nothing. But he set me on, an' now he's in a pickle. If the excise is all at this end he won't know nowt about it. And I told you last time, didn't I, his young wife was expectin' a bairn. It's his second wife. I told you. She was bonny, very bonny.'

The urgency in his voice seemed to have got all, except his father, on their feet, and John came with him to the door, saying, 'You'll still get across on the slack all right, but it's gettin' back; that little tub would be swamped by the incomin' tide. You couldn't battle against it.'

'I won't try; I'll go to me granny's.' Freddie looked back to where his mother was standing with her hand on his father's shoulder and addressed them both: 'Don't worry,' he said; 'I'll be all right. I'll be careful. I always am. Really, I always am.' Then for a ten-year-old boy he added words that made them wonder from where he came by his wisdom: "Cos it's daft to be brave,' he said, then ran out into the night. But immediately John followed him and, catching up with him half-way down the steps to the shore, he said, 'Hold your hand a minute! Look; I'll come along of you.'

'Don't talk daft. We *would* be swamped then.'

'What if the river scullers are lined up for the night and won't let you beach?'

'Oh, I'll drift down below them, or at worst camp on a sandbank. There's plenty of them.'

'Don't be funny, our Freddie, you could be in trouble either way; those river blokes across there are a real rough lot. And your size won't help you. Anyway, what's this bloke in the big house really like?'

They were running side by side now along by the row of cottages and on to the shore.

'Oh, gentleman like; but funny tempered I'd say. But, as I said, he's not stingy.'

'You can't go on like this much longer, our Freddie, you know that; you'll start sproutin' soon. An' you said you didn't want to keep on at the butcher's. I wouldn't neither. I don't like dead meat, not really. What would you like to do if you had your way?'

'Make shoes.'

'What!' John eased up in his run, but Freddie kept on.

25

'That's what I said, make shoes; not just be a cobbler, make shoes. For that you've got to make money though. But if I had money, John, I'd first get you out of the pit. That's what I think about an' all, I'd get you out of that pit if I had the money.'

'Aw, lad, you're a funny 'un; but ta all the same for thinkin' that way. It's the air I miss an' the sky. If it wasn't for the folks I wouldn't mind starvin' above ground, anything rather than go down into that bloody hole.'

It was Freddie who now paused in his run. He had never heard John swear before. His mother didn't allow swearing in the house, yet he once heard her swear like a fishwife when she was having a row with a woman at the water tap in the centre of the town. But then, John must hear a lot of swearing workin' with the men down below. He himself could swear roundly, but only when he was outside. His mother's hair would stand on end if she heard him at times. But it was still strange to hear John swear.

They were both breathing heavily when they reached a comparatively empty stretch of the water-front, and there, bobbing on the water next to a fishing smack was a small sculler.

'How you going to manage without a light?'

'Put me finger in me eye and make a starlight.'

'Don't be so damn funny!'

'Well, look across there! There's lights all along the shore.'

'Aye, yes, you can see them but who's gona see you?'

'Aw, John man, you worry too much. And look; I've got to look slippy or I will be in trouble.'

Freddie was quickly into the sculler and away; and John could soon hear only the dipping of the oar.

Freddie was well aware of the danger of a fast-running incoming tide as he made for the south shore,

26

and knew how easily he could be dashed against the moored river keels; and so was surprised when a few minutes later he did just this with a bump, and a voice yelled, 'What the hell!' Then a light shone down on him and the voice went on, 'My God! Where've you come from at this time of night?'

'I was lookin' for Mr Stoddart.'

'Billy Stoddart?'

'Aye.'

'Well, you're too late, he made the London trip with coal two days gone.'

Freddie knew about this but showed great surprise and disappointment in his voice as he cried, 'Aw. He lets me tie up me boat to his'n now an' then.'

'Your boat!' The man laughed. 'But what you over here for at this hour?'

'Me granny's bad; I'm gonna stay the night.'

'Aw, well, take your monkey-nut shell along to the end of the line and tie her up. I'll see she's all right till the morrow.'

'Ta, mister. Ta. I'll see you right.'

At this the man let out a bellow of a laugh, saying, 'Oh, you will, will you? Well, I don't want coppers mind, a tanner or nowt.'

Freddie laughed with the man; then hastily pulled himself along by the scuppers until he came to the end of the line. Here, steps led up to the quay, and just beyond them he tied up his sculler to an iron ring; then stretching, he drew himself back to the steps and scrambled up them.

He now ran like a shadow along the dock side, threaded his way through hovels, crossed the market square, up the bank, past a farm, across two fields, and so to the better part of town.

Even before he reached Westoe village the houses had the appearance of wealth: they were terraced,

27

but they were large with their own iron gates and front gardens.

He stopped and merged into the garden of one when he saw a swinging lantern approaching: a night-watchman, carrying a cudgel as well as the lantern, passed by. Through the village the dimly lit houses all suggested quality.

He was beginning to feel tired. It must be twenty minutes since he had crossed the river. Remembering the fields hereabouts must by now have been harvested, he decided to cross them and so skirt Harton hamlet. But oh! how the stubble hurt his feet.

He came out by the coach road and recognised the two big houses, both approached by long drives, but the bulk of each discernible as a dark mass against the night sky. Another hundred yards or so further on he came to the gate of The Towers.

He hung on to the bars of the iron gate for a while before thrusting it open; then he really had to grope his way along a verge to keep himself clear of the line of trees that bordered the drive. He had no idea of the layout of the grounds, he knew only that the house itself looked enormous and that there was a tower at each gable end. He had some idea of the size of the rooms because on his second visit he had stood gazing at the two long windows to the right of the front door, for they were lit up to a brilliance such as he had never seen before, and he had reached up and pulled himself onto the balcony that ran under the windows to give himself a better viewing point. He had then seen a lady and gentleman sitting at a table, and there was a lamp at each end and one hanging from the ceiling full of gas mantles.

The master himself had brought him on his first trip. He had pulled him up onto the front of his horse and, like that, had ridden right from Shields. He had brought him a little parcel. The faggot man had strapped it to his body underneath his singlet, and when the gentleman on horseback had asked for it and he had told him where it was, he had laughed and had then hauled him onto the front of his saddle, saying, 'Well, little fellow, if you're going to be undressed we'd better do it in private.'

That was the first parcel he had carried to him. Previously he had only taken messages from the faggot man to the men in the cottages or down the road at Cullercoats.

But tonight there were no lights on downstairs, not in the front of the house anyway, although a faint light was showing up part of a stairway and another brighter light appeared in a window which could have been a bedroom.

He was sweating profusely when he entered the courtyard and made his way to the far end and the kitchen door. Before reaching it, he could hear voices coming from there as if in argument; but when he knocked sharply on the door the voices became still. And it was quite some seconds before it was opened and he looked up into the face of Connie the maid. She was holding a lantern shoulder high and she exclaimed under her breath, 'Dear God! What are you here for this night?'

'I . . . I've got a message.'

'Who is it?' The man he knew to be Connie's father was now towering over him. 'Boy,' he said, 'what you after?'

'I have a message for the master.'

'A message? Come in. Come in.'

Their hands clutching his shoulders, together they almost lifted him into the kitchen.

'What kind of message?' The man was bending over him again.

29

'I . . . I've got to give it to the master.'

'God Almighty! this an' all; an' the night of all nights!'

'Well, Da, you'd better go up and tell him.'

'Not me. Not me. The state he's in he's likely to fell me, an' I don't want to see him choke the truth out of her afore the bairn's born.'

'You think as he does, Da?'

'Aye, I do. But I don't blame her, for she's had no life: he's past livin' with. Anyway, it was a mistake from the beginning. I said so. But this youngster –' He now turned his attention down on Freddie, saying, 'Is it so important? Who's the message from anyway, the same one?'

'Aye, the faggot man.' It was easier to say that than try to explain.

The elderly black-coated man turned and looked at his daughter and said, 'That's Mr Freeman from Newcastle; he gives him a penny for faggots. 'Tis important if it's from him. Look; go on up and tell your ma to tell him. He'll listen to her if nobody else.'

The young woman hesitated for a moment. She looked at her father, then down on Freddie, and he gazed up at her. He remembered the first time he had looked into her face, and he had wanted to laugh; but then he'd had a strange feeling, a kind of sad feeling for her because her face was pockmarked, and she was cockeyed an' all. As his da would have said, she had one eye in the pot and t'other up the chimney. Yet her voice was nice and her manner kindly as now she said, 'Come on along of me.'

'No, God! Don't take him up there with what's goin' on. Are you mad?'

'Well, d'you think he'll leave her and come down here, Da, when he's been out since early mornin' from he knew the Spaniard's ship was in? He

30

couldn't have found him though, else he would have spilled it before now that he'd murdered him.'

Freddie gaped from one to the other. She was actually yelling at her father. She didn't seem a bit afraid of him, although he was a big man. And now she went on, 'Two hours he's been up there with her; an' he's like a fiend, he won't leave her be. God help her! 'Tisn't that he ever cared for her; 'twas her money he was after 'cos, if you ask me, any human feelings he ever had were for Mistress Ellen. What's wrong with him is pride; it's been split open. And again I say I don't blame her . . . Come on, lad.' She held out a hand and pulled Freddie forwards. And now, with not a little apprehension in his eyes, he looked back towards the elderly man; but the man flapped his hand towards him as if pushing him on.

The kitchen was long and stone-flagged. The corridor they went into was also stone-flagged, with a number of doors opening off it. She pulled him through one; and now they were in a hall. Although only dimly lit by light from the stairs he could see the ceiling was beamed. The beams were big and black like those used for the keel of a ship. The bannister to the broad stairs was black and highish; he found it easier to grip the rails as she tugged him upwards. At the top they seemed to be in another hall with the same sort of rails edging it. She was now almost dragging him along another corridor. In the dim light it looked almost as long as three cottages put together. She brought him to a sudden stop as a high scream came from behind one of the doors and for a moment he found himself clinging to the young woman's side, and when he looked up at her her eyes were closed and her face screwed up as his had been. She had her hand round his shoulders now and she pressed him tightly to her, saying, 'It's all right. It's

31

all right.' Then bending down to him, she whispered, 'Don't be frightened. It's the lady of the house; she's havin' a bairn. You understand?'

He nodded but didn't speak. He understood all right. He remembered when Lily was born his mother had yelled out something like that and he had buried his head under the pillow tick. And now he had the urge to bury his head in the big white apron that this maid was wearing. 'Stay there,' she said now as she pushed him against the wall. 'Don't move.'

She opened the door which was only a foot away from him and a man's voice roared out of it, crying, 'Hold back on me, would you! Well, we'll know, won't we, when you decide to let it come; you can't hold on forever, you loose little whore!'

When the door was banged closed, a woman's voice, almost as loud as the man's but the words thick sounding like those of the voices he was used to, cried, 'Let up, Mr Roddy! You'll be sorry for this when you come to yourself.'

'Shut your mouth, Betty! I am myself. At this moment I am myself, never more.'

There followed a silence. It seemed to go on for a long time but it could only have been a minute before the man's voice came again, yelling, 'Bring him in then! Bring him in!'

'*No, no! Not in here, surely!* It isn't seemly. Go out and see the lad.'

'What! and miss the coming of the black Spaniard! Bring him in, I said. He won't faint at the sight of naked limbs; he's the scum of the waterfront. Bring him in!'

The door opened once again and the maid, without saying a word, gripped Freddie by the shoulder and pulled him into the room, where he stood within the doorway, his mouth agape at the sight before him.

It was a large bedroom. There was lots of furniture in it, but the main thing was a big four-poster bed, with all its draperies hooked back towards the head of it, so exposing the two bottom poles, the rumpled bedclothes and the woman lying on the high mattress, which was all of four foot or more from the carpeted floor.

The woman's face on the pillow was turned towards him. It was red and running with sweat. Her hair was spread out all around her head; it looked as if the wind had tousled it. The sweat was running down her face, and the old woman whom he knew to be the maid's mother was mopping it with a flannel. But of a sudden she put out her hand and pulled the nightdress over the heaving mound of flesh. It didn't cover all the woman's nakedness, her legs were spreadeagled, and if it hadn't been for her face and the expression on it he would have thought she looked awful. He had never seen his mother like that.

He watched the man turn from the bed; and then there he was towering above him, and he had to put his head right back to look up at him.

'Well! What is it?'

He found his throat was dry: the explanation why he was there was all in his head but he couldn't get the words out. And when the man bawled, 'Come on! Come on! Have you lost your tongue for once?' he stuttered. ''Tis . . . 'tis the excise. The . . . they're c . . . comin' the night.'

'What d' you mean, they're coming the night? Have you spoken to Mr Freeman . . . the faggot man?'

He nodded; then swallowed deeply before saying, 'He . . . he gave me a message for t'others that meant it was off the night. He . . . he said you would likely know that.'

'Yes, yes; of course, I would know that.'

33

"Twas my sis . . . sister.'

'*What!*'

'She's . . . she's blind.'

The man put his hand up to his head and ran his fingers through his hair, but he said nothing, only stared down at the small boy. And Freddie, his wits returning, went on quickly, 'But she makes up for it with sharp ears an' she can tell people by their smell.'

Still the man didn't speak, but his eyes grew wider and his expression indicated he didn't know why he was standing here listening to this prattle.

'She heard two strange men talking; they weren't from the town. She knows nearly everybody in the town from where they work 'cos of their smells. And what she heard was that it was all a put-up job that they were there on our side of the river, kind of puttin' everybody off the scent; what they were going to do was raid this end . . . an' you.'

The last word was almost whispered.

The man bent down towards him and in a much calmer voice said, 'Your sister heard all this? D'you mean to tell me that this kind of thing was discussed openly in the street?'

'Aye; well, outside the tavern. She was some distance off; but she's cute, she hears things, an' sees with her ears, an' 'cos she's blind nobody takes much notice of her. Any road, she thought they were talkin' about somebody in a tower an' she was tellin' us the tale after we'd had our supper, an' I jumped to it, it wasn't a tower it was this house, The Towers, and they're on to you.'

'God in heaven!' He straightened up and began to laugh, and the expression on his face changed: he wasn't the same man who had been bawling his head off a few minutes earlier. 'So I'm going to have some visitors, am I? But am I the only one?'

34

'Aye. As far as I could make out.'

He turned about now and looked towards the old woman who was still mopping her mistress's brow: 'What's in the dining-room, Betty?' he said.

Without turning towards him she answered, 'A bottle of rum, the remains of a bottle of whisky, that's if you didn't finish it after your dinner, and a bottle or two of port.'

'All labelled, authentic?'

'Aye.'

'You're sure?'

Now the old woman did turn towards him and she hissed at him, 'Yes! I'm sure. Why didn't you look yersel'? I filled the bottles the day afore yesterday. But I haven't done anything about the two kegs that are down the old well, and if it's them fellas, they'll rummage till they find that an' all.'

As he stared towards her it came to Freddie it was odd that a servant would talk to a gentleman like that, and he her master. It was like his mother might have done if she was in a paddy, and like the pockmarked Connie had done to her da.

He didn't even yell at her, although he spoke swiftly and definitely, saying, 'Tell Frank to get them up, Connie, *and right away*, and bury them in the midden.'

'In the midden?'

'Yes!' His bark was back now. 'That's what I said, in the midden and well down. It's not likely they'll look there. As for the rest –' He turned and looked towards the bed and, his voice changing, he added softly, 'Even God himself wouldn't disturb a woman in labour. Would he, dear?' He was addressing his words to his wife now while none too gently thrusting the old woman from her towards the foot of the bed; then bending over the panting writhing

35

figure, he said, 'You have something to tell me, dear?'

The young woman's mouth opened and shut a number of times before she whispered, 'Yes; yes, Roderick, I have something to tell you.'

But before she could get any further words out her knees came up and she let out another agonizing groan that caused Freddie to turn his face to the wall.

For a moment, both the old woman and the man seemed to have forgotten the boy's presence, for she now shouted at him, 'Will you, for the love of God! let up on her.'

The groans subsiding, the man began again: 'You were saying, Mirabelle, you had something to tell me. Come along, my dear, I'm waiting.'

'Yes, I have something to tell you, Roderick' – but the words were coming out between gasps now – 'and it's just this . . . I hate you now . . . and I've hated you . . . since the first week we were married. You want to know who . . . the father of my child is. Well . . . Roderick, you'll never know, never, never . . . If it comes out dark or fair you'll still never know because your mother . . . looks like a Spaniard, doesn't she? and the child might . . . hark back to her. I . . . I'll not live once it's . . . it's born because I have no desire to live. But wherever I am I shall . . . think of you sitting . . . in this mausoleum of a house . . . drinking your rum and your port . . . in between sniffing your opium . . . and all the time wondering . . . wondering, how many times we were together. What did we do when we were together . . . he and I? Perhaps you'll wonder if . . . if we did the same as you do when you . . . visit the brothels on the Shields waterfront . . .'

'*Don't you dare!*' The old woman had thrust him

36

aside. 'Lay a hand on her again an' I'll do what I promised you the last time: we'll up, the three of us, and go. I'm an old woman an' me time's runnin' out, like hers is, but I'll tell you this much, I'd open me mouth wide, aye wide, an' you know I've always meant what I've said. It shocks me that I have to say this to you of all people, but I'm doin' it, so move yourself away.'

He was glaring at her as if his hand would come out and deal her a blow when the door was thrust open and Connie Wheatley cried, 'They're comin' into the yard. There's four of them.'

'Did you tell your father? Has he got them up?'

'He's bound to. Oh, he's bound to by now.'

He turned and looked almost wildly round the room and, his eyes alighting on Freddie, he said to her, 'Get rid of him.'

'Where'll I put him?'

She had hold of his collar as she spoke and was pulling him from the room when the man cried, 'Hold! Hold a minute! They'll recognise him; like all his kind, a runner is stamped on him.'

'There's ... there's the cubby-hole.' Her voice sounded as agitated as his own, and when he answered, 'No, no; I wouldn't put him in there,' she thought: No; he wouldn't put a dog in there, which showed he had some feelings left that weren't buried deep below bitterness and recrimination.

'Under the bed,' he said.

'He'll never get under there.'

'*He will.* He's not as thick as two laths. Here!'

Three strides and he had Freddie by the arms, which brought a protest from the boy against he knew not what in crying, 'Eeh! no, mister. Eeh! no.'

'Still that tongue of yours! Not a murmur out of you.'

37

The hands now shook him like a rat. 'Lie flat. Put your legs out. Do as I say!'

He did as he was bidden. He saw the heavy valance of the bed being lifted up, and then he was being pushed along the carpeted floor and under what he imagined to be a shelf. The next minute he was in total darkness and the voices seemed far away but still audible, as was the scream that brought his eyes tight shut. Then he heard the old woman's voice saying, 'That's it, love, that's it. Here it comes. Here it comes.'

There followed the sound of a commotion, the vibration of feet thudding on the floor. They came to him as if they were going to walk onto him; then two loud voices seemed to tumble one on top of the other, saying, 'I am a customs officer, I have a warrant.' That voice trailed away as another, and recognizable to him now, yelled, 'What, sir, do you think you're up to? What is this anyway? I'll have the law on you, customs or not. Can you see what's happening here?'

Above him, in the room, the excise man and another stood open-mouthed looking at the man in his shirt sleeves, his hands covered with blood and the woman on the bed, his wife, giving birth.

The excise man gulped, turned and glanced at his companion, then said, 'I'm sorry, sir; but 'tis my duty.'

'Then carry on with your bloody duty: search the house, if that's what you've come for, search it from top to bottom, outside too, you're welcome. But let me tell you you haven't heard the last of this, no by God above! you haven't. I'll have that uniform stripped off you if it's the last thing I do, and I'll see you running in your bare pelt.'

When there came another cry from the woman on the bed he turned to where the heaving body was pushing the head out into life. Then his gaze swinging back to the men, he said, 'Get to hell's flames out of it!' And almost instantly they stepped back into the corridor and the door was closed once more.

He now looked to where old Betty Wheatley was cutting the cord; then he watched her lift the crying blood-smeared mass, cradle it in her arms and wipe its eyes, his own eyes riveted on the child's head and the small ridge of black hair sprouting from it.

'Look, love! Look, love! It's . . . it's all right; it's all over.' She was holding out the child now to the mother in the bed, and the young woman went to lift her hand but the effort was seemingly too much. Her lips moved as if asking a question, and, as if she had heard it, Betty said, ''Tis a girl; and she is whole and bonny. Sleep, love, sleep.'

When she stepped back from the head of the bed and the man went to take her place, she half barred his way and in a low voice and in which was a note of pleading she said: 'Not another word, Mister Roddy, please! In God's name! not the night. She's low, she's been low these many weeks. Have you no pity in you? What's done's done.'

He turned from her to the bed just as the door opened and Connie Wheatley came in, whispering, 'They're ransackin' the house, every nook and cranny.'

'Did Frank get the kegs up?'

'Aye; but just in time, for he only just got the muck off him, and the stink. He hadn't time to clean his boots' – she was now addressing her mother – 'he dropped them in the rain barrel. He won't be able to use them any more.' She now looked at the child in her mother's arms. 'What is it, Ma?' she asked.

'It's a little lass.'

'Oh, nice.'

39

She now glanced at her master and recognised the expression on his face which spelt trouble; then, glancing at the bed, she exclaimed, 'She's bleedin' heavy, Ma!'

'Here! take her.' Her mother thrust the child at her. 'Clean her up.' Then she added, 'The doctor should have been here! But he's another one that's likely skittering around burying his kegs in the muck,' and she indicated the urgency, saying, 'And you tell your da to go for him this minute.'

'You'll do no such thing.'

'She's got to have attention.'

'Attention or no, you won't find him there tonight. He was off to Newcastle earlier on to a meeting, and it's a sure thing that he'll have to be carried back. So get on with it, both of you. And' – his voice dropped – 'get rid of that. Understand me? Get rid of it.'

'*No, by God!*'

'*Oh, yes, by God!* Betty. Walk out, as you say you would, the lot of you, and split until your tongue runs dry, but *that* is not surviving in this house. Either you do it or I'll see to it; but I should imagine you'll be more gentle than me because I've had me answer.'

He now glanced at the deadly white face on the pillow, then stalked out of the room. And for some moments after the door banged behind him neither of the women moved but listened to his voice bawling at someone on the landing. Then Connie whispered, 'He means it, Ma. He would do it in.'

'Aye, he means it. And aye, he would do it in. But put it to one side for a minute, on the couch there, and help me to see to her because we've got to get the rest away.'

What time they dragged Freddie from under the bed he didn't know for he must have fallen asleep, but

40

his mind took in the voice saying, 'Eeh! we forgot all about him. Is he all right?'

'Oh, he's all right, lass; he's a tough 'un, although he looks such a bairn.'

'No more than six or seven.'

'Well, I should imagine he's twice that, the head he's got on him. He's been a runner for the last two years. They rely on him an' his little tub a lot across the water, just for that reason: like a bairn playin' about. Wake up, lad. Wake up. Get on your feet.'

'Poor mite; I'll carry him down.'

'Oh, let him walk.'

'He's dead asleep, Da.'

He felt himself being lifted up into two sturdy arms, and in a short while he knew he was in the kitchen again, and he heard someone say, 'He can sleep by the side of the fire with Tinker, she likes company.'

That was all he remembered, until the voices came at him again; but then it was daylight . . .

He had lain for some time between sleep and wakefulness because he felt warm and comfortable. He had his arm around someone, hugging them to him, the pulse beat of their heart was in his hand while his own heart beat was thumping through his ears. It often did when he lay on his left side. He knew he felt stiff but he was warm, and there was a nice smell in his nose. A voice above him said, 'They look canny together. Tinker's never had a child as a mate. I bet he's thinkin', better late than never.'

'You'd better wake him. He'll want to see him shortly if it's only to give him a tanner.'

'Oh, Da! I think last night's bit of work is worth more than a tanner. He saved the master's bacon if anybody did. But then, I suppose the master saved the boy's too as well as his own, for who knows but they would have made for the bed if he hadn't played up as he did; they've been known to pull beds to bits, them lot. And there was that poor soul. I'm glad she's out of her misery. She's where God pleases, but I'm gona miss her. Ma will an' all. She was a sweet creature.'

'Aye, she might have been but she shouldn't have done what she did: she should have realised that he wasn't the kind of man to play about with, made a cat's paw out of. An' God only knows what's gona happen to the bairn. He'll likely smother it and have it buried with her.'

'Oh, no, Da. No.'

'Oh aye, aye. I won't say he hasn't his rights. And he's had them since he was a lad but never got them. Funny that; you know he hated his father but he's like him in many ways. If only Mistress Ellen hadn't died; she made a different man of him for a time. But look what happened to their child. He couldn't stand the sight of him; and he was all of four when she went. He rarely goes to see him. It's a good job his granny took him. Anyway, he'd have a better upbringing with her than he would have here. But you can see, lass, if he turned against the legal one what care would he have for this one who's not his own?'

'You can't prove that, Da.'

'Oh, you've just got to look at it. Hair like pitch. And look at the eyes: new-born bairn's eyes are often blue, nearly always so; but look at hers, browny-black already. Well, God help her, she'll be happiest alongside her mother. An' she's puny, she wouldn't last long at any rate.'

Freddie was wide awake by this time with his ears stretched. He heard the kitchen door open and the older woman's voice came to him, saying, 'He wants to see him.'

42

'How is he?'

'Need you ask. Wake the lad.'

'Come on. Come on. Get up!'

He opened his eyes, and then pulled his arm from around the dog and stared at it in some amazement, and a gentle voice above him said, 'Aye, you've been cuddling a dog all night. Come on, give me your hand an' get on your feet, an' go and put your head under the pump in the yard. Then I'll give you a bite of breakfast afore you go an' see the master.'

Blinking his eyes against the strong morning light, Freddie made his way into the yard. Seeing it for the first time in daylight, he was amazed at the size of it. It was mostly bordered by stable doors, two being half open, each with a horse's head nodding out.

When the icy water hit the back of his head he shivered and groaned; but rubbed his face with his hands and squeezed the water from his hair, and felt somewhat better, at least refreshed; then he walked slowly back to the kitchen.

He knew the smell of bacon, but it was always of the fat kind in long strips; but there, on a plate, were two shives of lean bacon, and to the side of them an egg reposed on a slice of fried bread. He had never seen such a breakfast; but strangely he had no appetite for it.

The man said to him, 'Well, tuck in, lad. I doubt if you'll see many plates like that.'

'I'm . . . I'm not very hungry.'

'*What!*' It was a chorus from the three of them. And the man said, 'Not hungry! Across there you must be fed on fish most every day. Well, are you goin' to eat it or not?'

'I'll . . . I'll try.'

'He'll try.' They nodded from one to the other, and they chorused again, 'He'll try.'

43

'My God! the folks, tall an' short, you come across. Well, hurry up an' try' – Betty's voice was hard – "cos the master wants to see you an' then you'll be on your way.'

He ate one piece of the bacon and half of the fried bread, but he gulped at the drink the young woman placed before him: he had never tasted anything like it. It was a bit scenty and his face crinkled against it, and she, bending down to him, said, 'That's tea, China tea. Never had it afore?'

He shook his head.

'It's nice, soothin', make you feel better.'

A minute later, Betty said, 'If your lordship's finished would you mind comin' along of me?'

'Aw, don't take that attitude, Ma: he's but a bairn.'

'And an all too knowin' one if you ask me.' And in a lowered voice she said in an aside, 'And after last night he knows more than's good for him.' . . .

He was in the hall again. In the daylight it looked enormous, yet had dim corners.

They didn't go up the stairs, but behind them and along another corridor.

When the old woman opened a door she stopped just within, and he looked past her into a large room that seemed packed with furniture of all kinds and colours. But immediately she said, 'He was here a minute ago. He's likely in the study,' and swung him round with her hand on his head now and pressed him forward and further along the corridor. At the end she guided him up four shallow wooden oak steps and onto another landing.

Here she paused at the first door before knocking on it, and when there came a grunt from within the room she opened the door and pressed the boy forward.

The man was sitting in a deep leather chair to the

44

side of a fire that was burning brightly, and the first thing Freddie noticed about it was that it had big lumps of coal on it, roundies, the best, not slack dust like theirs at home.

'Leave him,' the man said; 'I'll ring for you in a moment.'

He was alone with the man now, standing in front of him. He looked different from what he did last night. His face looked different. His voice sounded different. Was he drunk? No; because men like him generally bawled when they were drunk, or angry. But now this man's voice was quiet, oddly quiet.

'You're a smart little fellow, aren't you?'

He gave no answer, for what could he say? He knew he was smart but it didn't do to brag about it.

'What do you think of last night's business?'

'I don't know.'

'Oh, come on, come on; you worked out what your blind sister told you. You said she was blind, didn't you?'

'Aye, she is.'

'You also said she saw with her ears. Funny expression that.'

Again he made no answer.

And now the man said, 'What would you think if I told you that the message you brought was just another red herring?'

'What d'you mean?'

'I mean, as far as my man Frank can ascertain, someone was playing double and treble games. What would you say about the two men over on the north side being fooled in their turn and the squad on the south side also being fooled? It would seem that somebody apparently gave us away, me and one or two others, but that in turn was another red herring in order to let the Newcastle lot distribute a load of

45

loads. Immediately they could after the tide crossed the bar they went over it with some precious cargo. What would you say to that?'

What would he say? His mind was trying to work it out. Yes, he could be right; but then the faggot man, and Mr Blaze and Johnson and Alec Crighton, they would have known about it, wouldn't they? Perhaps they didn't 'cos they were at loggerheads with the Newcastle lot. He'd heard tell a while ago that there was a man come up from Devon, a place in the West Country wherever that was, it must be as far as London town or some foreign territory like that. But this man was well up in the game and clever. It was said he had escaped the excise men and made his way here . . . He had thought it was just a story.

His head was beginning to swim with his thoughts and the heat of the room and not a little from the stare of the man's eyes on him.

'Well, what have you got to say to that?'

'Some men are clever.'

'Huh! Well, that's as good an explanation as any I've heard. Do you think you're clever?'

There it was again. He'd have to answer something.

'I have me wits about me.'

The man didn't speak for some seconds, and then he said, and with a change of voice for his words now came slow and deep, 'Well, I hope you have enough wits about you to keep a silent tongue in your head or else you could get into dire trouble. You understand me?'

Yes, he understood him, but he didn't say so. And the man went on. 'You heard a lot of talk last night and you saw a lot. You know my wife is dead, don't you?'

46

His mouth fell open. No, he didn't, not really. Yet he had heard them say something in the kitchen, but it hadn't really sunk in because they hadn't used the word dead. But the poor lady was dead, like Billy, his brother two years ago. He had cried when Billy died, because Billy had been like Nancy, gentle and kind.

'And the child was very sickly; it died too.' He stopped here, and Freddie watched him turn his head away as he muttered, 'But it'll not go along of her; her brat'll be put where it belongs in . . .' His voice trailed away into a growl as Freddie's mind yelled at him, Eeh! Eeh! What was he saying!

The man was talking directly to him again: 'Now you are to forget all you heard or saw last night. Do you hear? Now pay attention to me: if you divulge . . . I mean, if you talk about it to anyone it will come back to me, and I have ways and means of paying for services done, good or bad. Again, do you understand me?'

Oh yes, he understood him. But in this moment he had one wish, that he was grown up and big, oh yes, really big, with a big fist that he could bash in between this man's eyes, 'cos he was going to smother his bairn. That's what they had said in the kitchen, and they had been right.

'Hold out your hand.'

He held out his hand, and when a coin was put into it the man said, 'How much is that?'

He knew what a sixpence was and a bob and half a dollar and a five-shilling piece but he had never seen a sovereign before, or was it a half-sovereign?

'It's gold, it could be a half-sovereign or a sovereign.'

'You haven't seen one before?'

'No; leastways not close up.'

'What do you mean, not close up?'

47

'Well, I've seen such goin' over a counter.'

'Oh. Well, this is not a sovereign, it is a half-sovereign, and that is a lot of money, don't you think?'

'Aye, it is.'

'Boy.'

'Aye?'

'You say sir when you speak to a gentleman.'

There was a pause, and then he said, 'Aye, sir.'

'What is your Christian name?'

'Freddie.'

'Your full name?'

'Musgrave.'

'Well, Freddie Musgrave, that is the first payment for your silence; but once you open your mouth . . . and you've got to do that just once and I shall know, the payment will be very different. You understand?'

Again those two words; and again he paused in answering because now his heart was beating so quickly it seemed to be sticking in his throat. But he brought out, 'Aye, sir,' on a sort of gulp. And then the voice came cracking at him, no longer soft: 'Where do I store my stuff? Come on, tell me where I store my stuff.'

His body began to tremble. If he said he didn't know he would trick him, trip him up in some way. He gulped again, then said in a very small voice, 'In the bed underneath.'

'Good. You spoke the truth, so now you know. But that's one room my friends didn't search, isn't it? And it will come to some sharp-witted individual later, and likely they will return, but by then they will only find two horsehair mattresses and a feather tick, because it would be silly to leave the stuff where it is, wouldn't it, Freddie Musgrave?'

'Aye, sir.'

48

'And do you realise, Master Freddie, that we haven't seen the last of each other? You will be paying me further visits now and then . . . How many are there in your family?'

'Seven at home, sir. Nell, the eldest, she's married.'

'Your father, what does he do?'

'Nowt, sir; 'cept make bits of furniture for the house. His legs are broken.'

'Are you the only breadwinner?'

'No; there's John. He works down the pit. He's older'n me, twelve.'

'And the blind girl, how old is she?'

'Eleven, sir.'

'Well, Freddie Musgrave, your family seem somewhat in need, and this alone should help you to keep a still tongue, shouldn't it?'

'Aye, sir.'

'Here!' His hand had gone into his pocket again, and drawing out a wash-leather bag he opened it and now thrust another half-sovereign into Freddie's hand, saying, 'You should now be asking yourself how you are going to account for that money. So how are you going to account for it?'

He hesitated a moment before saying, 'Payment for warnin' you 'bout the raid, sir.'

'Yes; yes, quite good, payment for warning me about the raid. But –' Now the man was leaning forward, his nose almost touching Freddie's as he said, 'It wasn't payment for the raid, was it? Answer me!'

'W'well, not quite, sir, but you . . . you'd have likely given me somethin'.'

The man fell back into his chair now and, looking up towards the ornamental ceiling, he gave a hollow laugh, saying, 'This little fellow will go far. Perhaps, being such a wise owl, he could tell me how one should respond to sympathy in losing your second beautiful wife and her child.'

When the man said nothing further but still sat with his eyes fixed on the ceiling, Freddie stood as if frozen to the spot although the sweat was running down from his hair. Then he almost jumped as the man's hand was thrust out towards a side table from which he picked up a long-stemmed pipe and started to draw on it, pulling at it with his breath, but there was no smoke coming from the head of it.

'Go on, get out! . . . *Get out!*'

As Freddie hastily backed from him, he saw that the man was still looking at the ceiling, while still pulling on the pipe, and well before reaching the door he turned and ran; and his hand fumbled with the door handle before he sprang into the passage, looked first one way then the other, before remembering he had come up some steps. And now he was flying across the hall, and when he opened the kitchen door he stood with his back against it and gasped while he looked at the three people further down the room all gazing back at him.

'What is it? What is it, hinny?' The old woman's voice was soft now, and as she came to meet him he ran towards her and leant against her for a moment as he gasped out, 'He . . . he was acting funny, frightenin'.'

'There's nothin' to be frightened of; he's not well, he's ill, bad you know.'

His head was against her waistband, and he found himself looking towards the settle on which was a clothes-basket and in it the child. And of a sudden he was running from her towards it. The baby's eyes were open and it was sucking on a linen bag of some sort and its small hand was moving in and out. He turned and, looking from the old man to his daughter, he muttered, 'She's not dead! She's not dead!'

'Listen, youngster' – the old man was on his hunkers before him – 'the master's likely told you you've got to forget all that's happened here. Now, be a good lad and go home and do as he bid you, forget all about it. Speak to no one. I repeat that, do you hear? no one, because he has ways an' means of gettin' back at those who do him down. He can be a good friend an' all, and I should imagine you and your lot over there are in need of a friend. Now think on it. These things happen.' And his face now stretching into a smile, he added, jocularly, 'There's worse things happen at sea every night, for that matter on the sea front, on both shores.'

Freddie turned to the older woman and she nodded at him, saying, quietly, 'Do as my husband tells you, lad. And here; I've got a bag of stuff ready for you to take back to your family. There's a ham shank in there an' some butter an' cheese and a fresh loaf, an' odds an' ends. The bag's nearly as big as yersel'. My man's got to go an errand into the town, he'll take you on the cart to the shore. I should imagine you can afford a keel boat across the river the day. How much did he give you?'

He seemed to have difficulty in opening his fist because the nails had pressed into the flesh in his fright. And when he exposed the two half-sovereigns they all nodded, and the old man said, 'Well, that's good pay. I'll say it is. You can't say it isn't. Nor can you say he's not generous to his own. You stick on the right side of him, lad, an' he'll see you through. An' your family an' all. So come on now, an' don't look so white about the gills. Everything's gona be all right. But put that lot deep in your pocket an' don't let on about it to no outsider.'

51

In doing as he was bid, he began to walk towards the man, then turned and looked into the clothes-basket again. The child looked to him like Lily had done only a short while ago when she used to lie in the skip sucking a pap bag, and he asked a question, but in a very low apprehensive voice, 'He ... he won't hurt her, I mean, you won't let him, will you?'

There was a pause before both the old woman and the young one said together, 'No, no; don't worry. It'll be all right.' But as he stared at them he felt sure that neither of them could do anything. 'Go on now.' The old woman patted him on the head, and when she lifted the bass bag from the table and handed it to him the weight of it almost pulled him down, but he had to force himself to look at her and say, 'Ta, missis. Me ma'll say ta an' all.'

He saw the old woman bite on her lower lip before saying, 'Your ma's got a nice little lad in you. Tell her that from me. Go on now.'

At the front door the old man took the bass bag from him and hoisted it up onto the cart, then lifted him up onto the front seat before taking his own place and saying, 'Gee up! there,' to the horse. And so Freddie rode most of the way back home, for Frank Wheatley himself put him in a keel and paid his penny fare and an extra penny to have his little sculler pulled behind. And so he crossed the river on the morning tide, and for the rest of his life he thought of it as the morning after the night when things began to happen to him.

2

He had been landed at the far end of the town and as he wended his way through the long narrow street he was jostled by every kind of inhabitant and vehicle; twice he slipped on some garbage, and the contents of the bag were only saved from spilling by the strings at its top.

It was as he left the town and passed the row of cottages prior to taking the steps that led to home when he saw in the distance two of the excise men. One was Mr Dees who was the Principal Coast Officer, and he was with the Landing and Searching Officer called Robert Leitch. Mr Leitch lived at yon side of the town in a nice house and he seemed a nice enough man because he had spoken to him. But then you didn't get many nice men among the excise.

He had never seen them along this way before, at least not together, and this early. Mr Dees's office was just above the quay and that didn't open for business till ten in the morning.

Now, as if the bag was a featherweight, he sprinted up the steps, then along the path and into the house.

And his entry caused his father to jerk himself from the bed and his mother to rush out of the other room, and it was evident from the expression on her face that she was about to yell at him. But when she spoke her voice was even but very low. 'So you've got back,' she said.

'Aye, Ma.'

He hoisted the bag onto the table, and she approached from the other side and, looking down at it, she said, 'And what's that, may I ask?'

'Some bits and pieces from the housekeeper over there.' He jerked his head back towards the door.

'Why? What did you do to earn that?'

'Don't ask the road you know, woman.' His da was sitting on the floor near the edge of the table now, and he put his hand out and touched his son's thin shoulder, saying, 'You look tired, lad.'

His mother came round the table and stood at the other side of him. 'I've got some broth, still hot; could you do with a bite?'

'No, Ma, ta. I've . . . I've had me breakfast.'

She stared at him, then said, 'Well, you may have had it, but you look fagged, boy. Sit down.' She pointed to a cracket, but he didn't obey her; instead, he undid the strings on the top of the bass bag and, one after the other, he pulled out the eatables while his parents stared open-eyed at the array.

'By! it looks as if your boat's come in, lad.'

Robert placed his forearms on the edge of the table and hoisted himself up a little further. 'That must be a pound of butter if it's an ounce. And there's some ham on that shank. My! I've never seen so much stuff all at once for many a long year. They must keep a good table in that kitchen where you spent the night.'

He now slid back to the floor. 'Did you spend it there? Or did you go to your granny's?'

'Don't be daft, man.' His wife thrust out her foot towards him. 'Would he have brought this lot back if me ma had got her hands on the bag?'

'Aye, you're right there, Jinny, you're right there. Anyway, come and sit down, lad, and tell us all about it.'

54

As his father propelled himself to his favourite spot at the side of the fireplace to sit with his back against the wall, Freddie seated himself on the cracket; and he dropped his head and looked down at his hands pressed tight between his bare knees before he forced himself to say, 'Not much to tell, Da,' when all the time he wanted to fling himself, not against his da, but into his mother's arms and howl out all his feelings about what had happened in that house across the water, especially about the poor lady and her bairn.

'Did you get there in time? Did the excise come?'

'Aye, just, Da; just in time. And aye, they came, but they found nowt.'

'Was there anythin' to find?'

'Aye, two kegs of rum down the well; but the master knew that's where they would likely look and he had his man put them in the midden.'

'In the midden?'

'Aye. Well, they were in kegs, it wouldn't do them any harm.'

'And he just had two kegs? That's all he had?'

Freddie hesitated: he blinked and wetted his lips. 'I think he had other bits and pieces like baccy an' wine an' silks an' stuff, but it was where nobody could find it . . .' Then he added, 'I suppose, 'cos they didn't get anything.'

'Did . . . did they see you?'

'No.'

'Where were you in all this then?'

Things were getting difficult. He slowly looked from one to the other before answering, 'Outside, in . . . in the garden.'

'Freddie.' His father had hold of his hands now. 'You . . . you frightened about something?'

Yes, he was frightened about something. Oh! Lord

God, he was. For a moment his da's face seemed to have become another's looking into his, the nose almost touching his and the promise in the eyes of what would happen to him if he talked, at least about . . . He couldn't even tell himself what the special thing was he must keep silent about, and so he said, 'No, Da, except . . . except that I'm tired.'

'You didn't get much sleep then?'

'No . . . no, I didn't.'

'Well, if that's how you feel you're not doin' any butchering this mornin'.' It was his mother speaking now. 'You can get yourself to bed for a couple of hours. Tommy Preston called in earlier on. He said Mr Aynsley might take you on half-days 'cos Mrs Bing's takin' their Georgie away. She's sendin' him half-day to the Jubilee School. He was snobbin' boots for Fluts in Bedford Street an' she took him away from there, you remember? No prospects for her son, she said, in snobbin' boots. He hadn't been there but a couple of years, an' she expected Mr Flut to have put him on to ladies' slippers, silk lined at that.' She laughed. 'Anyway, you seem to get on if you're a Methodist. But, lad, there's a full half-day for you ready an' waitin' if you want it . . . Do you want it?'

He stared up into his mother's face for a moment before saying softly, 'I'm not taken with butchery, Ma, never was. I . . . I wouldn't mind goin' into boots an' snobbin'.'

His father pulled him round towards him again. 'But there's nothin' in it, lad,' he said; 'they tell me the town's full of boot an' shoe makers these days. You trip over them wherever you go. They even beat the butchers, an' they run the ship-owners neck and neck. And that's saying something.'

'Eeh!' his mother now put in, 'my gall rises when I pass the Dock Inn or the Duke of Bedford, or one or other of them bars that swarm the town an' see them comin' out with their peaked caps an' their brass buttons an' their bellies pokin' their trousers ready to burst. And the air of them. My God! I don't know about the Duke of Bedford, you'd think they were all descended from the Duke of Wellington.'

Robert laughed now, saying, 'Aw, lass, they're not all alike. There's good an' bad . . .'

'Few and far atween with that lot, an' what they make on the side in the bottom of their holds. Why doesn't the excise collar them?'

'They do, lass, they do. They all have to take their turn. What d'you say, boy?' He pushed Freddie gently, expecting his son to laugh. But when there was no response except an almost blank stare from this lad whom he imagined was so full of spirit that nothing could get him down, he said gently, 'Go and rest yersel', lad. Go on. And thank you for bringin' this grub. We'll have a beanfeast the night. Go on now.'

Without hesitation Freddie went into the other room. There was no one occupying any of the three shakedowns on the floor. Nancy, he knew, would be on the shore pushing the bogie which held Lily, and the driftwood Jessie was picking up. He went to the bed farthest from the door and which he shared with John and, sitting down on its edge, he pulled off his boots and his coat but kept on his breeches; then he crept under the patchwork pad and buried his head in the striped pillow tick.

It was only then that he remembered he hadn't mentioned the small fortune that reposed in the pocket in the lining of his trousers, and as his hand instinctively felt for the coins he wondered why he hadn't handed them straight to his mother. There must be a reason; he didn't forget things, at least

57

where money was concerned. There must be a reason, and deep down he knew that part of the reason was fear, fear of not being able to keep his mouth shut, because in his ma's and da's eyes that lot of food on the table out there should have been payment enough for any night's work. They would reckon he had done something big or even something bad to be paid a whole sovereign, when John worked six days down the pit for four shillings and he himself only got a shilling a week for sorting out bloody entrails. The thought of such work, as usual, upset him; and yet he was always thankful that the animal had been killed before he got there. Even so, the flesh was still warm, especially the heart. And his ma wanted him to work the full half-day there. Just because he might then be paid one an' six a week.

Of a sudden he felt sick. He didn't want to go back to the butcher's shop. For a moment he had the wild idea he could run away to sea and that would solve all problems. Mr Gallagher could hardly do anything to him then – could he? – if he was at sea. But that would mean he would have to go off to Newcastle, and who would sign him on at ten years old; especially when he only looked eight?

It was funny, but he didn't feel ten years old. In fact, he felt older than Mick Harper up the street, and he was fourteen; certainly older than Ernie Blaze or Tom Crighton, an' they were over twelve. Two of them worked in the brewery and one went out fishing, deep sea, but they talked daft, well not exactly daft, silly though. But even that wasn't the right word to describe the difference between him and them. The only thing he knew was that they didn't think about things like he did. They were slow on the uptake. Aye yes, that was it, they were slow on the uptake.

But what was he going to do about the money? How

58

many one and sixpences were there in twenty shillings? He reckoned on his fingers: thirteen and a bit. He could stay away from the butcher's for thirteen weeks and still give his mother his pay ... He discarded the idea, it was too complicated. What would he do when he wasn't at the butcher's? And Tommy Preston would certainly be here the first day he didn't put in an appearance ... It was a daft idea.

He could save the money. But only rich people saved, and Methodists. Well most of them. The Prestons were Methodists. His mother always reckoned that Mr Preston was a warm man on the side 'cos he neither drank nor smoked so he must have money.

But where could he save? ... He could hide it. Where? There was no place in the house or out of it.

Maggie Hewitt. Eeh! but his ma didn't like Maggie Hewitt 'cos she made money out of lending it. But some liked her: the men from the boats who wanted to change their money did. And another thing: Maggie Hewitt liked him. She always joked with him when they met on the quay. She would pull his hair or his ear and call him funny names. Jack-the-giant-killer, she said he was, or Fearless Freddie.

Fearless! She didn't know. Nobody knew. Of a sudden he wanted to cry, but he knew he mustn't 'cos that would bring his ma in, and he hadn't cried since Billy died. He jumped from the bed, dragged on his boots and coat, then went into the kitchen. The door was open and his da was sitting on the front step and he looked at him in surprise.

'Where's me ma?' he asked.

'She's gone to the pipe for some water.'

If his ma had gone to the stand-pipe in the main street for some clean water that would mean she wouldn't be back for an hour, 'cos that was her treat for the day when she met up with the other women and they jabbered, argued, and even fought. It was a known thing that the men kept clear when the women were round the stand-pipe. Men who had been foolhardy enough to try to enter their conclave had come away with broken heads and faces. So he said to his father, 'I can't sleep, Da; and . . . and I'm not goin' to the shop this mornin'; I'm gona take a walk.'

'Somethin' troublin' you, lad? There is, isn't there?' Robert's arm went out in a curve inviting his son to come into the comfort of it, but Freddie sidled past him, saying, 'I'll be all right, Da; I'll just walk it off.'

As he ran along the path towards the steps his father called after him, 'Look up Nancy an' the bairns; help them with the wood. That's a good lad.'

When he reached the shore he turned in the opposite direction from where he knew his sisters would be gathering and hurried towards the main quay. There would be bustle there, men milling about, and boats that had managed to avoid the sandbanks on the way down from Newcastle waiting hopefully to put out to sea; others unloading some of their cargo in order to lighten the load to help them up the river to Newcastle to clear their cargo and pay their dues to that hated city. But his mind's eye would always follow these boats leaving the river on their hazardous journey across the Black Middens that claimed so many ships and lives, and out into the German Ocean.

He stood on the quay looking at the *Africaine*. She was quite a big ship and new, a three-hundred tonner. She had been built in Jarrow, and was owned by the Coxon company who had their office along the quay there. His eyes travelled beyond the ship to another lying at anchor. She was a whopper that one, a five-hundred tonner likely. She was a New-castle one. Nobody liked the Newcastle boats; they always tended to be better and bigger than anybody else's along the river. For himself he fancied the smaller ones, like the *Anna*, the North Shields *Anna*. There were lots of boats called *Anne* and *Anna*, some from Newcastle, some from South Shields, and there were two from here; all with the same name, but belonging to different owners. What would it be like to own a boat? He'd rather own a boot shop.

The smells on the waterfront stung his nostrils: tar, fish, hides, baccy, wood. The wood came from the prop boats. He liked the smell of these. The props came from Norway. What was Norway like? Was it full of big men, like the ones who docked here with fair hair and ruddy faces? He knew one thing, they were nearly always big drinkers and big fighters, very pally and nice when they were sober but they raised hell outside the bars, especially the night before they sailed. Would he like to be a sailor? No, he didn't think so now. Anyway, he had been through that.

'And where is Jack-the-giant-killer off to this morning?'

He came to himself as if from a daydream and blinked at the woman who was now walking at his side.

'Nowhere, Miss Hewitt,' he said.

'Shouldn't you be at Mr Aynsley's?'

How did she know he worked for Aynsley?

'Ah, you're wondering how I know you work at the butcher's? For the simple reason, young man, that I deal with Mr Aynsley and I've seen you through in the back shop, your grubby little hands tearing at the entrails. How many hours do you work?'

'Three a day.'

'For how much?'

'A shilling a week.'

'Eighteen hours for one shilling . . . twelve pence. What's eighteen into twelve?'

He tried to work it out but couldn't. 'I don't know,' he said.

'You don't know, and you can't read or write, but you think you're a big fellow, don't you?'

He slanted his glance at her. What was she up to?

'Did you enjoy your trip across the water last night? You were late going and early coming back.'

He actually stopped and gazed at her. How did she know? She could have seen him coming back; but who could have seen him going?

'How do I know? I know lots of things, young fellow-me-lad, that would surprise you. Well, what did you do across there?'

'I minded me own business.' It came out before he could check it; and her reply was a short laugh and a thrust from her hand and, 'You cheeky monkey!'

The push she gave him brought him against a stack of barrels and although they shook just the slightest a voice bawled, 'What the hell do you think you're up to! Tryin' to climb on top?'

The man had come from behind the pile, his glare fixed on Freddie, but his tone changed immediately when he saw the woman, and his voice was a greeting, saying, 'Oh, hello there, Maggie.'

She didn't answer him but, looking at Freddie, she said, 'Come on, you.'

He felt embarrassed and slightly defiant. He wanted to say, 'I'm goin' back,' but then he had thought about her earlier on – hadn't he? – and the fortune in his pocket. So, apparently obediently, he walked by her side.

'Your father's a cripple, isn't he?'

He looked up at her but didn't answer. She wasn't very big, not like his mother. He reckoned she was just over five feet; and although she wasn't dressed ordinary 'cos she was wearing a black straw hat, she wasn't turned out like the ladies from yon end of the town. Her skirt was grey but it wasn't very full, and she had a three-quarter-length coat on. It was tight into her waist. She was skinny. He said, 'You seem to know a lot, don't you?'

'Don't be cheeky, young man. And I could say the same to you, and to my mind too much for your own good.'

He had heard those words before. When he shivered visibly, she said, 'You cold?' her tone expressing surprise, and he answered, 'Aye, a bit.'

'Well, you must be in for something because it isn't cold this morning. What did you do last night?'

He jerked his head and looked at her in some alarm, and she said, 'Oh, it's all right, it's all right. You went across to Gallagher's, but it was all a set-up job. You should have been over here; there was some fun. I don't know who Robert Leitch hates most, your lot or those two from Newcastle.'

She had said, your lot; she must know about Mister Blaze and the rest.

'Damn and blast it!' She stepped quickly to the side, shaking the excrement from her foot, and she glared at him as she said, 'Do you know what I'd like to bet, and I wouldn't lose on it, this is the filthiest town in the country. They're sitting on their bloody committees debating whether they should have a tunnel or a bridge across the bloody river that will vie with anything in Newcastle, while the pigs are still running the streets, instead of sweepers. By God! I'll do something about this, I will! I will!' and she stepped briskly towards some rotting hay lying

63

against a coil of chain and, swishing her foot, she cleaned the mess from it. 'You know something, boy? Pigs are cleaner than people.'

She hurried on, picking her way now until they left the quay, past the row of one-roomed cottages that looked like hovels and which also came in for her disdain as she thumbed towards them, saying, 'You know nothing about statistics, boy, but you'll know that practically every working man's house in this town and along the coast contains only one room.'

'We have two.'

She turned her head and looked down on him. 'You're lucky then.'

'And the other cottages in our row have two.'

'You're all very lucky then.' She bounced her head with each word, and they walked on again, up a cindery bank now and onto a narrow road. And as he continued to walk by her side he wondered why he was staying with her. Yet he knew why. But they'd soon be out in the country.

They walked on in silence for some way until she said, 'What are your plans for this morning, young sir, may I ask?'

She seemed to be laughing at him now, but his answer brought her to a halt when he said, 'To see you, to talk to you.'

'Really? You mean our meeting was not unintentional or accidental?'

He didn't quite get the gist of her words but his answer was, 'Well, I thought about you when I was lying in bed.'

The laugh she let out was, strangely, a nice laugh: it was high and sort of tinkling, different altogether from her face that looked leathery and old, older than his mother's.

'So you had been thinking of me in bed? Well! Well! all I can say to you is that your appearance is very deceptive and that you are starting early on a downward trail.'

He couldn't follow her now, but he said, 'I want to talk to you about money.'

'Ah!' Her mouth opened wide. 'So now we know . . . money. You want a loan?'

'No.'

'*No?*'

'I want you to keep some money for me.'

She remained silent, staring down at him. Then she said, 'You want to do business? Well, if that's the case, let us go on and quickly.'

They walked on. She didn't speak any more until she turned from the road onto a bridle-path. And as he walked up it, slightly behind her, he wondered why he had never been along this way before. But then he very rarely left the town, there was never any time, except on a Sunday. And he always had a long sleep on a Sunday and afterwards he would do whatever John wanted to do.

His open mouth showed surprise when her hand guided him through a white painted gate, then up the gravel path towards a house with green shutters. It was a real house, like those on the top of the bank in the town. He took in immediately it had actually eight windows; no . . . nine, there was one in the roof. The heavy door, he noticed, was of black oak, and when she inserted a big key into the lock and turned it and there was no grating sound, he knew it must have been well oiled. And now he was as surprised as he had been when he first stood in the hall of The Towers: this one was smaller, but as grand; well, not grand but better in a way, interesting. His eyes took in the wheels of two ships hanging on the wall right opposite the door and in between them a painting of a sailing ship, full blown. It was so real he could even imagine the wind in the sails.

She had taken off her hat and coat and was saying, 'Come along,' as she pushed him gently in the back and through one of a number of doors that went off the hall, and into a room that looked like one of the ship's offices along the quay, only a bit more comfortable. She pointed to a leather chair, saying, 'Sit down. Would you like a drink?'

'No, no; ta . . . thanks.'

'Like something to eat?'

'No; no thanks.'

'You want to get down to business, is that it?'

He said nothing; and so she walked over to the chair behind an oak desk placed in front of the window, and having sat down, she leaned forward with her forearms on the desk and said, 'Well now, if it's business you want to talk about, let's talk business.'

He stood up, put his hand down inside his breeches and into the lining pocket and pulled out a piece of rag and, placing it on the desk, he unfolded it and exposed the two half-sovereigns.

She now leant further forward and looked at them. She seemed to look at them for a long time before she raised her head and asked, 'What had you to do to get that amount?'

He could have answered simply, 'Keep me mouth shut,' but he said nothing, just stared at her.

And now she asked, 'Did you get more than this?'

He shook his head.

'Then why didn't you give it to your mother? You're in straits along there, aren't you? She has her hands full, so I understand. Your father being like he is, and with a blind daughter, she could do with this.'

66

'I know.'

'Then why – in the name of the Almighty! – haven't you given it to her?'

''Cos . . . 'cos it would make her worry; and she would ask the same questions as you, what did I get it for?'

'Then I ask again, what did you get it for? Did you do something bad?'

'*No*.' His voice was loud now, almost a yell. 'No, I didn't!'

'All right. All right. Don't blow your cap off. Well now, we've got to talk, you and me, haven't we? Why have you come to me? I could give you away, you know I could, couldn't I?'

'Aye, you could . . . suppose.'

'But you don't think I will?'

'No.'

'You're a funny one. Frank said you had a head on your shoulders that would fit your granny.'

Who was Frank? And he wasn't pleased at being associated with his granny because she was a crabby old scut. She didn't like him and he didn't like her.

'What do you want me to do with your money?'

'Keep it for me till I want it. I'll pay you.'

She chuckled now, saying, 'If I keep your money, laddie, it's me that will be paying you. Have you heard of anything like interest?'

'No. I just thought you charged.'

'Well, for your information' – her face was now grim, as was her voice – 'I am no money-lender, I am not a penny in the shilling woman. Do you understand what I mean?'

Yes, he understood her all right now, 'cos some of the old wives charged a penny a week for lending you a shilling, so his da said. And he had thought she was one of them.

67

Her voice still grim, she said, 'I don't deal in pennies, cents or sous, I'm what you call a commission agent for various things . . . miscellaneous. A commission agent you could say without a licence, for I am not registered in Newcastle, and I'm a thorn in the flesh of many males in this town, those who consider women fit only for bed and breeding.'

She was talking angrily now, walking about the room, and it wasn't as if she was addressing him: 'They don't know the difference between an American and a Spanish dollar, although it's only a penny at the present time, four and tuppence to four and threepence.' She now stopped in her walking and stabbed her finger at him; then went on, 'In one day I can deal with riels, eight to the dollar, sixpence ha'penny at best, or a gold rupee. And you know how much a gold rupee can bring? The last one I had through my hands brought twenty-eight and ninepence. And why am I talking to you, telling you this?' She stopped in front of him again. 'Because if you understood half of what I've said I could be in the soup. Your sideline is being a runner, my main sideline is exchanging money, but not ripping the poor sods off like Johnson and Rickmore up in the city or Tate along in the town there.' She bent over him, her hands on her hips, her body leaning forward. 'Now you know my secret, tell me yours.'

What secret? He didn't understand anything she had been saying except that she changed the sailors' money. Well, lots of people did that, so he understood. There was an office along the quay. And they could get it changed in the shipping company too. So he didn't really know what she was at; but he reckoned she was sly. Even so he felt tempted to tell her exactly what had happened. He didn't really

68

know why except he was sure that he could trust her, she wouldn't give him away.

He recalled how whenever he'd heard her name mentioned it was always associated with . . . what was the word? Not fear, no; he supposed it was what his ma called respect. She was always saying, you can respect this one or that one, or on the other hand, this one or that one breeds no respect. But still he daren't, for the life of him, tell everything, so he said, 'I . . . I warned the master that the excise were on to him, and . . . and he was glad I did.'

'As far as I can gather you've warned others that the excise were on to them, but did they give you a sovereign?'

'No.'

'What did they give you?'

'Some baccy for me da and a draw off of rum.'

'No white powder for your da?'

He screwed up his eyes at her. 'White powder? No.'

'Well' – she straightened up – 'that would likely do him more good than the rum, help him to blot out life. Still, every man to his taste. You take the powder across the river though, don't you?'

'I don't take no powder across the river. What kind of powder?'

He watched her face soften. She came towards him and put her hand on his head, and her smile was sweet and her voice soft as she said, 'No matter what they say you're still just ten, and one of these days that little shell of yours will be taken out on the tide if you're not careful . . . Well, I'm going to have a drink of cocoa. You like cocoa?'

'Never had it.'

'Aw, well, we'll have to see if we can tempt your palate, and also with a raisin bun. But first of all let us decide on our business association. You have,

69

young man, this day, pledged with me two half-sovereigns which I'm to keep for you for an unknown time. That's right, isn't it?' His head bobbed again. 'Well, as long as the half-sovereigns remain with me you will receive some interest. Usually interest is paid every six months, or once a year. Now at two and a half per cent you will be entitled to sixpence at the end of the year and I will be entitled to say, well, a penny of that sixpence for looking after it for you. You see what I mean?'

His eyes flicked from her to a side table on which there were a number of photographs, then to the desk, then to the fireplace to the right of him where a wood fire was still smouldering, and then, looking at her, he said, 'The penny would be your cut?'

He saw her close her eyes, put her lips tight together and swallow before answering: 'Right, partner. Right.'

She was laughing at him again. He knew this, and he smiled at her. But the stiff expression returned to her countenance again as she said, 'Of course, that's if you leave your money for a year. Are you going to?'

'I don't know. If . . . if things get bad I might have to take a bit out at a time; or if I decide to leave the butcher's, 'cos I don't like it there, I might take me wage out.'

'Oh' – her face stretched – 'I can see this is going to be a difficult proposition. Still, it is my job to face difficulties. Well now, sit where you are' – and she pointed at him – 'and don't touch a thing on my desk. You understand?'

He had the desire to answer her back but he didn't. And when she had left the room he let out a long breath and sank into the soft leather of the chair for a moment, telling himself that all this business was nearly as queer as last night, only not

70

so frightening. She was a funny card, but he liked her. She was cute in a kind of way. His mother would have said she was as fly as a box of monkeys.

He turned his head to look at the paintings on the wall opposite the window and desk. One seemed to be of the same ship as in the hall, only smaller; and to one side of it, there was a painting of a sailor with a beard and brass buttons, with a young lass by his side; and to the other, a painting of a young clean-shaven sailor, also with brass buttons and the same lass by his side. He looked at them for a long time trying to work out who they were. Likely her da and her ma. Her ma looked bonny. He got up and walked over to look at them more closely when the door was pushed open abruptly and she came in carrying a tray and on it two steaming mugs and a plate of buns. She paused a moment watching him as he looked, startled, back at her as though he had been caught out, and he stammered, 'I . . . I . . . I was only . . . look . . . lookin'.'

'Well, I won't charge you for looking,' she said and walked over to her desk.

He followed her, and as she placed the tray down he, seeming to have regained his usual composure, nodded backwards and said, 'They're nice. Is that your ma and da?'

'No, young sir, that isn't me ma and da. That is my father and me.'

His mouth dropped slightly open as he looked from her weather-beaten face to the pretty girl. And when she said, 'Oh, yes, yes, I have changed. Thirty years and salt spray and wind and –' She stopped, swung round and picked up a mug of cocoa and, handing it to him, she said, 'Taste that and see if you like it.'

He tasted the thick brown stuff. It was hot and sweet and the only thing he could couple the taste with was cinder toffee. ''Tis nice,' he said.

71

'I'm pleased you like it.' Then she said, 'Try a bun and see if you like that too.'

As he took a bun she walked back to the paintings, to the one of the girl and the young man. And she stared at it for a moment before, pointing now to the ship, she said, 'That was my father's boat.'

Her eyes were fixed tightly on the painting as she went on quietly now, 'She went down on the Black Middens and he with it, and Sam too.' She turned towards him. 'That is Sam.' She pointed to the young man. She didn't go on to explain who Sam was but said, 'We lived on The Lawe, you know, across the water in Shields. I was born there, almost within sight of the Middens.'

Having taken a long drink from the mug, she suddenly leaned towards him and, wagging her finger in his face, said, 'Never go to sea. Do anything: clean guts in the back of a butcher's shop, swill middens, anything, but don't go to sea. Of all the treacherous bitches in the world, she's the biggest, for she takes men from their wives and grooms from their brides; she deprives children of fathers; and even when she's kind she cripples men and makes women old before their time. Don't ever go to sea, boy.'

The next moment she was out of the room and he was left alone, a half-eaten bun in one hand, a half-full mug of cocoa in the other, staring towards the door. Was she potty? Bats? Up the lum? Well, there was something the matter with her. He looked at the bun. It was a nice bun. He'd never tasted one like it. And this cocoa was nice an' all, warming. But he'd better go. It had been a funny morning . . . it had been a funny night. Everything had been funny since he crossed the river last night.

But here she was, coming back into the room. And

72

her voice was soft again as she said, 'I got a bit carried away, didn't I, about the sea? But I don't often have visitors, especially in this room. In fact, I don't do business here at all. My office is on the quay, you know. Well, I call it my office but it's known as Maggie Hewitt's house, isn't it, because there's no brass-plated plaque outside. Anyway, finish your cocoa and your bun and then we'll put our business in writing, eh?'

'I . . . I can't write.'

'I didn't expect you could, but I can. And if you can't write you can't read, I suppose. Is that it?'

'No; I can't read.'

'Well, there's a school of sorts in the town; why don't you go there instead of skittering up and down the quays? What do you get for your skittering anyway?'

'Oh, sometimes a bit of fruit, an orange or some lemons, or when they're revictuallin' I get the old stuff.'

'Is that as far as you think, getting the garbage from the boats?'

'It . . . it helps at home.'

'Aye, it might. But what when you grow up? And you'll be grown up, you know; you won't always remain that size. What are you going to do then?'

'I would like to go in for a shoe-shop. Well, I mean, not a shoe-shop, just make shoes.'

She nodded at him now, saying, 'Well, there should be money in that, but not in this town. They're falling over each other here.'

'That's what me da says.'

'Then you have discussed your future?'

'Well, I've told them I don't want the butcher's.'

'If that's the case, then there's hope for you.' She turned to the desk, pulled a book towards her, flicked over a number of leaves, then dipped a quill pen into an inkwell and began to write. She hadn't sat down but was bending over the desk; and now she turned her head and said, 'See what I've written here?' He went round the desk and looked on the page and saw some squiggles and she said, 'It says, "Deposited with me on the first of September, eighteen forty-three."' Then stopping and turning her head towards him, she said, 'I'm dating it from the first: I'm being kind to you,' before going on, '"the sum of two half-sovereigns to be invested at two and a half per cent per annum. Interest to be half-yearly if so required. Signed this day, Margaret Hewitt, spinster, and Freddie Musgrave."'

'It should be Frederick.'

She glared sharply at him and started writing again, then said, '"Frederick Musgrave." Here' – she handed the pen to him – 'put a cross there where I'm pointing to.'

His hand shaking, he made a cross. She now took a rocker blotter and dried the ink before, pointing to the writing again, she said, 'You have this day, Frederick Musgrave, done your first business deal. And I don't think it'll be the last one. What do you say?'

'I . . . I don't think I'll get any more half-sovereigns.'

'Oh' – she wagged her head – 'you never know. And Frederick' – she stressed his name as she brought her face down to his – 'you haven't hood-winked me. Get that into your head. Do you hear? You haven't hoodwinked me this morning. Because you didn't get those half-sovereigns for carrying a message to Mr Gallagher, not just for carrying a message; but you'll tell me some day. Oh yes you will, you'll tell me some day. Or perhaps I'll be able to tell you before you tell me. What do you think of that?'

What he thought was, she would never be able to tell him what had happened last night or what had happened this morning, 'cos not even the staff knew what the master had said to him, although they knew what he intended to do with the bairn. Oh, that poor bairn.

At the door she said, 'Go on now; and if I were you I'd make up my mind quickly between the butcher's and the boots', because, let me tell you, you'll come to no good running the quay all day. You might be too young to be picked up by the press gang but there are still other ways to disappear, laddie. So get yourself into a settled job. Do you hear me?'

'Yes, miss.'

'And one last thing: if you get worried about anything, anything at all, just make your way here or to the house on the quay. I'm either in one place or the other, except on a Thursday afternoon and a Saturday morning when I'm in Newcastle.'

'Thanks, miss. Aye, I will. And ta for the cocoa an' . . . an' for puttin' me name in your book.'

Her face relaxed and she smiled now and, her voice low again, she said, 'Go on with you. You'll do . . .'

Before descending the cinder hill towards the beach he stood still for a moment and looked along the river as far as he could see both ways. It seemed packed with boats, large ones and small ones. In the far distance he made out a keelman sculling coal from the staithes to a boat in the middle of the river. It was one of those too big to come inshore the way the tide was at present. And from where he stood he could see over the other end of the town and the steam rising from the saltpans. And the noise of the

75

town and the river merged and rose to him, and it was like the sound of bees swarming, punctuated every now and again by the banging of hammers in rhythmic flow as if from a forge. And a voice rising above the rest and conveying to him that it would be carrying an oath from someone on the quay to someone on board ship, or the other way round.

It was said there were well over eight thousand people in the town. How many was eight thousand? He could count up to a hundred and that was a fair amount, but he couldn't visualise eight thousand.

What was he going to do now? Go to the butcher's and get his lugs clipped and his backside kicked, or go and see if he could be set on in a boot shop? But that would mean a full day, six days a week from seven in the morning till six at night, and then if he was lucky. And it would be mostly cobbling. Oh, he'd better go home first and talk it over with his da. But he wouldn't go the way of the quayside, or by the market and the main street, he would skirt the town 'cos it wasn't so mucky on the outskirts. But why was he bothering about it being mucky? It had never struck him until she had mentioned it. He could see her angrily wiping the muck from her boot. Aw, he was thinkin' daft. He would go the way he always went.

And so he ran down the hill and along the road to the quay. There was a fruit boat in at one place and he picked up a partly squashed orange that had got wedged between two crates, and as he did so there was a shout from the deck of the ship, and he looked up and saw two oranges come flying towards him. He managed to catch one and quickly retrieved the other; then turning, his face bright, he shouted, 'Ta, mister,' and the orange thrower laughed and answered in a foreign language. Minutes later he had reached the end of the quay where it merged into the beach when he saw Mr Tommy Johnson coming round from behind his boat. He was humping a creel of herring and he called to him, 'Hi! there, Freddie,' then waved him forward.

He hesitated a moment before approaching him because he knew there would be more questions. But when he reached the fisherman all Tommy said was, 'Take them to your ma,' and handed him four big herrings on a hook. Then he added, 'Tell your da I'll be popping in to see him later. Understand?'

Yes, he understood. 'Ta, Mr Johnson. Ta.' As he turned away and climbed to the road above the beach, he thought, That's funny, Mr Johnson rarely came empty-handed to see his da, so there must have been a run of some kind last night; or perhaps Mr Johnson was just bringing something from his own store. And he likely did have a store because he was a sober man was Mr Johnson; after a run he didn't get totally bottled like the rest.

Before he reached the house he knew they had company, and when he entered the room he stood in amazement looking at his granny. His granny never came across the water, she was frightened to be in a sculler or the ferry, but there she was, and a strange lass with her. His mother said, 'Look what the wind's blown in. And this is your cousin Lizzie from Darlington.'

He was looking at a young lass. She had a face like a full moon, or more like a turnip lantern that the lads made when they wanted a bit of carry on at night to scare folks. But the face that he was looking at wouldn't scare anyone, he thought it was too dull. And she was nursing a bundle on her knee. He didn't know what made him step forward and look at the baby without giving a greeting to his granny or this

77

new cousin. The thing was swaddled up to the eyes and it stank of pee. Last night's baby had looked clean and bonny this morning. What he could see of this one's face was red and puffed; it looked dull like its mother.

'Not a word of greeting; we mightn't be here.'

He turned and looked at his grandmother, then said, 'Hello, Granny.'

'Oh, he's seen me and he's just asked how I am an' how I managed to get across that flaming river; and would I like some of those herrin' he's holdin' to take back home with me, and one of the oranges an' all.'

As he handed the fish to his mother, he said, 'Mr Johnson gave me these, Ma, and' – he glanced now at his father sitting against the wall – 'he said he'd be along later to see you, Da.'

'Oh, that's nice. That's nice.'

'You haven't been to the shop then?' His mother spoke directly to him for the first time, and he shook his head and said, 'No, Ma. I . . . I wasn't feelin' like it.'

'My God! in heaven, did you ever hear anythin' like that?'

All eyes were on his grandmother now. She, like her daughter, was a tall woman, but that, apparently, was the only resemblance between them. She was wearing a black skirt and a blue-striped blouse. He could see it through her open knee-length bead cape that matched her bonnet. Besides her voice, her presence seemed to fill the room. His mother was now saying to her, 'Will you have a drop of broth, Ma?'

'Broth it is. Well, I could have got that at home, but beggars can't be choosers.'

He looked at his mother and she looked at him and he smiled inwardly at the thought that she wasn't bringing out the ham shank, nor the butter and cheese and white bread. 'Who gave you the oranges?' she said, and held her hand out for the fruit that was lying along the crook of his arm.

'A fella on a boat,' but he didn't offer them to her; instead he said, 'I'm keepin' these for the bairns, Ma.'

'Oh, aye, aye.' As his mother nodded to him her mother, addressing her granddaughter, said, 'Did y'hear that? He's keepin' the fruit for the bairns; no, can he, Ma? or, we'll share, Ma.' The old woman now looked towards her son-in-law, saying, 'Who's boss in this house anyway?'

And his father infuriated her more when he answered, 'Oh, he is, has been this long while.'

'It's no joke, but would seem so,' she said.

His father winked at him and the look in his eyes said, Come on, laugh at her; but he couldn't laugh at his granny; her joking was always pointed and hurtful for somebody. And he turned and walked from the room now and into the bedroom, and there, lifting the lid of a wooden trunk that held their clothes and was set between the girls' beds, he put the two whole oranges in the corner. Then closing the lid again he laid the squashed one on the top and sat down beside it.

He hadn't been sitting long before his mother came into the room and, closing the door quietly after her, she went to the small window and pulled the curtain a little to the side to let more light in. Then coming to him, she bent over him, saying, 'You all right now?'

'Aye, Ma.'

'Really? Better than you were?'

'Aye, Ma.'

She now put her hand on his shoulder and in a

79

conspiratorial voice murmured, 'I'm not fetchin' out that food while they are here no matter how long they stay. What d'you say?'

He smiled back at her, saying, 'You're right, Ma.'

'We'll have a do when they're gone, eh? By the way, she's just lost her husband . . . Lizzie. She's come to live with your granny, and the bairn's only six weeks. It won't last if you ask me; 'cos there's trussin' and trussin' an' bindin' an' bindin'. I wouldn't like to give a guess when she last changed it. She looks a lazy little bitch to me. Anyway, come on and be pleasant. It was nice of Mr Johnson to give you the fish. And you say he's comin'?'

'Aye, Ma.'

'And there wasn't a run last night?'

'No, Ma.'

'Well, he must have something. It'll please your da. Come on now.'

'I will in a minute, Ma.'

She straightened up, then stood looking down on him for a moment before going out. And he sat on, thinking. He thought about Miss Hewitt – he no longer said Maggie in his mind – and her house and the way she talked. His thinking seemed concerned only with the way she talked and what she talked about. She was clever was Miss Hewitt. By! yes, he would say she was clever . . . and different, different from them out there.

He didn't question whether he was including his mother and father in 'them out there'.

3

Three weeks later Miss Hewitt came to the house. She came because she hadn't seen Freddie on the quay for more than a week.

Jinny had been about to leave the house; she had got set on at the Rope Works half day, one o'clock till seven; but when the knock came on the door and she opened it and was confronted by a slight-figured neatly, even smartly dressed, woman whom she and everybody in the town knew as Maggie Hewitt, sometimes prefixed with Miss, her jaw dropped.

'Mrs Musgrave?'

'Aye, that's me.'

'May I come in?'

Jinny glanced back into the room where Robert was sitting on the floor, a bundle of shavings to his side as he whittled away at the leg of a chair. He'd had a stroke of luck. Buckhams, who had the shop in Saddle Street, had given him an order for three chairs. It was the first time for years it had happened. Lily was sitting on the mat playing with her clouty doll, and Freddie was in bed in the other room. But what did this one want?

She soon said what she wanted once she had stepped into the room: 'I . . . I haven't seen your son for some days. Has . . . has he gone away?'

'No. No, ma'am; he's . . . he's been sick.'

'Sick? Ill? What has been wrong?'

'It was his stomach, ma'am. But he's on the mend

81

now.' She nodded towards the bedroom. 'He'll be up and about in a day or two.'

The two women stared at each other for a moment: Jinny trying to weigh up this woman who spent her time on the waterfront doing business with men and who spoke like a lady and almost dressed as one, except that her clothes were plain, no frills or laces. But what did she want with her lad? She had never heard Freddie mention the woman's name. She saw her looking now towards Robert, and Robert was saying, 'Good-day to you, ma'am.'

'Good-day, Mr Musgrave. I see you know how to carve.'

'I'm a carpenter, ma'am. 'Twas my trade; still is.'

'Did you make this furniture?' Miss Hewitt looked around the room at the table, the chairs, the small sideboard, the carved wooden mantelpiece upon which were four brass candlesticks and all shining, and apparently not used for the purpose for which they were made for there was a tin candle holder at each end of the shelf. There was no sign of a lamp in the room; they must still depend on candles.

'Will you take a seat?' Jinny pulled the chair from under the table, and as she did so Lily rose from the mat and stumbled towards her, only to be checked by her mother, saying, 'Play with your doll, Lily; that's a good lass.' And obediently the child returned to the mat.

'I meant to come and see you before this, at least after I'd found out if your son was agreeable to my proposition.'

After I'd found out if your son was agreeable to my proposition. Jinny threaded the words through her mind. Whatever it was this woman was proposing she was going to talk to Freddie about it first. But she listened to her as she went on: 'You see, I need a

82

gardener and someone who can do odd jobs,' she was saying. 'I have two acres of land on the outskirts of the town and it is very badly overgrown. It hasn't been seen to for more than a year. The man who attended to it died and I've never bothered engaging anyone since. But I understood your son was looking for new employment and I wondered if you would be agreeable to his taking on the position?'

'Gardener?' It was Robert speaking. 'He knows nowt about gardenin', miss. Doubt if he's ever been in one; not many gardens round here.'

'I'm well aware of that, Mr Musgrave. But there are gardens round about, and there's only one gardener in the town; that is Mr Blyton of Union Street, and he is fully occupied.'

'I don't know whether he'd take to it, ma'am.' Jinny's voice was stiff. 'He's been used to the shore and the quay-front all his life. Boats are more in his line.'

'Perhaps, perhaps. But if he was willing, would you agree to his taking on the position? I can offer him at the beginning three shillings a week together with his food. The hours would be eight till six in the summer and nine till four in the winter. And, as I've indicated, his wage will rise according to his capacity for the work.'

According to his capacity for the work. What was surprising Jinny as much as anything was the way this one talked. She had heard she could swear like a trooper and handle men no matter what their class or size. But what was she saying? Three shillings a week and his food and a rise if he was worth it. And he'd be worth it because he'd put his heart into any job he was doing, even the butchery. That's why they wanted him round there. And that's why that pig of a man had given him that lump of meat; he was

83

never the one to give lumps of meat away. And it had been rotten. She knew when she was cooking it, it was rotten. They'd all had diarrhoea for days, but it had hit Freddie worst of all. Eeh, dear God! She thought she had lost him, yes she did. That morning around three o'clock she thought she had lost him, and if he had gone the spark would have gone out of her life. She had weathered Robert and his useless legs; she had weathered Mary, Joe, and Harry going; and she had just about weathered Billy dying, after getting him up to eight years old, too; but if Freddie had gone, oh no, she couldn't have stood that. And here was this woman offering him a position as a gardener. Funny that, to think of Freddie being a gardener when his main object in life was to be a cobbler. No; not a cobbler, a shoemaker.

'Do you think I could see him for a moment?'

Jinny paused, then said, 'Well, yes. And he's not 'fectious.'

'Oh, that wouldn't trouble me if he were infectious; I've got a leather hide that germs can't penetrate.' She smiled from one to the other; and Robert smiled back at her, but Jinny didn't smile, she led the way into the bedroom, saying, 'You've got a visitor.'

Freddie was lying propped up against two bare pillow ticks, and at the sight of Miss Hewitt he pulled himself up straight for a moment from the pillows before sinking back, and he looked from the visitor to his mother who was saying to Miss Hewitt, 'I'll bring you a chair.'

He continued to stare at the woman standing at the foot of the shaky-down. She looked tall from this angle, and it was as if she had gone back into one of the dreams he had been having about her, the latest only last night when she had been captain of that big sailing ship. He had watched her take it up the river.

84

He had stood to her side as she turned the wheel, and the sails had billowed, and the shanty man had sung as they rounded the sandbanks. But there she was, and his mother was placing a chair for her, saying, 'I meself have got to leave, ma'am; I'm due at me work.'

'Oh, are you working?'

'Yes, at the ropery.'

'Oh, yes, yes. Well, undoubtedly we'll be seeing more of each other in the future, Mrs Musgrave, at least I hope so.'

There she was smiling again, but his mother gave her no return smile or answer but turned about and went out; and they were left together, and Miss Hewitt did her best not to wrinkle her nose against the smell in the room. It wasn't the stench as in some houses she had been in, but it certainly reeked of humanity in all its processes.

'How are you?'

'All right.'

'I didn't know you had been ill.'

'It wasn't the plague or anythin'.'

'No, so I understand. What caused it, do you know?'

'Aye, rotten meat.'

She clicked her tongue, then said, 'I've been looking out for you.'

'Aye?'

'I want to offer you a position.'

'Me? Runnin' for you?'

'No, not running for me. I don't need that kind of a runner. Anyway, once what they call The Free Trade Bill gets passed that'll put a stop to your running. There'll be no need for it. Yet' – she shook her head – 'there are those who do it for the excitement, like Peter Morley. You remember him?'

Yes; he remembered Peter Morley. They caught him 'cos he had been too cocksure liftin' a cask from the river in the early dawn. A daft thing to do. He'd been manacled by the neck in the cellar of the customs house. They kept him there for a week before they took him to Newcastle. He was in the House of Correction now, and lucky to be there some said; a year or so back and it could have been Australia.

She was saying, 'How would you like to be my gardener, and see to my glasshouse and maintenance about the house itself?'

He jerked in the bed. 'Me? Gardener? I couldn't be a gardener, I know nowt about plants and things.'

'I suppose you can use a shovel and dig?'

'Aye.'

'Well, that would be your first job, clearing the vegetable garden that is all overrun and the brushwood from the grounds. And by the time you have finished that you will have learned that the first stages in gardening are digging, weeding, and sweating; knowledge will follow . . . three shillings a week, your food and moderate hours. What about it?'

As he stared at her the butcher's shop receded into the past, but the boot shop did not follow immediately. He saw the plate glass window: just such a one as he had seen in Newcastle, the only time he had been there. And behind were rows and rows of beautiful shoes and boots and gaiters, and leggings, and the colours rose from black to all shades of brown. There was even a pair of white doeskin slippers, at the very front, made to fit a bairn.

She could see his mind working, weighing up the pros and cons of the proffered situation.

'I can't start till next week,' he said; 'me legs are rocky.'

She looked at him for almost thirty seconds before she said, 'That'll be all right. Leave it longer if you must. The weeds have stopped growing anyway, and so you can work in the conservatory to begin with.'

'In the what?'

'The glasshouse. Didn't you notice it? It begins at the side of the house and runs its full length and has doors into the sitting-room and dining-room. Oh, of course' – she nodded now and her smile widened – 'you came on business that day, business only.'

This caused him to look towards the door and he wagged his hand at her, whispering now, 'They don't know I went along to you.'

Her voice was as low as his. 'They don't?' she said.

'No.'

She drew in a short breath before saying, 'Of course you're right. I'm very dim about some things. You couldn't tell them.'

She wasn't dim, she could never be dim, but she had thought he must have mentioned her in some way to his ma and da.

'You wouldn't have a job for two of us, would you?'

The look on her face expressed surprise and slight indignation. 'What!' she said. 'Two of you? What do you mean?'

'Me brother John. He works down the pit, I told you, but he'd give one eye and a thumb to be out of it. He rarely sees daylight he says, 'cept Sundays, and then he's so tired he sleeps half the time.'

'Well, I'm afraid I can do nothing for your brother' – she paused – 'as yet.' Now she gave a sort of chuckle and, leaning forward, she said mischievously, 'You're sure there's no other member of the family you want to put into business?'

Although he knew she was joking he answered her seriously, saying, 'No. Our Nell's married and set, and Nancy's goin' on the concerts again, singin'. She got two shillings last time and she's singin' in the Methodist Chapel come Sunday. She won't get paid for that though.'

'No, I'm sure she won't get paid for that. She's the blind one, isn't she?'

'Aye. And Jessie's only four, but works for her keep; she hauls more wood up than many twice her size.'

He saw her body shaking and when she said, 'As yet the baby is unemployed,' his face went into a wide grin as he said, 'Aye, you could say that.'

She stood up now, saying, 'Well, that's settled. You can start on Monday if you're able; if you're not I shall understand.' She put a hand out as if to touch his head, then drew it back; and she had reached the door when he stopped her by saying, 'I . . . I can still do me runnin' at night.' It was both a statement and a question, and she looked at him across the dim room for a moment, her face straight now as she said, 'I'd rather you didn't.'

'I want to. I . . . I mus . . .'

She'd had the latch in her hand but she didn't open the door, she kept it pressed closed as she said softly, 'You were going to say, you must. Does that mean someone's got something on you? You've done something?'

'No, no; I haven't.' There was a hiss in his voice. 'I didn't mean nowt; I just meant I want to do it.'

She looked away towards the small window where the piece of curtain obscured most of the light and she said slowly, 'Well, if you want to do it, you must do it, but not in my time.' And on this she went out.

If he wanted to do it he must do it. He didn't want to do it, not any more. It had somehow been fun up till a few weeks ago. And from what his da said there had been no run since then, well, not from this side, at least round about. But then nobody knew what went on across at South Shields or up the river. They said the Newcastle lot were well organised; and of course they would be 'cos all the boats had to dock there first. But what had she meant about this free trade?

A few minutes later his father propelled himself into the room and straight to the foot of the shaky-down; and he leant his arms on it and looked at his son as he said, 'Well, lad, it seems you're set for life. But who would have thought it? A gardener. With all the industry an' jobs that's goin' on in this town and along the river, you've got to be set for a gardener. There's breweries, and boat builders, and bakers, and booksellers, and butchers, that's just going through the B's. And there's clogmakers, and coopers, and couriers, and joiners, and nailmakers, and painters, and plumbers, not to mention the pawnbrokers. God above! I could go on with black-smiths, bottlemakers, and that's not touchin' on half. Everything to support birth, life an' death is created in this town. But have we heard of a gardener? No.'

'There is, Da, there's one.'

'Aye, that's what she said an' all. I didn't tell her he wasn't my idea of a gardener, more like a grave digger, he sees to the grass. Well, what d'you think of the idea?'

'I said I would do it, Da.'

'Aye; an' you're right to say that. You won't get another chance of a full-time job an' your grub an' three shillings a week. Aye, I bet John wishes he had the chance. But he'll be glad for you. He's been worried about you. There's one thing your ma an' me's certain about, you'll not go butcherin' again.'

'D'you like her, Da?'

'Who? Maggie Hewitt, or Miss Hewitt as she's

called to her face? Well, now you've asked me a question. It's hard to say if you like or dislike her. They say she's as sharp as a ferret about business, an' she's never been known to give much away. She does a lot of work on the side, I understand, for foreigners an' their money, and she's liked among that lot because she doesn't rip 'em off. They tell me she comes from a seafaring family. Her da was a big nob at one time, used to race in sail, captained a big schooner. It went down. Her and her mother used to live in a house outside the town. She still lives there, I hear, but spends most of her time on the front. Queer card; not quite what you'd call a lady but not quite anything else either. Anyway, you can but try workin' for her. And I'll tell you somethin', lad. If I can get a few more orders like the one I've got, an' you bring your three shillings a week home, with John's pay and the odd shilling or two Nancy brings in, we'll be in clover, an' your mother won't need to go to the ropes, for that's a hellish job that. Backwards and forwards up that hill, the blood runnin' from the hands in the winter pullin', pullin', pullin'. I'll be satisfied if we can get her out of that . . . She's a good woman is your mother, Freddie. Always remember that.'

He didn't say, 'I know, Da' or 'I will, Da,' but he looked at his father; and with a nod, Robert twisted around and eased himself through the door and into the kitchen again.

His da had just said they'd be in clover. He looked round the room, but he was seeing the house with the green shutters: no wind would get through them; the sea wouldn't shake its foundations; the putrid smell that rose from the streets wouldn't have impregnated its walls.

There were different beds of clover.

PART TWO

As it Happened When I Was Twelve

1

'Read that.'

'All of it?'

'Yes. Yes, all of it.'

'I don't know whether I can or not.'

'You won't know until you try.'

Freddie took up a small sheet of newspaper and, holding it well away from his face, he began to read:

FIVE GUINEAS REWARD

Whereas Sunday Morning last about Three o'clock, Three or Four Men landed from a Sculler Boat, at the Quay a little above the Custom House Quay; quar-relled with and ill-used the Water-man; pulled down a Coal House belonging to Mr Horner and also Water Spouts belonging to Mr Horner and Mr Tyzack; and com . . . mitted vari-ous other Dep . . . red . . . ations to the Terror of the Neighbour . . . hood, whose Windows were ass . . . as . . . sailed with Stones.

A REWARD of TWO GUINEAS will be paid by the said MR HORNER and MR TYZACK and a further REWARD of THREE GUINEAS by the NORTH SHIELDS and TYNEMOUTH ASSO . . . CI . . . ATION for prose . . . cuting FELONS, to any PERSON, or PERSONS who shall give such In . . . for . . . mation as may lead to the Con...viction of the Offender, or Offenders.

NORTH SHIELDS

26th November, 1817.

'Not bad. But what do you notice about that piece?'

'It happened years ago, and it was far too much money for the reward. The coal house and windows wouldn't have cost half that much to put up again.'

'That isn't the point. What else did you notice?'

'Nowt.'

'Can't you say nothing instead of nowt?'

'Everybody says nowt.'

'Everybody doesn't say nowt. And what do you notice about that piece, I've asked you?'

'Just what I said.'

'Did you notice that a lot of the words began with capital letters not just the paragraphs or the beginning of the sentence?'

'No.'

'No, I suppose not.' She sighed. 'Well, for your further information, Master Frederick Musgrave, every noun in that piece began with a capital letter. And a noun happens to be the name of anything.'

Freddie stared at her in some bewilderment. She was always bewildering him. He had been working for her now for over eighteen months but never a day passed but she seemed to spring something new on him, and not always pleasant either. He had never wanted to learn to read; write his name, aye, but you could get the gist of all you wanted to know by just listening to other people. But then on the other hand he must give her her due because he had felt different since he could read a bit. And then he had gained a sort of prestige in the house because, at home at night, he could read snatches of paper writing to them. His da was tickled to death. And Nancy loved listening, but his ma wasn't pleased about it, he knew that. His ma hadn't taken to the Miss: she hadn't a good word for her even when he brought the big bag of buns back on a Saturday night. The Miss made the buns herself; she was a dab hand at cooking. Oh aye, he'd say she was; he had never tasted food like what she put on the table. Of course, give his ma her due, as a rule she only had the neck end of mutton or tripe and chitterlings to deal with and bran flour for the bread. It was good wholesome food, he admitted, but it wasn't like the stuff the Miss dished up: a pudding made with white flour, milk and eggs, it melted in your mouth; and roast beef with gravy that you could suck up like soup. But still, at first, he didn't enjoy his meals very much 'cos she was always at him about how he was eatin' it. Apparently you didn't eat with your mouth open nor wipe your mouth with the back of your hand. As for your nose, he'd wished many a time in those first weeks that he hadn't got one. And then there was washing. She was worse than his ma about washing. His ma always made them dip their hands in the bucket before they came to the table, but the Miss made him scrub his nails. Still you had to take the good with the bad, and in the main it was good here. Oh aye, it was very good. He had to stop talking about it to John though, because John was a bit green. Anyway, it looked as if John would soon be seeing a lot of daylight, because there was a big strike about to break. Pitmen were always striking, it seemed; if it wasn't about one thing it was about another. It used to be about money, but now it was about conditions. Well, it was to be expected 'cos look

95

what happened in the last disaster. There were a lot of fatherless bairns in the town now, many of them in the poor house. And only this week three young lads went to the House of Correction for stealing.

'I saw you talking to Mr Freeman yesterday. What did he want?'

He didn't raise his head as he said, 'Just passin' the time of day.'

'Don't try to hoodwink me, Freddie Musgrave; remember who you are talking to. There's a run on, isn't there? But talking of runs, don't forget what happened last month to the Newcastle fellows they picked up; they're well and truly along the line now, aren't they? They won't come ashore for some time again, their bellies strapped tight with silk and such. Idiots they were, braving the daylight! And was it worth it for a dozen or so yards of lace? Yes, one had lace and the other silk.' Her voice changing, she said, 'You know what will happen, don't you, if you are caught anywhere near anyone if they've got the stuff on them? It will be no use saying you don't know anything about it, because those excise fellows are no fools: they've been picked for their job, they keep their eyes open. And let me tell you, they know that you're used. I've tried in my own way to put it about that that episode in your life is past. You're in a good job now and you're learning your letters and if you behave yourself you've got a good future afront of you.' She put out her hand now and caught his and there was a plea in her voice as she said, 'Tell me, Freddie, now tell me the truth, just answer yes or no. Has Freeman got something on you?'

He could look her straight in the eye and say, 'No.'

She let go of his hand and straightened up; then, in a characteristic manner, her body jerked forward and again she had hold of his hand, demanding now,

'Then who is it? You're frightened of somebody, I know that. I've known it from the day you brought your half-sovereigns to me. Is it Mr Gallagher?'

He couldn't answer, but in returning her stare his throat contracted and he had to gulp at his spittle. And then she said, 'Ah! Ah! I knew there was something. And it happened that night, didn't it? You were away all that night. It happened then?'

'No. No.' He was shaking his head.

'Don't lie to me, boy.' Her voice changed again, becoming soft and pleading now: 'Trust me,' she said. 'You know you can trust me, you know that. I'm your friend, your good, good friend. I want to see you get on and ... and I don't want to see anything happen to you. Mr Gallagher is a queer customer, not for him just French wines and a cask now and again, he goes in for bigger stuff, or I could say smaller stuff. Look! Tell me what you know about it.'

He could again say honestly to her now, 'I ... I don't know anything, miss, I don't honest, not about what he goes in for. All he had that night I was there was two barrels down the well, an' I told you his man stuck them in the midden. I don't know anything else that he gets.'

She sat back from the desk and her voice held a weary sound to it now as she said, 'Well, if it isn't that, what is it, boy? There's something, isn't there?'

'Yes, miss.'

'Ah, well, that is an admission. At last we're getting somewhere.'

'No, miss, we're not, 'cos I can't tell you, but ... but I will some day.'

'Why some day? Why not now?'

Why did he answer her with the next words?

'I want to grow up a bit, miss.'

Her face screwed up at him and the lines from her

97

eyes to the top of her ears formed deep furrows, and she repeated quietly, 'You want to grow up a bit, what do you mean?'

He didn't know exactly what he meant except that he wanted to live, and he felt that he wouldn't live long if he talked about Mr Gallagher killin' his bairn. It wouldn't be like murdering a grown-up or anything like that, but it would still be the killing of somebody and if that didn't mean hanging it meant gaol. And a man like Mr Gallagher would, as he had promised, pay anybody in full who would be the cause of his being found out. He looked at her face. It looked sad, worried, and it came to him that he liked her so much he would do anything so that she needn't worry; he sensed that she was a lonely woman. She had lost her father and the young man in the painting. He knew that he liked her, too, as much as he did his ma but in a different way, a sort of wider way although he couldn't explain the feeling that prompted the thought wider. But the next minute he was standing and bending forward across the desk towards her, saying, 'Don't worry any more. I'll promise you something. I have to run this one message an' that'll be the last. I'll tell him.'

She didn't smile as she often did when she was pleased, but her face seemed to relax and she said, 'Thank you, Freddie; but couldn't you get out of doing this last run? You know, I told you about the free trade coming . . .'

'No, not very easily,' he cut in on her words, his own tumbling over each other. 'I don't know where the faggot, I mean Mr Freeman, lives; and anyway, it's too late now to even try to find out.'

'You're crossing the river?'

'Aye.'

'To Mr Gallagher's?'

He looked downwards, then muttered, 'Aye.'

From under his lowered gaze he watched her rise from the chair, move round the desk, and as she passed him on her way towards the door, she said, 'Come on; let's have a bite, and then you can go home.'

As he followed her across the hall towards the kitchen she asked, without turning round, 'Do your parents know where you're going tonight?'

'No, not yet.'

'You must tell them.'

'Aye. Aye, I will.'

'What are you taking across?'

They were in the kitchen now and she had gone towards the fireplace that had an iron oven at one side and a boiler at the other and, before opening the oven door, she took down a towel from a brass rail running under the mantelshelf and, unhooking the iron latch of the oven, she took from it a large pie dish. This she set on the table, replaced the towel on the rod, took two plates that were lying on the top of the steel and brass fender and returned to the table, placing a plate at each side of it before she said, 'Well, what are you carrying?'

'I don't know. 'Tis the truth, I don't know. I've got to see Mr . . . well, somebody at this end of the Low Lights later on.'

'Sit down.' He took his seat at the table and watched her cut the pie crust, then ladle out chunks of steak and kidney and gravy on to his plate. But after she had passed it to him he did not begin until she had served her own portion which was not half the size of his. When she was seated she nodded to him, and he began to eat. Sometimes, when she was in good humour, she would say the funny grace. He had repeated it to his da, and it made him roar with laughter for it went:

> Meat and grains,
> Water and wine,
> Hold your hand, stomach,
> And it will be thine.

His da often said, 'Hold your hand there,' when he meant 'Wait a minute', so the rhyme was understandable. She always said it in a funny voice. And then during a meal she often talked about places that she had been to, like France and Italy, and three times to Norway. She liked Norway. She had once said to him, 'We'll go there one day. We'll get on a boat and we'll hie for the fiords.' He had said, 'What are fiords?' And she had told him.

It had been like a story, and he had described this, too, to them back home that night sitting round the fire ... He only wished his ma would like her. He didn't know why she hadn't taken to her, 'cos his da spoke well of her, and Nancy's opinion was she had a good smell: strong and clean, was how she described her. And she was right, she was strong and she was clean and she had a good smell.

He finished the meal with cheese and bread. There was still half the pie left. He wondered if she would give it to him to take home. After the meal she washed up the dishes in the wooden sink next to the fireplace in hot soapy water – she didn't use soda – and he had to dry the dishes. At first, he hadn't liked that; it was only women who dried dishes. He had never told his da or any of them at home that he had dried dishes, for in a way it would have taken some of the highlights out of his position.

When he was ready to go she walked to the gate

with him, and there she said, 'The tide'll be over the bank about ten. What time are you going?'

'I don't know for sure. I'll be knockin' about from dark.'

'You can't knock about without people seeing you, and you know who I mean.'

'I can. I'm good at hidin'.'

'You might have been, but you're not as small as you were. You're sprouting.'

'Aye,' he said; 'I am, but . . . but I'll be all right. I'll see you in the mornin', an' I'll be on time.' He now did an odd thing, at least he thought so, for he put his hand out and touched hers. It was the first gesture he had ever dared to make to her, not that he hadn't felt inclined to do so before this moment. Her other hand came on the top of his and pressed it tight and she said, 'I'm worried for you.'

'I'll be all right. I know I will.' He grinned, adding, 'I'm lucky. Didn't you give me a job and learn me to read and write a bit; I'm lucky, I tell you.'

She said nothing more but pushed him from her, and he went down the road feeling very odd as if he didn't want to leave her.

But he hadn't gone more than twenty yards or so when he heard her voice calling, 'Freddie! Freddie! Wait a minute.'

She came running towards him panting, 'Listen!' she said rapidly. 'If you promise to stick to your reading and writing and learn your figures, I'll take you into the office and your brother can have your job. What do you say?'

'Eeh! you would?'

'Yes, I would; but it will mean you spending most of your evenings for some months to come sticking to your books.'

'I'll do it. I'll do it. And I can tell him?'

'Yes, yes, you may tell him. But it all depends on you.'

'Oh, ta. Ta, miss. Eeh! What did I tell you, miss, I'm lucky. We're all lucky.'

He turned from her and raced along the pathway. He ran until he reached the top of the cinder bank. He ran the whole length of the Low Lights, then along the shore, past the row of cottages, up the steps, along the pathway and into the house. And, standing gasping, he looked around him.

They were all there. His ma and da; Nell who came in to do shoppin' because it was a Friday night, and with the sweat still on her hair from the saltpans; John who was home early because the strike had started; Nancy, bright-eyed, smiling kindly as usual; plain little Jessie; and Lily. They were all there and all had their eyes on him. It was his da who said, 'What's up, lad? You look as if you've lost a tanner and found a sovereign?'

'As good as, Da, as good as.' He went straight up to John saying, 'You always said you wanted to get out of the pit, didn't you?'

'What you at? I'm out of the pit, we're on strike.'

'But for good, I mean, for good.'

'What d'you mean?' John's voice was dull; his whole attitude was dull.

'Well' – he turned now and looked at his da and then at his ma and he kept his eyes on her as he said, 'The miss just said if I stick to me books and learn to reckon an' write I can go into her office and she'll give John here me job.'

There was silence in the room for a moment, then a complete clamour.

'Eeh! God above! that is news. I've just said to John there, "Don't worry, lad, when a door closes another one opens."'

'How wonderful, John! You've always wanted to work in the open air. Remember the Methodist minister last Sunday night, God always answers prayers.'

John didn't reply to Nancy but, looking at his younger brother, he said, 'You know what you are, you're a marler.'

'Aye, I suppose I am a bit of a marler. I said to the miss I'm lucky. Don't you think I'm lucky, Ma?'

They all turned excitedly and looked at Jinny for her confirmation, but her reply came out flatly: 'There's luck and luck,' she said; 'some kinds of luck has got to be paid for.'

'Aw! woman, what d'you mean by that? Don't be a wet blanket. It's the best news that's come into this house for years. First, the youngster here being started with a woman like Miss Hewitt.' Freddie had noted for some time that his employer was no longer spoken of as Maggie. And his da went on, 'And now the promise of gettin' John out of that hell-hole. Aw! lass, what's the matter with you? Be happy for them.'

'Do you think she wants a housekeeper?' It was Nell now laughingly asking the question, and Freddie answered, 'It's a pity, Nell, but I doubt it. I can't do anythin' for you in that line 'cos she's a good cook. She makes . . .' His voice trailed off because his mother had turned her back on them and was now walking into the bedroom. John had nudged Freddie with his elbow, then jerked his head in the direction his ma had taken. And Freddie slowly left them and followed her.

She was standing near the window looking out into the deepening twilight, and he tugged her skirt, saying, 'What is it, Ma? I've upset you, but I didn't mean to. All I want to do is to please you, to ease

103

things. Why . . . why don't you cotton on to me workin' for the Miss?'

She turned and looked down on him, then quickly she dropped on to her hunkers and, putting her arms about him, she pulled him into her embrace.

Never in his whole life, even when he was small, could he remember her hugging him like this. Her body was shaking. And when he looked into her face he saw that her eyes were moist and her voice was thick as she said, 'I'm a silly woman. I . . . I suppose I'm jealous; I don't want to lose you.'

'What! Ma. You lose me? Aw, don't be daft, Ma; you couldn't lose me if you tried.'

'You seem to like her very much.'

He paused for a moment before he said, 'She's very lonely, Ma. Her da was drownded and the young man she was goin' to marry was drownded in the same boat along of him. She yells and shouts on the quay and bosses people about and even some of the men are frightened of her, but she's not like that, she's got nobody and she's old.'

She took her fingers and combed his hair with them back from his brow, smiling now as she said, 'She's not old. Am I old?'

'No; not really.'

'Not really?'

'Well, I mean . . . you know what I mean. But she's a lot older than you.'

'She isn't, she can't be fifty.'

'Well, that's old, Ma.'

'Yes, I suppose it is, to a twelve-year-old that's old.'

'Ma.'

'Yes, son?'

'Try to like her, will you, 'cos she needs people to like her. I don't think anybody visits there at all. Well, nobody comes in the daytime except to deliver

the groceries an' that. An' you know somethin', Ma?'
He hunched his shoulders. 'Peabody tried to sting
her on one of the bills. They charged her tuppence a
pound extra for the butter. But she was on to them.
She wrote them a letter saying she was going to
move her custom. And you know, she deals with
Aynsley. Well, he got it in the neck an' all 'cos she
paid for the best stewing steak and they sent her
hough meat. She kept it till the next day and when
the lad came she sent it back with another letter.
There's no flies on her, Ma. You know something?
I . . . I didn't know whether I'd like her at first when I
went there. I even thought I'd go back to the
butcher's.'

'You never did!'

'Oh, aye, I did, 'cos she didn't only make me wash
me hands, she made me scrub them.'

'Right too.'

'And you know something else she made me do
and she still makes me do it? I don't like it but I've
got to do it. You won't laugh, Ma, will you?'

'No, I won't laugh.'

He knew that he had her smiling already. And so
he played on it, and he wagged his head a bit and
looked downwards before he said, 'She makes me dry
up the dishes.'

He lifted his head. Her face was stretching. She
said, 'Never! Dry up the dishes? She made you dry
up the dishes? I've never been able to make you dry
up the dishes.'

'I know, and . . . an' I refused at first.'

'You didn't!'

'I did.'

'What did you say?'

He looked away, then bit on his lip before he
answered her. 'Well, she put it like this, Ma. If I

105

didn't help to dry up the dishes she wouldn't wash me plate and each day she'd put me food on it as it was, greasy like, until I decided that I would do me share of the chores. That's what she calls them, the chores.'

'She's a funny woman.'

'Aye, Ma, she is; but . . . but she's kind an' she's . . . well, I don't know a word for it except sort of lost like.'

She was holding his face between her two big rough hands now and her voice was a whisper as she said, 'I love all me bairns, but you were always special. But mind' – her voice and expression changed – 'I'll break your neck if you ever take advantage of what I'm sayin', or repeat it, d'you hear, Freddie Musgrave?'

'Aye. Aye, I hear, Mrs Musgrave.'

They fell together for a moment and if he could have expressed his feelings in words he would have said he was experiencing a moment of ecstasy.

A moment later she opened the door into the kitchen and pushed him in, saying loudly now, 'This one's gettin' too big for his boots; he's tryin' to run this family. He's just told me it's about time I packed up; I'm about ready for me chair at the side of the fireplace.'

There was laughter in the kitchen; everybody seemed happy. And so it remained until eight o'clock, when the two children were in bed and the candles were lit and his ma and da and brother and sister were preparing to sit round the fire and listen to his crack, for then he surprised them by saying, 'I've got to go out, but I won't be long.'

His father pulled himself onto the mat in order to be nearer to him and, putting out his hand and gripping his shoulder, he said, 'I thought you were finished with that?'

'This'll be the last time, Da, the very last time.'

'Is it the faggot man?'

He looked at his mother, 'Aye, Ma.'

'Something big?'

'I don't think so, just an errand.'

'I don't like it, lad.'

He was looking at his father again. 'It'll be all right, Da. I'll be back straightaway, 'cos I'll have to make use of the slack tide . . . Ta-ra!'

The farewell was divided among them all, but as he went out of the door he was aware that no one moved to see him off, and, too, that there was no warning from his mother to be careful, nor did John say he'd come with him to look at the full moon, 'cos it would be that tonight.

He did not make his way straight down to the quay; there was plenty of time. His usual procedure before going on a run was to mingle with one or another set of lads, for he knew most of those that frequented the quayside in their spare time which was mostly late at night. One of the things they got up to was teasing Granny Brimstone's dog. It was chained up, and the lads would throw bones out of its reach and the poor thing would go wild, and the old woman would come out screaming blue murder at them.

Then again, he might join those who were doing the tin walk along the fancy houses at the top of the hill. The tin walk was exactly what it said, two holes were bored in the tin, some ropes slotted through and you stood on them pulling the ropes tight to keep them on your feet; then you clattered up a street. When there were a dozen or so of you and you walked on the flags, like some of the houses up there had for paving stones, the clatter that twenty odd tins made, especially if they did a sort of jig, was quite something. He had once had a chamber-pot emptied over his head, and so he tended to avoid the tin walk, if possible. But it was well to be seen playing about; and then it was easy to slip away to the appointed place.

But what was the appointed place the night? He didn't know. He only knew he'd have to be near Northumberland's Wharf. Some people called it Hall's Wharf because it was owned by a woman of that name. She was the wharfinger. He had never before been told to stick near this particular wharf; and so he decided to stay a good way off and keep an eye on it. There were men still working on the quay and their flares and lanterns would show up anyone coming along.

He took a position in the shadow of a bloater-smoking hut, and, his hands in his breeches pocket, he leant against the tarred wood and prepared himself to wait. He guessed he wouldn't be contacted for another half-hour because the water was not quite slack yet, and they knew he couldn't cross on a running tide. So when a voice came to the side of him, saying, 'You're in good time, that's right,' he would have sprung up from the shadow, except for the hand gripping his shoulder. He recognised the voice as that of the faggot man, but when he turned to look at him he appeared different. He knew him as the gent who always rode into town on horseback and was always well-dressed in knee-breeches and polished leather gaiters. But here, he could just make out a man looking like any other workman along the quay, even to his cap which was pulled down over his brow almost to his eyes. But he could see his eyes all right because they seemed to glint.

'Now listen to me, little 'un, and this is important. You scoot across now. Now! you understand?'

Before the man got any further Freddie said, 'I can't. Why, I can't! River's still runnin'. It'd take me out to sea.'

The next minute he felt himself being shaken almost like a terrier shakes a rat, his teeth seeming to come free in his head.

'Listen to me! Things are not as they appear tonight, quiet like. There'll be a lot of movement once the tide has covered the bar. Now, it's your business to get across before that. Understand? It's important, very important that you do. Is that clear?'

Freddie made no answer, for the man was now holding something in his face. It was a packet not more than three inches long and an inch or so wide, and it seemed to be wrapped in some shiny material, too shiny for calfskin.

'You have a pocket, haven't you, inside your breeks?'

'Aye.'

'Well, let me see you put it in.'

He undid the buckle of his narrow belt, unbuttoned the flap; then, taking the small parcel from the man's hand, he pushed it down inside his trousers.

'How deep is your pocket?'

'Deep enough.'

'Is there a button on it?'

'N'no; but I've n'never lost n'nowt yet from it.' He couldn't stop stammering; he sensed something different; he was fearful.

'Well, you can pray to God that you don't lose this. Now listen. When you climb the other side, don't take your usual route up through the town. That's the way you usually go, isn't it?'

'Aye; m'most times.'

'Well, not tonight, for as soon as you reach the top bank turn to your right. There's a row of boathouses along there and the road leads up to

109

Cookson's Wharf. Now, you'll see a man on horse-back; more likely he'll be standing by his horse. You know who it is, don't you?'

He said nothing.

'Well, you'll give him the package . . . That's all. It's as easy as that.'

He dared to say now, 'Well, if it's as easy as that why don't you take it across, or one of your men?'

'Do you want your ears rung or your lip busted just for a start?'

For all the man's big talk, Freddie realised it wasn't this man he was afraid of: he seemed no different at this moment from any man, any work-man in the town, and so he said, 'What do I get for it?'

The man thrust his hand into his pocket and placed a coin on Freddie's outstretched palm. And now as he peered at it, Freddie said, 'This is only a tanner; I never get less than a bob. Now you know that . . . even half a dollar.'

'Well, that's all you're getting now, at least from me, because you'll be well paid at the other end. Now, scat!'

'If I go now I'll get wet, sodden; an' I'll likely drift.'

'I'll be watching you, and I'll give you one minute to reach the quay and if you're not in that sculler of yours by then I'll come down there and hold you under just long enough for you to get wet all over. Now what d'you say?'

He said nothing but he walked away from the man, he didn't run, he just walked. Inside he was now feeling defiant. He had the strange wish that the Miss would suddenly appear on the shore and say, 'That's enough. You're not going.'

When he climbed into his sculler and pushed off into the river he noticed, in the moonlight, there was

110

another but bigger sculler bobbing in the water further along the beach and two or three men standing on the shore. They seemed to be messing about with nets, and his mind asked him why they should want nets in a sculler like that? Of a sudden the night became dark, the pale moon was obscured by a black cloud and for a moment he seemed lost as to his direction; and when his paddle hit a mound of sand he really experienced a surge of fear. He could evade the sandbanks in daylight but in the blackness it was a different thing, especially if you didn't carry a lantern. Swinging his thin body from side to side, he paddled furiously towards where he could make out the lights on the south shore.

The moon suddenly escaping from the black cloud, he saw he was more than half-way across; he also heard above the rush of the water a muffled shout. He turned his head and looked back; and, there, he made out two men in a sculler and they were rowing furiously, and like the rush of the outflowing tide over the sandbanks it came to him why.

The swell now lifted him to the outer row of hiring keels and he grabbed at them and pulled himself along to the steps, and a ring where he could tie up. Only habit made certain his sculler was secure before he scrambled up onto the dockside; but he didn't hesitate once his feet touched it and, following the faggot man's directions, he ran as fast as his gasping breath would allow past the boathouses and towards the figure of the man and the bulk of the horse standing waiting for him.

He almost threw himself against Roderick Gallagher's legs, spluttering, 'They're comin'! they know. Two in a boat just ahind me.'

As he pointed along the dark road the man swung himself up into the saddle and seemingly in one

111

movement he gripped the back of Freddie's coat, and the boy thought he was going to choke as his narrow collar clamped tight around his windpipe. Then his body jerked and it seemed that he would be bounced from the horse's back onto the road; but the man's arm came about him and his voice yelled in his ear, 'Straddle your legs and hold on to the pommel.'

He leant forward and gripped something. It was handfuls of horsehair. All the bones in his body appeared to be rattling. It was like a continuation of when the faggot man had shaken him. He didn't know which part of the town they were riding through because the moon had gone in again. But when it reappeared, he had time to realise they were just passing out of Westoe; then that they weren't taking the usual road to Gallagher's horse. He was aware, too, of the man cursing before drawing the horse to a skidding stop to listen. He too listened; but for some seconds he could only hear the gasping of his own breath; but then, like the man, he made out the sound of horses hooves in the distance . . . yet those men in the sculler didn't have horses.

He noted that they were now going along a narrow path one side of which was covered with brushwood and thicket. The next second he was gasping and he thrust out his hands in protest as the man gripped his collar again, crying, 'I'll come back for you. Lie low!' and he knew he was actually flying through the air into blackness. But for how long he wouldn't have known.

When he came round he lay still listening, thinking he would hear the riders passing. He was lying on his side and wondered why the moonlight was dappled on his hands; then realised he was lying amidst greenery.

Slowly he put his hand out and felt down the

length of his body. Part of it was lying on soft ground, but the side of his leg was against a stone, and when he touched it he winced. Oh God, what if it was broken. He immediately conjured up a picture of his father dragging himself from the low bed, and with it his foot jerked and he let out a slow, slow breath. Next he felt his face. The side of it seemed wet. He brought his hand before his eyes and shivered as he saw blood on it. Tentatively now, he felt the back of his head: his hair there was wet too, sticky . . . He'd cracked his head. That man could have killed him. Perhaps that's what he'd wanted to do. But he groped in his mind for something. Then he remembered: he said he was coming back for him. And yes, of course he would come back for him because he still had the parcel on him. The thought brought his hand down his trousers and into the pocket. 'Eeh!' The exclamation was loud. It was busted.

Slowly he pulled the packet out of his pocket, and as his fingers came in contact with the loose powder the word 'Eeh!' escaped him again, and, pulling himself into a sitting position, he looked at it.

The wrapping, whatever it was made of, was split. The inner wrapping which he saw was silk, that too was split. But what he noticed right away was there were two separate little packages: besides the one with white powder there was one holding brown powder. He moved his finger in the white powder and was amazed to feel pieces of glass. Dusting the powder slightly aside he saw the pieces of glass. And when he did the same with the brown powder, the pieces of glass he saw were red.

At first he thought of them as glass because his mind wasn't working properly. But of a sudden it seemed to spring back to life and he thought, God Almighty! These are jewels.

113

He knew traffic went on in jewellery, but he understood it was just the Newcastle lot who got up to that lark because it was so dangerous. Ten years or more you could get, he understood, if these were found on you. And this is what he had been carrying! He had thought it was just powder which was really a drug. Why people risked their necks for drugs he couldn't understand because you could go to the dispensary in the town and buy all kinds of drugs and have them made up into medicine. They were all arrayed in coloured bottles around the shop. Some of the bottles were more than a foot high and quite bonny. The lids were like helmets with points on. But this man's powder had been just a sort of package for stones, like these. Eeh! Dear God! He wished he would come and take them and let him get back home.

He was feeling dizzy again. He'd better wrap these up as best he could and put them back in his pocket.

He had just accomplished this when a bout of tiredness, as he thought of it, overtook him, and as the moon disappeared once more he slipped back into sleep . . .

When he next woke it was daylight, and he was so stiff he could hardly move. His head was aching and his hip was sore. With an effort he pulled himself to his feet. His head was just above the brushwood in which he had been lying and there, just a few feet away, was a narrow road. He turned about, to see that the brushwood stretched away into the distance to some houses and his muzzy thinking told him to make for them. But when he attempted to walk he almost cried out with the pain in his hip, and so, dropping on to his knees, he crawled further into the brushwood.

He had gone about ten yards when he was brought

to a surprising halt, for there before him was a shallow gully with a rivulet of water running along it. As if he were in a desert and had found an oasis he slipped down the side of the gully and, kneeling down, he splashed his face and hair with the water. And as he did so his tongue lapped it, and it tasted cool and fresh. He guessed it was from a spring.

The blood cleared from his hair, his fingers searched for a cut, but he could feel only grazed skin, and he wondered why, if that was the case, he should be feeling as odd as he was?

You could take your trousers off and look at your leg.

As if obeying a voice that sounded like that of the Miss he first took off his boots, then carefully slipped off his trousers, lifted up the tail of his rough shirt and saw that his leg was whole but black and blue from the hip down to the side of the knee.

He was lucky, he told himself, he had just hit the side of that stone. If he had landed full on it he could have broken his hip, or his back. The thought made him shudder; he was always careful about his legs, fearful lest he got a knock. That's why he rarely went barefooted if he could help it; Sandy Ramshaw had lost a foot after he had trodden on a broken bottle.

As he lowered his bruised leg into the water he gave a sigh as if of pleasure, but he crawled up onto the bank again and, bare from the waist down, he lay there until the sun dried his skin; then he put his trousers on and, lying flat on his back, he looked up into the sky. He wasn't hungry, he was just tired; but he mustn't go to sleep again. If only that man would come and take his package, he could then get home. There came into his mind a picture of home; but again it wasn't the kitchen with his father sitting propped up against the wall and Lily and Jessie on the mat, his mother at the table and Nancy sitting beside their father making bobbin lace, while John, worn out with work, dozed in the chair; no; it was the kitchen with the iron range and the table with the white cloth on it and the delph rack holding all the blue china, and the brass helmet coal scuttle that stood between the fender and the sink, and the pump that splashed water into the sink. The last picture in his mind was of the Miss cutting the crust of the meat pie last night . . .

What was the matter with him? He blinked his eyes and stared up into the darkening sky. It was just a minute since that he had been looking up and the sun had been on his face. He couldn't have been asleep all this time. What was the matter with him? Had something gone wrong in his head? He pulled his stiff slight frame upwards. Had the man been looking for him? Eeh! he'd have to get up and get to the house before it got too dark and he wouldn't be able to see his way out of this.

When he got to his feet he buttoned his jacket up because now he was feeling chilly; then he put his hand to his head as though to straighten his cap, and remembered feeling his head and finding the blood. He hadn't the cap. Then he remembered the stone. He must have left it there.

Standing up now, he limped his way back through the brushwood to where he could see the road. And he congratulated himself on his sense of direction because there was the stone and the place where he had lain, and he knew it to be the same place because there was some blood on the stone. That must have come off his hand. But his cap wasn't lying anywhere about. Somebody had got his cap.

He stepped onto the road and as he did so he told

116

himself that he didn't know where this led to, so the best thing to do was to go back to where it branched off and take the road he knew. This he did; and he met no one, not on this branch which wasn't much more than a path, nor on the road that led to The Towers.

He went up the drive, past the front of the house and into the courtyard.

When he knocked on the kitchen door it was opened by Connie the maid he remembered from time back with the pockmarks and the wobbly eye and what she said was, 'My God! it's you. Come on! Come on! Come on away in!' She pulled him into the kitchen and, looking towards her mother, she cried, 'He's here!'

Betty Wheatley stared at him for a moment, then as if he had just left the house earlier on that day or perhaps the day before, she said, 'Where on earth have you been, lad?'

'I hit me head. I must have fallen asleep. He . . . he threw me into a thicket.'

'Did anybody see you come? What I mean is, did you see anybody on the road?'

'No, not a soul. I was in a sort of field. I didn't know me way from there and so I came onto the proper road.'

Betty turned to her daughter, saying, 'Go and tell your da to tell him.'

'Me da's had enough of him for one day; I'll take him in. Anyway, Da's on the look out: you never know when we'll have another visit, they won't let up. As me da says, they've got their teeth in now and they won't let go. Where's it all gona end?'

She didn't wait for an answer but, grabbing Freddie's sleeve, she said, 'Come along with you!' then, 'What's the matter? You've hurt your leg?'

117

'Aye. When he tossed me I fell onto a stone.'

'It's a wonder you didn't break your neck.'

He followed her across the hall and up a corridor; but before she reached the end of it she stopped and, turning, whispered, 'Don't aggravate him by answering back. If I remember owt about you, you've got a ready tongue an' it won't have bettered with time. Now do as I say an' don't answer him back.'

He didn't want to answer him or anybody else back; he just wanted to hand over the parcel and get himself away from this house and everybody in it.

Connie didn't knock on the door but pushed it open, saying loudly, 'He's here!'

Roderick Gallagher sprang up from the chair he had been sitting in and in his haste he almost toppled over a table on which there was a decanter, a glass, and a long pipe and two blue stone jars.

Steadying the table with one hand, he watched Freddie limp towards him. And when the boy stopped by a chair at the other side of the fireplace he spoke, saying below his breath but almost in a growl, 'Where the hell do you think you've been?'

'I . . . I was lying in the thicket.'

'Don't tell me bloody lies. I went to the thicket. What's this!' He bent over, reached out and picked up the cap from the hearth. 'I was about to burn it. You forgot it, didn't you?'

'I kept fallin' asleep an' . . . and I felt funny. I was gona try to reach a house, so I crept back an' . . . and I came to a stream, a little stream, and I bathed me head an' me leg.' Now his voice dared to rise a little as he said, 'You could have knocked me out; you did for a time. I hit some stones when I fell and after that I . . . I kept fallin' asleep. Me leg's all black an' blue, an' me head's cut.' He pointed first to his side and then to his head.

118

'Where's the package you were given?'

'It's in me pocket here.'

'Well, let me have it. Come here!'

Freddie took two steps towards the man, undid his belt and the flap of his trousers, and as he put his hand down to his pocket he said, 'It got bust on the stone when I fell.'

'Bust? What do you mean, bust?'

'Well, it split.'

'And it spilt?'

'Oh, no, no; it just split. I put me hand in to see if it was all right and I felt it split.'

He drew out the package and placed it on the outstretched palm; then he watched the man look at it for a moment before moving his fingers in the white powder, and then in the brown. 'You knew what you were carrying, did you?'

He told himself he had to be careful here, so he said, 'Aye, powder, a kind of drug. I've carried it for you afore.'

'Have you looked into this powder?'

Freddie looked towards the palm now and shook his head, saying, 'No; I told you I was too tired to bother. As long as it was all right and the powder hadn't spilt. I was careful when I pulled it out and put it back again.'

He now looked towards the fire. The room was very hot; he felt he could fall asleep again at any minute. He said, 'Please . . . please can I sit down?'

He shrank back a little as the hands came out towards him, and felt surprise as he was lifted from the floor and placed in the big leather chair. Then a glass was being held to his mouth and the man was saying, 'Drink that. Sup it all up.'

He knew what rum tasted like, and ale, he'd had drops on the sly, but this was different, and when he screwed his face up and coughed the man said, 'It's a pity, but you'll never acquire a taste for fine French brandy.'

He sipped at the glass again. He liked it, and it seemed to take the tiredness away.

The man was sitting opposite to him now and he was saying, 'You kept your word. Do you remember the last conversation we had in this room?'

'Yes, sir.' He remembered that too: he had always to address him as sir.

'This is the first time we've met since that night; there's been a go-between at other times, hasn't there?'

When he didn't answer the man said, 'Too many cooks spoil the broth, and go-betweens get greedy. You were never greedy. What did Freeman give you?'

'Sixpence.'

The man put back his head and looked up towards the ceiling saying, 'Good God!' and the gesture brought back the time when he had watched him do that before. Then he was looking at him again and saying in quite an ordinary tone, 'I hate that fellow, you know. I hate meanness, but I'll fix him before he's finished. He's got enough stored away to fill Jingling Geordie's Hole. You know the hole?'

'Yes, the one above the short sands, near the castle. They say the Romans made it.'

'They say more than their prayers and they whistle them; they've got no authority for that, no more than they have for the subterranean passage that was supposed to run from there under the Tyne all the way to Jarrow so that the monks could trot through to visit their kin on the other side. But anyway, who knows? They were merely men with men's wants and women are always ready and

120

waiting; no need for enticing. How old are you now, boy?'

'Twelve, sir.'

'Oh well, it'll soon be on you.'

He didn't know what would soon be on him, but again he was feeling sleepy and the man's voice became a drone in his ears. He was talking about the money that was being spent on Lord Collingwood's monument that was to be erected next year. Something about it standing on a fifty foot pedestal. Now he was on about the Black Middens below the Spanish Battery. Now he was talking about South Shields and the Herd sands.

His eyes were closing and he seemed to be on the point of sleep with the voice saying, 'That bloody lot in Newcastle sucking the river dry. But their time's running out, did they but know it.'

Then he was shot into wakefulness by the bursting open of the door and Mrs Wheatley's voice crying, 'Frank's just signalled. They're here again.'

He was dragged from the chair as the man swung him round towards the woman, saying harshly, 'Get rid of him.'

'Where? But where?'

'Anywhere.'

'That's a daft answer.'

'Yes, I suppose it is, but where?' The man was now beating his fist against his brow. 'He can't go outside: he's been concussed; he'll fall asleep in the yard. Put him in the cupboard in the kitchen.'

'Oh, talk sense!'

Fancy her talking like that to him. But she still went on: 'The cupboard in the kitchen after they prised the floorboards up in the attic!'

'The attic.' He was wagging his finger wildly at her now. 'The cubby-hole.'

121

He wasn't fully awake but wide enough to listen and to see a look almost of fear on the woman's face as she stammered now, saying, 'You've always said . . .'

'Yes, I know: I wouldn't put a dog in there. But woman! what'll happen if they come in and find him?' And saying this, he thrust his fist now into Freddie's chest, causing the boy to stumble against the edge of the chair and to sit down; but only momentarily before he was whipped up again.

'Put him in there; it's the only place. God, damn it! he'll be the death of me yet, this one. Take him, quick!'

Holding a candle in one hand, the woman was now dragging him along the corridor with the other; then up the stairs; across the wide landing; up another flight and onto a bare landing; and from there into a carpetless room.

In the flickering light of the candle he saw that the room, except for a few trunks, was entirely bare. There was an iron fireplace built into one wall with a high grate and a small mantelshelf above it, and there was a window to the side. But there was only one other door in the room, and this she wrenched open and thrust him into what he imagined must be a broom cupboard. The Miss had a cupboard like this where she kept her brooms, buckets and cleaning things. And there was a brush in here and a bucket and what looked like rough dish-cloths hanging from a peg.

Holding the candle high, she put her free arm upwards and pressed her hand against the low ceiling. And now his eyes nearly popped out of his head as the whole wall of the cupboard slid away and there showed up before him a weird room. Even in the poor light of the candle he knew it was weird.

But what was more weird still was the movement in the far corner of it.

He was shaking visibly as he watched her pressing something in what looked like a mattress stuck to the wall while the door slid into position again.

When, his voice a whimper now, he said, 'Missis,' she said, 'It's all right, lad, it's all right. You'll come to no harm in here. And she won't hurt you, poor mite.'

His eyes were stretched wide, his mouth agape as he stared in amazement down on the child sitting on what looked like a half single mattress in the narrow slit of, he couldn't call it a room, just this place.

Again the woman was speaking to him. She had her arm round his shoulder and she was pointing to the child, saying, 'You remember the baby? He . . . he wanted to do away with it. Well, he . . . he thinks it's gone, but . . . but we couldn't. Connie defied him on the side like. He doesn't know she's here. He'd murder the lot of us if he did. We're at our wits' end. We don't know what to do with her. It's keepin' her clean an' fed, that's the trouble.'

He muttered now, 'What's . . . what's this place?'

'It's what we call the cubby-hole. He's frightened of it, the master; he'll never come near it. You see he used to be pushed in here when he was a young lad. I think it's gone a long way to make him turn out as he has. It was his father. You see, his grandfather built this place, I mean the whole house, he was a master builder, and he built this special room on with his own hands so he could put his wife in when she had one of her turns. He wouldn't have her put away to an asylum. You see there's no sound can get out; these are all hair mattresses.' She put her hand out and tapped the padded wall. 'An' behind them is another layer of padding. The grandmother didn't

123

last all that long but I think the master's father was given a taste of this room himself; then he passed it on to his son. Give the master his due, he always said he wouldn't put a dog in here. So the child's been safe so far. But God only knows what would happen if he found out. I tell you he'd murder the lot of us, 'cos he still has nightmares about her, the mother. You remember? He can't get over the fact that she made a cuckold of him.'

His breath was catching in his throat. He was still staring at the child who looked like an inanimate doll except for the rapid blinking of her eyelids in the candlelight.

'Is . . . is she left in the dark?'

'God forgive us! Aye. We've got to leave her in the dark most of the time. We can only take her out when we know that the road'll be clear for a few hours.'

'Tis terrible. 'Tis cruel.' His voice was high.

'I know that, lad. I know that, but what would you have us do? Bury her as he ordered? When Frank refused to do it he was for taking her down to the river himself, but Connie stepped in. She would bury her, she said. And that's what she did, supposedly. Oh, what a to-do it was, but our Connie's got more spunk than her da. But as I said, she's grown, and what we're gona do with her now, God alone knows. Anyway, this time I'll leave the candle for I must go down else that lot'll be trying to find me.'

'How . . . how long will you be?'

'Not long. He'll want you downstairs and out as soon as the coast's clear.'

'How d'you . . . how d'you get out without anybody seein' you?'

She pointed to the top of the padded wall to the side of the door, and she said, 'When anybody puts

124

their foot on the outside landing that gives a tinkle. As for air, up there.' She pointed to the high padded ceiling. 'There's a vent that lets into the chimney, and it's a tall one, and if any noise got through it just sounded like the rooks in the trees beyond.'

'He thought of everything, that man, didn't he? But what use was a bell inside here?'

'Well, I understand that the sound stopped her thrashing about, at least so I was told; it sort of calmed her for a little while. But it wasn't all that effective because he told me' – she now thumbed towards the floor – 'that he saw his grandfather come out at one time with his ear almost hanging off. Oh, he's to be pitied, for the only pleasure he seems to get in life now is cheating the customs. I daren't think of the times he's risked his neck. But they'll have him one of these days. An' you, lad, have nearly been the means of it. An' here's another time.'

'If they catch you going out what'll you say?'

'Once I'm in the cupboard I can hear a mouse on those stairs, and if they were to come in to the room then I'm at the old trunk in the corner taking out some of the mistress's clothes for cutting up. But don't worry about me, lad, only sit quiet, talk to her. She understands. She can say some words.'

'What . . . what d'you call her?'

'Belle. Just Belle.'

As she pressed the spring in the mattress he turned in panic to her, saying, 'You'll come . . . you'll come back quick, won't you? Eeh! Look, I . . . I can't stay in here.'

'Now, now, lad; steady on. Of course I'll come back, but if I didn't, laddie, all you've got to do is to press the spring and the door will open. So there's nothin' to worry about. But talk to the bairn, comfort her, 'cos she's not barmy or daft.'

125

Nevertheless, in spite of her words he almost yelled out when he watched the panel glide back as if it was on oiled hinges, then slip into place again and causing the candlelight to flutter just the slightest.

He stood as if transfixed staring down at the child; then he looked about him. He hadn't far to look. The place was about eight feet long and five feet wide. The only articles in it were the mattress, an enamel chamber-pot, a bucket and a tiny low table on which the candlestick rested.

His nose was wrinkled against the smell, but the air though heavy was breathable. He looked around the mattress-padded walls and, reaching out, he tried to put his fingers in between two of them, but they were so firmly packed he doubted he could insert even a fingernail. Then he looked at the thing in the corner again. He couldn't yet put the name child to it. There were two dark blots in a small round face, the whiteness emphasised by the blackness of the hair surrounding it. The child was sitting motionless like a dummy; the black orbs seemed fixed on him. She had said, comfort it. How? How was he to comfort it? He was afraid of it; scared to touch it: as yet it still wasn't really a bairn, even though his mind told him it was the baby who had been lying in the wash-basket the morning he had left this house all that time ago. But he still couldn't move towards it.

Then the child made a sound. It wasn't like ma or da but more like caw, like the sound a seagull made. Then she said it again, loud and clear this time; and now he recognised it as Con. The servant's name was Connie.

When she held out her arms he very slowly dropped onto his knees by the side of the mattress pad, and the next minute he found himself hugged to

126

the small body. At first the feeling made him shudder; then to save them both falling sideways he put one arm about her while supporting himself against the floor with the other. Now the small face was close to his, the tongue on his cheek as if kissing it or sucking at it. He heard himself say, 'There, there. There, there.' Then like a small animal burrowing into the flesh of its mother she snuggled her head into his neck and put her thin legs around the side of his waist, and then she became utterly quiet.

Oh, Ma. Ma. He found himself repeating the cry in his mind. He wished he was home: he wanted his ma to put her arms about him, as she had done in the bedroom last night. Running was one thing; he wasn't really afeared of running, it was exciting in a way; but . . . but this was different, he was afeared now. And this poor bairn. How long would they be able to keep it in this place? It would go mad here, like the woman who was its great-grandmother. It wasn't right. No it wasn't. He should be brought up before the justices. But . . . but then he didn't know anything about it; he thought it was dead. Well, it would have been better dead. But what when he found out, would he still kill it?

What was he to do?

Mind his own business.

He couldn't mind his own business; he wouldn't be able to sleep at night for thinking of this bairn in here.

He looked towards the candle. It was half down. He wished she would hurry up and get back. Yet she said he could get out when he wanted. Well, he wanted to now, the sooner the better. He went to unloosen the child's arms from around his neck but it clung to him. He had a picture of the day when the men had flung the cat over the dockside with a piece

127

of wood attached to its neck so it wouldn't drown straightaway. He could see its claws coming up and grappling with the wood which pressed it under the water. The men had laughed; all but Joe Armstrong, and he had knocked Bill Storridge into the water in the battle royal that followed. And Bill Storridge couldn't swim. But he had been the one who had thrown the cat in. Joe Armstrong had hauled the cat out but wouldn't give a hand to Bill Storridge, and Bill Storridge's blokes had fought Joe Armstrong's. They were always two warring factions working at either end of the quay, hitting out whenever they came together, mostly in the bars.

She was like the cat; she was still clinging tightly to him. But she was no weight; Lily, he imagined, could make four of her. He pulled himself to his feet, asking how long he had been in here. Well, he had been in here for as long as it took a candle to nearly burn itself out, and he just couldn't be in here in the dark.

Oh no, by God! not that. Oh no! not in this place in the dark because he, too, would start yelling out. And anyway in black dark he would go round in circles and he wouldn't find that spring.

He made for it, reached up and, his fingers on it, he hesitated and looked back towards the low table and the candle about to gutter. Then screwing up his eyes, he pushed his finger on the spring. When the mattress slid quietly past him, he remained standing where he was for a moment. His first reaction was to tear the child from him and push it back into the room, but he couldn't do it, he couldn't push it back into that blackness where it must have lived for most of its life.

He was in the cupboard now, and he didn't stop to put up his hand and press the door back but thrust

128

open the cupboard door and stepped into the comparative light from the starlit sky coming through the one small window in the room.

He stood gasping and hardly able to breathe for the child's bony arms were constricting his gullet. Its face was still hidden in his shoulder, but he said to it, 'It's all right. It's all right,' and it was as if he was comforting himself for being out of that hole. Eeh! Dear God! He couldn't believe this was happening to him. They wouldn't believe it at home; they would say he was stretching it. But when they saw the bairn. He almost sprang from the room onto the landing. What was he talkin' about? It was them downstairs that would have to have the bairn. And he would tell them they hadn't to put it back in that hole else he would split on them. Aye, he would. By God! he would an' all.

He had the opportunity of telling them this in the next minute or so when he stepped off the bottom stair into the hall for, there, Betty Wheatley and Connie were both hurrying from the kitchen doorway, and they both stopped dead in their tracks when they saw him. But before he could speak Betty had reacted and rushed forward, crying, 'You should have left her there, lad. What's up with you? He could be in at any minute. Oh God! in heaven, what now? Here, give it to me!'

When she went to pull the child from Freddie's arms the baby gave a high piercing cry, and Connie, putting her hand across her mouth, said, 'Eeh! Ma! God Almighty! Did you hear that? She doesn't want to let go; she likes him!' Connie was pulling at her mother's arm now. 'It could be a way, a way out. Let him take her. She'd . . . she'd be safe across there an' lost among the lot of them. We could send somethin' now and again.'

129

'No, no; you can't; me ma's got a job to keep goin'
as it is.' He was yelling now.

'Well, don't let's stand here. If he bursts in that
door we'll all be done for.' Betty was pushing him
now none too gently through the green-baized door,
along the corridor and into the kitchen now where
her husband exclaimed on an oath, 'Christ
Almighty! Are you mad, woman? Why did you let
him?'

'I didn't let him. Where is he?'

'He's . . . he's ridden over to Doctor Black's, likely
to see what's happened there. But he expects to go
visiting somewhere else because he told me to get
the cart ready. I've got Prince in the shafts.'

'Where's he for?'

'You ask me. I don't know. But wherever it is it's
too far to take Jumbo because he's been riding him
on and off all day. But what's up with you, woman?
Do you want us all murdered?'

'I've thought of somethin'. Let the lad take it
across the water.'

'Don't be so soft.' There was scorn in his voice.
'How is a lad like that to account for a bairn in arms?
The authorities would be on to it.'

'Not if he took it into his house. They all live like
rats.'

'No, we don't. We don't live like no rats.'

'All right, all right, you don't live like rats; but
you're huddled together in one room.'

'We're not, we have two.'

'Oh well, you have two. How many are there of you
in the two?'

'Seven.'

'Well then, one more won't make any difference,
will it?'

'Shut up, Ma. Go softly. Look, lad.' Connie was

bending down to him now. 'If you could take her across with you, your mother, being a wise woman, would find some excuse to give the neighbours for it being there; an' I'd come across every week, I promise, an' bring you a shilling or so and a bag of food to help for her keep. It'll more than help for her keep what I'd bring you.'

'You know what?' He looked from one to the other as he seemed to get worked up; then he stammered, 'Yo . . . yo . . . you're awful, the lot of you, keepin' a bairn up . . . up in a mad room.'

'Better than havin' it buried alive or drowned in a sack,' Frank Wheatley growled at him.

'Shh!' Connie held up her hand. 'Did I hear the front door?'

They listened; then Betty said, 'He wouldn't come in the front door, he'd come into the yard with the horse, wouldn't he? And oh, for God's sake! shut her up; I haven't heard her cry like that afore.' Betty was pointing to the child now whose head was raised from Freddie's shoulder. But lifting her hands, Connie commanded silence when she hissed, 'Shh! I tell you there's someone in the hall.'

'Well, go and see.' Her father thumbed towards the far door; and she moved immediately, only to stop at the far side of the table within arm's reach of her mother; and now they both stared at their master standing within the doorway.

Freddie too was staring at the man, and for a moment he wanted to throw the child from him. Then he found his arms tightening about it. The child of a sudden had stopped crying; it too seemed to be looking at the man advancing down the room.

Roderick Gallagher stopped within two arms' length of his housekeeper and his maid, and he looked between them to where the little runner stood

131

with a child in his arms. The child was pale-skinned with great dark eyes and black hair. It didn't seem to have grown or changed since the morning he threw it at his man and told him to bury it. He recalled that Frank had said, 'Why not just smother it and bury it alongside its mother.' But no; even dead, he wasn't going to afford her that comfort. But when his man had said, 'But you have no bairn to bury with her, master,' he had told him that he had already thought of that: there were ways and means of obtaining a dead child from the workhouse or hospital under the guise of dissection. Anyway, even if Doctor Black had been in at the birth he wouldn't, three days later, have noticed anything.

'You bloody lot of twisters!'

As Gallagher sprang forward, Connie thrust an arm back to the table and, grabbing up a long wooden rolling pin, she brought it in a swinging arched movement towards him. Fortunately for her it missed his head and struck him on the shoulder, causing him to stagger sideways for a moment. He was screaming now like a madman, and so was Betty Wheatley, yelling at her husband: 'Get them away!' she yelled to him. 'Use the cart. Get them away!'

As Frank grabbed Freddie by the coat collar and almost lifted him from the floor, he saw the two women fling themselves onto the man. Then, in the next second, it seemed he too was being flung into the cart, and as he fell on his side the child let out a startled cry. The next thing he experienced was being tossed from one side of the cart to the other while aiming to protect the child with one arm and trying to find something to hang on to with the other hand.

He knew when they had left the country road and taken the broader way into South Shields, for he

132

wasn't being tossed about so much. When they passed an inn he saw in the light from the lanterns that the child had its eyes wide open and its mouth was agape, but that it was no longer crying. It was still gripping him tightly, and every now and again he had to loosen its hands from the collar of his coat.

They were in the town now and he pulled himself up by the iron frame of the seat and yelled at the man, 'Where are you goin'?'

And Frank turned his head and yelled back, 'Where d'you think? To drop you nearest the river, then to make myself scarce or I'll be done for the night.'

'I . . . I don't think I'll . . . I'll be able to get across. The tide'll be high about now.'

'That'll be your look-out.'

'No, it isn't, mister. She's not my look-out . . . this 'un I mean.'

'Well, if you don't want to see her end up in the river you'd better let her hang onto you. And as my lass said, you won't lose by it. Although what'll happen now since he's found out God alone knows. Here's one though that's not waitin' to see. So prepare yourself, laddie, I'm goin' to dump you along the quay here.'

'But . . . but the bairn, mister, what'll I say to people?'

The horse had pulled to a stop now and Frank Wheatley called over his shoulder, 'Say it's your sister's like: you're mindin' her bairn. It's your sister's. Well, here we are; I daren't go any further. I'm goin' to drop you now and leave this lot at the ostler's. It's where he usually leaves it. He'll call for it the morrow; but he won't find me there, no, by God! Anyway, I've had enough, years of it. So come on, get down, an' look slippy.'

Easing himself to the end of the cart, Freddie dropped to the ground; but he had hardly time to relinquish his hold on the iron rail when he heard, 'Gee up! there.' And by the dim front lamps of the cart he saw it disappear into the distance.

He stood for a moment peering about him. He knew where he was all right, but he'd have to walk some way to get to his sculler, and from what he could see of the river below the dock wall the tide was rising high.

Two figures passed him but took no notice of him or of what he was carrying. A group of youngsters came racing from a side alley; they were having some sport. There were lasses among them, but they took no notice of him either. There were shouts from the river from where a boat was likely being coaled.

Then he saw a dim shape coming towards him. It was a woman; and he thought his mind was going a bit funny again because he seemed to recognise her walk. And as she came nearer he saw she was carrying a lantern in one hand and a cudgel in the other, and he thought . . . But no; it was only a night-watchman. He hadn't got over the knock on his head. And that must be true because he was feeling tired again. Then the figure stopped in front of him and raised the lantern and said, '*In the name of God!* And' – there was a pause – '*What have you got there?*'

'Oh, miss, miss, am I glad to see you. Oh, it's been awful, it has. You wouldn't believe, miss. You were right. Aye, you were right. I should've told you. You were right. This is it.'

'This is what, Freddie? This is a child. Whose child is it?'

'It's his an' the one he was gona dump that night a long time ago when I couldn't tell you.'

134

He saw that her face was all screwed up, and she said, 'Oh! boy. Oh! boy. Well, we'll hear all about it when we get to yon side. But, oh my goodness! you've had us all worried. Your people are distracted. You know that? Quite distracted. You've got to stop this.'

'Oh, miss, 'tis stopped, all stopped. But . . . but I'd better get across home 'cos I feel he's after us.'

'Who? Gallagher?'

'Aye. Aye; he went mad when he found it was alive.'

She was hurrying him forward along the dockside now. 'What do you mean, when he found it was alive? Did he think it was dead?'

'Aye; I've told you. Oh . . . oh dear me, miss, I'm tired. I fell an' I've been tired since. I don't know how I've kept awake all this time. I think it was the cart rumblin' that kept me . . .'

'Shh! What's that?' She had pulled him close to her. 'That's a horse coming, galloping. Who'd come galloping along the quay at this time of night? My God! It could be an' all, it could be him. Come on! We can run for it. I've got a sculler further along. Come on! Come on!'

They were on the longshore now and it seemed deserted, but there was no doubt who the man dismounting from a horse on the bank behind them was.

'Give me the child!' she cried as she ran; then immediately contradicted herself, saying, 'No, no! You go on.'

It was then the voice hailed them, shouting, 'Hold there! Hold!'

She swung the lantern up and it showed the tall figure coming down the bank, his high boots sending up sprays of sand while one raised hand brandished a horsewhip.

He was within an arm's length of them now when he stopped and, bending forward, peered at the figure who, likewise, had a raised arm. And as if in surprise he muttered, 'Maggie Hewitt?'

'Yes, Maggie Hewitt.'

'What have you got to do with this? I want that boy and the child.'

'Well, you're not getting the boy, or the child.'

'Don't try to stop me, woman! That's my child.'

'For how long? Till you throttle it?'

'What d'you mean?'

'You know what I mean. Your child was buried with your wife. Everyone knows that. Now get back or else you'll wish you had.'

'Woman! don't try to thwart me or you'll find yourself in the river. I warn you.'

She now made a backward movement with one foot, saying quickly, 'Go on! Go on, Freddie. Go on over; the sculler's just along there.'

But the boy didn't move. Whether it was he was petrified of the man or he didn't want to leave her, he wouldn't know; but he stood there, the child clinging to him and a portion of his mind aware that it was once again wetting and that urine was running up his sleeve.

When he saw the whip miss Maggie's head he did move, and that was forward, only to be stopped almost in his stride by a cry from the man as Maggie's cudgel caught him in the middle. The next moment his mouth sprang agape when, as the man's body seemed to tumble forward, Maggie delivered another blow which caught him on the back of the head. And there he was now doubled in two lying at the water's edge.

He watched her, in amazement now, raise the lantern and peer back towards the dock, then up the river. There were still voices coming from the loading boat and there were voices and figures moving along the far shore.

The next moment she had turned and thrust the lantern, then the cudgel, into his free hand and, without saying a further word, she now bent forward and began to roll the recumbent body further into the water. Then she was in the water herself urging the bulk forward; and only when the water reached almost up to her thighs and had blown her skirt into a bell did she stop.

In the flickering light from the lantern he saw the huddled shape sink beneath the water, and he stood in petrified stiffness looking to where her dark shape was bending down as if she was gazing at the incoming tide. Of a sudden he felt funny again: he wanted to go to sleep just where he stood with the water now creeping over his ankles.

He wasn't aware that she had turned towards him until he felt a hand on him, and then he experienced bodily relief when she took the child from him, gasping as she did so, 'On! . . . Go on!' He went on splashing through the water, the swinging lantern casting weird shadows before him.

When they reached the boat he saw that she had put the child inside her coat, and now she ordered tersely, 'Row!'

'I can't use two oars.'

'Nobody's asking you to. Give one here!'

A wind had risen and with the uneven rowing the boat rocked, and when she cried at him, 'Steady!' he said nothing; he was tired, frightened, even petrified: she had killed him; perhaps not at first, but she had made sure by drowning him.

'Put out the light.'

'What?'

'I said, put out the light. Quick!'

Gathering breath, he blew into the top of the lantern that rested between his feet. And when presently she said, 'We'll run in here, but be quiet,' he thought he knew the shore even in the dark, but apparently he didn't know it as well as she did.

She didn't take the first path up the bank leading to the Low Lights but kept on. He knew she was holding the child in the crook of one arm while still gripping the cudgel because she was guiding him very firmly with it pressed against his shoulder.

Lights showing ahead pointed out that they were nearing the quay where the work was still going on; but before they reached it he was twisted around to climb some slimy steps jutting out from a wall. There was no rail and as he neared the top he fell onto his hands and knees, and her voice hissed at him, 'You're all right. Stand up!'

They were now in a labyrinth of short streets where the lights from windows told him that they were nearing the top of the hill. She was walking slower now and she had taken her hand from him; but she still did not speak; neither did he, for all he wanted to do was to drop down and sleep.

At times he knew he was walking with his eyes closed, but when some time later – he had no account of how long, whether it was five, ten, or fifteen minutes – she pushed him through the gate and up the path, he couldn't believe that he was home. And in relief he did think of it as home at this moment.

'You're all right. You're all right.' Her voice was floating about him.

'I'm . . . I'm very tired.'

'Yes, yes, I know you are, lad. Have . . . have you been hurt?'

He was aware that she was stripping his clothes

off him and he said, 'When he threw me off the horse I hit a stone, or a rock.' And at this she said, 'Aha!'

He opened his eyes and was amazed to see she hadn't a skirt on, or boots, or stockings, she was standing in her petticoat and bodice. What was the matter with him? Oh, he was just tired. But the bairn?

He said now, 'Where's the bairn?'

'Don't worry, don't worry, she's all right, she's all right. Go to sleep.'

'You killed him.'

'Yes, I killed him. You wouldn't like to have seen me go to the House of Correction would you for bodily assault, while you were doing time there, too, for kidnapping? And he would have had us both. Oh, yes: Roderick Gallagher would indeed have had us both, because how could we prove that he intended to murder his child? His servants? Servants can be bought off. Oh yes; money talks loudly. And he was powerful in his own way, was Gallagher. Very powerful. We'll talk more in the morning. Go to sleep.'

And he went to sleep.

When he next awoke it was to look up into his mother's face. She was bending over him and stroking the hair from his brow, and he said, 'Ma. Am I home?'

'Aye, lad.' She nodded. 'You're home.'

He looked beyond her to a bedrail and beyond that to a mirror attached to a piece of furniture. They hadn't anything like that in the bedroom. He was at Miss Maggie's. When he went to pull himself up his mother's hand stayed him as she said, 'Lie still now. Lie still.'

'Ma.'

'Aye, lad?'

'There's a bairn.'

'It's all right. It's all right. You can talk in a little while.'

His eyes were wide open now. He stared at his mother, then asked, 'How did you get here?'

'On me feet.'

'Oh, Ma, don't be funny, 'tis serious.'

'I know 'tis serious, lad. By the way, did someone hit you?'

'No, no, Ma. When he threw me off the horse I fell against a stone and after that I kept fallin' asleep. Where's . . . where's the bairn, Ma?' He again attempted to rise, and again she pushed him back, saying quietly, 'She's all right. She's been fed and she's asleep. And clean for once in her life, poor bairn, at least as clean as we can get her at the moment until her scabs heal; she must have sat in wet for God knows how long. They should be gibbeted that lot.'

'They . . . they saved her, Ma, and . . . and had to hide her. Where's miss?'

'I'm here.'

The last time he had seen her she seemed to be almost naked. Now she was in a grey dress with rows of buttons down the front. Her hair was combed back, making her face look more weather-beaten still.

She came round to the other side of the bed and sat down, and said quietly, 'You hungry?'

'No; but . . . but I'd like a drink.'

'I'll get it.' His mother got up and left the room, and, his eyes widening, he looked towards the door through which she had just gone, saying, 'She knows where to go?'

'Oh, yes, yes; she's grown up enough to find her way to the kitchen.'

'Who . . . who brought her?'

140

'I did.'

'Oh.'

She moved up the bed closer to him now and, putting her hand against his cheek, she turned his head right round towards her as she said softly, 'Now listen. Can you remember what happened on the shore last night?'

He looked away from her up to the white ceiling, then down to the flowered wallpaper, and then into her face again before saying, 'Aye, everything.'

'Well now, listen very carefully. *Not to your mother*, nor to another soul must you describe what happened. We know nothing about a man who tried to take the child from us. You understand? You can tell your mother . . . and me everything that happened until I met you on the dockside. From then, we just got into the boat, crossed the river and came here. *Now this is important, Freddie. Do you hear?* Because he'll be found later, and . . . and there'll be bruises on him, and' – her voice dropped to a mere whisper as she went on – 'you wouldn't like to see me swing by the neck, would you?'

'Oh, Miss.'

'Now' – she was wagging her finger at him – 'your mother too must be given to understand not to mention a word of what you tell her because people would put two and two together if the whole story came out. I think those across the water that kept the child alive, they'll keep their mouths shut too, at this stage. Anyway, I'm going to get in touch with one of them. But listen, and carefully, the child is the *daughter* of my *cousin* who *died*. You understand?'

After a moment he brought his chin into his chest by way of confirmation, then said, 'She is the *daughter* of your *cousin* who *died*.' Then in a

141

normal tone, he said, 'How you goin' to bring that about? Everybody knows . . .'

'Everybody knows what? That I haven't got a cousin? I have got a cousin, two cousins: one's in London and one's in Darlington. But it's all worked out. I'm going to take a few trips, and one day very soon, and it will have to be very soon, within the next week or so, I'll come back with the bairn in me arms. It'll have to be at night, because china dolls don't cry. Do you follow me?'

He didn't, not quite, not about the china dolls because his head was muzzy, but what he said was, 'You mean to let her live with you? We won't have to take her?'

'Don't you think your mother's got enough to look after? And why shouldn't I take her? It's about time I took on some responsibility. I've had it too easy, don't you think?'

He knew she expected him to give no answer, but, a faint smile on his lips, he said, 'Aye; aye, I think you have.' She slapped his face gently with her fingertips, saying, 'Concussion hasn't dulled your wits.'

'What d'you mean, concush . . .?'

'That's what you've got, that's what's making you sleepy. You'll be like this for a couple of days yet. And you're very tired too, in any case.'

'But . . . but who's goin' to look after the bairn? If I'm goin' to do the garden an' things, I couldn't.'

'Of course you couldn't. Who'd expect you to look after a bairn?'

'I used to look after our Lily.'

'Well, your mother's going to look after . . . my bairn.'

'She is? Me ma? She's workin' on the ropes half day; an' then there's me da.'

142

'Shut up and go to sleep again, at least after you've had something to drink. Your mother's taken on a new job: she's working for me now, here. And close your mouth, you're nothing to look at any time but with it open you look like a gargoyle.'

'A what?'

'A gargoyle. Which reminds me, you're going to school.'

'No, by God! I'm . . .'

'And we'll have no more "by Gods!" either. You're going to school, at least part of the day.'

'I'm not though.'

'You are though.'

She rose from the bed as his mother came into the room and, speaking to her across the distance, she said, 'He's so pleased he's going to school and stop being an ignorant little lout.'

'You were goin' to larn me.'

'I haven't the time now. And anyway, it's not larn. And that's just by the way; there'll be lots of by the ways for you, young man . . . Sit yourself down, Jinny, for I must be off for a while else those cut-throats down on the quay will have collared half my business.'

He took the mug of cocoa from his mother and gulped at it; then he looked at the two women, sitting one at each side of the bed, at the big bony bulky form of his ma and the thin narrowness of the woman whom at this moment he knew he liked as much as he did his ma, but who last night had murdered a man, and it hadn't seemed to have affected her, for she was still acting the same.

He didn't know, but his mother knew that Miss Maggie Hewitt had spewed her heart up in the closet after she had come for her early this morning.

143

2

A fortnight had passed and tongues were wagging along the quay. Did you ever know such a thing? Maggie Hewitt had adopted a bairn. A cousin of hers had died and left it to her. She didn't seem over-pleased about it; you couldn't get a civil word out of her at times. And it must be telling on her for she looked peaky. Well, it was to be understood, wasn't it? because she'd had to spend out, and who had she spent out on? The Musgrave family. Taking on big Jinny as a part-time housekeeper, and the little 'un's brother as a gardener, and he himself, it was said, was going to school. Oh, they'd believe that when it happened because that would be like tying an eel up with silk ribbon. And then what would the gang do for a runner? It was also said there was one place he wouldn't run to any more, and that was across the water. Funny business that, for a man like Gallagher to be found in the river and been bashed about an' all, neck broken with a heavy instrument. So the coroner had said. He was missing for five days. The first inkling of his being missing was when his man came looking for him. He had been gone twenty-four hours. 'Twas then they knew who owned the horse that had been picked up at yon end of the sands. His man had said his master had ridden out to meet some friends. But the question now was: who were the friends? And the customs had been interested too. But there was nothing found on the body. It was understood he had a son by his first wife who would come into the estate;

but the boy was only ten years old and had been living in the care of his maternal grandmother.

Freddie himself had had a visit from two customs officials. One was from the excise office in Saville Street, a Mr Thomas Brayhay. It was the place where you went for permits. This man had asked him what he was doing on the river in the dark on a certain night and he had answered glibly he was going across to see his granny who had took bad; his ma couldn't go 'cos she had to see to his da and the bairns.

Was it not that he went to meet a certain gentleman with a message?

No, no. Anyway, he didn't run messages any more for anybody, the fish men or the butcher, 'cos he was going to have a half-time job in Miss Hewitt's office and go to school.

But the man had then wanted to know why he went across the river in a little sculler when the tide was going down; and, too, had he not heard someone calling on him to stop?

No, it was a windy night, if he remembered rightly, he had said.

Miss Maggie had come on the scene and she had laid about the customs men with her tongue and said in future she would be responsible for anything that the boy did and that they had to come to her. And the conversation had ended funnily because the man had smiled at Miss Hewitt, and had said, 'Oh! Maggie, Maggie.' And she had turned a funny colour and wagged her head, then showed him out.

Then another man had come across from South Shields and when he had asked the same questions he had answered in the same way, except he added, his granny hadn't been well and he had stayed with her 'cos she had nobody to look after her since her granddaughter had gone back to Darlington. Fortunately his granny had been primed with half a dollar and had kept to the same story. But it had given her something of a hold over his ma which he didn't like. But the excise man from the permit office had been the worst. He was still the worst, for he had collared him only yesterday and said, didn't he think it was funny that his mother should be walking the waterfront enquiring of the boatmen if any of them had seen him the day following the night he went across the river if she had sent him to his granny's. And the only way out of it was to cheek the man, and he said, Oh, his ma had funny turns, sort of fits and starts, which had brought the man's hand out at him; but he had dodged it.

When later, he had told the Miss about it she had said, 'Don't try to be a clever clouts with that lot. If they question you just say you know nowt or keep dumb, act stupid. They can't have much on you then. But there's one thing, they're not going to let this drop. They know there was something big afoot that night and they're going to find out what it was.' It was then she had looked at him and said again, 'Have you any idea at all what he did with the bag?'

And he had repeated for the countless time, 'No; I've told you. The last I saw of it was when the woman came in the room and gave the alarm. And the main thing that stuck in me mind after that was that awful room an' the bairn.'

Three odd things then happened before this chapter of Freddie's life closed. The Miss came to him and said, 'They've gone.' And for a moment he didn't know to whom she was referring and he said, 'Who's gone?'

'The staff. The lot from The Towers. I . . . I made enquiries. It appears they all got the push. There's an old lady in charge now, with a young boy, Gallagher's

146

son, and she brought her own staff with her. And she must be a woman of some substance because there's eleven of them and two carriages. And she's having the whole place torn apart and redone. I don't suppose you'd have an idea where those three went, would you?'

He had just shaken his head and felt sorry for them, for they'd be out of work. From what he could gather, too, they had been with the family from before the time *that man* was born . . .

But what had happened to that lot was made clear when one morning, as he was about to go down the garden the gate opened and the muffled figure of a woman entered. As he went towards her he gave a slight gasp when he recognised the pockmarked face. It seemed to be even more disfigured, although it was shaded with a deep-brimmed bonnet and the collar of her cloak covered her chin.

'Hello there, lad,' she said.

'Eeh! it's you. I thought you had gone.'

'On the point of. On the point of.'

'You all got the push?'

'Aye; we all got the push.'

''Twasn't fair.'

'Oh, don't worry, we're all right. How's the bairn?'

He looked back towards the house and said, 'She's lovely now.'

The woman's lids shaded her eyes and her head drooped before she acknowledged quietly, 'She was in a state, I know, but we couldn't do anything about it. I used to rub her with lard, but it was the mess an' the wet. And there were days when he was in the house and we daren't go up because he was restless, you know goin' from one place to the other. And if he'd seen us up on that floor where none of us ever really went 'cos there was no need, just to sweep the cobwebs

147

away now and again, he would have twigged and he would have murdered us. Instead he was . . . well, somebody must have done for him, mustn't they?'

He made no answer to this, and she said, 'We all wondered how you got across. We didn't know what had happened, only that you must have reached home and taken the bairn with you. We thought your mother had it, that was, up till yesterday. When me da came across the water he went in a bar and heard bits and pieces, and he put two and two together. Why . . . why did the woman take her? I mean the owner of this place?'

'Oh' – he hesitated – ''cos I suppose she's lonely. An' . . . and I work for her, an' you see it was her who helped me across the water that night. She happened to be just comin' back from some place over there. And I had to tell her . . . well a bit, not everythin',' he lied, 'about the bairn that nobody wanted. An' it just went on from there.'

'I . . . I couldn't see her, could I, the bairn?'

'Eeh! no. I don't think it would be wise. Me ma's in there; she might go for you, 'cos it was in a state, it's backside an' that.'

Her head was bobbing now as she said, 'I just thought. Anyway, we're off. We're goin' off to Scotland the morrow.'

'You lookin' for work?'

She gave a deep laugh now, saying, 'No, laddie, we're not lookin' for work. I can say this to you 'cos you've got a big head on those little shoulders, we won't need to look for work. You see we'd worked for that family . . . well, me da had from he was a lad, and me ma, she started when she was five, and I was born there, and we stuck by him through thick and thin. There was a time when things were thin afore he married . . . well, the bairn's mother. And she had a

148

bit. Oh aye, I'd say she had more than a tidy bit and he got the lot. That's all he married her for, the money. Yet she was bonny, beautiful, and the nicest lass you'd care to meet. But I think any good that was in him was buried with his first wife. Yet, he couldn't bear to look at her child after she went. Now isn't that funny? But good days or bad he never gave us a penny piece over our wages, an' they weren't big I can tell you; three shillings a week I was gettin', me ma five, and me da eight, never a penny more. And so when he didn't turn up . . . well I ask you! What would you have done? He had a few hidy-holes he thought nobody knew anything about. He thought he was the cutest thing on two legs. Of course, mind, when the old girl took over she found quite a bit in the safe, as well as his first wife's jewellery, and his second wife's an' all, at least most of it.' Her eyes widened under her bonnet as she bent towards him now, whispering, 'What I really came across for was to see your ma, 'cos I thought the bairn was with her, you see, an' to make it all right that she wouldn't be out of pocket for some time. But I can see the bairn's in clover, and if your ma's lookin' after her she'll be all right an' all. But anyway – ' She now put her hand into a pocket and pulled out a purse. It was chamois leather and was very like the one he had seen her master use. She drew out a half-sovereign and handed it towards him, saying, 'That's for yourself 'cos you're a good lad.'

He gave her no thanks but looked at the money in the palm of his hand, and he had the strange desire to hand it back to her and say, 'I don't want that, that's his.' But she was saying now, 'I don't suppose we'll ever meet again 'cos Scotland's a long way off, at least where we're goin'. So ta-ra! lad. It's been a strange do, hasn't it?'

'Yes. Aye, it has.'

She backed from him towards the gate, and now he felt forced to say, 'Good luck to you.'

'Thank you, lad. We've already got it. God looks after his own. An' good luck to you. He'll see to you an' all. As I said to me ma, you'll do things, go places, be somebody. It's in your face. Ta-ra!'

'Ta-ra!'

He'd do things, go places, be somebody.

Would he?

The second thing took place the next morning. It was the day on which he was about to attend half-day school. His mother had given him a clean pair of trousers, saying, 'Put them on. And there's a clean shirt as well. And put some blackin' on your boots mind. Anyway, I'll be over there later to see that you do.'

When he reached the house Miss Maggie said to him, 'You can stop helping John from now on. Anyway, he's better on his own. He's been at it for the past hour; I think he'd work all night if he had a light. You're coming down to the office with me. You're starting school today and a morning at my place will show what it will lead to if you can take it into that thick skull of yours.' She had smiled at him; then, looking at the parcel he had unwrapped, she said, 'Oh! clean trousers and shirt. Go and put them on now, so you'll be ready.'

The trousers he had on were the same as those he had worn on the night he had crossed the river carrying the little parcel in the inside pocket. He couldn't remember when he had first started to wear them or when he hadn't worn them, they seemed stiff with glar, but he considered they were still all right for gardening work. As he took them off he looked at them and thought, I've got a feelin' in me bones that I'll never don you again. And then, as if putting his hand into the inner pocket for the last time, he groped with it, only to bring it out sharply as if he had been stung under the finger nail. It seemed, he thought, as if there was a pin in there or something. There was a seam in the bottom of the pocket and it felt thick with fluff on both sides. So again he put his hand into the pocket and now gently scraped his fingernail along one side of the seam; and there he felt the sharp thing again. Now he used two fingers to scrape along the seam until he felt the prick, then pulled out fluff mixed up with black dust which he put on the table. Gently now he blew at the dust until what looked like a piece of glass was left.

He thrust his hand quickly back into the pocket and again his fingers travelled along the seam, and again they found something sharp. Once more he was blowing at the dust and revealing something red, red glass this time. For the third time and at a pace now, both fingers were raking along the seam, and for the third time he brought out a piece of glass. Now he turned his trousers inside out and tried to turn the pocket inside out, but this was impossible. So once more he scraped wildly with his fingernails. But there were no more pieces of glass to add to the one red and two white pieces of glass that seemed to be dancing on the table in the sunlight. But they weren't pieces of glass, he knew that; they were what must have fallen out of that package when his side hit the stone. Eeh! Eeh! dear God. What if they were . . . But they were. Where was the Miss? He looked round the room wildly as if to conjure her up.

'*Miss! Miss!*' He was out in the hall now and running towards the kitchen.

'What is it? What's the matter?'

'Come. Come an' look at this.' For a moment he

didn't realise that he was almost naked and that his middle was covered only by his shirt tails.

She followed him into the small back bedroom, and there he pointed to the table with the three pieces of glass on it.

She stood looking down at them but didn't touch them; and then, turning her head slowly, she said in a very stern voice, 'Where did you get these?'

He now pointed to his trousers lying on the floor and, picking them up, he tried to explain to her that they had got into the fluff, but his words were coming out in a stuttering gasp.

'Sit down. Sit down.' She pushed him onto the side of the bed. And now she picked up the stones and examined them, saying, 'You know what these are, don't you?'

'Aye. What I had in the parcel for him.'

'Huh! Huh!' She began to laugh. First, it was only her shoulders that shook, then her whole body and her head seemed to bob with laughter, and then it burst from her mouth and she laughed until the tears ran down her face. Of a sudden she threw her arms around him and hugged him. And when her laughter subsided it was she who now stuttered, 'Y'Y'Your interest will certainly go up with these, boy. Oh certainly.'

'I can keep them?'

'What else. What else. But keep them is the word, and for a long time, years in fact. They won't depreciate in value. Am I to be your banker again?'

His mouth now went into a wide grin; then he said, 'We'll have to discuss it, won't we?'

Her hand did not go out and clip his ear, but her voice was soft as she said, 'Oh! Freddie; this could be the rock on which you build your life.'

He looked from her to the stones. That young

152

woman Connie had said he'd do things, go places, be somebody. And now the Miss had said these could be the rock on which he could build his life. Funny the things people said.

The third thing worried him for a bit.

Mick Harper said to him: 'Why did you leave your sculler across the river an' come over with Maggie Hewitt in hers? You didn't think you were spotted, but you were.'

He didn't relay this conversation to the Miss, for he felt she would worry on the side; already she had been sick a number of times over the past weeks. Cheery all day when folks were about, but he'd heard her vomit at night, from what was his bedroom now, at least it was for two or three nights a week when his mother had told him to stay to help the Miss with the bairn when it was fractious and couldn't sleep and cried. At such times he would walk the floor with it and hum to it. It seemed to soothe it. It was then he had heard her vomiting.

His answer to Mick Harper had been, he had met up with the Miss and she had asked him to take an oar for the tide was running fast and she didn't think she was up to getting across herself. So now he knew. And did that satisfy him?

And Mick Harper had said, no, it didn't, and that he thought he was a clever clogs, but he'd be caught out one day and he'd be there to see it.

Freddie wasn't to know, of course, that Mick's prophecy, too, would come true.

PART THREE

As it Happened When I Was a Man

1

'Ben Hutton is going to swallow his spittle and choke himself when he gets this account. I can hear him yelling now: "Ninepence in the pound tax! I won't pay it. I won't pay it."' Freddie was leaning across the desk addressing Maggie who was sitting deep in a leather chair, her feet on the fender, soles upturned towards the roaring fire, and a glass of steaming liquid in one hand, and he went on, 'Remember in fifty-five when Gladstone put it up to one and tuppence? Eeh! He danced, didn't he? Actually left the floor in the office. Remember Andy Stevens was just the office boy then, and he burst out laughing and Ben Hutton brought him one across the lug and knocked him off his high seat.'

'Yes, and you, big fella, said, we'll have none of that. And you nearly lost us Hutton's contract.'

'You know something, Maggie' – Freddie now sat back in his chair – 'I've often wondered about his giving us the contract. His business now is big enough to take on two or three clerks.'

'Well, if he did that he'd have to pay two or three clerks, wouldn't he? And you know, when they first started they did all their own summing up between them, him and his fat bejewelled Bessie. Oh, how that woman gets on my nerves! And there's another thing.' Maggie now pulled her feet from the fender and placed her glass on the side table before swivelling round and pointing her finger at him. 'You know as well as I do he doesn't declare half, and I've told you you should probe into it a bit further and let him know that you know. I don't forget the dirty work he did at the new election of councillors sometime before then, in forty-nine he tried for the Tynemouth Ward when Solomon Mease got it, and Spencer got in for here. Old Tyzack got in too. Remember old Tyzack?' As she leaned back in the chair again he looked at her, as he often did, in genuine amazement. She had a wonderful mind and a wonderful memory. She could pinpoint people and dates back to those days when, as a girl, she lived on The Lawe in South Shields. At times he asked himself what he would have done without her, and what would he do without her were she to go. She had a pain now and again in her chest that worried him seemingly more than it did her. He had stopped asking himself why he loved her more than anyone in the world; yes, even Belle. But then, that was a different thing, a different feeling. Belle was a sprite, a joy, something as light as air, yet as dark as bog oak; but Maggie . . . Maggie was a rock. She was a mind that instilled itself into you, and she certainly had instilled her mind into him. It all went back to that night when they had come across the river, he, she, and Belle. Yet all she had put into his mind had not given him the power to put words to the feeling he had for her, which wasn't like the feeling he had for his mother. He felt guilty in knowing that that feeling for his mother was a faint shadow compared to the way he thought of Maggie Hewitt. It could have been the feelings of the son for the mother, yet it wasn't. It could have been those of a man for his wife. Yes; yes, it could, but it wasn't. It could have been for a teacher, a wise teacher, a stern, grim one at times, but nevertheless kind and wise teacher.

No, no; he couldn't put words to the feeling he had for the woman sitting in that chair. He only knew he wanted to hug her to him. He had done it twice. The last time had been on New Year's morning, and he felt he must never do it again because the result of it then had been her going into her room and crying so bitterly that he could hear her through the locked door. This woman with her weather-beaten face and her skinny body which he knew would harbour everlastingly the girl who had never been given the opportunity to become a real woman, was someone he loved and loved so much that he was daily fearful of losing her.

He said now, 'Belle finishes school tomorrow. What are you going to do with her?'

'What d'you think? Put her in a cage on show?'

'You could do; it would be the safest because you've got a problem on your hands. I suppose you've thought about that.'

'Yes, Mr Musgrave, I've thought about it. And so have you, haven't you?' She cast a sidelong knowing glance at him, and he shrugged his shoulders before he said, 'Naturally.'

'Well, would you mind sharing your thoughts with me?'

He picked up a mass of scattered papers, then tapped the bottoms on the desk to bring them into order, after which he laid them on the leather-bordered blotting pad before going round the desk and seating himself in a chair to the other side of the hearth from her. 'Finish that hot drink,' he said.

'Never mind the hot drink, answer my question.'

'Well' – he pursed his lips – 'she's got to be told sometime, but when, that's one problem; how, is another problem. And, as you've already found out, she has a lively enquiring mind, and so doubtless she will want to go across the water not only to see the house but also her half-brother so called. And that, Maggie, is as far as my thoughts go on the subject; except that I can't see any need for bringing the matter up unless something untoward happens, and my mind doesn't give me a picture of anything so untoward that would make you tell her that you are in no way related to her, that she is not the daughter of your cousin but that, nevertheless, you love her like you would your own daughter; in fact, the moment you first saw her she became the focal point of your life and everyone else was excluded.'

He stopped here, and they looked at each other for some seconds before she said quietly, 'You fishing?'

'Fishing? What would I hope to catch?'

'Well, talking of catching, I'm going to ask you again, what are you going to do about May Harper? Now, now! don't get up, and don't evade the question.' Her hand was wagging towards him. 'You know how I feel about May, always have done, but you should do the right thing, either marry her or give her up. It's five years now you've been dangling with her, and a little bird tells me she gets very nasty at times.'

'Your little bird wants its beak slapped, if not glued up.'

'You can't stop people talking, Freddie.' Her voice was quiet now. 'I said when you became engaged to her, such as it is without a ring, she wasn't for you; you've moved out of her world; you've risen and you're going on rising. Now, there is a vacancy coming up in the Tynemouth Council shortly, but can you imagine her acting as the wife of a councillor?'

He was on his feet now looking down at her, his face grim. 'Maggie, this is one thing I'll make me own mind up about. She's a good lass; she has her faults, haven't we all? but she's no more dying for marriage than I am.'

'Oh! don't talk so bloody soft.' She had sprung out of the chair, almost upsetting the little table on which was the tray and the empty glass. 'She's been ready for marriage since she was fourteen, that one, when she was skitting up the alleys after you. She took up with two or three others, as you know, to try to draw you on and got a name for herself, so much so that nobody would touch her, not for a wife, that is. Then, God knows why, because I don't, you take up with her when you could have had the pick of most of the town.'

His voice was unusually calm as he said, 'Pick of most of the town? Don't talk rubbish, Maggie! It's only over the last few years that even you have been considered fit to sail through the brass-studded doors of the – huh! – so-called gentry up the bank. As for me, all your training and polishing couldn't get *me* in. It was only as my sister's escort when she was singing at one of their soirées that I got past the door.'

'All right, all right, that may be so' – her voice too was quiet now – 'but things have changed over the last three years, and they'll go on changing rapidly from now on, and it's up to you to take advantage of it. You've got a head on your shoulders, you're well read. I'll say you're better read than any other man in this town, or up the river to Newcastle. And who knows more than you of what actually goes on in Parliament today. Half of them don't know the name of the Prime Minister. Palmerston, they'll say, who's he? Even those who are paying taxes

161

through Gladstone wouldn't know he's the Chancellor of the Exchequer. So now I'm coming out in the open, Freddie, and I'll say this once and for all, you marry May and you might as well go back to the time you were a runner. I hate to put it so bluntly, but there it is. What is more she doesn't like me and I don't like her; we both know where we stand, and you're in the middle.' As she turned and went towards the door he said quietly, 'Maggie, I'm sorry; but I can't see a way out.'

'Then I'm sorry too, lad.' She had the door handle in her hand when she paused and looked over her shoulder at him and said, 'By the way, don't hurry back here the night, I'm all right on me own.'

'I'll be back,' he said.

'Please yourself.'

He turned now and put his two hands on the mantelshelf and looked into the mirror above it. The light from the lamp behind him made his grey eyes look dark and his thick fair hair that fell below his ears take on a brown reddish tint. His full large mouth was set tight and his chin appeared knobbled with the thoughts passing through his mind.

She had said he might as well go back to being a runner. Had he ever been a little runner, a tiny mite of a thing? His mother said he was still a mite at fourteen. But after he had got up after that long spell in bed with fever, he had seemed to sprout like a bean pole and remain as thin as a bean pole. He couldn't recall when he had stopped growing. But there was a time, he remembered, when he feared he would grow too tall. It wouldn't have mattered so much, he had told himself, if he had grown broad with it, but his growing had come to a halt when he was just about six foot tall.

It wasn't until he was twenty that he realised that clerking all day and learning most nights didn't give a man strength to combat the quay prowlers, or even to row up to Newcastle in a sculler, so he had done something about it. When he started to run the hills first thing in the morning Maggie said he would kill himself by getting another fever. And when he took up Swedish drill exercises she said he was mad. But that was nothing to the opinion she expressed when he joined a boxing club, but not in the town or across the water in South Shields, no, in Newcastle. And what a waste she had said, and still said, because it hadn't put an ounce of flesh on him, muscles yes, here and there, but you couldn't really notice them.

He stepped back from the fireplace and stood gazing down into the fire for a moment before turning about and going upstairs and into his own room . . . his own room because for years now he had spent more time in it than he had done in his own home. Which fact caused his mother to show her spleen at times, although she had everything to thank Maggie for, such as a better house. It had three rooms and a separate kitchen, besides which it had a patch of garden with a workshop at the bottom of it in which his father spent most of his days. There was only Nancy at home now, for John had been married these six years. He was the father of twin boys and had a position as an under-gardener in an estate outside Westoe village across the water. Jessie, now twenty-three, had been in service in Durham since she was fifteen. She was with a good family and they were kind to her. She had though, at least so he felt, cut away from her own family for there were times when she didn't come home on her leave days.

163

Lily had died at four years old, another victim of the fever.

The move from the row to Bing Cottage had taken place only a matter of weeks following his mother's position of part-time housekeeper to Miss Hewitt, and it had caused a bit of a sensation. As his mother said, she'd have to live it down because no longer did she go to the centre of the town to the main tap to get her water, for there was a tap laid on near the house. She really did miss her daily trot with the bucket and her conflab with the women of the town, but because apparently she had gone up in the world she had lost a lot of her old friends. The bitterest against them had been their neighbours, the Harper family, that was until Freddie took up with May and then everybody seemed to be happy, for a short time at least.

Freddie now got into a Melton cloth great-coat, then took from a cupboard a high-topped hat and a pair of calfskin gloves, and went downstairs.

When he opened the front door, he did not immediately go out but, donning his hat and stuffing the gloves into his pocket, he took up a taper from the jar that stood beside the oil lamp on a marble-topped table to the side of the door. And he lit it, shielded the flame with his hand, went out onto the step, lit first the wall-lamp, then, bending down, he set flame to the wick of the glass-covered lantern standing on the side of the step. This done, he blew out the taper, returned it to the jar, put on his gloves, went out and closed the door and, picking up the lantern, he walked down the path, out of the gate and onto the road. It was necessary to have a lantern for this end of the town because it was not yet, as was the main thoroughfare, lit by gas.

It was a routine he had followed literally hundreds of times over the past winters and he looked upon it as

164

all part of his life with Maggie. Since that day she had
sent him to school, except for the time he spent in bed
with the fever, he had been with her every day of the
year, Sundays included; and he had slept in her house
until now it was his home, more so than Bing Cottage.
Oh, yes, much more so, although he would never dare
to voice it.

He did not, as once had been his custom when he
reached the end of the narrow road, drop down over
the cinder bank and make his way past the Low
Lights along the quays, then up the steps to home.
Instead, he turned abruptly left, went up another
bank and crossed the old coach road that led to
Newcastle and on to an open piece of countryside on
which were scattered a number of houses now distin-
guishable by the diffused light from behind curtained
windows.

Within minutes he was going up a short garden;
but before he reached the door it opened and there
silhouetted against the light stood Nancy.

'Where you off to?' he said.

For answer she said, 'Oh, hello there, Freddie.
You're late. I've been waiting for you. I'm going along
to see the Twaites.'

'The Twaites, is it?' he said. 'And what about Rob?'

'Oh, Freddie, don't be silly.'

'All right, I'm silly. You're going to see the Twaites
but give Rob my regards; he'll likely be on the look-
out for you.'

'What's kept you? I've wanted to talk to you about
tomorrow. You know we'll have to leave here at six
o'clock sharp. You'll bring Belle?'

'That's if she wants to come.'

'Of course she'll want to come. Stuck in a girls'
school all this time, she'll be like a bird let out of a
cage.'

165

He made no answer to this, but he thought, Yes. Yes, perhaps you're right, Nancy. She will act like a bird let out of a cage. And she'll be more than frustrated, having been kept at that school for another year when she had hoped Maggie would let her leave when she was sixteen.

'Come in or stay out, but close the door; the wind's raisin' your mother's skirts.' They both laughed at their father's voice; then he said, 'Don't worry; I'll be here at half-past five. Go on; but mind how you go.'

Her voice sinking to a whisper, she said, 'It's you who had better take that warnin', our Freddie. May's been round an' she didn't sound pleasant. She expected you to be here an hour ago. I told her you were likely staying on with Miss Hewitt because she wasn't very well. But then I think I said the wrong thing there. Anyway, I wouldn't dither in the house too long. 'Bye.'

''Bye, Nancy.'

He stepped straight into the living-room and closed the door behind him. His father was sitting in a low hide-padded chair to the side of a roaring fire. He looked comfortable but old. His mother too was waiting beside the fire, but further back from it, and she was busily turning the heel of a sock. Glancing up at her tall son, she said, 'You've got here then?'

'Now don't you start. Let me get in, and my coat off.' He had already taken his hat off.

'I wouldn't bother if I were you, lad.'

'What d'you mean, Da?'

'May's not long gone.'

'So I understand. Nancy told me. But why all the fuss; I never keep to time, not strictly speaking.'

'Well, apparently you should. An' you know you disappointed her on Sunday.'

'Well, what did you expect me to do, Da? Leave

166

Maggie on her own and her almost coughing her guts out?'

'She should see about that chest of hers.'

'Well, she's like you, Da, she's mutton-headed and stubborn and she doesn't like doctors. So you've got that much in common.'

'How was she when you left her?'

He turned to his mother now. 'Not too bad, except her temper was a little frayed.'

'What about?'

'Oh, this and that and the other. You know her.'

'Is she looking forward to tomorrow and having Miss Belle on her hands from now on?'

'Well, she's looking forward to having her home. But what d'you mean by, on her hands? I would say there's what is known as an inference in your tone.'

'You can leave your book learnin' outside the door, lad; you know what I mean. That lass is goin' to prove a handful. And Miss Maggie is goin' to find herself gettin' tired with her about the place day after day. It was all right when she came home for holidays. She got everybody tuned up, as our Nancy would say, and hit the high notes, but you can't go on livin' on the top of high notes. And have you thought about her future an' what's gona happen if she wants to get married or such?'

'No, I haven't, Ma. Anyway, it's got nothing to do with me.'

His tone was more than testy; and his mother now brought the three needles of the heel into line, stuck the fourth needle through the leg, then placed the sock on her lap before saying, 'Got nothin' to do with you, you say? You turning stupid all of a sudden? Why, in my eyes you could have almost fathered her. All right, all right, I said almost. That's a funny thing to say but that's how I see it:

167

from what went on she wouldn't have survived very much longer if you hadn't lifted her that night. I can still see the sight her poor little body was in. And what you seem to forget, lad –' and now, lowering her voice and inclining her head deeply towards him, she said, 'You're the only one who knows the true facts of her beginning. What Miss Maggie an' me knows was just hearsay but you were there from the time she was born. And you might have forgotten some things but it's my bet that one day, an' not too far into the future either, you'll likely be called on to remember because you'll be the only one who can. Those three servants have disappeared as if from the face of the earth. You said the daughter came and had a word with you; well, that's over fourteen years gone, to my reckoning. I also reckon that because they were makin' for Scotland they had greased their palms afore they left the house an' God knows to what extent. They said Scotland, but likely enough to take them across the water out of the country to Canada or the Americas. So when you stand there, lad, an' say her life has nothin' to do with you, I say think again.'

'You finished, Ma?'

'Yes, for the present.'

'Ta . . . thanks, and looking back over the last hour or so I seem to have run the gauntlet in one way or another; and so now I think I'll go and find a little solace in the Harper family.'

A smothered laugh from his father brought him around to ask, 'You find that funny, Da?'

'Aye, lad; aye, I find it funny after the way May went out of that door a while ago. Aye, I do, I find it funny.'

'Ah well, forewarned is forearmed, Da, so here I go.' He now picked up his hat, bent over his mother and flicked his thumb against her cheekbone, then said, 'I'll give you all the news of the battle in the mornin', Ma; that's if you arrive on time because I'll be setting off for Newcastle shortly after eight.'

She made no reply, just slanted her glance sideways at him, but his father, still laughing, said, 'Good-night, lad. Mind how you go. Swing your lantern well 'cos someone was attacked by a footpad the night afore last up your way. Time they had lights up there.'

'All right, Da, I'll swing it, and I'll swing it off their heads if the opportunity arises.'

Going out the door he called loudly, 'Good-night to you, Mrs Musgrave,' and his father's high laughter followed him.

But once on the road again he didn't bother swinging his lantern wide but walked slowly and steadily towards Jimmy Harper's house.

The Harpers too had moved from the row but not into such a salubrious part of the town as his parents. In fact it was a house merely higher up the same hill, still with two rooms but with an attic and a washhouse. Jimmy Harper was still a keelman and his son Mick, now a tough loud-mouthed stubby built man, was his partner. Mick had been married these past ten years and had added to his family each year, and all had miraculously survived in a two-roomed shanty lower down the hill. So there remained at home only May.

May had started work at eight years old as a part-time maid and washerwoman, but at sixteen she had graduated to shop assistant in Dixon's the fruiterers in Union Street. This elevation had naturally caused her to have ideas above her station in life. At the time she considered herself on an equal footing with Freddie Musgrave, because what was he after all but a little tin clerk in Maggie Hewitt's office on the quay?

It took some years and some thinking before it was forced home to her that if Freddie Musgrave didn't think he had become too good for her, Miss Maggie Hewitt did and that she had stuffed him with education to point out the difference.

Freddie was well aware of all this and in a way he was sorry for May: she had waited for him when he didn't want her to wait. In those far gone early days he had avoided her. He had laughed at his father's chipping: 'May'll net you yet, lad, you'll see.' And always his answer had been, 'Not if I've got me eyes open, Da, and me fins flapping.'

How had he become entangled with her? How had the word marriage been approached? Oh, he knew how he had become entangled with her. It was that night when the sap was rising in him. No; it had been rising in him for some long time and she was there ready and willing, and by Harry! she had been willing. He had felt scared for weeks afterwards in case she should come to him and say, 'I'm goin' to have a bairn.' And that was something very odd, she had never fallen with a bairn. Of course, he hadn't given her much chance this past year or so.

When he had thought about it, he could say to himself he had been lucky. Many a fella being as free as he had been and her as willing would have been tied for life . . . What was he thinking about? He was goin' to be tied for life to her; he was goin' to marry her, wasn't he?

Oh God! no. The thought brought him to a dead stop. He was standing at the foot of the steps leading up the hill, the lantern hanging still but slack in his hand. His teeth ground together, his chest became tight within. In the light from the lantern he could see the steam from his breath dispersing like a silver spray into the blackness now.

How could he get out of it? Could he tell her straight . . . but tactfully? Oh, God Almighty! there was no tactful way to tell a woman that she wasn't wanted any more, particularly if she had been used and had been promised for five years. But that was it, he couldn't recall any promise, any talk of marriage, except from her. It was at that New Year's do when they were having a party and Jimmy Blaze had opened up a full barrel of rum he'd had put by for years and everybody was merry, very merry. They toasted everything and everyone, and one of the toasts had come from May. Lifting her mug up she had said, 'Here's to Freddie and me, we are gona be married.' And they had all slapped him on the back. He might not have remembered but the accompanying comments surfaced the next day: 'Glad to see, lad, you're stickin' to your own,' and, 'That Maggie Hewitt hasn't turned you into a proper upstart yet,' and, 'You've got a fine lass in May, made for each other you are.'

When, a few minutes later, he knocked on May's door it was she herself who opened it with the greeting, 'So, you've got here then.' In a way, she sounded like his mother or his wife, but she wasn't his mother or his wife; and looking at her round high-coloured face with its peevish expression which he had come to recognise spelt trouble ahead his mind said, And she never will be.

'Yes, I've got here in the flesh.'

'Been very busy I suppose?'

'Yes, as you say, May, I've been very busy.'

'You're always very busy, if you ask me.'

He looked around the dull kitchen. There was a

171

brass fender in front of the fire, but it wasn't shining. The wooden table top had never seen sand and salt for many a day, nor had the clippy mats that covered the floor been shaken for some time either. And it offended his taste to see pieces of food sticking to the black rags that went to make the mat that was set alongside the table.

'Are you alone?' he said.

'Not quite; me ma's in bed, an' me da's gone to bring our Mick.'

'What for? Is your ma worse?'

'No, me ma isn't worse, but me da thinks it's about time we had a talk, an' our Mick an' all.'

'Have a talk? Your da and your Mick, and me, about what?'

'Oh, don't play the innocent. You know what about. It's five years now since I've been promised, an' I want to be married. You know I do.'

He stared at her before saying flatly, 'Well, what if I don't want to be married, May?'

'Oh, don't you come that with me. You're gona marry me, or else.'

'Yes? Or else what?'

'Well, me da an' our Mick'll tell you. Aye, they will. I've kept them back till now. But the morrow that one'll be back in Miss Maggie's fancy house, the one you're never out of, an' I know what happened last time when she was on holiday. I hardly saw hilt or hair of you an' I'm not goin' to put up with it again because now I understand she's home for good. With the airs an' graces she puts on you would think she was the Duke of Northumberland's daughter instead of some homeless waif that Maggie Hewitt took under her wing. And that's another thing, whether you know it or not, she's supposed to be the daughter of Miss Hewitt's cousin. Well, me

172

da was talkin' to a man some time gone by who knew her and her da and the family, an' he couldn't remember her havin' a live cousin. Her mother was an orphan, but her father had one brother, and he had two daughters and they were the same age as Maggie Hewitt but they died in their teens, both were hit with the cholera. He said he helped to bury them. So you explain that if you can.'

He shook his head, saying, 'I can't; but perhaps if you had a word with Miss Hewitt herself she would explain it. All I know is that Belle is the daughter of Miss Hewitt's cousin, and if you ask me I can't think that Miss Hewitt, being who she is, would take on anybody else's child. Can you?'

'Funny things happen. Me da says lots of funny things happened along this coast years back, an' that's one of them, that Belle.'

'Well, as I said, you'd better talk to Miss Hewitt about it. But with regard to us, May . . .'

'Aye, with regard to us, what about it?'

He stared at her. What could he say? In this moment I dislike you . . . I'm sorry for you but I dislike you? And: Yes, I've used you but you've wanted to be used, not only wanted but you've almost eaten me alive at times; and I've sickened myself when I've touched you? Could he say that?

What he said was and quietly, 'May, I don't think we'd make a go of it. I must face up to it. Quite candidly it isn't because I don't want to marry you, it's because I don't want to marry anybody. I'm . . . well, you could say I'm not the marrying kind.'

'Oh my God!' She was moving her head slowly from side to side now while keeping her eyes on him. 'You know what I could do to you this minute, Freddie Musgrave? I could stick a knife into you. By God! I could. But I'll leave that to me da and our

173

Mick. When they've finished with you you'll wish you'd never been born, I can tell you that. You're a dirty rotten sod! You're a bloody upstart, a dirty big-headed nowt . . .'

'May! May!'

She turned her head in the direction of the bedroom, shouting now, 'Shut up! Mother.'

He was about to turn from her and go towards the door when she almost sprang across the room and, standing with her back tight against the door, she said, 'Oh, no, you don't! You dirty bugger you! You'll stay there if I have to claw you to bits until they come in. An' I hope they've had a drink on the way 'cos then they'll be able to use their feet better on you.'

'I don't want to manhandle you, May, but get away from that door.'

'You try it, big fella. You try it.'

He looked behind him: one door led into the bedroom and another into the washhouse.

She realised his intention before he could make a move and she screamed at him, 'You try that way an' I promise you I'll do me best to tear you to shreds. You know me strength, don't you? You've had a taste of it in other ways, haven't you?'

There was the sound of footsteps outside and the next minute she was pushed forward as the door opened, and there entered her father and brother.

They were small and thickset men, and although they were muscular due to their work as keelmen they were also bloated with heavy beer drinking. Jimmy Harper's protruding stomach gave him the appearance of being nearly as broad as he was long, and his son was almost a replica.

They stood staring at him now, and it was Mick who, looking at his sister, said, 'Been havin' a chat like, eh May?'

For answer she said, 'The dirty bugger says it's all off. He says he's not the marryin' kind.'

'Oh, he does, does he?' The words were ominous.

'Look, lad,' said Jimmy Harper; 'let's talk this over, eh? What d'you say? You've been welcome in this house for years; we want no bad feelin'. You're gona marry me lass, aren't you?'

'No, Mr Harper, I'm not going to marry your lass; and I've just told her. And if you think your bashing and kicking' – he glanced towards Mick – 'will make any difference, you're wrong. And I'd just like to tell you that when there's any bashing and kicking to be done I can do me share.'

'You can?' Jimmy Harper's lower jaw jutted out, and in the short silence that followed Freddie heard the grinding of his teeth; then with an almost lightning jump he missed the blow that had been aimed for his face.

When next Mick made to come for him his father yelled, 'One at a time! lad. One at a time! I'll leave some for you; just let me deal with the pink-livered lily.' And his hobnailed boot came out and contacted the side of Freddie's knee and sent him stumbling towards the table, which in preventing his falling also enabled him to spring around and almost in the same action to deliver his fist between Jimmy Harper's eyes. The elderly man stumbled backwards, his two forearms across his face now. But his son had already taken his place and was pounding at Freddie's body; and Freddie, in turn, was lashing out at him. For a moment they were locked together until the toe-plate of Mick's boot tore down the length of Freddie's shin. Perhaps it was the agony of the flesh being ripped from the bone that brought his own knee up and into the man's groin with such force that sent him reeling back.

175

Freddie's vision was now partly blurred with the blood running into one eye from a tear in his brow, but out of the other he could see the two men lined up against the door, with May to one side of them. Not only was she screaming but her mother's voice had joined hers, for the elderly woman, looking like a witch, had appeared in the bedroom doorway.

Freddie was aware that the two men together could do for him, then dump him in the river. Such things had been done before, and the fear of this caused him to bend swiftly and grab at a two-foot iron poker leaning against a fire blazer to the side of the grate. And now brandishing it, he cried, 'Open that door because if you don't I'll brain the first one that comes near me. You're out to do me, well, it's the same from this side. And I might not only finish one but the two of you.'

There was a silence in the kitchen for a matter of seconds, yet it was a silence full of hissing breath.

'Let him be!'

No one took notice of the voice from the bedroom door until it came again, screaming now, 'Let the bugger be! He's not worth it. If he maims you that's your job gone.'

Again there was the silence, until once more the woman screamed: 'Our May, you stupid bitch! Get them from the door. D'you hear me? Get them from the door.'

He watched May glare at her mother; then, reaching out a hand she grabbed her father's arm and without a word pulled him to the side. Now there was only Mick left, and it was his mother's voice that moved him: 'Have I got to come across there and shift you?' she yelled. 'Let him out! There'll come other times. Let him out!'

As if pressing against a force Mick Harper stumbled sideways and joined his father. And now, slowly,

176

Freddie, side-stepping and his eyes riveted on them, made towards the door, with the iron poker held ready to strike.

When he opened the door he did not immediately step outside, but he thrust it wide because he knew that once he made a step through it they would bang it on him and likely knock him flying again. Before going through it, he shouted, 'Move to the table!'

And he watched them, like wounded animals ready to spring, slowly make a move towards the table. But not May, until he said, 'You an' all!'

Her head moved as though this was more than she could bear; but then she joined her father and brother. And when he had them in full vision he stumbled backwards onto the stone slab, then reached forward and pulled the door closed with a bang, and seemingly all in the same motion grabbed up the lantern and broke into a staggering run.

He had no fear of their following him now for he guessed they were in as bad a condition as himself; and he knew he was in a pretty bad state and must get home.

On the way down the slippery stone steps towards the quay he stumbled once and only just saved himself from an uncontrolled hurling to the bottom by grabbing at the broken balustrade to the side. He lay over it gasping. He had instinctively managed to hang on to the lantern, which he now placed on the step, then sat down and let his head droop forward between his knees for a moment to get rid of the faintness that was overtaking him.

The blood was still running down his face and he was aware that his mouth was stiffening and also that there was something wrong with his leg; and this for a moment filled him with fear, the old fear of anything happening to his feet.

He'd have to get home. But which home? His mother would look after him, yes; but not in the way Maggie would; nor had she the facilities. And what was more, Belle would be home tomorrow and if she knew he was ill she'd be along to Bing Cottage, and would stick around. And his mother wouldn't like that.

He pulled himself to his feet and stumbled down the rest of the steps and made his way slowly and erratically, which brought occasional and ribald comments from passers-by, to the house he really thought of as home . . .

After he had pulled at the bell and the front door was opened by Maggie, he literally fell into her arms. And as she gasped, 'Oh, my God! What's happened, man?' she lowered him onto the carpet while reaching hastily out and picking up the lantern that had fallen from his hand and was now lying on its side, its oil spilling and aggravating the flame.

A minute later, the door closed, she helped him to his feet and into the sitting-room and, peering at him now, she again said, 'Oh, my God!'

'Mag . . . Maggie.'

'Yes, lad, yes, what is it?'

'Give . . . give me a drink, will you?'

She seemed to fly out of the room and fly back again; and then she was holding a glass of raw spirit to his lips; but in his efforts to gulp at it, half of it ran down his chin.

'Let's get your things off. Come on, get up.'

She had to help him to his feet, then lead him into his room; and there he dropped as he was onto the bed and made no protest as, for the second time in his life, she undressed him.

It was when she finally pulled off his trousers and

178

his small clothes and saw the sight of his shin from the knee to the top of his foot that she brought her lips tight together for a moment before saying, 'Well, the buggers did a good job on you here. Who was it, a mob?'

His lips scarcely moved as he muttered, 'My in-laws to be.'

'Oh, now . . . now I understand . . . It's over then?'

'Aye . . . Aye, you could . . . say . . . it's over.'

'Well, my God! they've made you pay for it. You could have them jailed for this.' She straightened up for a moment, then said, 'I should get the doctor.'

'Maggie.'

'Yes, lad?'

'Just . . . just wash my leg will you? The rest will be all right. Just wash my leg.'

'I'll do that. I'll do that.' Her voice was soft; it was as if she knew of his fear.

While she washed his leg he had to make a great effort not to scream, and all the while he thought of his father and what he must have gone through when they were trying to push the bones back . . .

When he went to sleep, he had no idea, but he faintly remembered waking up several times, once thinking he had died and was in hell, another time there was a young girl bathing his head and he knew her to be Maggie, but she was only seventeen; another time he was aware that it was Maggie as she was.

When he finally awoke it was to see his mother standing at one side of the bed, but he couldn't see who was at the other because his eye was bunged up. And when he tried to turn his head he thought his neck was broken. Then Maggie's voice came at him, saying, 'Here's Doctor Wright.'

'Well, well! I thought the Crimean War was over.'

179

The jovial tone irritated him. He felt ill. What was wrong? He tried to recall what had happened to him, and for a moment he had the queer feeling that he was lying in some shrubbery and he'd hit his head upon a stone. But . . . but that was years ago.

The voices were talking across him now. 'It must have happened just after he'd left our house, Doctor.'

'You should have come for me last night, Maggie.'

'How could I? I couldn't leave him in this state and he was raving half the night.'

The doctor's hands were moving over him now, and no one spoke for a time until he said, 'I would say this is a case for the Justices. You could put those two Harpers along the line and right into the House of Correction for a time.'

'No, no.' His voice sounded like a croak to himself. ''Tis over, finished.'

'Well, that's up to you, but during the time you got this I hope you left a little impression on them.'

He said nothing, but he knew he had left a little impression on them for he could recall the pain in his knuckles as they landed between the dark baggy eyes.

Gradually he became aware that every inch of his body was paining, but his main concern was still his leg.

'My leg, Doctor.'

'Oh, it's nasty but it's clean, stripped to the bone in parts. It must have been some iron toecap to rip through your trousers and take the flesh off and that deep. But don't worry, it'll be all right. It remains to be seen if you've got good healing flesh. And by the look on your face I can see you will be on liquids for a few days. Well, there's nothing so sustaining as gruel and rum, and hot milk and whisky for a change. You won't come to much harm if you keep to that diet. Now I don't need to tell you to lie still, do I? But I may pop in later; if not, I'll see you tomorrow. You've got two good nurses here so you needn't worry. But the next time you want to finish a courtship I would think about doing it in a different way, if I were you.'

Laughing at his own joke, he went out, and Maggie followed him. He was left with his mother, and what she said to him was, 'Well, the finishing of that courtship could have finished you. You've had a lucky escape; and it's a wonder you got clear of those two. But anyway, you're free. You can thank God for that. You're free.'

He was free. He was free. For a moment he could feel no pain, no stiffness, no ache, no thumping in his head. He was free from May . . .

He went to sleep again, only, later, to wake with a start, thinking, I've got to go and collect Belle. And then there's tonight. Who'll take Nancy?'

He opened his eyes. There was no one in the room, and when he tried to raise himself the pain in his body was so excruciating that he fell back on the pillow, groaning aloud.

The door opened and Maggie came in. She was dressed for outdoors, and, on seeing her thus, he attempted to speak but his mouth refused to open and the sound that came from his throat could have issued from the far end of a tunnel.

'Belle.'

'Don't worry yourself about Belle. I'm all ready for the road, can't you see? in my best bib and tucker. All you've got to do is to lie quiet and do what your mother tells you. We should be back middle of the afternoon.' And then she smiled

181

before adding, 'Goodbye, peaceful and quiet house . . . How you feeling?'

Again the tunnel sound as he emitted, 'Terrible.'

She bent over him: 'It'll pass,' she said softly. 'But oh, I'd like to have those two up before the Justices. Anyway, I'm going down to open up first and I'll tell Andy to keep his ears open and find out if they've managed to get to their keel this morning.'

When he attempted to speak she caught the word, 'fleet,' and she said, 'Don't worry about the fleet; Roy will see to our interests in that line. Anyway, there's a glut of fish at present and you know what that means, poor returns. But we'll survive, won't we?' She grinned at him. 'You have nothing to worry about, not any more, only' – she straightened up – 'to prepare to protect yourself from the flying angel that'll be here in a few hours.'

He couldn't smile; he could make no response either with his face or his voice, but he managed slowly to lift his hand towards her. Then he lay thinking.

She had said we'd survive. That indeed was a joke. She always said we, and so included him when talking of business. She had her fingers in so many pies that if half of them sank she'd still swim. The half share in three fishing boats was just one of them, a minor one. Yet he himself owned nothing. Well, he didn't expect to. She paid him a spanking wage, and over the years she had sold the diamonds and the ruby for him and even the Roman coins that had long reposed in a tin on the mantelpiece. And so now it could be said he was a man of property; and as such, although his property reposed in the bank, he was entitled to vote. But then hadn't he been eligible to vote for a long time, since he first had ten pounds; any man with more than ten pounds could vote.

He touched his swollen and battered face. Would he

ever get his looks back? he wondered. He wasn't vain but he was naturally pleased that he was pleasant to look at. He had been called handsome once or twice, but that was soft-soaping him. But he had been lucky in the last pox epidemic that he hadn't been touched, as many had in the town.

His mother's coming into the room broke into his thoughts and he beckoned her and croaked, 'Nancy.'

'Yes; what about her?'

'The night?'

'Oh, don't you worry about the night, she'll find somebody to take her; there's always Rob; so settle yourself.'

There was nothing he could do but settle himself.

He slept fitfully all morning; then when at midday his mother had spooned gruel and rum into his mouth he had the desire to heave it up, but his ribs didn't seem to be capable of the effort. And when she went to spoon liquid from a bottle he flung his arm wide and, enduring the pain of opening his mouth, he brought out, 'No laudanum. No, Ma: no laudanum,' nodding his head in emphasis, and Jinny, tipping the spoon back to the neck of the bottle, said, 'Well, if you enjoy the pain, carry on; you'll have plenty of it in the next few days.'

The lamp was lit and the fire was burning brightly in the small iron grate when he heard the commotion in the hall and her voice. It was different from any voice he had ever heard: it held no trace of the northern accent; in fact, at times some of her words sounded as if she was a foreigner speaking English. He had always loved her voice. He had always loved her. She had been his little sister for years; but then, as Maggie had pointed out, he could have been her father, so attached had she become to him.

It was some months since he had last seen her, and he had realised then that she was no longer a little girl. What would she look like now?

He saw what she looked like when the door was thrust open and there appeared a slim young woman, five foot six in height or thereabouts with alabaster skin in which were set two oval-shaped eye sockets each filled with a dark shining glow, a nose that just missed being large and a mouth that was large, and the whole topped by a mass of raven black hair that fell straight from the crown of her head onto her shoulders.

She had stopped just within the doorway for a second, but now she skipped across the room to come to a halt at the side of the bed; and, her hands going out, she caught his, saying, 'Oh! Freddie, Freddie, what have they done to you? Your face. Your poor face.'

'Don't slaver over him; he's had enough of it, he's enjoying it.'

Maggie's voice brought the young girl's head sharply round and she said, 'Oh, Aunt Maggie, he looks dreadful, shocking. Will it ever come right again?'

For answer Freddie pulled his hands away from hers and croaked at her, 'What if it doesn't?'

'Well, in that case you'll have to wear a mask.' Her voice was as chirpy as Maggie's now.

'You've . . . you've grown.'

'Yes, I know I have. I'm an old lady, as Miss Rington pointed out to me before I left: "You have now entered your eighteenth year," she said; "try to act accordingly, Mirabelle." But you know what Madame Evette said?' She hunched her shoulders now and glanced at Maggie and pursed her lips before saying, '"Live, laugh, and love, child, so that

184

when you are old you will have at least your memories to keep you warm."'

'If you ask me she wanted her lugs smacking, that one, a flighty piece if ever I saw one. Frenchie all over.'

'What are you talking about, Aunt Maggie? You once said she was the only one that had any life in her in the whole school.'

'Well, you know me, I talk through the fat of me neck sometimes. Anyway, leave him alone now and come and get your meal. Jinny's wanting to get away; she's been here long enough the day.'

She took hold of Belle's arm and turned her from the bed, saying now to Freddie, 'You can take heart: neither of your friends got to their keel today. I called in at the office on my way back. Andy tells me it's the talk of the quay. You won't recall anything, but there were lots of eyes watching you stagger out of that door last night and there had been lots of ears listening in to the commotion that took place when Freddie Musgrave chucked May Harper.'

Belle now tugged herself from Maggie's hold and, turning to the bed, she said, 'Oh, I was so pleased to hear that. You should have – chucked her – years ago. I never liked her and I know she *loved* me.'

Her hand came out swiftly to pat his face, But she checked it, and, her face now hanging over his, she said softly, 'Oh, it's wonderful, Freddie, to be back. I'm never going to leave home again, or this wonderful house, or . . .'

'You'll leave it in a minute for I'll swipe you so hard that you'll find yourself sliding off the face of the earth and leaving all your mush talk behind. Come on with you.'

For answer, the young girl turned and flung her arms about Maggie and, kissing her boldly on the

185

mouth, she cried, 'You know what you are, Miss Margaret Hewitt, you're a bossy old crab, but' – her voice dropped – 'I love you.' Then glancing over her shoulder, she looked towards Freddie and added, 'And I love you.'

She could say nothing more before Maggie pulled her, laughing, from the room, and Freddie lay staring towards the door. 'I love you,' she had said. But what did that mean? That she looked upon him as her brother, even her father?

Look! – A voice was yelling loudly in his head – You've just got out of one tangle, and barely with your life. You are her brother, her loving brother. Get that into your napper. What place you take in her life from now will be seeing to her future.

Later on, when Maggie came to bid him good-night, she sat on the side of the bed and said, 'Well, what d'you think of the finished article?'

- 'She's grown.'

'Is that all, grown? You should have been on Newcastle station. She had them goggle-eyed, especially when she pushed her bonnet back. She hates bonnets. I'll have to get her a hat and a pile of new clothes; the things she's got will soon be up to her calves. But on that station their eyes were sticking out like pike shanks.'

She smiled softly now as she added, 'We're going to have trouble ahead. They'll be beating a path to the door, so we'll have to be careful in our selection.'

He drew in a painful breath before he spoke from the side of his mouth, saying, 'I think you'd better face up to the fact that the selection won't lie with us. She's headstrong, she'll do the choosing.'

'Well, she'll be guided; and anyway, she's got a head on her shoulders; she'll pick right.'

186

As if to change the subject he said, 'How did you find things up there? Any change?'

With an impatient movement she rose from the bed, saying, 'That's a daft question with the boats stuck in the river like frozen dummies.'

'I meant, have they got the big steamer free yet?'

'No; and not likely to, although there's a steam tug at her. Eeh! that river. You've never seen anything like it. You know something? Before long there'll not be a pennorth of trade on this side, or yon, I'm telling you. Most of them are going into Sunderland, and no wonder, them advertising deep water there. Men are fools, fighting against each other like children. They thought when Newcastle lost the charter the sandbanks would disappear overnight, just melt away and leave free passage. And what's happened? There they are, boats stuck in the river for months on end. And you know what? They're starting to unload part of the cargoes across the water in Shields in order to lighten the boats so they can get up the river. Did you ever hear anything like it? No wonder that inspector said last year it's the worst river in the country. They're all for dredgers now when they should have been using them ten or fifteen years ago. Oh, it gets me mad. Even a little sculler couldn't get up there on low tide now. By the way, I saw a lad in yours yesterday. He was skimming across at slack tide. It's amazing how that little thing's lasted. Well, here I am off to me bed. Is there anything more you want?'

'Just a new face and a new body.'

'Well, yes, it would be an improvement.' She grinned at him; and he flapped his hand at her; then she went out.

He lay thinking, not about her or Belle, but about

187

the little sculler, for it was that that had started it all. If his da had never built it for John and he himself hadn't toddled into it from he could walk, he wouldn't be lying here now in this house at this minute. No, he wouldn't; he would have been married to May for sure.

2

It was four days later. He was up now but he hadn't yet been out of the house. He was at his desk in the study going over the rents that had become due from Maggie's property. And over the years, this had spread far and wide up the river, from a row of one-roomed hovels in the town here, to three terraced houses in Newcastle, to mention but a few.

She was a shrewd business woman, was Maggie, with an eye for a bargain, and she seemed to have the knack of buying at the right time as well as selling when the market was favourable. And besides the half share in the fishing boats she had financed a number of small shops. Even so, all this was only part of the business. Most of her money came in from the interest on loans; and she could have had twice as much business in this way because she didn't skin people like the banks did. She was chary though, and picked her customers where she willed.

She had never dealt in a penny a week or a month for a shilling loan; this she considered daylight robbery; but she had advanced ordinary sailors money, until they could get signed on a boat, and often she would promise to keep their families going when they were beginning a long voyage and when the half-pay note they left was so meagre that it wouldn't supply a grown family with bread, let alone meat.

So she had a good name on the waterfront and was

respected; but at the same time she was also feared and envied and resented, for was she not a woman in a man's world. There were a few such about, though in different capacities, up and down the river, and there was a natural dread in many male quarters that their number could grow.

'We are off then.' Maggie appeared in the doorway. 'I can see I'm going to get some work done these days gallivanting about the place.'

'Isn't there anything in the shops here that would suit her?'

'Don't be silly. Do the so-called ladies patronise the local shops? And me ladyship here knows what she wants. Listen to her.'

He listened. She was singing, and his face broke into a twisted smile as he said, 'Her musical voice won't get her very far.'

Maggie laughed, saying, 'No, she's no Nancy. What d'you think about letting her go tonight?'

'Well, it's seemingly all arranged, isn't it, with Mr and Mrs Twaite?'

'You wouldn't risk going like you are?'

'Don't be daft, Maggie; one look at me and they'd have me thrown out.'

The sound of singing came nearer and then it flooded the study. It certainly wasn't musical, but then it wasn't unpleasant.

'What's that you're jabbering?'

She approached the desk, saying, 'It's a little French song about two birds: one sits on the nest and one goes off gathering food; then a big crow comes and takes the poor little mother bird, and when the father bird comes back he finds his wife gone and his chicks dying. It's very, very sad.'

'Get yourself away.'

She reached out across the desk towards his

190

cheek, saying, 'The colour's changing. It's yellowish now; in another six months you should be all right.'

He picked up a paperweight and pretended to throw it, but she didn't move. Straightening up and in a haughty tone, she said, 'You cannot intimidate me. I am a young woman of fashion, at least I shall be in a short while when Auntie Maggie empties her purse.' She glanced over her shoulder. 'But recalling what my dear headmistress used to say, "The world is your oyster, girls, but you've got to learn how to open the shell" . . .'

'*Get out!*'

'Yes; let's get out. And my purse-strings, my dear girl, are tight; and that's how they're going to remain. Come on.'

Her hand near her cheek, Belle now wagged her fingers at Freddie; then skipped from the room.

And he sat looking at the ledger for some minutes before he picked up the quill again.

A short while later his mother entered, carrying a cup of tea on a tray and, laying it on the corner of the desk, she sat herself on the chair to the side of it, saying, 'It's a pity you can't go along with them the night; it's goin' to be a big thing for Nancy. Second time in a week at the same place. She must have gone over well.'

'Naturally, she would. What is she going to sing?'

'Aw. "Molly Bowen", "Comin' Through The Rye", "The Keel Row". They always ask for these. Then, of course the usual local ones, the favourites that they can all join in. You've never been in that place, have you?'

'No I haven't; in fact, I've never heard of it before. Cora's: it sounds like a ladies' tea-room.'

'Oh, from what Mrs Twaite said, it's far from that. But there's no strong liquor sold; coffee mostly, but

191

you can have tea. It's the food though that's the attraction, an' the entertainment. But the food sounds plain to me: potato hash and rabbit pie, and for their pudding, plum duff with honey; and then she has what they call savouries, bacon pancakes, which is just a slice of bacon rolled up inside a pancake. But they seem to have taken on. They've been there nearly a year. And Mrs Twaite said the customers all seem to be respectable, good class ones, nothing rowdy. Well, she wouldn't take Nancy to anything rowdy, would she?'

'I don't know.' He laughed gently now. 'If she thought there might be a bigger cut in it, who knows?'

'Well, she's got to charge for the travelling and her time, hasn't she? And I don't begrudge her what she gets because she's put Nancy on her feet. Without her, Nancy wouldn't be where she is the day.'

'No, that's right. That's right.'

'What's the matter?'

'What d'you mean, what's the matter?'

'You seem down in the mouth.'

'Well, Ma' – he sat back in his chair, his two hands resting on the desk – 'look at me. How d'you expect me to act? I'm still aching from head to foot.'

There was a moment's silence before she said, 'Belle's grown into a bonny lass.'

He turned a sharp glance on her. 'Yes, she has,' he said.

'An' she's nice with it. In spite of that smart school learnin', she's ordinary like. Well, not ordinary, but you know what I mean.'

'Yes, Ma; I know what you mean.'

And yes, he did know what his mother meant. His mother was a very discerning woman.

'Well, I'd better be gettin' on; this won't get me

work done. By the way' – she turned about – 'our Nell's threatened to leave him.'

'Not again!'

'Aye. He's never sober. He's got in with that lot on the quay. And there's a couple of hussies down there that would strip off for a tallow candle. They live in one of those filthy lodgin' houses, sleepin' twelve to a room an' the pee runnin' out of the door. They raided one the day afore yesterda', I hear, and one of the polis spewed with the smell inside. And Nell's got her suspicions he's been with one of 'em. Well, she knows for a fact, so she means it this time.'

'Well, as bad as the lassies might be they'd have to be badly in need of a man to take up with Joe.'

'Oh, some women would take a clothes prop with trousers on. Anyway, she says she's gona move, to Gateshead of all places, across the river and right up yon side . . . it's opposite Newcastle.'

His pain-racked body shook now as he muttered, 'Ma, yes, Gateshead's opposite Newcastle.'

'Oh!' – she was indignant – 'What you laughin' at? Everybody isn't as travelled as you, smart arse.'

When the door closed after her none too gently he stopped chuckling to himself and repeated, 'Not so travelled as you.' And where had he travelled to? Newcastle mostly; no, he'd been as far as Durham.

Travelled! she had said. It was pitiful in a way how the lack of education stunted the mind. *God*, that did sound pompous, and against his own mother.

'Tell me how I really look, Freddie?'

'I've just told you, Nancy, you look beautiful, really, really, beautiful. I've never seen you in a dress like that before and it . . . what is the word? Enhances. Yes, it enhances you. But you were beautiful before you put it on.'

'Oh, Freddie.' She put out a hand towards him. 'You were always kind.'

'I'm not being kind; don't be so daft, you're a beautiful woman. But that dress . . . velvet. I suppose you'd call it plum?'

'The lady in the shop called it pale magenta.'

'Oh, that's what it is? Anyway in local jargon, you're a bonny lass. Yes, I'd say, a real bonny lass.'

'I wish you were coming, Freddie. I always feel . . . well, different when you're with me. And it's such a nice place.'

'What kind of place, a cross between the George and the Methodist Chapel?'

'Dead in the middle, I'd say. The voices are different, the smells are different. Oh, they are not smells, they are scents.'

He laughed. 'Mixing with the smell of the tatie hash? And tell me, do they go on eating while you are singing?'

'Strangely, no, Freddie. I . . . I do wish you'd come and see the place for yourself. Anyway, you will soon and then you'll get rid of this feeling against it.'

'I haven't any feeling against it. How could I?' His voice sounded indignant.

'Well, you seem to scoff at it.'

'Oh, it's the name, Cora's; it sounds utterly female.'

'Well, it's owned by a female; at least the family run it.'

The door opened and Belle came in. Freddie didn't speak, he just looked at the figure walking slowly towards him; it was Nancy who said, 'Oh, you smell beautiful, Belle.'

Belle made no reply to this, but she looked at Freddie who had risen from the chair and it was a long moment before she said, 'Well?'

He swallowed, then said, 'Aye, well. So this is what the money's gone on! Is . . . is that what is called a dance frock?'

'No.' She shook her head. 'Just . . . oh, I suppose a party frock. But Nancy tells me they clear a space on the floor on a Saturday night and they waltz –' she now bent slightly towards him as she ended, 'decorously.'

'And what colour might you call it?'

'I might call it forget-me-not blue, and I might inform you that the material is chiffon on top of silk. And my cloak is of a similar shade but in velvet, and at the present moment Aunt Maggie and Jinny are attaching a hood to it because I am not going to wear a hat, and I couldn't possibly go out without a covering to my head, could I?'

'You're being saucy.'

She stared at him, then said quietly, 'You haven't said yet if you like it or what I look like.'

How could he say what she looked like? For the very sight of her was bringing a heat to his body which a large hot rum had never accomplished. Of a sudden he had the urge to dash upstairs and change and say, To hell! with how I look, because once she was let out in public looking like that she'd be eaten alive. She didn't look as if she belonged to this earth. That would never be made apparent to anyone until she spoke and they discovered she had a mind of her own. He forced himself to say, 'It looks bonny. You both make a bonny pair.'

She turned now to Nancy, saying, 'Do you hear that, Nancy? We both make a bonny pair. What does that word convey to you? A new Easter frock, or a clean pinny? Couldn't he say, we are two beautifully dressed women, charming, fascinating, full of female wiles? Anything but not just bonny.'

Nancy's laugh rang out. 'Oh, Belle, don't tease him, you know he thinks you look wonderful.'

'How can you tell that, Nancy?'

Belle's voice was quiet now, a solid note of enquiry in it. And Nancy, after a moment, answered, 'Oh I can always tell.'

A voice from the doorway now interrupted, saying, 'Are you two ready? Mr and Mrs Twaite are here.'

Nancy moved towards the voice and so to the door, but Belle remained standing looking at Freddie. And now she said softly, 'Your face isn't too bad, you could have come.'

'I will next time.'

'That's a promise?'

'Yes, that's a promise.'

'I'll see you in the morning then.'

'You'll see me later on tonight. I'll be here when you get back.'

Without further words she turned from him and went from the room, and he sat down again by the fire. And when Maggie came in a few minutes later, she began abruptly, 'We'd better get more steak on that face of yours and pull it together quickly, because if that one hasn't an escort soon I'll have to see about engaging the militia.' Then sitting opposite to him, she sat quiet for a moment before asking, 'Did you ever see anyone so beautiful in your life?'

And he answered simply, 'No; I never have, Maggie. I never have.'

3

A week later, on a Tuesday, he made his way by train to Newcastle. His visits to Newcastle he always found interesting; and this morning's was no exception for in the first-class compartment there was a man who told him he was due to appear at the Court of Conscience in the Guildhall, and, as everybody knew, this court was held for debts under forty shillings, yet this man was travelling first class, and he had wanted to ask him why he could afford to travel thus if he was in debt for under forty shillings. But he refrained, for 'mind your own business' was part of his motto.

In the city, he would make for the quayside, not to do business at the Harbour Master's Office or the Town Dues Office, or yet at the Assay, but, as he put it, to have a crack here and there and pick up bits of information that might assist Maggie in her next deal.

Then he liked walking the main streets: to stop at the Theatre Royal in Grey Street, and then the Assembly and News Rooms in Westgate Road. He had dropped in there once or twice; you could learn a lot if you had time to stay; as you could in the Central Exchange and News Rooms in Grey Street. Oh, he could spend a day, a week, even as much as a month in the city and not get tired of the sights and sounds. As for the churches, God in heaven! they were spewed all over the place. A close second were the Baptist chapels, then the Methodists, and places that housed denominations he had never heard of before. But there was only one Catholic church in the city, that was in Clayton Street. He remembered old Mr McNeil as far back as twenty years ago: he used to walk from North Shields right out here on a Sunday morning just to go to Mass. Everybody thought he was strange. Well, weren't all Catholics strange; and in his case it was proved so when he left a decent job and moved to Newcastle and to a starvation wage so that he could be near his church. Religion was a funny thing. He was glad he had nothing to do with it.

But today he wasn't here specifically to roam the quayside, nor to satisfy his desire to know more of the city and what it held; he was here to find the whereabouts of the eating house called Cora's. And he found it. It was tucked away in a side street not a stone's throw from Grey Street. The street was narrow but it would take a carriage. There was a swinging sign above the door, and it said simply, Cora's Coffee House. Both the door and the big window beside it had panels of bottle-glass to prevent passers-by peering in, but which evidently let in a great deal of light, as he saw when he opened the door and stepped into a long room.

He stood for a moment looking about him. Half of the room, he saw, was taken up with tables of various sizes, some to hold twelve, others simply for two people. It was only half-past twelve in the day but most of the tables were occupied. There was a quiet buzz of conversation, threaded here and there with laughter.

He walked down an aisle between the tables and when he saw a small and unoccupied table he sat down at it. He was now at the end of the dining area. In front of him was an open space that took up the width of the room and was about twelve feet deep. This, he imagined, was the floor on which Belle had joined in the dance with the man who had requested the pleasure of her company, and to whom, as the Twaites said, they gave their permission because he was a gentleman, one of a small company dining at a nearby table, all of whom had clapped long and loudly when Nancy had sung. Behind the space was a narrow stage, in the corner of which was a pianoforte, and beyond this was what looked like a small glass-partitioned office. The door to the side of it apparently led into the kitchen quarters, for from it now there emerged a waitress carrying a tray on which were three plates of steaming food. Behind her came a youngish man; he too was carrying a tray and on it two brown jugs of steaming coffee, and as he passed close to him he could see that it held four colourful mugs and a bowl of brown sugar too.

Slowly he turned his head and took in more closely the other occupants of the room. They were mostly men of a business type by their dress. The few women present seemed to be in a family group.

The waitress came up to him now, saying politely, 'Yes, sir, and what can I serve you?'

'Well, what have you got?'

'Tis hot-pot the day or rabbit pie. Now, that's got a very nice crust. But if you want something cold and light there is pork brawn with red cabbage and new bread. That's very tasty.' She nodded at him.

Pork brawn, red cabbage, and new bread. He'd never heard of such a mixture, but he'd try anything for a first time. So he said, 'I think I'll have the cold.'

'You'll like that, sir, I think . . . an' coffee?'

'Yes; coffee, please.'

Within the next twenty minutes or so and during which he ate and enjoyed the strange meal, a number

199

of people passed up and down the long room making their way to and from the glass office, from where he caught glimpses of a face that looked plastered with powder; at least that's what it looked like from this distance. It wasn't until some minutes later that he went to the partition and had a clearer view of the face through the glass that he drew in a sharp breath as the person spoke, asking, 'Did you enjoy your meal, sir?'

His mouth opened twice before he answered, 'Yes. Yes, thank you.'

'That'll be one and fourpence, sir.'

He now placed one and six on the narrow mahogany counter, then pushed it through the arched aperture in the glass towards her. And when he said hesitantly, 'That'll be all right,' she said, 'Oh, thank you, sir. I hope you come again.'

He made no answer to this but just inclined his head towards her while his eyes took in once again the heavily powdered face.

Out in the street he walked slowly. It couldn't be, but it was. She hadn't recognised him. Well, would she? How many years ago was it since she clapped eyes on him, fourteen? fifteen? Yes, it must be fifteen. He had been a scrap of a thing, and look at him now. But she hadn't changed, not really. Well, she couldn't change her face, no powder could hide all those pockmarks. And then there was the eye dropping into the corner.

How strange. Yes indeed how strange that she would own such a place as that. But did she own it? Yes, he imagined she did. But where would they get the money to start a place . . .?

Don't be an idiot, he was yelling at himself. Think back to the day when you last saw her in the garden. And what had she said? 'Oh, don't worry; we're all

200

right. And he thought he was clever with his hidy-holes.'

They had likely left just enough to satisfy the old lady who came to take over.

Well. Well. Well. Cora's Coffee House. And her name was Connie. Should he tell Maggie? No; at least not yet because she would be made to wonder why not one of the three of them had come over to North Shields to see how the child was faring. But then hadn't they gone to Scotland? Yes, but according to Nancy they had been open about a year here. And there was something else to worry about. Belle had been there and she would likely want to go again. Yet, it wasn't likely, if they hadn't kept track of her, that they would recognise her. But should it come to their ears that Maggie Hewitt was her guardian, they wouldn't have to put even two and two together.

But then what could they do? What would they want to do? They hadn't done anything so far, and there was only one thing sure, they wouldn't want their own affairs to be looked into too closely, because where could three such people get enough money to start a business in Scotland and then take such a place in the centre of the city where rents were high. And they would be high for a place like that. Then they would have to have a licence for their entertainment side of it. Yes, where would they have got the money?

Well, the only thing he would have to see to now was that Belle didn't go back there again.

It was as he was making his way through yet another side street that would bring him out into Northumberland Street that he saw ahead of him a man coming out of a jeweller's shop with the name of Taylor in faded lettering above the door. It was, you

could say, a small insignificant shop which had no
fine display of expensive rings, bracelets, and neck-
laces, no gentlemen's watches and chains or ladies'
fobs, but seemed to deal mostly with the mending of
old clocks, an assortment of which was displayed in
its narrow window.

Freddie had become acquainted with the shop
some years ago through Maggie, for she had not
been above acting as go-between for a little mer-
chandise brought into port by some sailor. But, as
she admitted herself, she had never really dealt with
anything big until she took the two diamonds and
the ruby to Mr Taylor. And that was only five years
ago when their value had trebled, for up till then
they had lain in her wall safe between the years
eighteen forty-five and eighteen fifty-five.

Maggie had seen she was given a good price for
those three bits of 'glass', even though, as she had
said at the time, it was nothing to what Mr Taylor
would have got when he deposited them in London.
Yet she liked Mr Taylor, and so did he. As far as his
underground trade went, he was fair.

How Mr Taylor had escaped the law over all these
years, Freddie told himself, he would never know,
unless he had a friend up in the High Court. And
that could well be possible. Oh, yes, yes, quite
possible. As he was sure had Mr Larry Freeman who
was now walking ahead of him and who no longer
galloped about on his horse but drove in a fine
carriage and pair between his equally fine house on
the outskirts of Newcastle and his office where he
transacted most of his business.

But now, seeing him come out of Mr Taylor's
jeweller's shop, it was apparent to Freddie that he
still had his hand in the old games.

Freeman had evidently seen him, for he stopped

and, when Freddie came abreast of him, he greeted him in a manner that was both condescending and jocular.

'Well, well! Who do we have here on this fine day? If it isn't Freddie Musgrave. It must be all of six months since I saw you. I believe you're still sprouting.'

Freddie forced back words his irritation was prompting him to utter. By now he should have become used to this form of address, for such it had been over the years. What he did say, with a smile which flummoxed Mr Freeman not a little, was, 'The day, Mr Freeman, when you address me as man to man I shall know then that you have reached maturity, as I myself did as far back as when I was fourteen.'

It was as if a dark shadow had passed over Larry Freeman's face. And, aiming now to come back with a retort to equal the young snipe's, as he thought of him, he said, 'As a dirty little runner you were always nimble on your feet, and now seemingly the quality has gone to your tongue, which is a much more dangerous place to harbour a talent.'

'Quite right. Oh, you are quite right, Mr Freeman. As is a fact that when one person knows so much about the other it is advisable for both to be civil. What d'you say?'

The joviality went out of his tone now as he added, 'And to remember, Mr Freeman, that I was a child when I was connected with your racket, and that I was used by elders. But since I was taken under the wing of Miss Maggie Hewitt, I was, as the preachers would say, saved, and have since lived a blameless life, a state which can't be claimed by everyone.' A slightly mocking note had returned to his tone, and with the merest lift of his tall hat he left the older man glaring after him.

He made his way now down an alley leading to the

main thoroughfare, but when he reached it he found that he was shaking slightly. It wasn't exactly with fear, but he had to admit to a certain apprehension. It was rarely he came in contact with the man, but when he did he remembered Maggie's warning to play dumb with him, because she saw him as a dangerous fellow, but today he had forgotten her warning. And recalling it, he knew he had been stupid in rising to the man's bait. Where there had before been merely condescension on Freeman's part, now there would be the desire to get even and to bring him low in some way. He knew the type: there were many Freemans kicking about, and back in the home town too. Oh yes, he was reminded time and time again that he had come up from being a bare-arsed quay brat.

It wasn't a good day, he decided. That business of finding out who owned Cora's made him ask himself, if Connie Wheatley found out who Belle really was, would she keep her tongue quiet? He didn't know, he just didn't know. And then there was this encounter with Freeman. No, it hadn't been a good day; and being such he should be looking forward to getting home to Maggie and Belle. And he was . . . to Maggie yes, but not to Belle.

4

He was rather late in getting back for he had walked slowly from the station to the house, wondering whether he should tell Maggie about the identification of the owner of the coffee house. But the choice was settled for him once he entered the house because not only was Belle in high spirits but Maggie too seemed to be quietly pleased about something, for she did nothing to quell Belle's exuberance as she rushed to him, crying, 'Where do you think you've been all day, Mr Frederick Musgrave, leaving two lone, helpless females to wander the waterfront where anything can happen, as you've told me time and time again, especially to young ladies who will be so foolish as to wear skirts that only reach to the top of their boots?'

'What's this? What's this?' He took off his hat and coat and hung them in the cupboard in the hall, then followed both her and Maggie into the sitting-room.

'Have you had a nice day, or should I say, a successful one?' It was Maggie looking at him now as he sat himself down in a chair by the fire. And in a flat voice he said, 'Yes. Yes, miss, I've had what you'd call a moderately successful day business-wise, nothing though to make me jump about and act like a hill goat while the mother goat looks on approvingly.' He looked from one to the other. 'Well now, I'm just bursting to know what's happened to brighten your day.'

'Nothing much.' Belle had taken a seat opposite

him and she shrugged her slim shoulders now as she said quietly, 'But it's been a very pleasant day, hasn't it, Aunt Maggie?'

'Yes; yes, you could say it's been a very pleasant day.'

'For all concerned?' He again cast his glance between them and they looked at each other now and laughed as they said together, 'For all concerned.'

'We've been in pleasant company; that is, up till now.' Belle made a prim face at him. And when he made no response, Maggie, her voice returning to normal, said, 'Go and put the kettle on, Belle, that's a good lass.'

It was noticeable to them both that Belle hesitated for more than a moment before obeying. And when the door had closed on her, Freddie, looking at Maggie, said, 'Well, tell me. What's all this about?'

'Nothing really; yet it could be something. It's like this. You remember the Twaites told us about a man who asked her to dance at that coffee house? Well, there he was in town today. They recognised each other, and I must say, Freddie, he's a gentleman. Well, of course, I'm going by his manner, his speech, and his attitude. He asked if he could walk with us, and he came down to the quay. Well, I wasn't going to the office and leave her with him, so the three of us walked further along and we chatted. He seemed to know quite a bit about shipping, but from the Newcastle end, and he was as worked up about the river as any of us. Apparently he has a small house in Newcastle and another in the country somewhere. Well, the top and bottom of it is I could see she was happy and a bit smitten. And who wouldn't be, because he was quite charming. But as I said, I wasn't leaving her with him; and apparently he didn't want me to, and so when he asked if we would join him in a glass of wine, there we were, sipping wine together in the best hotel in town. Following this, we said goodbye, he with the hope that we would meet again. Well, Belle and I went down to the office, and she stayed with me and seemed to be very interested in all that went on. And it must have been about half-past three when I left Andy to finish up, and we made for the town again, because she had decided there was a hat in Franklyns that she would like. So there we were and there he was again coming towards us as before. There was nothing planned; we all laughed. It happened that he was on his way to the station, but he said the trains run every half-hour so would we like to have a cup of tea with him. Well –' She made a small movement with her head and her voice was low and sad as she went on, 'I could see she was happy. And she's on eighteen, Freddie, and youth goes so quickly, so I couldn't put a spoke in. If he hadn't been so nice and of the class he is I likely would have. But you know what I want for her, and you know what she's entitled to.' The last words were stressed. 'The top and the bottom of it was, we had tea, and he asked us to a musical evening in Newcastle. Really, as you know, under these circumstances he was asking her but he couldn't have her without me, but he's a very, very pleasant sort of fellow. So there it is.'

Freddie stared at her in not a little astonishment. If the man had been interested in her herself she couldn't have seemed more pleased. He said flatly, 'What's his name?

'Marcel . . . Baxter, that's how I think it's pronounced. It sounded French to me, and there could be a little of the foreigner in him. Anyway –' She reached out and put her hand on his knee, saying now, 'Be happy for her, Freddie. He mightn't be the one, he could just be passing through sort of, but he's a good start. After mixing with someone like him she won't pick lower.'

'*Maggie!* You've had enough experience to know that a smooth tongue and a velvet jacket doesn't go to make the man.'

'Oh, I know, I know, nobody better. And don't you forget' – her voice was harsh now – 'it was me that taught you to distinguish between the gold and the dross.'

After a strain-filled moment, he said, 'How old is he, a young boy?'

'*Oh, no, no.*' She shook her head. 'I would say he's your age. Well, perhaps a little younger.'

'I hope you know what you're letting her in for.'

'Well, she's got to be let in for something before much longer. You know that, don't you?'

'Yes, yes. I know that. But whoever she marries will have to be put in the picture. Have you thought of that?'

'Yes, I'm well aware of that. And don't shout at me. Anyway, here she comes. And for goodness sake take that look off your face and' – she was hissing now – 'face up to facts, she sees you as a brother. Face up to it, man.'

As Belle entered the room he rose, saying, 'I'm going to have a wash.'

Belle, now looking at Maggie, asked, 'What's the matter with him?'

'Oh, don't take any notice; he's at sixes and sevens with himself.'

'Aunt Maggie' – she bent towards her – 'is there something wrong with him? I mean, he hasn't been the same since I came home. Well, not since he was

208

knocked about that night. Do you think he regrets breaking it off with May?'

'*Oh, no.* I should say not. I think he's been trying to break away for some long time before now.'

'I get upset when he acts like this, because he wasn't pleased about my enjoying that evening with Nancy, just because I danced with that man.'

She laughed now, adding, 'Why did I say, that man?' And her smile widened and her voice softened as she went on, 'He is nice, isn't he, Aunt Maggie? Different.'

'Yes, he's nice and he's different, but you'll meet a lot of nice and different men before you're much older, so don't get too excited about this one. But I admit, he's quite good to start on.'

'Oh, Aunt Maggie, good to start on! What do you think they're going to do, line up for me to choose from?'

Her voice serious now, Maggie said, 'Yes, yes, girl, be patient and they'll line up for you to choose from.'

'I . . . I don't like to think that way, Aunt Maggie.'

Maggie looked up into the serious face. 'Well,' she said, 'it shows that you're not a flibbertigibbet. But all I say is, don't set your heart on the first man that's nice to you.'

'I won't.' She bent and put her arms round Maggie's neck. 'But he was nice, and so amusing and entertaining.' Then mischievously she added, 'Are you looking forward to going to the concert, the musical evening with him, Miss Hewitt?'

'Yes, I am. But you never know, I might have a cold that night and neither of us will be able to go.'

'Oh, you wouldn't, Aunt Maggie, would you?'

'You never know. Anyway, just remember this' — she put out her hand and stroked the pale cheek — 'whatever I do for you it will be done for the best.'

5

It was almost two months later when Freddie met the 'gentleman', and emotions in the house had been alternating between very high and very low throughout that period. But the height and the depth were experienced during the morning of the day in early December when the 'gentleman' was to come to tea. Maggie had decided it was time they returned his hospitality for, since they had first met him, he had accompanied them to two concerts and an exhibition. But on that day instead of the 'gentleman' turning up for tea he sent a messenger with a letter, not for Belle, but for Maggie. The letter from an address in Newcastle had expressed his apologies and his keen disappointment at not being able to keep the appointment, explaining that he had been called away on business and that he would get in touch again when he returned. Would she please convey his deep regret to Miss Belle for the loss of her company? He remained, her faithful servant, Marcel Birkstead. The writing was small and neat.

Freddie had repeated the name aloud after Maggie had handed him the letter; he had looked at her and said, 'You said his name was Baxter.'

And she had answered, 'Well, it sounded like that.'

'It reads like Birk . . . stead, to me.' And he had added, 'Where have I heard that name before? We have no one on the books of that name, have we?'

'No, but we've got a couple of Baxters.'

'But this isn't Baxter,' he had insisted.

Belle's reaction had been one of keen disappointment. And when she had said to Maggie, 'He could have stated when we could expect him back,' Freddie had turned on her sharply, saying, 'Has it reached that stage where he's got to be accountable for his actions to you?' And to his amazement she had cried at him, 'Yes! Yes, it has;' then rushed from the room. And he had looked at Maggie and said, 'Well now, what about that? You've never indicated that things have gone as far as this.'

And she had replied simply, 'Because I didn't think they had. In fact, there's been times of late when I thought she was going off him, especially last week after he had cut into her telling of an incident at school rather sharply.'

'You didn't see him last week. At least I wasn't told of it.'

'No; you weren't told of it' – her tone had been harsh – 'because I didn't want to go through another black period when you never open your mouth until you're forced to. And let me tell you, your mother's noticed it too, and Nancy.' Then, her tone changing, she had said in a voice a little above a whisper, 'Look, Freddie; you've got to let her go,' and on this he had turned on her and yelled, 'Why? Tell me why.' And she had hissed back at him, 'Because as I've told you she doesn't think of you in that way, and if you brought such feelings as you harbour into the open nothing would be the same between you ever again. She'd even become afraid of you. I know. I'm sure of it. You're like her father. What I mean is, you've taken the place of him over the years.'

'Ten years older and like her father.'

'Ten years can appear like fifty to a girl of eighteen. *Thirty* is old. I know myself how I thought of age at that stage of my life. But that's beside the

211

point.' She had paused as though thinking back; then she had ended, 'What is the point, and you must get it into your head, is that she'll never think of you but in the light of some sort of a parent.'

Christmas had not been very gay. He had accompanied the two of them to the coffee house because Nancy was singing there again, and only Nancy had seemed to enjoy the evening. But then she had reasons of her own for her added happiness, for a young man, also from North Shields, had come to hear her sing. She had known him for some time: he had often spoken to her in the town. From the beginning she had liked his smell, his voice, and his hand on her arm as he had guided her across the road, which, of course, was quite unnecessary as she knew her way.

At first this acquaintance with the young man had caused laughter in the house especially from her father; but now both he and Jinny were very concerned for he was a customs officer and, as such, was considered an enemy of the people, especially of Robert's mates, who still at times kept him supplied with a decent drink and baccy. As Jinny had said to Freddie, it couldn't have been worse if she had taken a fancy to a polisman.

The meeting with Marcel Birkstead finally took place on the third Saturday in January when the sky was low and the air was so cutting it penetrated the thickest of clothes, and the general opinion of the weather was that they were in for it. There had been a slight fall of snow earlier in the month but nothing that could stop traffic. But on this day the sky was laden and everyone knew that the snow was coming and that it would be heavy.

There was a blazing fire burning in the sitting-room.

Maggie had acquired what was called a Chesterfield. The couch was set opposite the fire and Belle was curled up in one corner of it, reading, while Maggie sat in the other crocheting a shawl. She liked crocheting, and Saturday and Sunday afternoons were the only daytime hours she allowed herself to relax in this way. She closed the quay office at one o'clock on a Saturday which caused a certain amount of upset in other offices on the quay in which the clerks had to work till five o'clock.

Jinny now appeared at the door. She was holding a large bass bag. 'I'm off now, miss,' she said. 'An' I hope I'll be able to find me way back on Monday. If not the big fellow there' – she nodded towards Freddie, sitting in the leather chair – 'better come and dig me out.'

'Now have you got everything you want?'

'Yes, thank you, miss. With this lot I could last out a week if we were snowed up.' She jerked the bag in her hand; then said, 'Well, so long now;' and added, 'By! you all look nice and comfortable there.'

Freddie rose from the chair and was about to make a remark when the sound of the front door bell ringing brought their eyes questioning each other.

It was Maggie who said, 'Who can this be? 'Tis neither the butcher, the baker, nor the candlestick maker on a Saturday afternoon.'

''Tis likely the Duke of Northumberland.'

Maggie thrust out her hand towards Belle, saying, 'Could be at that, miss. You never know.'

Belle was smiling back at her as she said, 'No, you never know; but there are some people who wouldn't be impressed.'

'I'll answer it.' Freddie was following his mother out of the room, and when she crossed the hall to leave by the back door, he checked her, saying,

'Come out this way;' and she laughed into his face. 'Why not? Why not indeed?' she said.

When he opened the door they both stared at the man standing on the step. But before he was able to speak Jinny sidled past them, saying, 'Well, see you on Monday, lad.'

The two men stared at each other, the visitor looking as surprised as Freddie but not so straight-faced. 'Yes? What can I do for you?'

'I . . . I have called to see the Miss Hewitts. My name is Marcel Birkstead, and I'm sure you must be Frederick Musgrave.'

He did pronounce it like Baxter, only drawn out.

Freddie nodded and glanced towards the sitting-room door before he said, 'Come in.'

'It looks as if we might have snow.' He was offering his high hat to Freddie now.

'I'll take your coat.'

'Oh, thank you. Thank you.'

Freddie could already see what had got the women, both of them: there was a quiet courteous charm about the fellow. But he was asking himself, and loudly, where he had seen him before; he could swear he had met up with him somewhere.

He now walked towards the sitting-room door and, thrusting it open, he said, 'You have a visitor.'

Both Maggie and Belle were on their feet now, and Freddie could have described Maggie's face as a beam, she was smiling so widely, but not so Belle. Belle's manner, he was surprised to observe, was what could be described as decorous, quietly decorous.

'Good-afternoon, Mr Birkstead,' she said.

'Good-afternoon, Miss Belle; and you, Miss Maggie. I'm sorry if I'm intruding.'

'You're not intruding, man, sit down. Sit down.'

214

Maggie indicated a chair, and once he was seated she began, 'You got your business over then?'

'It wasn't quite all business; I . . . I was rather unwell for a time, caught a bit of fever.'

'Oh, I'm sorry to hear that. And yes, I can see that you still look peaked. Well now, what would you like to drink? Something to warm you on this cold day? I could offer you tea, or something very much stronger and hotter.'

He smiled widely now, saying, 'Tea will be excellent. I'm very partial to tea.'

'Well, tea it shall be; and I'll go and make it.'

'You'll do no such thing; I'll see to it.'

Maggie turned on Freddie now, saying, 'And you'll do no such thing. Sit yourself down there. Anyway, you've never made a decent cup of tea in your life.'

She laughed, and the visitor laughed, and Belle smiled; but Freddie, sitting down on the corner of the couch, looked at the visitor who was now looking at Belle and explaining that he had been as far as Harrogate over the past weeks.

Where had he seen him before? He was a man of more than medium height, not quite as tall as himself, but much broader. He had deep blue eyes and thick fair hair that framed his longish face; his mouth was wide and full-lipped; his skin at the present moment, pale. He had very expressive hands. He seemed to talk with them, which to Freddie's mind bore out the idea that he could be partly foreign as his Christian name suggested, because the few Frenchmen he had come across always seemed to be waving their hands or their arms around. His voice was pleasant, what he supposed Belle would call cultured.

But where had he seen him before? He had come across him somewhere; he could swear on it.

215

The man was addressing him now: 'I was saying to Miss Belle that there is to be a Grand Ball at the Assembly Rooms in the city. It would complete a foursome if you would join us, Mr Musgrave.'

Freddie looked from one to the other. He had missed what had gone before, but Belle must have already accepted his invitation. He replied coolly, 'I'm afraid I'm no hand with my feet, so to speak; I've never had time for dancing.'

'Don't be silly, Freddie; you've danced here in this very room. On New Year's morning you jigged.'

'I don't think they would appreciate our jigging at the Assembly Rooms, Belle. However, we'll see.'

'Will one of you gentlemen kindly take this tray from me?'

Maggie had pushed the door open with her buttocks, and when they both sprang forward it was the visitor who reached her first; and she said, 'Thank you. Thank you.'

There was a silver tea service on the tray and the best china.

The tray set on the table, Maggie began to pour out, saying as she did so, 'You take lemon with your tea, don't you, Mr Birkstead?'

'Yes. How good of you to remember.'

'Well, it isn't everybody who has such tastes. Here, Belle, pass that to Mr Birkstead. Freddie, you'll have milk as usual?' She cast what could have been a naughty glance towards Freddie, and he nonplussed her for a moment by saying, 'No, I'll take it straight.'

'Oh, you'll take it straight. Very well, very well.'

The conversation turned to the weather: the snow being imminent; how long it might last; whether it would go on for weeks as it had done in past years; would the ice in the river hold up the shipping more than the sandbanks have done? And this went on

216

until Freddie asked a straight question: 'What is your trade, Mr Birkstead, or should I say, profession?'

'Oh –' The man shrugged one shoulder now and, picking up his cup again from the small side table, he looked at it before he said, 'I don't think I can lay claim to either. I was left at school too long, and then I went to university, but didn't shine there and I came down before I should. I then had what they called scarlet fever, which laid me low for a time; since when I have dabbled a little in this and that, buying property mostly. My grandmother owns mills and warehouses in the city; and so now and again I might supervise a cargo coming in or going out. Which reminds me, speaking of my grandmother, she has expressed a wish to meet you all.'

He included Freddie in his glance. 'And so when the weather is a little more clement, fit for travelling, especially for crossing the river, I would like you all to come to tea one day.'

'Your house is at yon side of the river? I thought it was in the country.'

'Yes; yes, it's what you call the country. It's well past the outskirts of the town and the villages. It was, at first . . . well, just an ordinary country house with a minimum of land, but over the years my grandmother, who is a real innovator, has extended the property, and the land. Oh yes, certainly the land. She loves land, more so than I do, I'm afraid. Now we have nearly fifty acres whereas in the beginning it was about six. How much land she would have acquired had she always lived there I can't imagine; but she only took over when my father died. I was ten at the time, and The Towers in those days seemed a gaunt, dull . . .'

Freddie had sprung to his feet. What he would

have done next he didn't know because he was seeing a man sitting in front of him, his nose almost touching his, and saying, 'You are to forget what you heard and saw last night. If you divulge . . . I mean, if you talk about it to anyone it will come back to me and I have ways and means of paying for services done, good and bad. You understand me?'

But the vision of the man was swept from his mind when he heard the clatter of Maggie's teacup dropping onto the saucer and her squeal when the tea spilled over her lap.

'What is it, Auntie? What is it?'

Belle had her arms around Maggie's shoulders, and when Maggie muttered something about feeling faint Freddie pushed Belle aside and, bending down, he almost lifted Maggie from the couch and led her from the room, shouting over his shoulder to Belle as he did so, 'Come along! Belle, and see to her.'

Belle turned a startled and apologetic glance on the man who had been in her mind every day for weeks now, and she said, 'I'm sorry.'

'Please, please, don't be. I'll take my departure; and I'll call again, if I may?'

'Oh yes, please do.' She was backing from him, and he, walking towards her, asked softly, 'You would like me to?'

She nodded twice, then gulped before answering, 'Yes. Yes, I would like you to.' Then she turned and ran from the room . . .

Maggie was in her bedroom sitting by the side of the window and Freddie was bending over her, saying, 'Drink this. Drink it all up.'

As Maggie took the glass from his hand, Belle said, 'What is it, Aunt Maggie? that pain again?'

Maggie nodded just the slightest, but Belle said, 'Then we must call the doctor.' And she looked up at Freddie. 'Call him at once.'

'Be quiet!'

'What did you say?'

'I said, be quiet. She doesn't need a doctor, not at the moment.'

'Well, if she doesn't need a doctor now I wouldn't like to see her when she does.'

'Belle.' Maggie's voice was soft. 'It's as Freddie says, I don't need a doctor at the moment. Now be a good lass: go and set the table for dinner; I know Jinny left a pie in the oven, see if it's done, will you? And you could put the vegetables on.'

'You want to get rid of me, don't you?' The young girl's face was stiff, as was her body. 'There's something here I don't understand. I'm not a child any longer, and I feel there's an explanation.'

'By God! there's an explanation, girl, and when you get it you won't like it. Go and do as Maggie says.'

Perhaps more so than the words the fierceness in his face and tone made her shrink back from him. Then the tears spurting from her eyes, she turned and ran from the room.

'Oh, my God!' Maggie put up her hand and lifted the hair back from her brow. 'What lies before us, lad? I knew it would come sometime, but not like this. And she's gone on him, deep, and he on her. And he's a nice enough fella. You could see for yourself.'

'Anything that's sprung from Gallagher can't be nice, Maggie. I felt something the moment I saw him. I knew . . . I knew I had seen him before; I'd had that face close to mine. He's a spitting image of his father, almost like a twin only a bit younger. Well, there's one thing sure, she'll have to be told, and right from the beginning.'

'No, Freddie. How can we do it!'

'How can we not do it, Maggie?'

'Yes, you're right, how can we not do it? But –' She pulled herself further back into the chair and somewhat eagerly now, she said, 'You did mention, if you remember, that there was some question of her mother having gone a bit astray with a sea captain or somebody. If that was the case . . .'

'Don't lay any stock on that, Maggie. The woman, as I recall, was raving at the time, in the throes of labour, and she likely wanted to get the better of him. And who wouldn't! because he was a beast of a fella, frightening. Those three who looked after the house only stayed on because they were on a good thing, as regards food and pay, and both of these were hard to come by in those days. And by the way, Maggie, there's more you should know. I've kept it back from you to save your peace of mind, but that Cora's Coffee House is owned by one of them, if not the three of them. Connie, as I told you, the daughter, is the cashier. She didn't recognise me but I recognised her in spite of the flour on her face. As I told you, she's covered with pockmarks and has a deep cast in her eye. And I'd like to bet my life now, she knows who he is because if I recall the resemblance, it's nearly sure she would. And it's almost certain she's found out who Belle is an' all. Oh aye. She came here, as I told you, surprised that it was you who had taken the bairn and not me ma; but, if me guess is right, she's thinking it's best to keep a still tongue in her head because they didn't get that coffee house on the savings of three servants. You can bet your life on that.'

'Well, trouble always comes in three's they say, that's the second. What'll be the third?'

'I can tell you that right now, Maggie. He'll have to be told an' all.'

'*Oh, dear God!* Oh, I'm sorry to the heart for that, Freddie, for as much as you say he's like his father, to my mind it might only be in his looks, 'cos I admit, I took to him and can understand Belle's feelings.'

'Funny you can understand hers but you can't understand mine, Maggie.' It was a quiet statement, and she looked up at him sadly for a moment before she replied, 'Yes; yes, I can, Freddie, but as I've told you before, I know her feelings and they don't lie in your direction, not that way ... not the way you would want. And, as God's my judge, I'm sorry at this moment it's so.'

He turned from her and stood looking down the room for a long moment before he said, 'Well, we can't let her go on in this fashion; we'd better get it over with.' He turned to her again. 'It's too cold for you to sit in here. Come on back into the sitting-room.' Slowly she rose from the chair and dispiritedly said, 'Yes, we'll go into the sitting-room and there take the sparkle out of a young lass's life, because let's face it, once she's got knowledge of her beginnings and such as they were, she'll never be the same again.'

6

It was seven o'clock the same evening. The snow had begun to fall. The two lamps with their pink glass shades were filling the room with a warm glow while the fire was crackling and burning brightly. The atmosphere emanated warmth and comfort, but not one of them felt it in any way.

Maggie and Freddie were sitting on the couch now, but Belle sat apart, not in one of the easy chairs set each side of the fireplace, but in a straight-backed chair set a good yard from that end of the couch where Freddie was seated. Her skin had lost its warm tint and even in the glow from the lampshades it looked a pasty white; and this had the effect of making her eyes look larger still, giving the illusion that they were set deep back in the sockets, and all was emphasised by the black abundance of her hair.

She had sat without speaking for the past half-hour: that was when Freddie had stopped talking and Maggie had taken up the story of the night she had brought her across the water. Neither of them, however, as arranged, had made any allusion to what had happened to the man who had pursued them. In fact, they had not mentioned being pursued. But Maggie had gone on to relate that the next day Roderick Gallagher had been missing, and that when, eventually, his body had turned up in the river, it was evident he had been attacked. And at that point Maggie had added, 'You need never feel sorry for him, my dear; he wasn't a good man.'

It was at that point Belle had spoken when she said quietly, 'But he was my father.'

Maggie and Freddie had exchanged a quick glance, and it was Maggie who said, 'Well, yes, I suppose so.' And Belle had raised her voice and cried, 'Why do you say, suppose so? He was or he wasn't. Is there something else you are keeping back from me?' – to which Maggie had given the non-committal answer: 'I wasn't there the night you were born, and you must realise that Freddie here was a little lad.' And to this Belle had cried, 'Well! for a little lad he seems to have had a very good memory,' and then sat without speaking further for almost half an hour until Maggie pleaded: 'Say something, dear, please. We . . . we did everything for the best to save you pain.'

Such had been Belle's tone that Maggie now expected the girl to retort in anger, but what she said now, and in a quiet tone while looking at Freddie, was, 'Is that why I'm afraid of the dark, because I was kept in that room?'

He stretched out and unwound her clasped stiff fingers and just as quickly, and softly, he answered, 'Yes, dear, that is the reason. It . . . it was a dreadful place. Even now when I remember it at night, and though the time I was in there was short, I know how riddled I was with fright.'

'But why should he want to kill me if I was his own child?'

Freddie swallowed deeply before he said, 'He was a jealous man. From what I can gather he imagined your mother might have been . . . well, associating with someone else. You understand?'

'Yes, yes, Freddie, I understand.' She withdrew her hands from his and her body moved in the chair as if she was about to rise; but she remained seated and, looking across at Maggie now, she said, 'You seemed to hesitate when you were about to confirm that he was my father, why? I can't see that a man would want to kill his child if it was his child. Could . . . could my father have been someone else?'

'I don't know, dear. I don't want to sully the name of your mother.'

'Hell! Hell!'

They were both startled. The young girl they looked upon as being incapable of any coarseness was standing glaring at them and swearing at them. And she went on, 'Does it matter what my mother did as long as that man doesn't prove to be my father? She could be a whore . . .'

'We'll have none of that! Now calm yourself down.' Maggie too was on her feet, but Freddie remained seated, his head bowed. He knew what was inspiring her to wish to prove that there was no blood relationship between her and Marcel Birkstead, a name he had no right to use for his true name was Gallagher.

'Anyway' – Maggie was shouting now – 'there's nothing you can do about it. There's no way you can prove you are or you aren't that man's daughter. But as things stand, you are, and that makes our visitor today your half-brother.'

'He's not. He's not. There's no resemblance. He is very fair and I'm very dark . . . Was my mother dark?' She was addressing Freddie now. 'You saw her on the bed, you said. Was she dark?'

'I cannot recall what she looked like, only that she was a very ill woman.'

'If you were there all the time, as you say you were, and pushed under the bed, you must have heard her say something.'

Yes, he had heard her say something, but he couldn't remember her words, only the impression that Gallagher was trying to get a confession out of her that he had not fathered her child. Even now, when the memory was dim in his mind, he knew deep within him that Gallagher had not been the father of the child, the proof of which lay in his determination to get rid of it. So why couldn't he now stand up, put his arms about her and comfort her, saying, 'You are not Gallagher's daughter. There is no blood relationship between you and Marcel Birkstead or Gallagher or whatever. So don't look like that, don't change.' But she was already changed. She would never be the same again. His Belle, Maggie's Belle, was gone. In her place was an angry young woman.

She brought his head sharply up as she said, 'That woman Wheatley, who owns the coffee house, you said she was the maid, she could know something. She was bound to know if my mother was meeting another man. I'll go and ask her.'

'You'll do no such thing, girl.' Maggie was now standing in front of her. 'I've looked after you all these years. I've brought you up as your mother might have, in fact, better, because you have been happy in this house and you would have never known happiness in that place across the water, because that man was bad, evil. Now, go to bed. We will talk more tomorrow when we are all in a calmer frame of mind. But remember this' – her hands went out and clutched the thin arms – 'I want your happiness. I've always wanted your happiness. So has Freddie. I've always thought about you as my daughter, a daughter I was deprived of having because the man I was going to marry was drowned and my father along of him. For years I was lost. I led a lonely life, and then Freddie came onto my horizon and he altered it. And then he brought you

225

into it, and you've got him to thank for saving your life, don't forget that, girl, always remember that. But when he brought you into my life my existence changed: I became a different woman. I've got that to thank you for too. But at the same time you've got a lot to thank me for . . . and Freddie. Oh, definitely Freddie.'

She now watched the face before her crumple, the lips quiver, the eyelids blink, and when a sob burst from her Maggie drew her tightly into her embrace. And her own eyes were wet and her voice had a break in it as she comforted her: 'There now. There now. It'll work out. We will do all we can to find out the truth.'

Belle slowly withdrew herself from Maggie's embrace and, gulping in her throat, said quietly, 'Will he have to be told?'

Maggie turned and looked at Freddie, and they both waited for his answer. And then it came: 'Yes, he'll have to be told. Whichever way it works out he'll have to be told.'

The trains were running on the Sunday but not as
frequently as the weekday half-hour periods. Freddie
boarded one at ten o'clock on the Sunday morning. It
was snowing heavily when he alighted at Newcastle.
There were no cabs for hire as the horses were finding
it difficult to keep their footing on the hilly streets. So
it was near eleven o'clock when he reached the coffee
house. It was closed, as he had expected it to be on a
Sunday. But he went down an alley-way and knocked
on a side door for he had been given to understand
that the owners lived upstairs.

He had to rap hard a number of times before it was
opened, and there stood a man, old and bent with a
shrivelled face in which he could see no resemblance
to the driver who had dropped him on the waterfront
all those years ago.

He said, 'Mr Wheatley?'

'Aye; what d'you want? This is Sunday, we're not
open.'

'I know that but can I have a word with you and
Connie?'

'Who are you?'

'You wouldn't remember me, it's a long time ago:
the twelve-year-old lad you drove one night down to
the Shields dockside and dropped him off the cart.'

The man took two steps back from him, then muttered something that was like, 'God Almighty!' He
then pulled the door wider and made a motion with
his hand and Freddie stepped into a passageway, and

227

when the door was closed he followed the man up some narrow stairs and onto a landing. It was dimly lit by a small window at the far end, but his feet told him he was walking on carpet. Then he watched the old man thrust open the door and he followed him. It was quite a large room and very comfortably furnished. He saw at once an old woman sitting in a chair by the fire. She had her legs stretched out on a stool and her feet looked swollen. And at the other side of the room and rising from behind what looked like a small mahogany desk was Connie, almost as he remembered her, for she had no flour or powder on her face today: the pocks were evident as was the eye. She came forward slowly, saying, 'Good-morning, sir.'

''Tis no sir,' her father was bawling now. 'Can't you see who it is! Well, who he says he is, the nipper . . . the runner.'

'Eeh! Dear God.' The woman in the chair had pulled herself more upright, and she now peered towards Freddie, saying, 'I'd never have believed it. You looked stuck there as a little lad, no promise of sprouting. Eeh! I wouldn't have believed it.'

He said politely, 'How are you, Mrs Wheatley?'

'As you see me, lad, as you see me. Dropsy I've got, so they say. That's what the good God gives you for working hard all your life. Well, I never expected to see you again. Yet why not? Why not? But we haven't been here all that long.'

Connie was standing close to him now, looking up into his face.

'You came in a while back,' she said, 'didn't you?'

'Yes, Connie, I did.'

'Funny, I had no inkling, yet there was something about you made me uneasy, I remember.'

'You needn't be uneasy through me.'

228

'What you after?' It was the man speaking again, and Connie, turning on him sharply, said, 'Let him get in first, Da, and then he'll tell us what he's after. Sit yourself down and shut your mouth.'

'You'll tell me to do that once too often, you will, you'll see.'

'Sit down, Frank.' This came from his wife, and the old man sat down in a rocking chair on the opposite side of the fire. And now Connie, indicating a large comfortable leather chair, said to Freddie, 'Take a seat.'

When he was seated he looked at Connie again, saying, 'I got a bit of a start when I recognised you; I never expected to see you at this end again.'

'We never really expected to be here.'

She had now sat down to the side of her mother and she laid her hand on her mother's where it was resting on the arm of the chair as she went on, 'It was the cold. Ma couldn't stand it. We think we're badly off here but it's nothing to what it's like in Scotland. We stuck it for as long as we could. And then there were the people. We didn't get on: they seemed to speak a different language. Well they do, don't they?' She gave a small laugh; and after a short pause she said, 'How are you faring?' but didn't wait for an answer and added, 'Well, I heard you were still with that Miss Hewitt and doing well. But I've never probed, although Ma here wanted me to go down to North Shields and see how . . . well, you know, the little miss was faring. But there never seemed to be time as I have it all on me own hands, I mean, downstairs, and when you're startin' a business like this you've got to keep behind people; nobody works like yourself. You've got to keep your eyes open, although they're a decent lot; you can't trust anybody these days. We had one in the beginning who used to bring her family in for meals, an odd one here an' there, an' slip them plates. Oh, you've got to be on the look-out. And another thing why we don't hear much is, we keep ourselves to ourselves.'

'Speak for yourself.' It was her father again. 'I get about now and then an' I hear things, an' I know a thing or two an' all.'

Both his wife and daughter ignored him; and it was Connie who asked quietly, 'How is she?'

'Well, you've seen her at least twice in your coffee house.'

'I have?'

'Yes. She accompanied my sister, the blind girl who sings.'

'Never! Never that one, the one with eyes as dark as sloes who comes with the blind girl? I thought their name was Twaite.'

'No; Mrs Twaite does the arranging for Nancy. She's my sister; Mrs Twaite is no relation.'

'She's a beautiful girl, your sister, and has a lovely voice. But the other, to think . . . And I remember seeing her dance once with –' She stopped and slowly her hand went to her mouth and pressed her cheeks tightly inwards. Now she rose to her feet and looked down at her mother, and then at Freddie before she said, 'Oh my! Oh my! For such a thing to happen, because do you know who she was dancin' with?'

He evidently surprised her by saying, 'Yes; yes I know. That's why I'm here.'

'You know about him . . . I mean, who he is, the Mister Birkstead, as he calls himself, when it should be Gallagher? He's taken his granny's name. I recognised him the first day he stepped in the door. And when I heard his name I knew it was his granny's. I can see her standing now in the hall, her nose turned up in distaste, saying, "This place has

230

been neglected." Then looking at me and saying, "I'm not really blaming you. It was impossible for one person to keep this house clean, but I won't require you or your mother's services in the future. I am bringing my own staff." That was Mrs Birkstead . . . And then there he was that day – I saw him from the office as he came in – he was with two other men and they ordered rabbit pie. I couldn't take my eyes off him; it was as if I was looking at the old master like he used to be when I was a young girl. And I used to think he was handsome in those days, and kindly. He was kindly, wasn't he, Ma?'

'Oh, aye; in his young days he was kindly enough, except at times when his temper got the better of him. That's when he took to the powder to calm him down, I think. But he changed altogether after the first one died. Oh, I'll say. And he married the second one just in time else he wouldn't have had a roof over his head, up to his eyes in gambling debts he was . . . Would you like a drink, lad? Well, I shouldn't call you lad any more – should I? – because you're a well set-up man now. We've got a good port. It comes from the right place. My! I never knew there were so many underhand dealings went on until we moved to this city.'

'Shut your mouth, woman.'

'And you shut yours.' She now pointed at her husband. 'And use your napper, have some sense, 'cos if anybody knows about underhand dealings it's this young man here. He was the best runner the river ever had 'cos the ones that came before him would have bought you at the fore end of a boat and sold you at the aft. Anyway, what about a drink?' When she inclined her head towards Freddie, he said quietly, 'No thank you. I take very little, and never any this early in the day.'

231

'Chapel are you?'

He laughed now. 'No, no; Mrs Wheatley, not me, never Chapel.'

'What have you come for anyway?'

He looked towards the old man but didn't answer him; instead, turning to Connie, he said, 'They've become attached, not knowing who they were exactly, it just happened. He called yesterday and I almost recognised him right away. As you said, he's like his father. He came with the intention of asking Miss Hewitt and' – he paused – 'Belle to tea. It was then he mentioned his grandmother and that house. I'd understood, and so had Miss Hewitt, that he lived mostly in Newcastle. He seems to have a house here too. Well, she had to be told, we couldn't let it go on. Naturally, she was very upset. I told her everything she should know about the night of her birth and what her supposed father intended to do with her. And it was this word, supposed, that aroused her curiosity and the fact that there was something odd about a situation where a man would want to kill his own daughter. I had to indicate then that there might be a doubt as to her parentage. But of course there is no way of proving that now, at least I have no way of proving it, but I wondered if any of you' – he cast his glance over them – 'could confirm that she wasn't Gallagher's daughter, or on the other hand that she was? I've thought about it a lot and it's probable that she was and that the man was mad jealous of a young and beautiful wife who dared to smile on another man. It happens.'

They all sat in silence now, and when he said, 'Well?' Frank Wheatley cried, 'Well, what d'you want us to do? Look! We want nowt to do with this business. We want to be left alone. We mind our

232

own business, always have, kept ourselves to ourselves. So you can go out the same way that you came in.'

'Da, if you don't shut up you know what'll happen, don't you?' Connie nodded slowly at her father and he stared back at her for a moment before looking away and growling something under his breath.

Connie now turned to her mother and said one word, 'Ma.'

And Mrs Wheatley, addressing herself to her daughter, said, 'Well, almost her last words to me were, "Hang on to it, Betty, for there might come a time when it'll need proof of its true identity," or words of that kind was what she said. So go and get it.'

Connie now turned and went to a bureau in the corner of the room. She pulled open a drawer and seemed to press something; then to his amazement he saw the top of the bureau rise to reveal a six inch high cupboard with a small alcove at each side. He now watched her press what he supposed must be a button inside the right-hand alcove, and then the door of the little cupboard sprang open. From where he was standing he only had a glimpse of the contents but his impression was there were two small chamois leather bags lying on the floor of the cupboard, and stuck at the back was a letter. Quickly she picked up the letter between her finger and thumb as if it was something hot. Then she closed the door, pressed the top of the cupboard down until it once more formed a level shelf on the top of the bureau.

Bringing the letter to her mother, she put it into her outstretched hand. He saw that the flap was open; whatever was in it was certainly no secret to those present. When Mrs Wheatley handed him the envelope, he mouthed the words, 'Thank you,' but no sound came out. Then he was reading simple words on a single sheet of paper headed with a crest and the address of The Towers engraved in fancy script.

I, Mirabelle Gallagher, am about to give birth to a child and I wish to state truthfully that my husband is not the father of this child. The father is one Captain José Fordyce. He is of Spanish extraction on his mother's side. But I lay no claim to him as he is a married man with a family and his ship is registered in Spain. He was honest with me and I with him. I am leaving this letter with my faithful servant Betty Wheatley in the hope that she will at some stage give it to the child in order that it should know that in no way is it a part of that demon, the man who is called my husband, Roderick Gallagher.
I place myself in God's hands.

Slowly he folded up the single sheet and replaced it in the envelope and handed it back to the old woman, but found he was unable to speak; when he could he looked at Connie and said, 'You know, if you don't mind I'll have that drink now.'

Quietly Connie stood up and went straight from the room; and after a moment her father pulled himself up from his chair and followed her, banging the door shut as he went out.

'Sit down here, lad.' Betty Wheatley indicated the chair that Connie had sat in earlier; and as he lowered himself down into it she pointed to the door, saying, 'There's a changed man for you if ever there was one. Some men can stand having money like they can stand drinks, others haven't the stomach for it. We had a little windfall, you know, and it went to his head.' She glanced knowingly sideways at him, then went on, 'If it had been beer he could have managed it, but it was rum. And if you want to slide to hell quickly the best way to do it is on rum, constant like. But Connie keeps him in his place. You know something? He's frightened of her. Not of me, mind, not of me, but she's threatened to throw him out time and again. But then she can't, can she? If one goes, we all go. But our time is runnin' out anyway. Connie will be all right, she'll always make a livin'. She's got a head on her shoulders for business so she's set. Aye, lad –' She smiled at him a weary smile as she ended, 'We had a little windfall one day. Have you ever had a windfall?'

He smiled gently at her as he said, 'Yes, I've had two. The first one was a handful of Roman coins I found in the sand.'

She laughed out loud now. 'I bet that's when you were a little nipper runnin' the sculler,' she said.

'Yes, it was.'

She laid her head back on the padded top of the chair and was silent for a moment; then she said, 'All that happened such a long time ago. It seems two lifetimes ago. Yet how long is it?'

'Fifteen years.'

'Just fifteen years . . . What you goin' to do about the letter then?'

'I'll tell her.'

'And him? Are you goin' to put it all to him?'

'I suppose so, but between you and me, if you want the truth, I'd rather nothing happened between them. The fact is, no matter how nice he looks, how charming he appears, he's still that man's son.'

'Aye, well. But you cannot put the blame on the children for the sins of the fathers. This fellow must have been brought up by his granny. Now his father didn't have a time like that. In fact, there's something to be said for his side 'cos his old man in his turn gave him hell. I told you once didn't I, how he was pushed in that room . . . I wonder if they still kept it?'

'I doubt it. I understood from what he had said yesterday the house had been practically rebuilt from the inside by the old lady . . . Mrs Wheatley,' he said.

'Aye? What is it?'

'Do you think you could trust me with that letter?'

She looked at the letter that she was still holding in one hand, and she sighed as she said, 'Well, that's what she said, didn't she? She said, if the time ever came when I thought the child should know from where it sprang, I had to show it the letter. So there you are, lad. Take it to her. But you know something? It's lucky . . . it's lucky it's still here, 'cos both of them, both Connie and him' – she nodded towards the door – 'plagued me to put it in the fire in those early days when the bairn was upstairs because in one of his rages he was not above ransacking every place in the house. And, as Frank was always saying, if he got an inkling he would tear our quarters apart. But then, as I said, who was goin' to give him the inkling? Yet many's the time I was tempted to do just what they said and burn the thing. But when he didn't come back that next day, nor the next, nor the next, and his horse was found by itself and he hadn't been to the ostler's, well, we knew that wasn't like him, and we knew we were for the road in any case, so we made our plans. And it was a good job we did 'cos it was just two days after he was found that there she was, his mother-in-law, as I told you, and among the odds and ends,' she stressed the last three words, 'we took away with us

I fetched the letter, and it lay in the tin trunk for years up in Scotland quite undisturbed and at times forgotten during the three moves we made. Then when we came here Connie bought that bureau because of its secret drawer, and she put it in there.'

Connie now entered the room. She was carrying a tray with three mugs on it, steam rising from each, and her mother, looking at it, said, 'Where's he then?'

'He's gone out.'

'Has he anything on him?'

'Enough . . . enough to get him a pint, no more. Don't worry,' she said as she handed her mother a steaming mug; 'he'll be back, 'cos it'd freeze you out there.'

When she herself sat down she looked from Freddie to her mother and back to him again, and she said, 'Ain't life funny. Who'd ever think that one day we'd be sittin' here talkin' like this and that the whole thing that happened all those years gone is about to come to light.'

'Come to light?' Mrs Wheatley was sitting up straight now. 'You're not goin' to bring all this to light, are you?' She was looking at Freddie, her face and voice expressing her anxiety. And he answered her: 'Not if I can help it, oh no! so don't worry.' He tapped the pocket of his jacket now, saying, 'I always believe in letting sleeping dogs lie.'

'Aye, but this one seems to have one eye open,' Connie said. 'The fellow mightn't see it like you or us.'

'If he wants to marry her' – he drew in a long slow breath – 'and I suppose he does if his attention is anything to go by, then he'd want the business kept as quiet as anyone. I should think more so, because although he mightn't have seen much of his father

237

he won't relish his being exposed as the man he was. Anyway –' He now lifted his mug and drained it; then putting it back on the tray, he said, 'If you don't mind I'll be making a move because the way it's coming down I think I'm going to have a job to get from the station to the house.'

He stood up; then bending over Mrs Wheatley, he took her hand and said; 'Thank you for your help. Thank you very much.' And she answered, 'That's all right, lad. Will you pop in when you're this way again an' let us know how things have turned out?'

He hesitated a moment, then said, 'Yes. Yes, I will;' and turning to Connie, he added, 'You've got a good business going downstairs. Who does the cooking?'

'I do most of it, but I've got two good lasses in the kitchen. They're learnin' my ways.'

'I'm glad things are going right for you.'

'Well, as I see it, in this life you've only got yourself to blame if they don't. It's hard goin' at times but if you work at it you'll get there.'

'Ah, shut up! lass.' They both turned sharply and looked at the woman in the chair. She was sitting bolt upright now and pointing to her legs. 'Work hard, you said, and you'll get there. What good did hard work ever do for us? Slaved we did from morn till night an' for what? Don't talk rubbish, lass. What you need in this life is luck and opportunity and money an' to hell with hard work. That's what I say.'

As she lay back in her chair seemingly exhausted, they went out of the room together and on the landing Connie said, 'She gets bitter at times, 'cos now, when she could be takin' it easy, she's troubled with the water and there seems no cure for it. Doctors or herbalists all say the same, take the medicine. But the swelling goes on. I can understand

238

her being bitter. And she's right, you know' – she nodded her head – 'you do need luck, and more so opportunities.'

On the dim landing they held each other's gaze for a moment before she turned sharply about, went down the stairs, and opened the door for him. Then saying abruptly, 'Mind how you go,' she let him out into the street; and as he was about to turn and say a final word of farewell, the door closed.

He remained standing where he was for a few seconds, the snow falling gently on him, and he thought, poor woman. And pity for her enveloped him as it had done when he first saw her face.

Now, as he made his way through the thickening snow underfoot and the struggling traffic towards the Central Station, he was lifted back to the night when as a lad he had gone across the river in the little sculler and had felt that his life was changing and that things were about to happen to him . . .

As he opened the door the house greeted him with warmth and the smell of roasting meat. He had shaken the snow off himself outside, but as he stood now divesting himself of his coat both Maggie and Belle appeared from the kitchen. And as Maggie, ever the housewife, said, 'Don't let that drip on the floor! Give it me here. You look frozen. You've been some time. What happened?' he replied quietly, 'Give me a chance to get in and I might tell you.'

Belle was looking at him intently. She had a white apron over her dress, and she undid the straps and rolled it up on her way into the sitting-room, her Ladies' School training acting unconsciously telling her that a lady, even of a small establishment, must not enter her sitting- or drawing-room attired in an apron.

239

She dropped the rolled bundle onto the couch, then turned and, going close to him now, she gripped the round collar of his jacket, saying, 'Freddie, listen to me for a moment before you start. I . . . I don't know what *you're* going to say but this is what *I* want to say. I want to thank you for all you have done for me. In the first shock I could only think of myself and what this discovery meant to my future, but now I realise that I could have been brought up under such conditions I can't bear to imagine had you not risked your life in trying to save me.'

When her arms came round his neck and her head rested on his shoulder he stiffened for a moment. It wasn't the first time she had hugged him. Like a child, she was always free with her embraces; but this was different. His arms went about her and for a moment he was holding a woman, and he pressed her to him and when she raised her head and looked up into his face he had to use all his will power not to let his mouth fall on hers. But when her lips touched his cheek and seemed to linger there, he pushed her hastily from him, and as he did so Maggie entered the room, saving him from making some verbal response.

'Well, let's hear it,' Maggie said as she took a seat to the side of the fire.

Belle had hold of his hand now and they both sat down together on the couch.

He began simply: 'It's all right; there was a letter left. Mrs Wheatley's hung on to it all these years. Your mother' – he turned now and looked at Belle – 'made a statement in it which clarifies things once and for all.' He now pulled the letter from the inner pocket of his jacket, but he hesitated on whom to hand it to first. So, to get out of this little dilemma, he said, 'I'll read it.'

And he read it. And when he had finished he handed the sheet of paper to Belle, and she looked down at it for a moment. Then her fingers moved round the perimeter of it as if feeling the texture as one would of velvet or silk: he realised that this was the only material connection she had with her mother; her mother had handled that paper the day she was born.

Maggie broke the girl's inmost thoughts when she said hoarsely, 'Well, that's settled then; at least at this end. But what now? Do you make things clear to him?' She looked from one to the other; and it was Belle who answered hastily, 'Oh, no! No; there's no need, is there? I'm your niece, Aunt Maggie, and you'll always be Aunt Maggie to me; in fact, the mother I never knew.'

'Hold your hand a minute.' Freddie was pointing a wagging finger from one to the other now. 'There's three other people that know. Two of them I could trust . . . well, a bit; but the third, Mr Wheatley, I wouldn't trust him as far as I could toss him. And he's got a drink habit and he gets about. He's just got to let his tongue go loose once and that would be that. No, I think the man should be told, that's if' – and now his voice took on a harder note – 'he shows his real intentions. Up till now he's given no indication that he wants to –' he paused, shrugged his shoulders as he paused, then finished, 'to marry you.'

He was looking at her and she turned her head away, saying, 'No, but . . . but I like him.' She looked from one to the other now, a shy almost embarrassed expression in her eyes. 'And I –' she swallowed before finishing, 'I get the impression that he likes me.'

'Oh, there's no doubt about that.' Freddie was on his feet now, his voice loud, aggressive. 'All the lads on the quay like you. As Maggie here said when she brought you from school, the eyes were popping out like pipe shanks on Newcastle Central Station. Oh, yes, quite a number of people like you; but there's degrees in liking. At first I liked May, but what did it come to? Dislike, even worse, and we weren't married. Feelings change.' He was nodding slowly at Belle now. 'Believe me, dear, feelings change. There's a great deal of difference between liking and loving.'

'But of course it's better if you like the one you love.' They both turned and looked at Maggie now, and she raised her eyebrows, saying, 'That's true. I must admit it's better to start with liking because if you're fool enough to fall head over heels in love at first sight that has the habit of blinding you to liking. And there's many a lass woke up one morning to find that the last thing she feels for a man is liking. But, Freddie's right in many ways, lass. Anyway, the dinner'll be kizzened up to cork so let's eat, because, as I see it, whichever way it goes we'll all need sustenance to face the future.'

8

The snow became thicker under foot; then it froze and for a fortnight most traffic was brought to a standstill. People had to be dug out of houses, horses out of snowdrifts, and here and there in the country there were tales of people actually starving to death. These might have just been tales, but when a shepherd was found frozen to death in a ditch and another man found dead, together with his horse, people said they had known nothing like it in the last thirty years.

Yet the feeling of affection between liking and loving was proved when the great thaw set in and rivulets up in the hills became streams and streams became rivers and the Tyne swept away low bridges. It was really feared it was going to be another big flood. But in spite of this there came a knock on the door at eleven o'clock on the Saturday morning. And when Jinny opened it there stood facing her the man, in high boots and leggings and a three-quarter-length coat, the tails of which were dripping water. And she greeted him with, 'By! you're wet, sir.'

'I am a bit. May I come in?'

'Oh aye. But Miss is out and so is Freddie. Miss Belle's in, though.'

'It's Miss Belle I've come to see.'

'Eeh! well, you'd better take that coat off and let me dry it by the kitchen fire. But I'll go up now and tell her, she's in her room, if you'd like to go into the sitting-room, sir, and wait.'

'Thank you, but I'm afraid my boots are rather . . .'

'Oh, don't worry about your boots, sir. These floors are used to all kinds of feet tramping over them.'

Jinny hurried up the stairs and, knocking on Belle's door, she said, 'Miss! Miss!'

'Yes, Jinny?' Belle appeared at the door.

'Didn't you hear the front door bell go?'

'No. Someone called?'

'Aye, somebody's called, an' they want to see you. So straighten your hair, it's all tousled.'

As Belle dashed back into the room and grabbed up a comb from the dressing-table she called to Jinny, 'Who is it, on a day like this?'

'Aye, that's what I said to meself when I saw him.'

Belle was on the landing now and she stared at Jinny for a moment, but neither of them spoke except that Jinny inclined her head forward.

Belle did not hurry down the stairs, she walked down slowly and as slowly across the hall and into the sitting-room.

He had been standing with his back to the fire. His legs were steaming. But now he came hurriedly forward, saying, 'I'm sorry if I've called at the wrong time.'

'How . . . but how did you make it through all the slush and the . . .?'

'Oh, the trains continue to run and the roads are running too' – he smiled now – 'some in two feet of water, I'm afraid.'

'You're very wet.'

She looked at his still steaming leggings.

'Oh, that's nothing; they'll soon dry. I'm used to being wet anyway, very often through to the skin when out riding.'

'Oh, well; won't you be seated?'

He sat in the chair she indicated to the side of the

244

fire; then she took her seat on the couch; and for a moment there was silence between them until he said, 'I hope the news is that Miss Hewitt is better.'

'Aunt Maggie? Oh, yes, yes; it was just a short spasm. She has a pain in her side at times and . . . and on that day it was a rather severe attack.'

Again there was silence; then she was startled by his rising swiftly and seating himself beside her. Then taking her hand, he said, 'I've missed seeing you. It . . . it seems like years.'

She forced herself to smile and say, 'It's only a little over a fortnight,' while remembering there was a time not long ago when he hadn't bothered to see her for weeks. But he was away on business then; yet still, there was pen and paper. But why was she questioning herself: he was here beside her, close, and looking into her face, and her heart was racing because she felt he was about to say something that she longed to hear. But she knew he mustn't utter those words until he had been put in the picture of their relationship . . . or their non-relationship.

When she in turn now sprang up quickly, he gazed up at her in some amazement, saying, 'What is it? You're . . . you're not pleased to see me? I . . . I thought.'

'Yes. I mean, I am pleased to see you, but before you say anything . . . I mean. Oh, what do I mean!' She put her hand to her brow and swung round. And now he was at her side, his hands holding her arms and he was saying, 'Yes, Belle; what do you mean? You know what I'm going to say.'

'Well, you mustn't say it.' She almost thrust him off. 'Not yet, not yet. You must talk to Freddie.'

'Why should I talk to Freddie? He . . . he has no jurisdiction over you. He's no relation as far as I can understand.'

'No, he is no relation' – her words were spaced – 'and neither is the woman I call Aunt Maggie.'

His brows drew together and a look of bewilderment came on his face. 'What are you trying to tell me, something about your parentage? My dear' – he put his hand out towards her again, in a gentle gesture now – 'wherever you came from makes no difference to me. You are what you are as I see you: someone beautiful and good, so lovely I can't get you out of my mind.'

'Please Mr . . .'

'My name is Marcel.'

Her head was bowed now as she said softly, 'Please bear with me. There are things you should know, *that you must know.* I . . . I can't tell you, but Freddie can.'

'Freddie? Then he *is* some sort of relation?'

'No, no. As I said, he's no relation, but . . . but he knows all about me, much more so than Aunt Maggie.' Her voice was a mere whisper now. 'Will . . . will you please say no more at the moment until you have talked with him . . . with them both? Please!' She was looking at him again.

'Yes; as you wish. But I repeat, nothing that he has to tell me about you can make the slightest difference to my feelings.'

She said now, 'Do sit down again. And may I get you a cup of tea?'

He did not give her a direct answer, but surprised her by putting his hand to his head and running his fingers through his hair and laughing silently before saying, 'We could be enacting a play. You playing the little lady to a T, as you were no doubt trained to do at school, not refusing the suitor yet not accepting him, but offering him tea . . . Oh! Belle.' She was forced to smile, but it was a weak gesture, as she

246

said, 'Yes; that's what it might appear like, but to me it is no play unless you look upon the play as a tragedy.'

'What!' The laughter died in him, then he added words that could have been a question or a statement: 'As serious as that?'

'Yes, as serious as that.'

'If that is so, please don't distress yourself any further. I will wait and talk to . . . your Freddie who seems to be such an important factor in your life. When may I expect him in?'

'Any moment. They only expected to be gone an hour because there won't be much business contracted on the waterfront today, except that of sweeping out the flood. If you'll excuse me, please, I'll get you that cup of tea.'

He said nothing but stood up as she went to leave the room.

It was as she was crossing the hall that she heard the commotion outside the front door and then Maggie's voice saying, 'Never again! I don't go down there until the sun is splitting the trees.' The door burst open and they both came in shaking themselves, only to stop in the process and look at her, and she, in a dumb show, pointed to the sitting-room: then hastily approaching them she whispered, 'He's . . . he's here.'

'He? You mean?'

She nodded, and Maggie said, 'How has he made it in this? It's like Noah's Ark out there.'

'He was very wet.'

Freddie had said nothing so far: he had taken off his coat and boots and was now holding his hand out for Maggie's boots, and for her coat too. But now he said, 'You go on in, I'll be there in a minute.'

'I can't go in,' Maggie said, 'not like this in me

247

stockinged feet,' only to be told, 'He hasn't come here to look at your feet. Go on in.'

'Get my slippers, girl, the pair in the office.'

Belle ran past Freddie, and he slowly made his way to the kitchen carrying the wet clothes, but Maggie turned about and went into her sitting-room, saying loudly as she entered, 'I'm in my stockinged feet; I'm a sight but I'm not making any excuses. I'm lucky to be alive. We've had to practically swim along that front. How are you?'

'Very well, Miss Hewitt, very well. It's a dreadful day. It's been a dreadful two weeks. You were very brave to go out in it.'

'And you' – she turned and looked at him as she seated herself by the fire and held her feet out to the blaze – 'are very foolish to risk the journey from Newcastle. They tell me the river's up to the arches there.'

'Well, not quite but it's pretty bad. I think it reached its highest in the night.'

'Have you had a drink of any sort?'

'No. Belle . . . was about to make one.'

'Oh, well, sit yourself down, don't stand about.'

He smiled at her words, a rather sad quiet smile, and when she said, 'What's amusing you?' he answered, 'you sound exactly like my grandmother; she still treats me as if I were ten: I must have warm underwear; I mustn't go out without a coat in certain weathers; I must take a potion of medicine once a week.'

Maggie smiled now, saying, 'She sounds like a sensible woman, your grandmother.'

'She is' – his voice was quiet – 'a very sensible and wonderful woman.'

'It's good to hear someone speak well of a relative. Ah' – she turned – 'here's the family en masse.'

248

Jinny had entered the room carrying a tray holding cups and saucers and a plate of scones, while behind her Freddie carried another tray bearing the silver teapot. Belle followed, and she closed the door behind her. But their greeting by Maggie, looking from one tray to the other, was, 'We haven't reached the time for afternoon tea yet. Why all the palaver? A cup of coffee I should imagine would have been more suitable.'

'I asked if . . . I suggested tea, Aunt Maggie.'

'Oh, well, if you suggested tea this is the right way to serve tea, I suppose. Thank you, Jinny.'

Jinny said nothing, but her face expressed her thoughts and her voice would indeed have been loud if she had given vent to them.

The noon tea-party was a very strained affair, so much so that Belle, of a sudden turning to Freddie, said, 'Mr Birkstead has called to . . . to, I think' – she drew in a long shuddering breath – 'put a proposition to me, but I told him that first of all he must listen to you and' – she now looked at Maggie – 'and to you, Aunt Maggie. So . . . so I will leave you to . . . to tell him all you know about . . . me.' And looking at Freddie again, she said, 'You may add to it my gratitude for the goodness and kindness I've received from you all these years.'

To say that the three people she hurriedly left were embarrassed would be to put it mildly; but at the moment the least so was the visitor. That was until Freddie, looking at the man he wanted to dislike but found he couldn't, not wholeheartedly anyway, said, 'I can put it all in a nutshell to begin with by saying that but for her mother having an affair on the side with a sea captain, you and she could be half-brother and sister.'

Freddie watched a look of incredulity pass over the

249

man's face, and when he added, 'I was in the bedroom the night she was born and heard your father trying to prise the truth out of his wife and also, when the child came into life, ordering it to be destroyed.'

'*What! What are you saying?* What is this all about anyway?'

'Well, sir, I would take that seat again because there's a lot more you haven't heard yet, and it's somewhat of a long and detailed story. So if you please, will you be seated.'

The man sat, and for the next fifteen minutes he listened to the details which began with a little boy used as a runner because he had a little sculler boat.

The room was hot, they were all sweating, the visitor most of all, and when he spoke his voice was thin with almost a snarl to it as he said, 'You've made my father out to be a scoundrel.'

'Well, that's how I saw him, and that's what he really was, although the servants seemed to think that circumstances had made him like that, because his father had given him a hell of a time when bringing him up. Anyway, hasn't your grandmother ever indicated what kind of a man her daughter married?'

'Not to that extent. Hot-tempered, taciturn, but not a potential murderer, or a receiver of stolen goods –' He paused now and his head swung from one side to the other before he said, 'and an opium addict. That's what you make him out to be. And now you tell me his servants own the coffee house. How is it that servants such as they must have been, of the lowest order, come to own a place like that?'

'I don't know anything about that. They had a little saved up, I suppose, and they started in a small way in Scotland. Most businesses start in small ways.'

'And his death? Was nothing ever discovered about his death?'

Both Maggie and Freddie resisted an exchange of glances; they looked ahead for some seconds, but when Maggie was about to speak Freddie put in, 'He seemed to have been attacked, likely for what he had on him that night. That's all that was known.'

'My God! He in his turn must have been murdered then?'

'I know nothing about that part of it. Anyway, you must have enquired before, or been told how your father came to die. You weren't such a small child then; you were ten when you moved into The Towers, weren't you.'

'Yes. I understood he had an accident and was drowned. The matter was not discussed after. I knew that my grandmother had no love for him so she didn't talk of him. The only thing she did tell me was that he loved my mother dearly and was a changed man after she died.'

'Yes, he certainly was, and this was demonstrated in the way he treated his second wife, who, by what I was given to understand those years ago, was a beautiful young girl and rich, and he married her not for her beauty but for her money.'

'I don't see how she could have brought him much money when he only kept three servants in that big house.'

'Again I understand he had kept more, but they didn't stay. Those three were faithful to him, as they had been to his father before him. Servants, sir, are human beings: there's some things they'll stand and some things they won't.'

'I'm well aware of that, sir.'

251

'Please. Please.' Maggie closed her eyes and lay back in the chair. 'Don't let us get on to the merits of servants. The question now is, has all this altered your intentions towards Belle? Don't say yea or nay.' She thrust out her arm and held up her hand in a warning gesture. 'Give yourself time. It would please us both if you would go now without seeing her and think about it, and take into account that if the relationship or the non-relationship was to leak out, and you never know because there's three other people in this secret, and as you've just stated they were common servants, there could be a scandal even if that letter there' – she pointed to the letter lying on the table to her side – 'was produced. There's no way of proving that it was written by Belle's mother. There's only Freddie's word of what he witnessed that night and why the man, your father, would want to get rid of the child, and why those servants risked their necks to keep her alive in what must have been that madwoman's hole up in the attic.' Maggie's head went back now because he had sprung to his feet again, and it was evident he was finding it difficult to speak. And when he did his voice was low: 'I will do as you suggest,' he said; 'I . . . I shall think about this. But one way or another, you, I mean, Belle, will hear from me. You can understand this has been more than a shock, it's been a . . . devastating . . .'

Realising the difficulty the man was in, Maggie rose too and she said quietly, 'You're right, and whatever you decide we shall understand.' She cast a glance towards Freddie, but he said nothing; instead he hurried from the room and went into the kitchen and collected the man's coat and hat. But in the hall, as he passed them to him, he said, 'If you care, I'll see you to the station, the roads are still very precarious.'

'Thank you; but I managed to get here alone, I'll

manage to find my way back.' He inclined his head towards Freddie, then turned to the door, and on Freddie's opening it he stepped out without further words. He had given Maggie no formal goodbye, but they stayed and watched him splash down the path towards the gate. Then they closed the door and what Maggie said was, 'Pray God he finds it too much to stomach, because I fear there is another side to him. I expected him to be shocked, but not to look and speak as he did.'

9

Three days later a letter arrived by hand. The bearer said he would wait for an answer. Jinny took the letter into the kitchen where Belle was trying her hand at pastry making. When Belle opened it she saw four words written in a small scrawly hand: Will you marry me?

She put her hand to her throat, an action which caused Jinny to ask, 'Bad news, lass?' She shook her head; then hurried from the kitchen and into the sitting-room, and took from the bureau drawer a sheet of paper on which she wrote one word: Yes. She folded it up, put it in an envelope which she sealed; then went to the door where the messenger was still waiting and handed him the envelope and a shilling, for which he thanked her gratefully.

When the hall door was closed she leant her head back against it and her mouth was wide open; and it was like this that Jinny saw her and said, 'What is it, lass?'

Smiling now, she said simply, 'I'm going to be married, Jinny.' And what Jinny said was, 'Well, all I can say is, that's quick work,' before turning about and returning to the kitchen.

Maggie and Freddie came in for their dinner at quarter-past twelve, and immediately they could see from her face that something had happened, for she met them in the hall and before they had time to take off their clothes she said, 'I've . . . I've had a letter from him.'

They both stared at her, and it was Freddie who said, 'Aye? Well, what had he to say?'

'Come into the sitting-room for a minute, will you?' she said, and there was an appeal in the way she looked at them. And when they were in the room she said, 'It couldn't have been more brief,' and handed the letter to Maggie; and she, after the glance that was all it needed, said as she passed it to Freddie, 'Well, there's truth in that.'

And he, after reading, retained it in his hand as he looked at Belle and said, 'No word of affection, nothing to say he cares for you.'

'Oh, Freddie! What's the matter with you? I know he cares for me.'

'And you care for him? Enough to marry him?'

'Yes; yes, I do.'

'And I suppose you've told him so?'

'Yes, I have.' Now her tone was sharp. 'I . . . I should have imagined that you would be happy for me that someone like him should . . . should want to marry me.'

'*Don't be daft, girl!*' It was a yell. 'Half the country would want to marry you if they knew you were available. What's the matter with you? Don't you know yourself? Don't you look in the mirror? Jumping at the first chance that's offered, and to him of all people, the son of his father!'

He turned about and stamped from the room, leaving Maggie to go to Belle where she was standing with her head bowed, the tears running down her cheeks, and to say, 'It's because he's concerned for you, like I am. And it's true, you know, lass, we know nothing about this fellow, only that he's the son of his father. And God in heaven! we both know a lot about his father.'

She turned away as if she had said too much; and

255

she knew she had indeed said too much, for now she was thinking, I wasn't supposed to have met the man. But anyway, the girl was in such a state that that slip wouldn't be questioned; at least, please God it wouldn't, for her mind wouldn't be able to stand that business coming into the open at this stage: murder was murder, whichever way it took a life. Self-defence would be no excuse. And she had paid for her deed, she had paid in nightmares, if in no other way. By God she had.

She said now, 'Come on and have your dinner; at least I want mine, I'm starving. And don't worry, everything will pan out; Freddie will come round. You've only got to remember it's you and your happiness he's thinking of.'

The meal was eaten mostly in silence, and when later Freddie went into the kitchen his mother remarked caustically, 'That was a merry meal,' and when he didn't answer she went on washing the dishes and talking to them, saying, 'Well, it would be best if you put a good face on it. If she wants to marry him she'll have him. I don't know the ins and outs of it, I haven't been told, but I think there's somethin' fishy going on. I'm not one to pry; I can wait until I'm put in the picture. I think you could have trusted me though 'cos over all these years I've never told your da the rights and wrongs of this affair.'

'All right, Ma, later. We'll have a talk later. But at the moment I'm worried. I'll tell you that, I'm just worried.'

'And a bit more.'

As he was leaving the kitchen he turned and looked at her, but stilled the retort on his lips.

Yes, and a bit more, as she said, for the fact was he was burnt up inside with jealousy of the man. Yet

256

that was not all: there was a fear in him concerning the fellow. Perhaps it was because he couldn't get it out of his head that the man was the son of his father.

And he had another niggling little worry on his mind. He'd had a message passed on to him this morning from Mr Taylor the jeweller. Apparently Andy Stevens went up to Newcastle yesterday on an errand for Maggie and while there had called into the jeweller's to see if his watch had been repaired, and Mr Taylor had said to him, 'Would you ask Mr Musgrave to call in and see me as soon as he can?' Now why should the jeweller want to see him? He himself had never done any business with Mr Taylor, but Maggie had. As yet he hadn't said anything to Maggie. It had been a busy morning and he'd thought it might be better left till dinner-time when they were up home.

He went back into the sitting-room now and said to her, 'I'm going up to town.'

'Why? Andy did all the necessary up there.'

'It's got nothing to do with that deal at all. If you want to know, Mr Taylor gave Andy a message when he called to pick up his watch. He wants to see me. Now why should Mr Taylor want to see me?'

Maggie didn't reply for some seconds, and then she repeated, 'Yes, that's a question, why should he want to see you? You've had no dealings with him, have you?'

'No, but you have.'

'Yes; yes, bits of odds and ends for the sailors. And there were the stones remember. But that's the only thing we would have to worry about. I've had watches mended and I've bought silver from him now and then, such as the tea service. I suppose I've been a good customer over the years; why didn't he ask for me?'

'Well, I won't know, will I, till I see him.'

'No; and the quicker you see him the better I'll feel. Oh it's that kind of a day. But hurry back, for there's a lot of discussion to be done. Yet I can't see that any of it is going to alter how she feels, and what I feel in my bones is, she'll go through with it. So you, lad, might as well make up your mind to it.'

As before, he gave her no answer, but went out.

Newcastle was a-bustle, yet everything looked grey and dull. The river had gone down but debris lined the banks. Warehouses had been swamped and were thick with mucky slush.

When he entered Mr Taylor's shop he sniffed; the atmosphere seemed thick. A gas jet was spluttering and an elderly man, standing below it, was bending over some article on the counter. He had a black spyglass pressed close to one eye and he was talking to a customer, saying, 'Very nice workings, beautifully done. But of course age tells. I'll do the best I can with it.'

The customer said, 'When will it be ready?'

'Oh, it could be two weeks, three; I have a number in and there's only myself now. I've lost my assistant. He was a promising young man but he had trouble with his chest and it took him off.'

'Oh,' said the customer; then turned and walked out.

Mr Taylor now peered at Freddie, saying, 'Ah, I know you better than you know me . . . Maggie's boy.'

'Yes, you could say that, Maggie's boy.'

'It's nice to see you. Well –' the old man jerked his head back on his shoulders, saying, 'There's no customer in sight, if you'd like to step into the back shop with me.' He now lifted up the flap in the

258

counter and allowed Freddie to pass him; then he replaced the flap gently as if any untoward noise it might make should disturb the clocks. Then he led the way behind the curved counter and through a door to a room into which the atmosphere of the shop seemed to have penetrated. The only furniture it held, besides countless clocks of all shapes and sizes, was an old battered table, very much like a butcher's block, and a high stool and a chair.

He now offered Freddie the chair by pointing to it, then hoisted himself up on to the high stool and, leaning his bent body so that his elbow could rest on the block, he peered at Freddie through the dim light afforded by a window that hadn't been cleaned for some long time and, coming straight to the point, he said, 'Do you know a man called Freeman?'

After a slight hesitation Freddie said, 'Yes; yes, indeed, I know a man called Freeman.'

'Well, somehow I thought you would. Have you ever had any private dealings with him?'

'No; no private dealings. Perhaps, if you know Freeman, you will know from him that I was a runner when the smuggling was at its height on the coast. I was very small for my age then and had a little sculler and so, in the main, could cross the river without comment. I was' – he paused – 'always on the way to me granny's.' There was a touch of humour in these last words, and the jeweller took them up, saying, 'Well, it's good to have a destination to make for. Now may I ask if you knew what you were carrying across the river at times? As you will gather, there's a purpose in my asking these questions.'

'Yes, I can gather that, and except for once, I wasn't aware of what I was carrying. But then, I carried very little, my job was to run messages.'

'Yes, I can gather that, too, but at one time you must have carried a precious cargo. You know what I mean?'

Freddie remained quiet and the jeweller went on, 'Maggie brought me three stones some time ago, and she got a good price for them. I'm always fair and I admit I got a good price for them too. Now no one knew about that transaction, only you, Maggie, and me, at least that is what I thought till recently when I had a visit from Mr Freeman. Between you and me, young man, I've never cared for Larry Freeman. I'm of the opinion that money is badly divided in this world and if you can sort it out a bit all to the good, but some people get greedy and he's one of the greediest men I know. And he's got fingers in many pies, not only in Newcastle but up in the big city too. And that is where the exchanges are made . . . well, with the special pieces of *glass*.' It looked as if he was endeavouring to straighten his bent back and he looked towards the dull window as he went on, 'It's always been a mystery to me why women and men go mad about such pieces. Anyway, he wanted to know if you had been in here and passed on some stones to me. Now, I said, lots of people had been in here and passed on stones to me, besides other things, as he was well aware, and, as I didn't keep any record, I couldn't remember if you had or not; that in fact, I was sure you hadn't. Then he said, if you hadn't been in, had Maggie Hewitt? Now I had to lie very glibly at this, and I repeated again I had no memory of Miss Hewitt bringing any stones to me, but I did know that she was a very good customer for my silver both new and second-hand and that I had sold her two of the best grandfather clocks in the county. Well, from the conversation that ensued I gathered that the stones in question had reached a certain person in London – amazing how news travels – and that this person felt that these pieces were part of a consignment that should have reached him many years ago via Mr Larry Freeman and then a Mr Gallagher, the man that you used to take messages to. Isn't that so?'

Freddie's throat was dry, and not just from the atmosphere of the shop. He said flatly, 'Yes, he was the man I took messages to.'

'Well, the two diamonds and the ruby that landed eventually in a certain house in London was but a small part of a larger package which has never been seen since. Now, recollecting all that happened, when this man Gallagher was found in the river there were no such stones on him. Apparently he had been attacked and someone had stripped his pockets before throwing him in the water. Now, although he didn't say outright, Mr Larry Freeman has worked it out that you, as a nipper, but not such a nipper because you were twelve years old at the time, was the last person likely to see him alive other than his servants, of which there were three. Is that correct?'

'You're correct about the servants, but I needn't have been the last person to see him alive because I delivered my message that night and that was that.'

'Well, apparently by someone else's statement it wasn't. One of those servants is an old drunk, the father of a woman who has taken a coffee house here. She's a very disfigured creature, one that can't be missed. Anyway, having been given some cheap liquor this man tells Freeman a very strange tale, quite unbelievable, which Freeman says he discounts, about a child whom his master means to kill and doesn't, and the servants hide it in a room, and you come along and you rescue the child; and Mr

261

Gallagher chases you and this man who was the servant right down to Shields waterfront. And there the servant leaves you, knowing that his master is hot on your heels. Now, I think as Freeman, that that's all fantastic rubbish, but what Freeman doesn't consider rubbish is the possibility that Gallagher met up with you. And although you were only a nipper you were wiry and quick on your feet and, to use his words, you could have felled him with a stone or anything else, stripped him of what he had in his pockets, then pushed him in the river. The three stones that arrived in London were part of the haul and he reckons it's more than likely you've hung on to the rest.'

'Oh, my God!' Freddie got to his feet. 'Do you think if I'd had a haul such as I carried that night, and it was a big haul because the package broke and the three stones that Maggie brought you had fallen into the seam of my trouser pocket, do you think if I'd hung on to the rest I'd still be here? It must have been a big fortune and I would have made a small fortune out of it and you a comparatively large one before it reached London.'

'Well, Mr Musgrave, I thought it better to put you in the picture as to what is taking place and for you to be on your guard from now on. Between us both, Freeman is a nasty piece of work, but like lots of other nasty pieces of work he is high up in several quarters in the city. Nobody really knows what he's worth. But I know he stacks a lot of his money abroad, perhaps for a rainy day when things become too hot for him, as it generally does for his ilk.' He too rose from his seat now, adding in a sad tone, 'The smuggling and the running, the narrow squeaks through the customs and the excise men, the bargaining that took place in this very room, mostly in the dead of night, all lent excitement to life. And there was honour among thieves in those days, and everyone got their fair share of what they managed to haul. But all that is past now, gone like so many other good things. Do you know something, young man? I am glad I am old. Ah, there's the bell, another customer, so I'll say good day, Mr Musgrave. I hope I've been of a little help to you.'

'Thank you. Thank you, Mr Taylor, you have.' He did not add, 'And an added source of worry with regard to things to come, as if I hadn't enough.' . . .

Maggie was perturbed at his news, but one thing she said and with which he agreed was that Freeman would bring nothing into the open: he himself stood to lose too much to risk exposure; everything that followed from now on would be underhand.

Here Maggie was mistaken.

The following day Freddie made another journey to Newcastle, this time to the coffee house. He went straight up to the counter. Connie was behind it. She didn't seem surprised to see him, and he began without any preamble: 'Your father's opening his mouth, do you know that? There could be trouble all round.' And to this she answered, 'My mother died the day afore yesterday. They're burying her the morrow. And me da broke into the cash box upstairs and has gone on the spree. D'you think I'm worried about anything more that can happen? My mother was more than a mother, she was my friend, the only one I had.'

He said, 'I'm sorry. I'm very sorry, Connie.'

'So am I,' she said, 'and for meself now.'

He had to move to the side to allow a customer to pay for his meal, and he stood for a moment longer looking at her through the blurred glass; then he turned and went out.

When he reached home it was to find that Maggie had had a bout of that pain, and so severe had it been she had had to be helped up from the office. Belle had put her to bed and sent for the doctor.

He had met the doctor in the hall, and had asked straightaway, 'What is it? What is really wrong with her?'

Shrugging his shoulders, the doctor had merely answered, 'Well, it's the old stomach trouble gathering momentum.'

He had wanted to say, 'What d'you mean by that?' but that apparently was as far as the doctor wished to prognosticate for he was on his way to the front door. And when a moment later he had stood by Maggie's bedside and asked, 'What's all this about then?' her reply had been even more non-committal: 'Oh, I'm sick of work, at least for this week; I've decided to put me feet up properly this time,' she said.

'And not afore time, I should say.' He looked across at Belle standing at the other side of the bed and said, 'When did this happen?'

And she replied, 'Shortly after you left. She tried to stop me sending for the doctor.'

'Well, what has he done?' Maggie looked from one to the other. 'Written out a prescription for the apothecary. It must be something nasty for he usually does his own dispensing. I'll get a bill for that all right. You could have gone down there and got me usual bottle for a shilling, but I'll bet he'll charge five bob if a penny.'

'Shut up! and rest yourself.' He bent over her and smoothed the hair from her brow; then casting a glance at Belle, he said, 'Is there anything hot going? I'm chilled to the bone.'

'Oh yes. Yes, Freddie, I'll get you a drink.'

As she hurried from the room he pulled up a chair in order to sit closer to the bed, and when she said, 'Did you see her? How did it go? What happened?' he said, 'Oh, I'll tell you later. It's nothing to worry about. But about this pain, Maggie. Was it all that bad?'

'Bad enough.'

'What is it? D'you know? Is there a name to it?'

'Well, I would give it the name of cramp, to be kind; like, you know, you get in the calves of your legs. But I suppose them doctors have a name for it. The guts get twisted or something, spasms. We all have spasms of one thing or another. She's in a spasm.' She motioned with her head towards the door. 'In spite of her worry over me she can't keep it hidden, it's shining out of her. Freddie' – she gripped his hand – 'try to be happy for her, be gentle with her. Married or not, she's going to need a friend through life, and you should be that one. At the bottom of me I'm worried about her.'

He wanted to reply, 'And you're not the only one;' instead he said, 'Don't worry about it. As to my attitude: knowing how I feel, you wouldn't expect me to react in any other way, at least not at the moment. But –' He pressed her hand against his chest, saying, 'It's you that's on my mind, not her. Now . . . now listen to me. You've got to take care of yourself, so be a good lass and stay there for a week.'

'Oh my God! no. I'd go mad lying in bed for a week. Look, lad, this thing just comes in spasms. I might go days, weeks, even months, and not have another.'

'You haven't had days, weeks, or months between the last . . . spasms, as you call them; you had more than a touch of one three days ago.'

Her voice was very low and soft as she said, 'Lad, we've all got to go sometime or other.'

'*Don't say that.*' He thrust her hand from him. 'Don't talk like that, Maggie. Don't scare the wits out of me. What would I do without you?'

'Oh, oh, come on, come on, man; everybody can be done without. There never was a good but there's a better.'

'Don't talk such bloody rot.' He was actually gasping now, and again he grabbed her hand and, his face coming close down to hers, he said, 'Maggie, for God's sake don't leave me. I can do without Belle because I've got to, but I couldn't do without you, because I know . . .'

'Now! now! stop it.'

'I won't stop it, I've got to say this. I've never said it to you afore: I've got a feeling for you that I can't explain even to myself, from the first time you took me under your wing. I don't think of you as another mother, Maggie. I can't, as I said, put a name to how I think of you. Perhaps if you had been a bit younger and I a bit older, even twenty years between us wouldn't have made any difference. I . . . I love you, Maggie. And . . . and this is the first time I've ever said that to a woman. I never said it to May, and I've never said it to Belle, but I say it to you.' His head now dropped onto her chest and her hands came on it, but she was unable to make any comment on his words, either derisory or otherwise, for at this moment the pain in her heart was obliterating the growling pain in her stomach. But after a moment, when she raised his wet face up to hers, she said, 'Then take comfort, Freddie, because I too couldn't put a name to the feelings I have for you.'

He now went to take her face between his hands when the door opened, and this caused him to rise abruptly and, with his back towards Belle now, he muttered to Maggie, 'See you later.'

She made no response, and he went out. In the hall, he hesitated whether to go to his room or down to the kitchen; but he knew that if he went to his room he might break down altogether, and he had an afternoon's work to face and people to meet.

His mother was in the kitchen and she cast a quick glance at him but said nothing, not until he asked a question: 'What is really wrong with Maggie, Ma, do you know?'

'Well, I can't put a medical name to it,' she said, 'but it's either what you call a tumour or an abscess in her guts, and it's been growing this long while.'

'Is there any cure?'

'No, as far as I know there isn't.'

He swung round from her and went to the window and looked out onto the garden, and Jinny, from where she stood at the table, said, 'It's no use lettin' go like that. You must have guessed she's been bad for a long time, and time's runnin' out now.'

Swinging about, he cried, 'Don't say that, Ma! Don't say it!'

'And don't you shout at me, lad. You asked a question and I answered it.' And her lips trembled slightly as she said, 'I hope when my time comes you show as much concern, but I doubt it, aye I doubt if you will.'

There it was, the old jealousy that he had thought dead this many a year, but it still festered. His voice just a mutter now, he said, 'She's been good to me, Ma. She's been good to all of us.'

'There's nobody sayin' nay to that. But what you seem to forget, lad, and often, is that I'm still your mother. I may be a servant in this house but I have me pride an' I can tell you this for nowt, you've hurt it many a time. I like the Miss; at least half the

267

time, but the other half . . . I hate her for havin' taken you from me.'

'You're wrong there, Ma; she hasn't take me from you, you're still me mother.'

'Aye, I might be in name but not in affection. Oh, lad, don't start givin' me any of your high-flown explanations. There's somethin' atween you two, and has been for years, that shuts me out.' She turned round now, took up a tea-towel and, stretching the hem between her fingers and thumbs, she shook it out straight before hanging it on the rod above the fire, when she said, 'By the way, I have a message for you from our Nancy. She wants a word with you. I think you had better call in home on your way down. It seems important enough to me for you to take the trouble to call in home.'

The angry retort that was on his tongue was quelled, and he marched from the room, all the while heavy with guilt now because he knew that everything she had said was true even to the last remark concerning his spare visits home.

When he was dressed for the road he looked in on Maggie again, saying briskly now, 'Do what you're told and stay put.' Then turning to Belle, he said, 'See that she doesn't move out of here, will you?'

'Don't worry; I'll see to her.'

Maggie watched him all the time, and as he made for the door she said quietly, 'Wrap up well; it's biting, and you left the hot drink Belle got for you.'

Wrap up well; it's biting. No frost or icy wind could make him feel colder than he was already inside. And when he reached the house – he didn't now think of it as home – he found Nancy alone in the kitchen-cum-sitting room.

'Where's Da?' he said.

'He's having a lie down.' She indicated the bedroom

268

door as if she could see it. 'His legs have been worrying him of late.'

'You wanted to see me, Nancy?'

'Yes.' She walked towards the fireplace, which was farthest from the bedroom door and there, her voice low, she said, 'You know I've been seeing John Pratt, and I don't care what the neighbours or people think. Do you?'

'What d'you mean?'

'Just what I say, Freddie. D'you care what people think?'

'No, not much.'

'That's just as well, because they criticise you for making a new home and neglecting your old one.'

'That isn't fair, Nancy.'

'Nothing is very fair, I find, Freddie. For instance, I've never thought it unfair that I was blind, up till recently when a man told me I was beautiful and asked me to marry him and I refused.'

'Why?' His tone changed. 'Why on earth have you refused him? Because he's in the customs?'

'No, of course not.' Her voice was scornful; and as he stared at her he couldn't believe this was Nancy who was talking, sweet, quiet, placid, Nancy, everyone's comforter. But this is what love did to one, opened one's eyes so to speak; and it was a poor simile but it had opened hers. He put out his hands and drew her to him, and she didn't resist his embrace. And when he said, 'You are beautiful, Nancy; and if this man loves you you must take him. Do you care for him?'

After a short silence she said, 'Yes. Yes, I do. All the things about him that I sense I like, much more than like.'

'Well, what has stopped you? What made you say no?'

'Da's upset because of what his cronies might think. As he said, I was bringing a spy into their midst. To hear him talk you would think the smuggling was an everyday affair. He lives in the past.'

'I'll soon settle Da in that quarter; you leave that to me.' He shook her now gently, saying, 'When are you seein' this fellow next?'

'I hope tomorrow. He's taking me into Newcastle. I have an appointment.'

'Tell him you've changed your mind. Now promise me? Because he sounds a decent bloke. I've only caught a glimpse of him. There's still so many of them around the town and along the front, it's practically as bad as Newcastle, but I could pick him out. Medium height, isn't he? Sandy hair, brown-eyed. Of course, you wouldn't know all those particulars.'

'I do, and what's more, why I wanted to see you was to give you a message from him.'

'*A message* to me from *him*?'

'Just that. Apparently there's something afoot. He couldn't explain what, but there are enquiries being made, especially on the river and even in the city. He says you must have an enemy or two. It's something connected with what happened years ago when you used to be a runner. Although how they can hold you responsible for anything that happened then I don't know, because you were just a tiny little chap. But he pointed out that you were twelve years old or thereabouts and, as he said, they used to transport lads for stealing a loaf, never mind valuables. Did you steal any valuables, Freddie?'

'No, I didn't, Nancy, and you can tell him that. I have never stolen anything in me life, except giblets from the butchers, and bits of fruit when I could.'

'Well, what do you think they are getting at? Why

270

are they suspicious? Can you guess why anybody should want to cause trouble?'

'Oh, yes, yes, Nancy, I can guess. I can pin-point the very person; so don't worry, I'll deal with this. But you give Mr Pratt my thanks and tell him I appreciate the gesture he's made. Apart from all that, though, you take back that no. Will you?'

'I'll think about it, Freddie.'

'You'll not think about it any more, you'll do it. If you don't I'll go to him and tell him how you feel. Nancy' – he gripped her arms – 'you must get away from here. Now don't think I'm actin' the upstart, but Ma and Da are used to this, they were bred to be used to this kind of life. As long as they've got their belly full and a good fire and something to drink they won't worry, but you . . . you are made for better things. Your voice could carry you far if you had somebody behind you, and this fella could be the very start you're lookin' for. Now think on it, because what's the alternative? You'll end up like Maggie, lonely inside and lost. And you couldn't stand life with one of the lads from around here. They're good chaps, many of them, but coarsegrained. By the way, did your friend give you any indication of how this matter had started? I mean people, somebody put on to me?'

'Oh' – she nodded quickly now – 'I think it was an anonymous letter sent to the headquarters in Newcastle first. I sort of gathered that.'

'Huh!' He gave a short laugh. 'There's two can play at that game. But I don't need to write my information down, I can speak it. Anyway, thanks, love. I must be off now.' He bent and kissed her, saying, 'Do as I tell you now. Get your life sorted out and think of yourself for once. I'll look after the both of them here; you need never worry about that.'

'Thanks, Freddie.'

'Ta-ra.'

'Ta-ra, Freddie.'

Anonymous letter. Of course Freeman wouldn't want to become implicated, would he? Well, by God! he would show him. He would go up to Newcastle now, and damn the business.

A few minutes later he burst into the quay office, startling Andy Stevens and the new clerk having a quiet smoke in short pipes, their coat tails lifted up to warm their backsides at the small fire in the office grate, and he bawled at them, 'Miss Hewitt's away sick but I'm in good health and there's a line of clerks wanting jobs up in the city. Think on it when next you want to warm your backsides at two o'clock in the afternoon.' But then, his voice dropping, he said, 'I'm surprised at you, Andy.'

'We were both froze, Mr Musgrave.'

'You've never complained about being frozen before. And I ask you, what would it have looked like if a customer had popped in, eh? Now don't let me have to warn you again on this. I'm surprised at you, I am that. As for you, Hooper: you learn and you learn quickly or you go. And now I want a message taken to a Captain Hannan. Tell him I can't come aboard at three as I said, but I'll see him in the morning when they dock again.'

'Yes, Mr Musgrave.'

He went out, and as he marched along the quay and up through the town to the station his thinking calmed somewhat and he thought he had perhaps been a bit high-handed, because it was the first time he had seen Andy slacking like that and taking advantage. But why had he taken advantage? Simply because he knew Maggie was out of the way. Well then, in future he would have to learn who was

272

boss, wouldn't he? And it came to him that it might take hard work and acting high-handedly on his part to convince them, whereas Maggie had just to appear at the end of the quay and they seemed to smell her presence and would be hard at it when she entered the office. Oh, but what did it matter? What mattered now was the meeting with Freeman. But where would he find him at this time of day? In his office? In which office? He had his fingers in so many pies. If it took till midnight, though, he would find him.

But he didn't have to wait till midnight, he found him in the first building he entered.

There was a brass plate alongside the highly polished door which read: Freeman & Son: Builders & Contractors. There was a reception desk in the hall and the hall floor was tiled in a special pattern of a star with beams radiating from it. The young man behind the counter raised his head from a ledger and asked politely, 'What can I do for you, sir?'

'I wish to speak to Mr Freeman.'

'May I ask if you have an appointment, sir?'

'No, I haven't; but will you tell him that Frederick Musgrave would like a word with him.'

The man stood up, saying now, 'Mr Frederick Musgrave. I'll see if Mr Freeman is in.'

'Do that.'

He stood looking about him, particularly at the wood-work. It was all mahogany doors, window frames, and skirting boards. The man was away four minutes, so did the brass clock on the wall in between two doors tell him. And then there he was, saying, 'Mr Freeman will see you now. Will you come this way, please?'

He was ushered into an office that made Maggie's quay room appear like a slum in comparison. The

273

swift impression was the continuation of the mahogany and the sumptuous brown upholstered leather chairs.

Freeman was standing by the side of his desk as the man announced him, saying, 'Mr Frederick Musgrave, sir.'

Not until the door closed did Larry Freeman speak, and then he said, 'By! you've got me puzzled, and I'm asking myself the question, why should he want to come and see me? He's never done this before. Could it be he wants to tell me something I've been trying to find out for years.'

'Don't take me for a fool, Mr Freeman, and don't act the innocent bystander. You know why I'm here.'

'I do?' Freeman now walked from the desk towards the marble-tiled fireplace and there, stooping down, he picked up the tongs and took a piece of coal from a highly polished brass bucket standing to the side of the equally highly polished brass fender. And having placed it on the fire, he repeated the process four times. Then straightening up, he dusted his hands and, his voice changing, he said, 'What you after? But before you start, don't think, young man, you can blackmail me in any way. You were a sly little nipper and I don't suppose that mind of yours has improved. No, it certainly hasn't. You're known as a sharp business man on the quay – Maggie trained you well in that – but don't think you'll use your expertise on me because . . .'

'Would you like to be quiet for a moment?'

Freeman now brought his teeth tightly together, and he remained quiet as Freddie said, 'You're putting up a very good show, but let me tell you this, Mr Freeman. You can send your anonymous letters to the customs or the police or who you like, but they won't carry the weight of a feather to what will happen to you when I open *my* mouth. Not only what I know from when I was a runner but from what I've learned since and . . .'

Freeman was now glaring at Freddie, and he brought the words out slowly, saying, 'What the hell! are you talking about? Anonymous letters? I've written no anonymous letters. That's not my way. What's all this?'

Freddie was nonplussed for a moment; and it was some seconds before he could speak, when he said, 'I've been given the tip that the customs are on to me for something that happened years ago and it could only be connected with you and the running across the river, and I thought that . . .'

'Then your thinking proves that you're not as smart as I imagined you were, or as you think you are. What the hell! would I be doing in writing an anonymous letter to give you away when the first thing you would do, as you've just said, is open your mouth wide. And who would come off worse in the deal, eh? A bit of a lad, as you were then, you would get all the sympathy, and me . . . the bad man using you . . . Don't be so bloody dim, man. Who knows what happened that night anyway?'

'No one knows, except Gallagher's three servants who now run Cora's Coffee House, and the mother died the day before yesterday. But the father's a drunk and he . . .'

'Oh, I know all about the father' – Freeman brought his hand across his face in an impatient movement – 'and I've got a version of what happened that night, if you can believe it. But the old fellow's half barmy and most of it was fancy, and I wouldn't think that old sop would be capable of writing a letter. He could though get somebody to write it for him. But why should he, eh? Why should he? And it wouldn't be his daughter because she keeps a tight rein on him. But there's a point. Where did that lot get the money to set up a place like that coffee house? There's a lot of questions to be asked here, and one I've been wanting to ask you too, for years: what did you do with the rest of the stones?'

'What d'you mean, what did I do with the rest of the stones? I never saw the stones.'

'Now look, don't try to hoodwink me. Maggie sold three of those stones to old Taylor. It's funny how things come about. They can lie dormant for years and then just a word and a door opens. I was in London not long ago seeing a friend of mine, in fact he was the friend who was waiting for that consignment that you took across the river that night. It was a very precious consignment that, and this man knows a lot about stones and their quality. I do a bit myself, but I'm a child compared to him. Well, he recognised the ruby; it happened to be one of a set of six; and the diamonds were all out of a special tiara. Do you know what a tiara is?' Freddie remained silent but his lips curled slightly. 'Well, these three stones had come to him through Taylor. He has a great respect for Mr Taylor and Mr Taylor hinted that they had come to him through a lady, a lady of North Shields who was a very sharp business woman. So what did I do but put two and two together. So I ask *you* now, *you* who were the last person likely to see those stones, what about them, I mean the rest of them?'

For answer Freddie took two steps towards a chair, then said, 'May I sit down?'

With an exaggerated wave of his hand, Freeman answered, 'By all means. By all means.'

'Then I advise you to do the same, because I am going to tell you a tale that is perfectly true. Yet you may not believe half of it. But before I start you can give up any hope of seeing the rest of those stones, as you call them, through me, as I don't know what happened to them.'

Freeman was now sitting opposite to him, his body pushed well back in the big leather chair, his hands resting on the padded arms. And now Freddie said, 'I'm only telling you this now because I believe you when you say you didn't write that letter.'

And so he started, from that night when he reached the Shields side of the river and was picked up by Gallagher, then thrown into the scrub field. He told all that transpired even to the finding of the child. He even went back to the day when it was born. But he finished his tale when Maggie met him on the front and bustled him into the boat.

It was a good minute before Freeman spoke, his head was making small movements as he said, 'The old bloke wasn't lying then, it wasn't drunken fantasy. But . . . but he said Gallagher was after you that night . . . Didn't you see him?'

Freddie's reply was quick and sharp. 'No. No.'

Freeman drew himself up in the chair and, leaning forward, he said, 'And that Spanish-looking girl, Maggie's ward, she's Gallagher's daughter?'

'No, no; as I said, she's not. She's the daughter of a sea captain.'

'Oh, aye. Yes, yes. Well now, would you believe that? . . . But haven't you left yourself open telling me all this? What would Maggie say?'

'Under the circumstances she would have done the same as me. The fact that you didn't write that letter proves somebody else did, and apparently they're not only on to me but also on to those I was mixed up with as a boy. So, have you any ideas?'

Freeman thought for a moment; then he said,

'Your one-time friends, the Harpers. You don't throw a lass over and get off with a black eye and bruised ribs. The bully boy Mick came to me and told me that, years ago, on the night Gallagher went missing, his dad saw you and Maggie leaving a sculler, and Maggie was hugging a pile of stuff to her. And what he suggests now is that it was very profitable stuff.'

'It was the child.'

'Yes, I can believe that now. But to return to this letter business. I'll admit I'm more troubled now than when you first entered the room, because I could have dealt with you and the blackmail I thought you were hatching. Strange, isn't it, that we now find ourselves on the same side as we were years ago, in fact, before Maggie took you under her wing?'

Freddie did not speak his thoughts on this matter, but he said, 'What evidence d'you think they'll need before they attempt to pick me up?'

'Oh, it would have to be pretty strong. Of course, if they have knowledge of the transaction of the stones it could be any time, because, like me, they'll think if you had three, then you had the lot, but unlike me, they might not be convinced by your strange tale of finding them in the muck of your trouser pocket.' He scratched the side of his chin now, saying musingly, 'I wonder where that lot got to? I'd give quite a bit to find out. But now this is the question: where do I stand? If you are picked up are you going to tell them my part in it?'

Freddie stared at Freeman and he knew that it would be unwise to make an enemy of this man: he mightn't be a good friend but he'd be a damn bad enemy. And so he said, 'That wouldn't do me any good. I could say a man, a stranger, gave me the package and the instructions.'

'That would be wise.' But the tone in which this was said and the inference caused Freddie's natural repugnance to come out in a flash, as he said, 'But don't take that as weakness, Mr Freeman, because believe this, I'm not afraid of you.'

A slow smile spread over Freeman's face, and he gave a short laugh as he said, 'No, you're not; and you're not telling me anything I don't already know. I've always realised that from when you were a nipper. But, as I've already indicated' – and now he almost voiced Freddie's thoughts – 'I can be a tolerable friend but a very bad enemy. Anyway, we'll certainly keep in touch after this.'

Freddie didn't confirm this statement but, rising abruptly, he said, 'Good-day to you, Mr Freeman.' then he went from the room, and as he did so he admitted to himself that he was now more troubled going out than when he came in, for whoever had sent that letter to the customs wanted him out of the way for some reason. The question was, who and why?

10

Maggie stayed in bed for five days, and the rest seemed to have done her good, for now she was up and in the sitting-room and apparently free from pain; and during this time Belle's suitor had made two visits.

The first and very brief one was on the day following Freddie's meeting with Freeman, his purpose being to ask formally for Belle's hand in marriage. Maggie duly gave her consent and he put a ring on Belle's finger, kissed the palm of her hand, and then her lips, to which she had not really responded even though it filled her with excitement, because this was love, a different love that aroused emotions that were new to her and more than a little disturbing.

But the second time he called things were very different. He had come in a hired cab accompanied by a servant bearing not only a large basket of fruit and a bunch of hot-house grown flowers for Maggie, but for Belle, a large box of crystallised sweets and a bottle of exclusive French perfume. He had also brought with him an invitation from his grandmother that they should all go to tea, not to his Newcastle home but to the house across the water, just as soon as Miss Hewitt was able to travel.

Maggie was up from her bed and sitting beside the fire in her bedroom, Belle and her future husband were alone in the sitting-room. Freddie was at work.

And now Marcel kissed her. He began with a peck

on her nose; then he kissed her brow, her eyes, her cheeks, and lastly her lips, and this time, and for the first time, her arms went about him and she held him almost as tightly as he held her. And when at last their faces parted, they stared at each other, their eyes bright, and when huskily he said, 'I . . . I can't believe that you love me, Belle. Over the last few days I've had to stop myself from dashing down and begging you to say it. You haven't yet said it in words, but now I know that you do love me, don't you?'

And to this she answered, 'Yes. Oh, yes, Marcel, I love you. From the moment I first saw you when you led me into the dance, I liked you. And, you know, Aunt Maggie says that the best way to start loving is to like. Do you like me?'

His head went back and he laughed, 'Oh no, I don't like you, I love you and I adore you, and I know I can't live without you and I want you for myself alone; no one else in the world has to have any part of you. That is how much I love you. As for liking you, well, can one love without liking?'

'Aunt Maggie says you can.'

'Your Aunt Maggie is a very wise woman, and I can say I like her, I like her very much but I don't love her. Well now' – his head was tilted slightly to the side – 'it wouldn't be right, would it?'

They were both laughing now. Her head had dropped onto his shoulder and his arms drew her tightly into him again; and what he said now and very quietly was, 'We must be married soon, very soon.'

Her head jerked up. 'Oh! Marcel, we've only just become engaged, there'll be so much to do. The wedding . . . well, there's a lot of arrangements.'

'Do you want a lot of fuss, all the parade?'

'Oh no.' The statement was firm but not emphatic.

'Then it could be simple and soon by special licence.'

She withdrew from his arms and turned from him, saying, 'I don't think Aunt Maggie would agree to . . . well, rushing things.'

He turned her towards him again. 'Your Aunt Maggie, as you call her, my dear girl, is a very sick woman. You know that, don't you?'

She made no reply, only her eyes widened as she looked into his, and he went on, 'I feel sure that she would like to see you settled, happily settled, while she's able to.'

'What makes you think she's a very sick woman, Marcel?'

'Simply because, the other day when I was here, I had a talk with Jinny. Her prognosis wasn't good.'

In her heart she knew herself that the prognosis wasn't good, but when it was voiced it filled her with fear, and already she could feel the loss. Of a sudden she thought of Freddie and how he must be feeling now, and what would happen to him if she should die, for die she would.

When she voiced her thoughts, saying, 'Freddie will be devastated when anything happens to her. He thinks the world of her and he owes her so much,' he stared at her silently for a moment, then said slowly, 'Freddie's a man and he has a mother of his own and a father and a brother and sisters, he won't be alone.'

'Yes, you're right, Marcel. And I, too, love Freddie.'

'*Don't say that.*'

She was actually startled, for now he was gripping her arms and saying, 'From now on I never want you to say you love any man but me.' But almost as quickly his manner changed and, laughing gently now, he said, 'Don't look like that. Isn't it natural? I must warn you I'll be a very jealous husband.'

'I'll never give you reason to be jealous of me, Marcel, never.'

'You promise that?'

'Yes, I promise that.' She, too, was smiling now as if it were a joke.

Almost as soon as the tap came on the door it was opened and Jinny stood there, saying, 'The cabman wants to know, sir, if he's still to wait? Your servant's in the kitchen, but the cabman wouldn't come in, not to have a drink. He's a surly bloke, he wants to get off.'

Marcel had swung round and was looking down the room at Jinny, and it was evident he was about to make a sharp retort, but then, on a laugh, he said, 'Tell him I'll be there in a moment,' and, turning to Belle again, he said, 'That's the last time I'll come to see you by cab. I'll be here tomorrow again. I want to talk to ... Aunt Maggie about future arrangements.'

'Marcel.'

'Yes, my darling?'

'Will you also have a word with Freddie? Because you see, Freddie ...'

'Yes, yes, I know; you owe such a lot to Freddie too. All right, anything you say, I'll have a word with Freddie. I'll say, please, sir, I want to marry your adopted daughter within the month.'

'Oh no, no.'

'Well, within two months.'

'Oh, Marcel, it couldn't be arranged in ...'

'My dear, dear one, it could be arranged within the next two or three days if necessary.' He now swiftly pulled her into his arms and his kiss was so

283

breathtaking that when he released her she was left gasping. And now turning from her and in an almost boyish fashion he ran from the room.

Freddie had never known what it was to experience the feeling of fear since the night he had been chased by Gallagher, then witnessed his end. Of course, he had been worried when the Harpers got at him, but the fear that was filling him now was twofold. The main one was concerning Maggie and her illness, which he couldn't believe was fatal because here she was going about on her pins like a lintie. And for the last three days she had been down at the office ordering everybody about and disproving the rumour that she was on her last legs. But the other fear was a niggling growing fear and it was gathering momentum now as he looked at John.

John had asked his employers for leave to take a journey in the middle of the week across the water to see his brother. He said it was important, and he was saying so now as he stood in the back room of Maggie's office. 'I thought I'd better come, Freddie . . . I mean, as Cissy said, although they weren't in any kind of uniform they were officials. You know, she's cute, and she said she could smell them a mile off and the way they talked. Well, they wanted to know if we owned the cottage, and she bawled at them and said, "Own the cottage! We pay two shillings and tenpence a week and it's kept off me husband's wages. You get nothin' for nothin' these days." You know how Cissy goes on. It was then they asked if I got help from me brother? Wasn't he well off? And Cissy came back at them on that and said, "Why should we expect help from him? He's workin' like the rest of us for his livin'." Then one of them, she said, laughed, and said, "Oh, but he lives pretty comfortably; I would have thought he would have looked after his own." At this she had said, "What the hell d'you want, the pair of you? If you want to know anything more, go up to the estate, me husband's workin' there. Who are you anyway?" she had asked. And one of them replied. "We are making some enquiries about some lost property." And to that she said, "Well, what the hell d'you expect to find here? Would you like to dig up the garden?" They then went away laughing, she said,' He now paused before ending, 'What's it all about, Freddie? Are you in trouble?'

'No, no, John, not any more than I was when I was a runner. It all goes back to then.'

'No! never.'

'Oh, yes, yes. There was a lot of stuff went missing presumably, and they're still looking for it. I might as well tell you there's somebody determined to get me one way or the other. They sent, you know, one of those anonymous letters to the customs and excise lot and this is what started it off. It's nearly sixteen years now since that all happened.'

'Oh, time means nothing to the polis or to the excise. They're like that sayin' about the elephant, they never forget. Well, I must be off; I said I would be away two hours. I'll have to put it in the night. By! they get their pound of flesh, don't they?'

'I thought you liked it across there.'

'It's a job, Freddie, it's a job. I like gardening, but when you're under an old fella like Bainbridge you get the muck and the grubbing jobs and he gets the smiles and the thanks for keeping the garden so lovely. D'you know somethin'?' He laughed now. 'She complained, the mistress, because she saw a blade of grass sticking up atween the paving stones.'

'Never!' Freddie was smiling too.

'It's a fact. Bainbridge took me almost by the scruff of the neck and bent me over that slab, saying, "Look there! That's annoyed the mistress."' He started to giggle now. 'Me eyes were on a level with his bloated middle and I had a job to restrain me fist from diggin' it in.' When he turned to go he said wryly, 'If you've got a horde put away, Freddie, I wouldn't mind risk sharing it.'

Freddie thumped him on the back, saying, 'Same cell in the House of Correction?'

'Aye . . . aye, that's where we'll likely end. Goodbye, lad.'

'Goodbye, John; and thanks for comin'.'

'Freddie.'

'Aye?'

'Be careful. Ma worries about you. Although you've been in clover all these years she still worries over you.'

'I'm a big lad now, John. I've been a big lad for a long, long time. Go on with you. You've got plenty to worry about without puttin' me on your books. And keep those flags clean; don't annoy the missis.'

The office to himself, Freddie sat at his desk and asked himself what was going to happen next? It felt as if a web was closing around him, a web of no silken threads, rather of steel hawsers. Since talking to Freeman he had racked his brains as to who might want him out of the way. He dismissed the Harpers: not one of them could write; although, like old Mr Wheatley they could have got someone to write the letters for them. That was a point . . .

Maggie had left early and when he arrived home he didn't tell her what had transpired with John, but she in turn had something to tell him. 'He's wanting to rush things,' she said. 'And she's more than half in agreement with him. All right, all right, all right' –

286

her finger was wagging again – 'I know what you're thinking and your thoughts are the same as mine, I might as well tell you now. But she's young and headstrong and, as we've found out before, she's amenable up to a point only. Remember when she was fourteen and I wanted to move her from that school to what I thought was one of higher standard: she went missing for a day, and then she told me that if I insisted on sending her to this place she would just walk out again, and she would have done. So, we've both got to go steady and meet her half-way. And another thing, about this invitation across the water to that house. I could no more go into that house where he had lived than I could sprout wings and fly. You mightn't know it, Freddie, but I have nightmares still about that business. Many's the time I wake up in a cold sweat 'cos I can see him goin' down.' When she put her hand across her eyes he immediately went over to her to allay her feelings and said, 'As I've said before, it was either him, or you and me and her, because he certainly would have done for me with the child in me arms, he would have swiped me into the river, I knew that. Then you being a witness to it, you would have gone after me. It was self-preservation, so don't let it worry you. I had thought you had put it out of your mind.'

She smiled wanly at him. 'You don't put a thing like that out of your mind, lad. You take a life and the loss of it is with you for the rest of your days, be the victim good, bad, or indifferent. Anyway, you'll have to go over with her yourself.'

'*Not on your life.*' He was on his feet now. 'Remember the fear in me about that man, well, believe it or not, like you it still comes back at times. It was as if he was two different beings: one minute he was an

287

ordinary man, the next an evil devil. It showed in his face. And –' He turned about now and although he lowered his tone, he hissed, 'And that fella's that man's son. There was a doubt about Belle's parentage but there's certainly no doubt about his, and that's why I'm not happy.'

'Oh, I don't think you need worry on that score. He seems a nice enough fellow in his own way, and he's more than likely taken after his mother's side.'

'Well, I don't care which side he's taken after, I'm not going across there. She goes on her own.' And with this, he stalked out of the room.

11

Belle went across the river on her own. Freddie put her into a hire keel at the quay, and she was met on the Shields side by Marcel himself. He it was who handed her up to the quay and led her to the waiting carriage. The driver, in livery, placed a footstool for her to mount; and then they were sitting side by side bowling through Shields.

Holding her hand tightly in his now, he asked, 'Excited?'

'Yes, very.'

'Then you're not alone; I've hardly been able to contain myself for days. As I said to Grandmama, it won't be like showing you your future home, it's like bringing you home, to the house where you were born. It's amazing, isn't it?'

She remained silent. Yes, it was amazing. She had lain awake half the night thinking about it. You read stories that dealt with such tales but you knew they were the fanciful imaginings of the writer. Yet she had been and still was the main figure in this fanciful tale which was not fanciful at all but made up of stark reality.

She had realised over the past few weeks that her eyes had only of late been opened to reality. She traced this revelation back to when Maggie told her about a man who had been found dead in an alley-way down at the Low Lights. His death was the result of foul play, but the culprit had not been discovered. The poor man had left a wife, and nine children all under eleven years old. They had been previously classed as a lucky family for they had managed to rear all but one child; now, however, they were all in the poor house. Maggie had been distressed about this.

That was reality, as Maggie had pointed out to her. And when the fishing fleet came into port with hardly enough herring among them to fill two creels and all those men had mouths to feed, that too was reality.

There was a lot of reality about, and she was just wakening up to it and realising more every day how sheltered she had been by that wonderful woman and that more than wonderful man who was now causing her pain, because she knew, no matter how he acted, he hadn't taken to Marcel.

Of course, when she used her reason on this matter it was understandable. He had known his dreadful father, the man who would have definitely murdered her had he had his own way.

Yet here was Marcel looking into her eyes, his face soft and beautiful . . . and he was beautiful. She had seen a number of pretty men but Marcel's looks went beyond that, he was beautiful.

He was saying, 'You'll find Grandmama ensconced on her chaise-longue; she doesn't get about very much these days, but' – he leant towards her – 'between you and me she loves being waited on . . . she's been waited on all her life, spoilt. I've told her that . . . you'll like her, and she'll love you as I do.' She was in his arms now and he was kissing her long and hard until the carriage, going over a rutted stretch of road rocked them both forward and almost onto the other seat, and they laughed like children.

'Where are we now?' She looked out of the window.

'Oh, entering the salubrious part of the town,

Westoe village. There used to be great fields between the village and the town proper but they're building like mad now all over the place. Still, I doubt if they'll get any further.'

'They're lovely houses.'

'Wait till you see yours.' He turned her to him again. 'Of course you won't remember anything of it, although if you did they would be pretty ghastly memories. I can recall when I first saw it I thought it was a dreadful place, so dark and dingy. But Grandmama performed her usual miracle with houses, she had it almost stripped bare inside, walls taken down, rooms extended, and then beautifully decorated. She's an artist of sorts is Grandmama, very clever in many ways. Oh yes, in many ways.'

He turned now and looked out of the window, and when he didn't speak for some minutes she said, 'Marcel.' And she had to repeat his name before he turned to her, his lids blinking, and she couldn't stop herself from saying, 'What is it? You look so sad.' She could find no other word to express the look on his face.

'Sad? Nonsense!' And then he added, 'Ten minutes more and we'll be there. My dear —' he took her face between his hands and there was a deep emotion in his voice as he said, 'You are so lovely, breathtaking. I'll soon be the envy of every man in the world.'

She did not contradict him for it was lovely to hear someone talk like this to her. No one had ever done so before. At times Freddie had teased her about her looks: when she had put on something new and asked him, 'How do I look?' he had pursed his lips and put his head on one side, studied her, then said, 'Passable, miss, passable.' But then Freddie hadn't been looking at her through a lover's eyes . . .

When the carriage drew up on the drive in front of

the house and she stepped out of it, she stood and gazed about her. She had tried to imagine the house but her imagination had fallen short of what she was looking at now. The house was so much bigger, built of warm pinkish stone, with deep mullion windows and two tall stone pillars holding up the portico over the front door. His hand on her elbow, he led her up the three shallow steps to where a servant in green livery bowed slightly towards them, but Marcel Birkstead gave him no recognition. However, when a middle-aged woman came across the hall towards them and said, 'Good-day, miss. Allow me to take your cloak,' he said to her, 'Is Grandmama upstairs, Cummings?'

'No, sir. She insisted on coming down into the drawing-room.'

'Oh, that's good.' Then in an offhand manner he made a small motion with his head towards the woman, saying, 'This is Grandmama's maid.'

'How d'you do?'

'Very well, ma'am, thank you.'

'Come along, dear.' He again had his hand on her elbow, and she hadn't really any time to take in the splendour of the hall, only that it was beautifully warm and that the warmth came from a great wood fire in a recessed fireplace at the far end.

She would have liked to stand and look about her, because no matter how it had changed this was the hall that Freddie had carried her across and amazed the two women by the sight of her.

They were now entering the drawing-room, and her first impression of it was that everything was blue from the ceiling to the carpet.

He was leading her now towards where a lady was propped up on a chaise-longue set some distance from but opposite another huge fire, and the next moment she was standing looking down into a face so delicately skinned it appeared like that of a china doll, and the round blue eyes helped the impression. And some part of her dared to be slightly amused when she realised that the lady was wearing a wig, because it was such a young looking wig in a beautiful brown shade, the hair lying in soft waves about the ears and supported on the crown by two pink bows.

Belle's impression of her was that of an elderly child, if that could have been possible; but only until the elderly child opened its mouth, and the voice that said, 'Well, my dear, so here you are,' gave the lie to the appearance, for even in those words it conveyed a note of authority. And it went on, 'And I can see the reason for all the fuss. Do sit down, my dear. Did you have a pleasant journey?'

As Marcel Birkstead placed a chair for Belle she answered, 'Yes, it was very pleasant.'

The old lady was staring at her now and her chin was moving in small jerks as if in agreement with her thoughts. And then she said, 'Ring for tea, Marcel.'

Belle watched him go to the side of the fireplace and pull on a thick red betasselled cord that apparently disappeared into the ceiling. Then returning to his grandmother's side, he said, 'You're very naughty to come downstairs, you know that;' and she glanced at him sideways for a moment, then said, 'My dear boy, I have never been naughty in my life, and you know that.' When he laughed she laughed and Belle smiled.

At this moment and for the first time that she could remember in her young life she was feeling very ill at ease. She had imagined that the training she had received from Miss Rington had prepared her for all occasions: she knew how to enter a drawing-room, and how to leave it; she knew the correct greeting with which to address a lady or a gentleman; but she knew now that that training hadn't taken into consideration an occasion such as this one, for she doubted if Miss Rington had ever met such a personage as she was now sitting beside.

The tea must have been ready and waiting, for there came a tap on the door and the butler entered carrying a heavily laden tray, and behind him a maid, in a grey uniform and wearing a tiny white frilled apron and a cap to match, pushed a trolley.

When the servants had departed the old lady said, 'Are you used to pouring tea, my dear?' And Belle's answer was rather stiff: 'Yes, quite used to it, madam,' she said.

The delicate pencilled eyebrows moved upwards; the head inclined towards her, which was permission that she should go ahead and pour now . . .

After two cups of highly scented china tea the old lady said, 'Do eat a sweetmeat. I know it isn't usual to eat with tea but I have never stuck to rules, have I, Marcel?' She turned, as though for confirmation, towards her grandson, and he, smiling at her, said, 'No, Grandmama; you have never stuck to rules. You are a rule unto yourself.'

She returned his smile as if he had paid her a compliment . . .

The tea over, the bell again rung, the servants having taken away the trolley and the tray, the old lady turned to Marcel, saying, 'I understand Yarrow thinks that Prince's leg has worsened. Would you like to go and see for yourself.'

It was a veiled order and he smiled at her, saying, 'Yes, of course, Grandmama; but you could have got me out of the way with a less subtle excuse.'

The old lady's lips puckered, her hand wagged at him and he went out laughing. And now as if she had shed the wig and the enamelled face and definitely her autocratic manner, she held out her hand towards Belle, saying, 'One can never be oneself in front of men, old or young, relations or not. Now, my dear, come and sit closer to me.'

Belle drew her chair to the side of the couch and, taking the extended hand, she waited while the round blue eyes remained fixed on her in silence for a moment. Now, the voice low, the old lady said, 'Let me say how glad I am that Marcel has chosen you to be his wife. I have never felt happy with any of his acquaintances before. But you, my dear, with this very, very, strange connection with this house, and the story is strange, isn't it?' She did not wait for an answer, but went on, 'I found it at first quite improbable until I remembered the man Gallagher, and how I was against the marriage of my daughter from the first. Yet . . . yet, it must be said, that he loved her and loved her dearly. And such was she that she made a different man of him during the short time they were together. But recalling that he had no use for his own son, my dear, dear Marcel, it is understandable that when his second wife, your mother, did what she evidently did, his reaction should be horrific, even to the extent of destroying you. But it seems, and I have been thinking a lot these past few days, that destiny has turned the wheel and that you should come back into this house, your rightful place. Of course, my dear, as you see it now, it wasn't then, because from my daughter's death he had let it go to rack and ruin. And your mother must have found it so dreary. No wonder she sought consolation elsewhere. But, my dear' – Belle's hand was being shaken up and down now – 'I want

295

you to promise me one thing. You see, I love my grandson very much. He has been for the past twenty-one years or so my life-spring, and he is very precious to me, and I would do anything to bring him happiness. So, my dear, will you promise in a way to take my place, because you know' – she now took her free hand and, in a long sweep that started from her brow, drew it slowly down the shape of her body underneath the silken cover – 'I am a very old lady, but, as I said, I want a promise that you will always love him and care for him . . . yes and care for him as it says in the marriage service, in sickness and in health.'

The blue eyes were staring straight into Belle's again, waiting for an answer, and Belle, her lips trembling slightly, said, 'Yes; yes of course I promise, because, I . . . I love him very much.'

'Oh, my dear, my dear, that is so good to hear. And he loves you. He adores you and he will never leave you, I can assure you of that, except when he may have to go to Harrogate on business. We have business interests there. Well, you know, our ancestral home, Wellindean Hall, is near there. Oh yes' – she nodded at the expression on Belle's face – 'the estate is now in my elder brother's hands. The old part of the house was two hundred years old when I was born there; it has been added to since; and our land covers quite an area.' She now lay back on her satin pillow and, releasing Belle's hand, she went on, 'I often, oh yes, so very often think of the old days, so wonderful yet so sad. My husband died in the hunting field, such a wasted life. I had no one else but my daughter. As you know' – she slanted her eyes towards Belle now – 'families don't always agree, and when my dear child married Gallagher I was devastated, and more so by her death; but then God has a way of recompensing the ills of life: Marcel came into my charge and I seemed to be born again to a new form of happiness.' Then the old lady made a movement that startled Belle: she gripped her hand again, and tightly, and as she leaned towards her, her whole expression was changed. It was no longer that of the wax doll nor yet of the kindly old woman that had been talking for the past few minutes, it was a face suffused with dark anger and hate, and the next words conveyed this: 'You know something, child, I hate the very name of that man, Gallagher. When I think of what he has done to my . . . Oh dear God in heaven!' She now fell back on her pillow, her hand to her throat.

The action brought Belle to her feet, apprehensively crying, 'Oh! madam, are you ill? Shall I call . . .?'

'No, no child; I'm all right. Forget this. I'm all right. I'm all right. Ah, here comes Marcel.' The door was opening now, and as if the sun had suddenly come out and shone on her face her expression was now as it had been when Belle first saw her.

'Ah!' she was saying; 'And how did you find Prince?'

'Not very good, I'm afraid, Grandmama; the leg is still swollen, the sinews strained. I think I'll get the horse doctor to him later, although I doubt he'll be able to do much more than Yarrow, as we've found in the past. Well, have you had your little chat, both of you?'

'Chat? Why should we chat? We have talked; only useless feather-brain women chat.'

'As you say, Grandmama, as you say.' He was smiling now at Belle, and she at him; she was feeling quite at ease. There were one or two things she might have questioned but they were of no importance. She knew that eventually she would come and live in this

297

house and that she would have a champion, if she ever needed one, in this wonderful old lady who had so many sides to her, almost like a play actress, one who, she imagined, must have been very beautiful.

'Now I'm going to show Belle round the domain. Where do you suggest we start, Grandmama?'

'In the servants' quarters. This will give the lie to the popular belief that the gentry house their servants in less comfortable abodes than they do their cattle.'

'Oh, Grandmama.'

'Well, that is what the common people think; and they're right, perfectly right, for their kind are housed in hovels. My father was the first to point this out to me. And by the way, introduce her to the staff because she'll be ruling them . . . er – one day.' She was nodding at Belle now; then as Belle was moving away with Marcel, the old lady said, 'Strange, you don't blush.'

'Excuse me, madam?' Belle had turned and inclined her head forwards.

'I said, you don't blush. You've just got to mention the word marriage to some young girls and they blush and go all fey. Sickens me. I'm glad you don't blush.'

In the hall they both stopped for a moment and Marcel said, 'She's a character, isn't she?'

'She is indeed.'

'She's taken to you. I knew she would; but she has, and in a big way.' He caught at her arm and pressed it to his side as they walked across the hall, and he said softly, 'I'm so happy, Belle, so very, very happy,' which made her want to turn and fling her arms around his neck and say, 'It's impossible for you to be as happy as I am at this moment.'

They had reached a swing door, and as he went to

push it open he said, 'We haven't a large staff, thirteen all told, but they have been with us for years; in fact, Benedict the butler started in our family service when he was six; he is now in his sixties. And Grant, Alan Grant, who is my man, is Benedict's nephew. He is comparatively new: he joined the service at the same time as I went to stay with Grandmama, that's over twenty-one years ago. He was footman then; later he took me on.' He smiled now. 'Then there's Grandmama's maid, Sarah Cummings. You saw her in the hall. Oh, you'll see a lot of Sarah.' He now pushed open the door and they entered a small hall from which a number of doors went off. Outside one, he said, 'Now here we are,' and opened it and she entered the kitchen, and a small round little woman was dipping her knee to her as Marcel said, 'This is Mrs Welch, our cook.'

Ada Welch said, 'Ma'am.'

'And this is Anderson.' He pointed towards a woman well into her thirties. 'Anderson is the kitchen-maid. And there's Summers. She has something to do with the scullery.' He laughed then looked about him before asking, 'Where are Chambers and Everton, Cook?'

'Mary, sir, will be upstairs, and Linda, sir, in the dining-room.'

'Oh, yes, yes.' Then turning to Belle, he said, 'Now, as Grandmama dictated, I shall show you their quarters.'

Belle hesitated just a second. He had not asked if it was convenient he should go into their quarters, but was walking away now towards the far door, and so, before following him, she turned and smiled at the cook and the kitchen-maid saying, 'Thank you,' then added, 'It's a lovely kitchen you have, and so beautifully clean.'

The little woman's knee went deeper now, and she said, 'Thank you, ma'am. Thank you very much.' And Rosy Anderson smiled broadly at her and dipped her knee almost to the ground and gave her a nod.

The servants' quarters were indeed different from those she had glimpsed in the school where two maids had slept in one bed, and that had taken up most of the room. There had been no wardrobe or dressing-table, only hooks on the back of the door. She had told Maggie about the conditions, and Maggie had said, 'Oh, child, that's the usual attitude: What are servants anyway? They're not human beings.'

When she now remarked to Marcel, 'You don't address them by their Christian names?' He turned sharply to her, saying, 'Use the servants' Christian names? No! No! Except Sarah, and that's because Grandmama calls her by her Christian name. But for the others, no, no; that would be too familiar.'

'Oh, Marcel.' Her laugh was a little derisory and, realising that he was displeased, she quickly endeavoured to alleviate his displeasure by saying, 'But you see, of course, how would I know anything about it; we've only had Jinny to see to the house.'

'Yes, that is right: how would you know anything about it?' He was walking ahead of her. 'This leads to the dining-room,' he said.

After the dining-room he showed her the morning-room, the library, the study, and the conservatory before mounting the stairs to a small gallery, where he said, 'I think this is the part of the house Grandmama left untouched when she made the alterations, the stairs and this.'

From the gallery two corridors led to seven bedrooms, all beautifully furnished, and three of them

300

very large. His grandmama's room, Belle saw, was like some pictures she had seen of grand boudoirs, silk lace and French furniture abounding.

They were now standing in another large room, at the end of one corridor and with windows on two sides looking into the garden. He turned to her and, pulling her into his arms, he held her almost fiercely while saying, 'This will be our room. This will be our abode for the rest of our lives. Do you know that?'

'It's a lovely room.'

'And you are lovely, and you will adorn it and I shall adore you.'

She mightn't have blushed, but a heat had come over her body and it wasn't all pleasurable because a little pocket of her mind was saying, It's strange, the way he talks, Freddie would never say things like this; while at the same time she wanted to return the fierceness of his hold and the hard pressure of his lips as they traced every feature of her face. But when his hands began to move beneath her shoulder blades, she drew in a long breath and, putting her hands on his chest, she pressed him from her, endeavouring to make the action gentle even though she was having to use quite a lot of strength in order to disengage herself.

He was standing straight-faced now looking at her.

'You don't love me.'

'Oh. Oh, Marcel, how can you say . . .'

'You don't love me in the same way as I love you. It would be impossible. Perhaps it's just as well: we would burn up.' He now drew her hands in between his own and gently placed them on his chest and, softly, he said: 'We must be married soon, Belle, for so many reasons. As you see, my grandmama is an old lady and, as you know, your . . . Aunt Maggie . . .

301

is an ill woman. What would happen if either of them should die? Decorum would demand that we put off the wedding, for how long? Oh, it would be torture. I'm going to come across and talk with Miss Maggie.'

Tentatively she said, 'You . . . you must speak to Freddie too.'

'Freddie! Why Freddie? Always Freddie. I don't see why, darling.'

'Oh . . . well, you know the whole story: I wouldn't be here now if it wasn't for Freddie.'

'You might have been, and my father too, if it hadn't been for Freddie.'

She stepped back from him. 'What do you mean?'

'Well, as I see it, if he hadn't run off with you my father wouldn't have chased you and somebody wouldn't have caught him and done him to death. If he had left you where you were things would have worked out.'

'In that!' She now pointed upwards; then put her hand to her head, saying, 'I'd . . . I'd forgotten about that room. Is it still there?'

'No,' his voice was harsh, 'it isn't still there. It was stripped and blocked up.'

'Marcel! Marcel!' – she put her hand out towards him – 'Don't be angry. Please don't be angry. But you know I wouldn't have survived in there, or out of it. He . . . he must have been so vicious against my mother for what she did that he would have taken his revenge on me, as Freddie said.'

'All right. All right, my dear, let us forget about it . . . about Freddie – yes, about Freddie – and everything. Come on, and I'll show you the rest of the place, and outside. But you must wrap up because the wind is cutting.'

He had reached the bedroom door when he stopped and turned her towards him once again, saying, 'I suppose you've realised by now that I'm a very jealous individual. I can't bear the thought of any man, father, brother, guardian or whatever capacity having anything to do with you. In the olden days I would have taken a sword and run them all through one after the other.' He was smiling widely now, and she smiled, too, tolerantly as she said, 'Oh, Marcel, you must have a very poor opinion of yourself if you think that I could even look at anyone else or think of anyone else when you are in my life.'

Gently he brought her hand and cupped it against his cheek. It was such a gentle gesture that it warmed her heart and definitely decided her that when she returned home she would have a firm talk with Freddie and Maggie and tell them that she, too, wished to be married soon.

12

On the Wednesday following Easter Sunday they were married in South Shields by special licence in a church of no consequence except that it practised Christianity. The same kind of ceremony could have been performed in North Shields or, as Maggie wanted, at any of the fine churches in Newcastle. But no, it had to be in this little church because it should happen that Mrs Birkstead was acquainted with the parson who happened to be the grandson of a friend of hers. At least, that is why she and, apparently, Marcel Birkstead had insisted that the ceremony should take place there.

It was raining heavily and blowing a gale. The weather had reverted to that experienced in the early part of the year; the church felt cold and smelt damp.

After the opening words of the ceremony: 'Dearly beloved, we are gathered together here . . .' Freddie asked himself once again how all this had come about. And why the rush? But more so, how could he bear to see her go to this fellow of all people . . . But to this there were really two answers . . .

'Therefore if any man can show any just cause . . .'

Well, he knew of a just cause. This man was Gallagher's son: that was just cause enough surely. No; that alone couldn't stop the wedding. But the other impediment . . . How could he name it? Only that he knew there was something wrong somewhere, and it was with this man, as charming as he was. And oh aye, he could be charming; it ran off him like hot butter at times. But there were other times when, taken off his guard, 'Those whom God hath joined together let no man put asunder . . .'

. . . It was done. It was done. And he didn't know how he would be able to bear it. He had kissed her pale cheek and her beautiful eyes had beseeched him, Be happy for me, Freddie, please. But he knew he would never be happy in his life again, nor know peace, because he had lost her and he was soon to lose Maggie. And God, that would be another kind of agony altogether. How many agonies could the mind tolerate?

Mrs Birkstead had declared herself too frail to come to the church, but it was arranged that they all return to The Towers and join her for a wedding breakfast, after which the happy couple, and it was evident to all eyes that they were happy in each other, would take the train to London where they were to spend their honeymoon.

Why weren't they going abroad to France or Italy? That seemed to be the pattern of young wealthy married couples these days, and Belle had even put this to Marcel. But no; he had pointed out that his grandmama was very frail and he didn't want to be too far away from her. And of course she understood.

But now, standing outside the church, Maggie said quietly to Belle, 'My dear, I won't be able to attend the wedding breakfast. I feel I must ask Freddie to take me home.'

'Oh! Aunt Maggie. Oh! do try.'

'My dear' – Maggie forced a smile to her pain-filled face – 'you wouldn't want me to cause an upheaval at your breakfast, now would you? I'm all right . . . really, but I feel I must get home and rest.

305

I'll be anxious though to hear from you. Send me a letter. You will, won't you?'

'Oh! Aunt Maggie. Aunt Maggie.' Belle was holding her tightly. 'I hate to leave you like this. I feel . . .' She didn't go on to say that she felt she shouldn't go away, that she was sorry it had all happened so quickly.

'Oh, Aunt Maggie, this is unfortunate.' Marcel's voice was full of solicitude, especially when he added, 'I tell you what we'll do, we'll come across and have a bite with you. My grandmother will understand.'

'You'll do no such thing. Now get yourselves away, and be sure to give our apologies to Mrs Birkstead. Goodbye, my dear.' She turned again to Belle who now hastily put in, 'We'll only stay a week.'

'Don't be silly. Go on with you, girl! Freddie' – Maggie turned to him – 'let us away.'

On this, he led her to the hired cab that had brought them to the church, and he helped her in, and was about to follow her but turned and looked to where Belle was looking at him, and she would have certainly made towards him but her husband was now firmly holding her arm.

After taking his seat beside Maggie he put his arm about her and pressed her gently to his side, but neither of them spoke; nor did they when they left the cab and took the ferry across the river. But once on the quay there, he said to her, 'Would you like to go to the office and rest before you take the road up the hill?' And she replied quietly, 'No; I can manage.'

When at last they entered the house Jinny greeted them with, 'Well, it's over then. It didn't take all that long.'

Freddie made no reply, but Maggie said, 'No; it didn't take all that long, Jinny; but how long it'll last, God only knows.' And she added to herself, And I won't be here to see it.

306

In the sitting-room, she said to Freddie, 'Get me a glass of whisky, lad, a tall one.'

'You sure? Don't you think you'd better take your pills?'

She looked up at him and said quietly, 'A glass of whisky, Freddie.'

A moment later he returned to the room carrying two glasses, and as he handed one to her he said, 'Take it slowly.'

She took two or three sips from the glass before heaving a long sigh; then she lay back in the chair. 'Why is it I'm worried sick, Freddie?' she said. 'She's in love with him and he seems to dote on her. Oh yes, I'm sure he dotes on her; but in spite of that I've got this awful feeling on me.'

'You're not the only one.'

'Oh, I know that.' She nodded at him now. 'I know what you've been going through these past weeks. But it wasn't to be, and I told you that from the first. She didn't see you in that way.'

'She was never given the chance; at least, I didn't give her the chance, and I should have. I thought, being ten years older . . . but then he's nearly as old.'

'It's done now, lad, and you've got other things to think about, and deeply I should say since this latest news from Nancy. My God! who would be on to this? We know for a fact it isn't Freeman, and we know for a fact too it isn't Connie Wheatley, and, as you say, she's scared the hell out of her father; and if you ask me, I think there's good reason there because we've always reckoned they feathered their nest before that old dame turfed them out. Not that I blame them. Odd, isn't it, how we've both managed to avoid meeting her? Yet I have a vivid picture in my mind of what she's like. An old autocrat by all accounts; yet Belle says she's got another side to her altogether and they seem to get on like a house on fire. Well, she'll likely need support . . . Now why should I say that?'

Freddie looked at her, took a drink from his glass, and placed it on the table before he replied, 'For the same reason I keep asking myself questions every time I think of him. Anyway, let's forget about them for the minute, if we can; and I would suggest you get yourself to bed.'

'Oh no. As long as I'm in me own house, I'll be all right; I can trot about. And Freddie' – she held out her hand to him – 'come here.' And when he came to her side he dropped on his hunkers and took hold of her hand and her words seemed to pierce his heart as she said, 'I'm not going to pop off today or tomorrow. I know all about this trouble: I'll have me good days and me bad, but I could go on for many months yet. And you know me, if I make up me mind to do something I do it, don't I?'

He dropped his head onto the arm of her chair as he muttered, 'Oh, don't, don't Maggie, please, not today.'

'We've got to face it, lad. We both have to face it. And I want you to know that I've left everything in order. Everything I have, every penny, every off-shoot is yours. Before, I'd left half and half, but now she's settled, and money-wise she'll never want for anything. Only yesterday I altered the will, because yesterday was as near today as made no matter.'

His voice was thick and broken as he muttered, 'I don't want the money or the businesses, Maggie. Getting them would mean nothing to me. Oh no! If it would give you one extra day of life, I would give up a year of mine. I could get by without the businesses. I could take up running for a start.' Maggie remained silent for a moment while she patted his bent head. Although she really knew what he meant when he

308

denied the businesses, nevertheless the stark words saddened her somewhat; but then she gave a little laugh, saying, 'Eeh! I can see you goin' up and down that quay. You always wore boots and no stockings. Your breeches were almost up to your backside. Who they belonged to in the first place I don't know because as small as you were they were too small for you. And you wore a jacket that was too big, you had to roll the sleeves back.'

He lifted his head and looked at her through misted eyes, saying, 'You remember that jacket?'

'Oh yes, I remember that jacket. Don't you recall I once said to you, your trousers'll never trip you up but your sleeves will?'

'You said so many things to me. Jack-the-giant-killer you used to call me.'

'Yes, Jack-the-giant-killer. Funny that. I used to wonder why I was interested in you, why you appealed to me, why I envied the woman who had borne you. Yet, I ceased to envy her years ago. But you know something else, Freddie? She still holds it against me, does . . . our Jinny.'

'No, no, she doesn't.'

'Oh, yes she does, and you know it. You've had to do a lot of placating in that quarter. And it's natural. My godfathers! if I'd been your mother and anybody had tried to take you from me I would have wiped the floor with them. So I understand Jinny's feelings, always have. And later on I think you should do something for them. Get them into a better place than they're in now, and set John up in something of his own. There'll be plenty to do that.'

'Oh, Maggie, for God's sake! will you be quiet?' He got to his feet now. 'And d'you know?' He turned to her, thrusting his arm out. 'If the one who's onto me with those letters gets his way, I'll likely be along the

309

line, never mind distributing largesse to the family. Have you thought of that?'

'Yes, I have, and I've thought of this an' all: they've got nothing on you, nothing at all. A lad of ten or twelve, you were. You can tell them everything that happened, but you told Freeman you wouldn't implicate him; tell them it was a man who gave you the package. And you could even go as far as to say, yes, you found the three stones in your pocket, and yes, I sold them. No, that would give old Taylor away. But then somebody's got to be given away; you're not going to sacrifice yourself. Just stick to the fact that you didn't see Gallagher after his servant said that the excise were coming. That's all you've got to do. Anyway' – she shook her head – 'you were just a bit of a lad, not any bigger than two penn'orth of copper. If you had taken the stones you wouldn't have had the wits to keep silent about them; they would have shown up before now somewhere or another.'

'Yes, I suppose you're right, Maggie. But, nevertheless, you can understand I'm worried. Strangely enough, not so much about the polis but about who's in on this that we don't know of. And I can tell you that Freeman is worried an' all. He hasn't said so, but it's in his mind. If the writer of this letter knows about these stones he's bound to know about other transactions that happened around that time and which Freeman himself was in up to the neck. But' – he paused – 'what I can't understand is if they've been getting these letters, and I must have definitely been mentioned in them according to Nancy's friend, why haven't they shown their hand before now?'

'There's still plenty of time. They'd have to feel sure before they accused anybody; and you're no longer a little nipper of no importance, you are known as Maggie Hewitt's lad or, in some quarters, man, and somebody to be reckoned with. So don't let's look for more worries to put on our plate. I think we've got enough at the moment, don't you?'

He didn't answer her but said, 'I'll go and have a word with me mother; she'll want to know all about it.'

She noticed that for the first time he had called Jinny his mother and not his ma. Odd that. In a way it only went to prove the distance he had moved from the far end of the town.

The new worry made itself evident on the Saturday morning at eleven o'clock when Jinny opened the door to two men who asked if they could speak to Mr Musgrave. One, she faintly recognised; the other was a complete stranger. She showed them into the sitting-room.

Maggie had decided to stay in bed this morning. Freddie was down in the greenhouse in the garden, so she picked up her skirts and ran out of the back door and across the yard, through the shrubbery, over the lawn and down to the walled vegetable garden.

The door of the greenhouse was open and she could see him, and so she began to call: 'Freddie! Freddie! There's two fellas here.'

'What?' He'd come to the open doorway.

'One I seem to know, the other I don't. The one I know is from the quay, he's something down there.'

'Maggie still upstairs?'

'Aye.'

'Well, don't let on who's called yet a while.'

'Oh, she'll be ringing down 'cos she heard the bell, you know that.'

He dusted his hands, took down his coat from a

peg, put it on, buttoned up the neck of his shirt, then followed her back to the house. But before entering the sitting-room he pressed his shoulders further back, took a deep breath, then opened the door slowly and walked in. He immediately recognised one of the officers from the Custom House, but the other he hadn't seen before.

The two men were standing in front of the window and they turned but didn't move towards him, while he made for the fireplace, to stand on the hearthrug before greeting them: 'Well! gentlemen. You wish to see me?'

It was his tone that brought an exchange of glances between them; then they came forward and both of them stopped near the head of the couch, and the customs officer said, 'We would like a word with you, Mr Musgrave?'

'May I ask what about?'

'Well' – there was hesitation now in the man's voice – 'it will become clear during the course of our conversation. This is Mr Mitchum.'

Freddie refrained from replying, 'Mr Mitchum of what, the excise or the police?' Instead, he extended a hand towards the couch, saying, 'Well, if we have to have a talk we might as well sit down.'

It was evident that both Freddie's manner and his way of addressing them had taken them somewhat by surprise. One at least of the pair felt he had been misinformed about this man, and more so when Freddie had seated himself and then continued briskly, saying, 'Well now, gentlemen, let's get on with this interrogation, for it appears that is what you're here for; but the reason escapes me.'

'Well . . . sir' – the title was hesitant but nevertheless firm – 'we will have to go back a number of years to when you were a boy.'

'Yes, and what about that?'

'Now look here, Mr Musgrave.' It was the customs man speaking, his tone showing some impatience. 'It's well-known that when you were a boy you were used as a runner for a number of men who were breaking the law in bringing contraband stuff into this country at that time.'

'A runner?' Freddie's eyebrows moved upwards. 'That's simply another name for a messenger, and, yes, I ran messages for anybody who would pay me in those days. You may recollect, times were hard then for quite a large section of the people in this town, and a penny was a penny. I would have run from here to Newcastle for sixpence, but unfortunately I wasn't able to pick my clients in those days.'

The customs man was now looking down and to the side as if he was studying the carpet, and Mitchum, with a more diplomatic approach, put in, 'It is understood, sir, that on a certain night in eighteen-forty-five a certain gentleman gave you a parcel to take across the water. Is that right?'

'Look, sir, we are going back all of sixteen years. I carried parcels and notes all over this town.'

'This was a particular night, Mr Musgrave, when you were given a package that held some valuable jewellery and you went across in your little sculler.' The man smiled now. 'I saw it on the river this morning; it looks still in good fettle.'

Freddie did not take up the pleasant tone nor reference to the sculler, but said, 'I can recall a night when I was given a parcel, a small parcel, and I took it across the water and delivered it.'

'To whom did you deliver it, Mr Musgrave?'

'To a man called Gallagher who lived out at The Towers.'

Freddie knew that they were well aware of all this and that it was best to play them at their own game.

'You had taken packages to him before?'

'I don't recall. Perhaps I did; I took him messages.'

'What kind of messages?'

Freddie now put his head to one side as if he was trying to remember; then shaking his head, he said, 'Oh, they were bits of rhyme or some such. I couldn't remember back the very words I carried.'

'You know who gave you the messages to carry?' It was the customs man again.

'Now you've set me a problem.' Freddie had turned towards the man. 'You deal with the customs, did you ever know who you were looking for?'

'Yes, we had a very good idea.'

'Oh, well, that's your business; it wasn't mine as a child to remember the faces.'

'But you remember who it was that passed you the parcel to be taken across to Mr Gallagher on that particular night?'

'No, I don't.' He spat the words back at the man. 'The only thing I recall was that it was black dark,' which was true, 'and this fellow gave me a little parcel, not as big as the palm of your hand, and told me who it had to go to. But I didn't see his face.'

'Perhaps you remember his voice?'

'Oh, man' – Freddie now made himself turn his head away as if in disdain – 'asking me, a man of twenty-eight, did I remember a voice of someone who spoke to me in the dark when I was . . . what? eleven or twelve years old. Have sense.'

When he turned back again to him the customs officer's face was grim, his lips tight together, but the other man was smiling gently, and because of this it came to Freddie that this man was probably the more dangerous of the two: he was the kind that

314

wouldn't lose his temper, he would probe gently until he caused you to trip yourself up. So, addressing him bluntly, he said, 'Would you like to get to the point? Am I being accused of something?'

'No one is accusing you of anything, Mr Musgrave. We would just like some information. You see, we are not only dealing with the theft of some precious stones but we are also dealing with the murder of Mr Gallagher on that particular night.'

'Well' – there was a touch of laughter in Freddie's voice now as he cast his glance from one to the other – 'huh! you're not thinkin' that I did him in, are you? Remember, I was a kid at the time.'

'No, we are not actually thinking that you . . . did him in, but we feel you may have knowledge of what happened to him.'

'How would I know?'

'Mr Musgrave' – the pleasant man was nodding his head slowly now – 'you know quite a bit about what happened that particular night. Now, I think it would be advisable if you would come down to the town with us where we can have further discussions because, as I understand it, there was more to the event that night than the theft of jewellery, now wasn't there?'

He stared back at the man and was about to say, 'I'm comin' nowhere unless you have a warrant that states exactly why you're takin' me there,' when he heard a movement up above, which meant that Maggie was getting out of bed. She must have got it out of Jinny that there were two male visitors. Getting abruptly to his feet, which caused the two men also to rise, he said, 'Very well, I'll come with you; but only because Mag . . . Miss Hewitt isn't well and I don't want her disturbed further in any way; and I fear she's already about to join us. Would you

315

kindly wait outside? I'll be with you in a moment or so.'

At this, he hurried from the room, bounded the stairs and rushed into his own room. He put on a narrow tie that had been hanging over the back of the chair, and pulled a fresh coat from the wardrobe; then, hurrying out, he tapped on Maggie's door and called, 'I won't be long; just popping down the town.'

'Freddie! Freddie, wait!'

He didn't wait but ran down the stairs, took up his hat from the hallstand, and joined the two men on the path.

'We do appreciate your co-operation, Mr Musgrave.'

Freddie cast a sidelong glance at the suave Mitchum and again he thought, He's a clever one . . . do appreciate your co-operation.

He didn't know where they were bound for, nor did he ask, but, by the road they took, it wouldn't be the Custom House in Low Street; it was when they entered Norfolk Street he knew they were making for the Magistrates Court, and he could not help a slight tremor passing through him. He had known so many people who had passed through that court, especially after a customs raid, when the penalties were so harsh that the men wouldn't have been much worse off if they had attempted to murder someone: for what other crime were they manacled by the neck in the cellar of the Court House?

As he entered the building between the customs officer and the suave gentleman, as he was now thinking of him, he told himself: Do what Maggie said in such circumstances, play dumb.

He was guided into a small room that had a bench attached to one wall and six chairs in a row along another, and between them an oblong wooden table.

316

The customs officer placed four chairs round the table; then he left the room, and the suave gentleman indicated that Freddie should sit; then he himself sat down, but he made no attempt to open a conversation. He didn't speak until the customs officer returned with another man whom Freddie recognised immediately as the Chief Constable. For a moment he thought the man was going to give him a friendly smile, but his face retained its formal expression, and he too sat down. And it was he who first spoke. Looking at Freddie, he said, 'Ah well, now for this little chat that might straighten things up, Mr . . . er . . . Musgrave.' Then he added in a quite kindly tone, 'There's nothing to be afraid of; we're just making some enquiries.'

Before he could stop himself Freddie was slapping back: 'I am not afraid because I have nothing to be afraid of. And I would thank you to let me know what all this is about. Moreover, I would ask if you have a warrant to bring me here.'

'Oh. Oh.' The Chief Constable wagged his head. 'Don't let's talk of warrants. We just want a little conversation with you to get to the bottom of something.'

'Well, would you kindly get on with the conversation and as quickly as possible because Miss Hewitt is far from well and I wish to be at home with her.'

It was the customs officer who was now stabbing his finger at him, only to be checked by the suave gentleman, saying to him, 'Leave it. Leave it.' And he himself, turning to Freddie now, said, 'It's like this, Mr Musgrave: we will put it plainly to you, we have had information to the effect that on a night, many years ago now, you not only carried a message from, as you said, a man you didn't know, you didn't recognise, to a Mr Gallagher of The Towers, beyond

Westoe village, and which you later realised was stolen jewellery; and there is also a witness who claims to have seen you and Miss Hewitt landing on this side of the river in the dead of night with a strange bundle. But the most important point is, when did you really last see Mr Gallagher? Was it not on the South Shields dockside when he tried to prevent you taking his child?'

The man stopped talking, and Freddie stared at him, actually open-mouthed. How did he know all this? If it was old man Wheatley, he could have pieced together what had happened on yon side of the water; but he couldn't have known anything about their landing at this side, that would have come from Harper. But neither of them knew the full story, Harper very little of it except what he surmised. There was no one else . . . When a thought entered his mind he flung it aside, then to the man he said, 'I knew nothing about what happened to Mr Gallagher. You've probed so much why don't you work out the rest and find out who did him in?'

'Oh, we will find out who . . . did him in . . . never fear.'

'You've taken a long time over it.'

'Keep a civil tongue in your . . .'

Freddie now swung round towards the customs officer, crying, 'Don't tell me to keep a civil tongue in my head! You have got me here without warrant or justice note. I can get up and walk out and you can't do anything about it. So *you* please keep a civil tongue in *your* head.'

'Now, now, now!' The Chief Constable's hand was wagging now, 'Mr Musgrave, mind . . . mind your words.'

'I am minding my words, sir. You tell your subordinate here to mind his words. I am not a prisoner.'

318

'As yet.'

It looked for a moment as if Freddie would strike out at the glowering customs officer, but he gritted his teeth and returning his attention to the suave man, he said, 'You do realise that I was but a lad when all this happened? I can scarcely recall anything that took place.'

'Then you wouldn't know what happened even to a very valuable hoard of jewels that you carried across the river to Mr Gallagher?'

'*No, I wouldn't.*' Each word was emphatic. 'Anyway, what would I, a lad in my position, have done with a hoard of jewels? I would have been terrified of handling them in the first place. And who in my family or neighbours could I have trusted them to? What could they have done with them that wouldn't have landed them right here or in the House of Correction or further up still? Jewels!' He tossed his head.

'I see your point, and believe me, Mr Musgrave, I take your word for it. But unfortunately there are more serious matters to go in to. For instance, you did come across the river that night with Miss Hewitt, did you not?'

Freddie returned the man's stare but said nothing.

'All right, we will let that pass. But it has been suggested.'

'Who suggested?'

'Mr Musgrave.' The suave man's voice spoke of patience. 'And it is known that Mr Gallagher was murdered that same night.'

. . . 'And you think I murdered him? A little strip of a lad twelve years old?'

'Oh, Mr Musgrave' – the man was smiling now – 'I understand from those who remember you, you were a very spritely little strip of a lad with a lot about you, a clever mind, even in those days. You may not have done any such deed but you may be cognizant of the facts and perhaps could enlighten us as to what might have happened, I say might have happened, that brought about Mr Gallagher's death.'

Cognizant of the facts. He hadn't heard that word before but he got its meaning. Oh yes, he was that all right, and he was now feeling sick to the depths of his stomach. These fellas were clever. They had probed this far but they were stuck, and my God! they would have to remain stuck. He would have to be careful from now on of every word he ever uttered. And so, sighing, he looked at the man and said slowly, 'Cognizant or aware of, or anyway you like to put it, I've told you when I last saw Mr Gallagher. I can tell you no more and I ask you one and all' – he now cast his glance around the other men – 'can you remember back to things you did as a lad? I mean, to pinpoint things and to people you met?'

No one answered for a moment, but then the customs officer spoke, saying, 'Yes, if it was a time when there was a robbery, a murder, and an abduction. Yes, I'm sure we could all cast our memories back to that time; in fact, I'm sure it would have caused us some sleepless nights for many years after. Do you sleep well? . . .'

It was the suave man holding his hand up in the direction of the customs officer while he looked at Freddie, saying, 'I think it would be best, Mr Musgrave, if we leave the matter in abeyance for a little while, don't you think? Perhaps if you talked the matter over with Miss Hewitt, she being an older person would be able to recall incidents . . . pertinent incidents that will refresh your memory and doubtless hers too.' He rose to his feet now, adding, 'I thank you very much for your co-operation. I'm sure you won't mind if I were to call on you at a later date, say Monday when we could have a ride into New-castle.'

'Newcastle?' Freddie was on his feet too now. 'Why Newcastle?'

'Well –' The man gave a slight smile and his voice had even an apologetic note as he went on, 'You see, my office is in Newcastle and it is more accommodating than here, although I thank the Chief Constable' – he inclined his head towards that worthy – 'for the use of the Court House. Yes, I would rather we talked in Newcastle. Shall we say then Monday morning at ten o'clock?'

Freddie made no answer, he simply stared at the man, for now he was knowing real fear and it was creating a sickness deep inside him. All he wanted to do at this moment was to get back to Maggie, and yes, yes, talk to her, for no matter what happened she must be protected from an enquiry such as this. She wouldn't be able to stand it. God Almighty! What was happening to them? Why had this come about after all these years? And who was it who had supplied the information? Well, before Monday he'd pay a visit to Connie Wheatley and that father of hers. He dismissed the thought of the Harpers, theirs was only surmise created by what they had seen when the boat landed on the north side; they would know nothing whatever about what had taken place at the other side of the river. So who had started all this? After all these years the whole business had been forgotten. At least, so he had made himself believe.

He was about to turn away when he forced himself to look at the man again and, in tones as firm as he could muster, say, 'You'll get me to Newcastle, sir,

321

when you can present me with a note from the Justices.'

The man made no retort. And now Freddie went from the room, but not before he levelled his glance at the other three men. In the hallway he had to stand aside while two policemen dragged a drunken man in, and from the look of the man's clothes and the smell that emanated from him he had been dragged through the mire of some particular street.

Outside, he found that his stride was impeded by the shaking of his legs. He had the desire to run, to scamper as he had done when as a lad he sensed danger was imminent.

When he reached the house he fully expected to find Maggie dressed and downstairs, but it was his mother who greeted him, saying, 'I had to put her back to bed' – she jerked her head upwards – 'she was for gettin' into her clothes. But she had a spasm; it doubled her up. I've given her a dose. What's the matter anyway? What's happening?'

'Nothing at present, Ma.' He stood before her, for a moment feeling the need of her strength, at least her physical strength. He had almost a childish feeling that he wanted her arms about him. He said slowly, 'They're on to the business, Ma. Somebody's been writing letters, somebody who's been puttin' two and two together.'

'About Belle?'

'Yes, and other things.'

'What other things can they get against you and her?'

'They're probin' into where the jewels went that I was carrying that night and, more so, into how Gallagher met his death.'

'My God in heaven! They don't think that you . . . ?'

'Ma, you never know what a policeman thinks, much less a customs officer or excise man. Anyway, keep your tongue quiet, don't mention this to me da, 'cos you know how he gets chattin' to his cronies, and the less said from our side about this the better.'

As he moved from her towards the stairs she said quietly, 'This could be enough to polish her off.' And as he mounted the stairs to Maggie's bedroom he thought to himself, Yes, she's right; it's enough to polish her off.

As soon as he entered the room she said, 'Police and customs?'

He nodded once, then drew up a chair to the side of the bed.

'What happened?'

'They questioned me – the two who came here, and the Chief Constable.'

'In the Court House?'

'In the Court House.'

'Who could have done this? Look lad, I've been thinking: that Wheatley lot not only feathered their nest that night with a lot of loose change which could have meant a hoard of sovereigns, enough to get them started, but they likely took that bag of jewellery because it wasn't on him, was it, when he was taken from the river? And a thing like that doesn't float away out of a pocket or a body belt. When he got on his horse he had left that bag of stones behind, and they knew it.'

'I can't think that Connie Wheatley would do anything like this, Maggie, she would be potching herself. Yet I've made up me mind to go and have another talk with her, 'cos there's her father and he's already opened his mouth to Freeman.'

'Were the stones mentioned, I mean did they ask

any questions about me taking those three stones to Mr Taylor?'

'No, no, that didn't come up; so let's hope they know nothing about that.'

'Well' – Maggie pursed her blue lips now – 'I bet your life that those Wheatleys picked the lot up and likely got rid of them in Scotland for not a crumb of their worth but enough to set them up, together with what else they took.'

'I'm goin' to see her tomorrow.'

'Yes, I would do that, but' – her hand came out and she clutched at his now – 'about the other, they ... they could never prove anything, could they? There were no witnesses, it's just all suspicion.'

'Yes, Maggie, it's just all suspicion. There's nothin' for you to worry about, not a thing.'

'Huh!' The sound seemed to come from deep in her throat. 'I'm not worryin' about meself, lad, my time is so short. It wouldn't matter to me if they found out this minute, I'd be gone before they could carry me downstairs.'

'Maggie, for God's sake!' He tried to pull his hand from hers. 'Don't talk like that, woman, I can't bear it.'

'All right, all right, calm down; but this is another thing you've got to face up to, as I've told you before. And anyway, we've all got to go sometime. That's an odd sayin', isn't it, we've all got to go? And where are we goin?' I've been lying here on and off these last few weeks askin' meself just that question, where do we go? Certainly not to the heaven that so many people are hanging their coats on, expectin' to be walkin' in flower gardens with God. No, I threw that idea over when I was twelve because I reasoned out' – she gave a little chuckle now – 'that if there were flower gardens up there the rain would sometimes

324

fall the opposite way, it would have to, to keep them goin'.'

'Oh, Maggie. Maggie.'

When she saw the slight smile on his face she said, 'Well, don't you think it is as good reasoning as any. Anyway, I've got a sort of assurance inside meself that wherever I'm bound for it will be peaceful, like a dreamless sleep. And after all, there's nothing more refreshing than a dreamless sleep . . . But tell me, have they finished with you?'

'Oh, no; no, Maggie, they certainly haven't finished with me. He's comin' back on Monday to escort me to Newcastle.'

Her breath caught in her throat, and as she attempted to heave herself up onto the pillows she brought out between gasps, 'But . . . why? They . . . can't, they can't . . . have anything on you. You were . . . a bit of a lad.'

'Don't agitate yourself, woman. Yes, I was a bit of a lad, but, as they say, I was a bright boy. Oh, yes, they stressed that, I was a bright boy.'

'But not bright enough to murder a man.'

He closed his eyes tightly, saying, 'Maggie. Maggie, don't put it like that. If you hadn't done what you did, you wouldn't be here today, neither would I, nor Belle. It was he who meant murder.'

'Yes, Freddie, I know; but who's going to believe that?'

'Nobody, 'cos it won't come out. It can only come out through me.'

He didn't add what had just come into his mind: And I could be called an accessory after the fact, or some such, and be in for a long stretch. He didn't say it because likely the thought hadn't occurred to her, as it hadn't occurred to him until a minute ago. And once again there the feeling was of sickness in his stomach. To change the subject, he said quickly, 'She was goin' to write straightaway when they got to London, wasn't she? If she had we would have received it this morning.'

'They wouldn't get there till late on Wednesday, and if she wrote it on Thursday, it would be with luck that we got it today. You know what the post is like here on a Saturday.'

He rose from the chair now, saying, 'You've had your medicine?'

'Yes, I've had my medicine.'

'Then you should be ready for a dose.'

'I've already had the dose and woken from it.' She smiled wryly. 'Go on now and get something to eat, because your mother will want to get off home.'

He stood looking down on her for a moment, then turned and left the room; but before descending the stairs he stood for a moment and covered his eyes with his hand.

Connie Wheatley opened the side door to be confronted by Freddie.

'May I come in?'

'Yes, yes, of course.'

She led the way up the stairs; but as soon as they entered the sitting-room she went hastily across to the door at the far side and closed it; then coming back to him, she said, 'Sit down.'

When he was seated he looked at her where she was perched now on the edge of a chair, and he said, 'There's trouble brewin', Connie.'

'Yes, yes, I guessed that.'

He stared at her for a moment before he said, 'You wouldn't write an anonymous letter, would you?'

'Anonymous letter? Me, write an anonymous letter? What would I write about, if I could write? I can

326

hardly write me name. I can reckon up figures; I'm good at that.'

'No, I didn't think you would; in fact, I felt sure you wouldn't, Connie. But then, there's your father.'

She glanced now towards the far door. 'Yes,' she said, 'there's been me father and what damage he's done. He must have done it before three weeks ago because he's had a stroke.'

'Oh. Oh, I'm sorry.'

'Oh, you needn't be sorry because if I was speaking the truth the only one I'm sorry for is meself at the moment, because, I can tell you, since we left The Towers all those years ago he's been a trial. I think me mother would have been here the day if it hadn't been for the worry of him; at times I've even thought he would see me out. He was all right when he could keep off the bottle, but a couple of glasses of the hard stuff and God knows what he would say . . . what he has said. It got that way that the polis brought him back twice in the last few months. Once I understand he ended up in the polis station, the Central in the city, yelling his head off. God only knows what he came out with. For days I could hardly sleep expectin' a knock and somebody to walk in and say, "Where did you get the money to start all this?" She now looked straight at Freddie. 'It could be the first question they would ask, couldn't it?'

He hesitated. 'Yes,' he said, 'yes, I suppose so, Connie.'

She drew in a long breath, then joined her hands tightly together in her lap and her voice was low as she now said, 'They say that no one prospers from ill-gotten gains; but when we rifled through those places and the stuff he had stacked away, we all thought we had earned what we took.' She now raised her head and said, 'But we didn't clear the place, just took enough that we thought would start us up, except . . .' She stopped abruptly and placed a hand on the top of her head as if she was trying to press it down onto her shoulders.

'Except what, Connie?' he asked her.

'It doesn't matter, it doesn't matter . . . Can I get you a drink?'

'No, thanks. But can I ask you this: have you any idea of what your father let slip? Could he have told them about driving me and the child to the dockside?'

It was some time before she answered, 'I don't really know, Freddie. I don't really know. The only thing I can say is that he came in here yelling one day that he had . . . well –' her head wagged now before she finished, 'potched you. And when he was sober I tried to get it out of him what he had said, but, you know, he couldn't remember a thing. And now he's lying there' – again she motioned her head towards the far door – 'as helpless as any child, unable to speak or move. He's lost the use of everything except for one hand, and the doctor tells me he could lie there like that till God knows when. During the week I've got a woman who comes in and cleans him and washes him because I've got to be downstairs. But how long I'll carry on there, I don't know. You know' – she leant towards him – 'I've got the feeling, a silly feeling as if I want to pick up my skirts and run right back into the past when I was a little lass, or more than a little lass. Anyway, before this happened' – she now tapped her face from one cheek to the other – 'when I only had me eye to worry about and I was happy workin' in The Towers . . . But we can't go back, can we?'

'No, Connie, we can't go back.' He now rose to his feet and went over to her and put his hand on her

328

shoulder, saying, 'I suppose it's a silly thing to say, me being in the precarious position that I am, but if I can help you in any way you've just got to give me a shout.'

She rose to her feet and gripped his arm, saying, 'I liked you as a lad, Freddie, and I like you as a man. And you know something – I can say this to you – I envy the woman you'll eventually take. I'm thirty-eight and past marriage, but you know' – she gave a cynical laugh now – 'I had an offer and only last week. Yes, yes, I had. He's got a shoe business along the street, but it doesn't make a quarter of the money that I do, and so he's willin' to put up with me face.'

'Aw, Connie' – he was gripping her hand now – 'beauty is as beauty acts and once anyone gets to know you they forget about the rest. And you say this fella has a shoe-shop? Well, you know' – he brought his face down to hers – 'that could have been me, because that was what I wanted more than anything else in life when I was a lad, to have a shoe-shop, not a cobbler's mind, but a real shoe-shop. I'd seen one here in Newcastle full of boots and bonny ladies' slippers and things, and I used to dream about it at nights. Yes, that fella along at that shop could have been me.'

'Oh, Freddie.' She smiled now. 'I wish to God it had been. But then you wouldn't have looked the side I was on.'

'Don't you be so sure. I have me eye on the main chance; I'd have married you for your money.'

'Not you, Freddie, not you.' . . .

As he walked into the street he thought: How strange! He had entered the house fearful but had come out laughing. And it was odd about the man in the shoe-shop proposing to her. Funny, but he hadn't thought of his desire for the shoe-shop for years. One thing, though, that had come out of his visit: Mr Wheatley was likely the man who, in his drunken state, had talked of the jewels and had undoubtedly insinuated, if not pointedly said, that the youngster, the runner, must have taken them. How other would the police have brought that up in the questioning? And if he said that, then he could also have hinted as to how his master died. But what about the letters? Connie had said her father couldn't write. But then there were plenty of professional letter writers that would have done the job for him. Among these men would probably be some who, if this knowledge had come into their hands, would surely have used it in a form of blackmail.

A letter arrived on Monday morning from Belle. It was very short. It said,

> 'My very dear Aunt Maggie and Freddie,
> We arrived in the hotel at seven o'clock last evening. It is a very nice place. I am looking out of the window now and London seems vast. The sun is shining. We are to spend the day sightseeing.
>   I miss you both so very much. I send you my fondest love.
>
>   Belle.

After reading the letter Maggie handed it to Freddie, and he, now slowly folding it up, said, 'Terribly informative, is how that could be described.'

'Yes, that's right, Freddie, terribly informative. Not a word about how she feels.'

'Oh, yes there is: she says she misses us both terribly.'

330

'And that shouldn't be on the first day of her honeymoon.'

'She's merely being polite. You've paid a lot of money over the years to have her taught to be polite and, what's more, to hide her real feelings.'

'You think I was wrong in doing that?'

'No, no, not at all. No, of course not. But' – he pointed to the letter now lying on the bed cover – 'there you have the result, an educated young lady.'

'She never hid her feelings when she was here at home.'

'No, but she's not at home now, she's a married woman, Maggie.' And God! how he knew she was a married woman, for on the first night of her marriage his imagination running rife had at one point almost driven him mad.

'Oh, it doesn't matter.' She picked up the letter from the quilt and put it on the side table near the bed, then said, 'There are more things to worry about. What time is it?'

'Quarter to ten.'

'If they have a Justice's warrant, you'll have to go with them.'

'Yes, but I won't otherwise.'

'But, Freddie . . . if they have a warrant it will mean they've got something concrete to go on. What then?'

He sighed now, saying, 'I don't know, Maggie; but don't worry, they won't get anything out of me, and that being the case they can't hold me.'

'I wouldn't be too sure of that.'

'I can't see how; there was no eyewitness as to what happened on the dockside. As for that bloomin' bag of glass, because after all that's all they are, as Mr Taylor said, bits of glass, they'd have a job to trace that to me, the remainder of them anyway.

They'll likely want to go through the house and I bet already they've been through my bank.'

'I doubt if they would get any information from them what you have there. There's a kind of law . . .'

'Oh, Maggie, you know as well as I do the polis can twist laws, especially the kind of polisman that is calling for me in a few minutes time. Anyway, I think that fella's lost in the polis force, he should be up in the government, in the Diplomatic Service or something like that. He's so smooth, his words slide out of his mouth. Anyway, dear . . .' He bent over her and looked into her face for a moment before kissing her; and then her arms went round his neck and held him close. When she whispered something that he couldn't catch, and he said, 'What is it?' she shook her head. But the tears were in her eyes and she pushed him gently from her, saying now, 'Go on. But hurry back. D'you hear? Hurry back.'

He nodded; then turned abruptly and went out.

His mother met him at the bottom of the stairs. 'They're here, there's two of them,' she said. 'They got out of a cab; it's at the gate.'

'Open the door; I'll be in the sitting-room.'

The men came into the room slowly, and he made himself rise just as slowly from a chair.

'Good-day to you, Mr Musgrave.' It was the same suave gentleman, as he called him; and he gave no reply to the man's greeting but waited. 'I happen to be Inspector Mitchum,' the man introduced himself; 'and this is' – he pointed to the other man – 'Police Sergeant Pringle. You know why we are here?'

Freddie knew why they were here; he also knew that the man's manner had changed, it was not as suave as it had been on their previous meeting.

'You stated, when we last met, that you would not accompany us to Newcastle unless it be on the order

of a warrant. Well now, here is the required article.'
He withdrew a folded paper from his inner pocket
and handed it to Freddie who, unfolding it, scanned
it, picking out words here and there which ran:

For questioning with regard to jewels that went
missing . . .
. . . And being of knowledge with regard to the
demise of one Roderick Gallagher on the same
night . . .
You are required to . . .

'You will allow me to get my coat and hat?'
'Certainly.'
It seemed now that the inspector put out his hand
and stopped the sergeant from following Freddie into
the hall.
A moment later when Freddie reappeared in the
doorway he said, 'If you are ready,' and the men
followed him, both eying the big bony woman standing to the side of the front door. And when she said,
'When will you be back, lad?' he answered, 'Later on
in the day, Ma.' She was glancing at the men and
slowly she said, 'You sure?'
'I'm sure. Don't worry, Ma.' He put out his hand
and touched her arm.
Outside, the inspector said in a polite enquiring
tone, 'Your mother?'
'Yes, my mother.'
Seated now at one side of the cab, he looked at the
two men who were looking at him. 'We are not
taking the train then?'
'No; out of consideration for you, we thought a cab
would be more discreet.'
'I see, out of consideration for me, not in case
you've made a mistake?'

333

'We rarely make mistakes, Mr Musgrave. We do our homework first.' The inspector said no more, only continued to look at him. It was the sergeant who leant forward, saying, 'You wouldn't like to begin talking now to save time and trouble later?' only to draw back swiftly as if to avoid a blow because Freddie too had moved forward and was now sitting taut on the edge of the seat, his knees almost touching those of the sergeant as he cried at him, 'Now listen here! Both of you listen here: I'll talk when I know what I'm accused of and it's put into direct words. And let me tell you this, you cannot stick any crime on me because I've never committed one, and by God! I'll see that there'll be a song and dance about this, and there'll be some people doing hornpipes. So, until I'm confronted by a magistrate or whoever's going to accuse me of what I haven't done, I'm saying not another word. Understand?'

Both men were now grim-faced, eyes narrowed, lips tight; and so was Freddie as he sat back against the smelly leather of the cab. The journey continued thus in an almost nightmare silence until they reached Newcastle.

The cab stopped outside the Court House. He had passed it dozens of times before on his meanderings through the city but had never imagined that one day he'd be entering its doors almost as a prisoner, for that's what he felt he was already. Such was the turmoil in his mind that he only dimly took in the surroundings. There was bustle all about him, but it was a quiet sort of bustle, not like that in the Court House in North Shields; but then this was a different kind of Court House altogether. He was guided across the spacious hall and up a staircase that was bordered by a fine balustrade – he always had an eye for wood – and to a sort of waiting-room where the inspector indicated that he should sit. There was an officer in uniform standing by a door at the far end of the room, as if on guard. The inspector and the sergeant now went through another door leading from the room, and he was left alone, and, strangely, he was no longer feeling sick or fearful, rather he was experiencing anger, an anger that wanted to give voice to itself. And the longer he sat waiting the more fierce his anger became, until, after fifteen minutes the sergeant returned.

Standing before him, he said, 'Come along.'

For a moment longer Freddie remained seated, then rose slowly and followed the man through the door at the end of the room and into another, larger room. To one side were three wooden benches, at the other a desk with a police officer sitting behind it. But facing down the aisle between the benches and the desk was a long table, and behind this three men sat. And one of them was the suave Inspector Mitchum.

The sergeant pointed to the first bench and indicated that Freddie should be seated, and as he did so the man who appeared to be presiding at the long table turned his gaze on him. And it was he who now spoke and the voice, Freddie recognised, indicated that this man was from neither north or south of the river, nor was he a Scot or Irish. He seemed not to have an accent at all, but his words were clear and his tone not unkind as he said, 'You are Frederick Musgrave?'

'Yes, sir.' When Freddie made to rise to his feet now, the man said, 'It's quite all right, you may remain seated. This is just an informal enquiry, you understand that?'

Informal enquiry that took a warrant to bring him

335

here. He could not stop giving voice to his thoughts as he replied, 'I was brought here on warrant, sir.'

'Yes, yes, I understand that; but nevertheless you are not being charged with any crime. All we want at the present moment is information about incidents that happened some years ago. The inspector has already questioned you at some length, I understand, but your answers have been rather evasive and not satisfactory. So shall we begin at the beginning and take your mind back to the night when you were given a small package to carry across the water to a certain Mr Roderick Gallagher at The Towers in the village of Harton.'

'I can add no more, sir, to what I have already told the inspector.'

'Come, come, Mr Musgrave. Let me now inform you that we have, from three separate sources, been given details of what transpired that night and these sources all implicate you. On my part, I shall now be frank and tell you that, taking the third source first, this is of the least importance, yet it has its bearing because it deals with what you brought across in the sculler from the south side to the north side on the night in question; a bundle of some sort. You were also accompanied by your employer, Miss Margaret Hewitt. Now for our second source of information. This suggests that the packet of stolen jewels that you delivered to Mr Gallagher did not remain with him, for they were not found on his body when it was recovered from the river some days later. But it is suggested, only suggested, Mr Musgrave, that you know what became of that stolen property. Our other source of information, however, brings us to a far graver matter. It suggests that you also know how Mr Roderick Gallagher came to meet his end. Now, do

336

any of these things refresh your memory, Mr Musgrave?'

Freddie stared back at the man. His eyes were fixed on his alone although he knew that every other person in that room was staring fixedly at him, and his mouth became dry. His anger had left him as if drained through a sieve. This man was even more suave than the inspector and he appeared more kindly, which, he considered, made him more dangerous at this moment.

'Well, will you answer, Mr Musgrave?'

'I can remember nothing more than I've already said.'

'Will you answer me just one question? What were you carrying when you came across the river that night? It was something bulky.'

Before he could stop himself he answered, saying, 'You don't think it was Mr Gallagher, do you?'

There was a single titter, but the expression on the man's face didn't alter and his voice remained the same as he said, 'No, I don't suspect it was Mr Gallagher.'

Suddenly Freddie said, 'And it couldn't have been the jewels, because if I had been carrying such a notable bundle it must have been the Crown Jewels, all of them.'

'No, I don't think they were the Crown Jewels; they would have been too heavy, wouldn't they, for a boy of twelve to carry? But you admit to carrying something?'

He hadn't admitted to carrying anything, had he? No, he hadn't. The only one he had told that part to was Freeman, and after that talk Freeman wouldn't have said anything, he was sure. No, he hadn't admitted to anything, and he said so now: 'I haven't admitted to carrying anything.'

The man leant back in his chair, sighed, put his hand on what looked like a blotting pad in front of him and patted it. The action spoke clearly to Freddie of impatience. And so, now and in earnest tones, he said, 'Sir, believe me, I have no knowledge of what was in the package I carried that night or what became of it and' – he had to swallow deeply before saying the next words – 'I did not kill Mr Gallagher.'

'Oh' – the flat hand came up from the blotter now and patted the air between them – 'you are not being accused of stealing the jewels or of murdering the man you gave them to. But we feel you have knowledge of both events and that you are withholding this knowledge and so obstructing justice from taking its rightful course. You understand me, Mr Musgrave?'

'Yes, sir, I understand you very well, but I have said all I can say.'

'*All you can say*, Mr Musgrave, but not all that you *could* say. I must impress upon you that this is a very serious matter that has come to light and that because it has come to light it will be pursued to its end. Again I ask if you understand me?'

Freddie wasn't absolutely sure if by this 'understand' the man was meaning what he thought was meant by it. It was in his mind first, that they could keep him here until he told them something, or secondly, that they could definitely accuse him of the theft or the murder. And it was no use putting forth that a boy of twelve couldn't murder a man because it had been done before, if he was to go by what he read.

His eyes wavered from those of the man and his head drooped forward; and presently the man's voice came to him, saying, 'Well, as you are seemingly determined not to be of help to us at the moment I

338

can only hope that we will be supplied with further information very soon from one who was apparently a confederate of yours in those far off days, and who apparently does not wish you well. You know the saying, when thieves break up enemies are born. So until then I'm afraid you will remain in custody.'

Freddie's head snapped upwards. 'I . . . I have no enemies, not . . . not like that, and I had no confederates, as you call them, and . . . and I can't remain in custody. I won't. I have done nothing wrong, except act as a runner when I was a child. And then I would run for anyone who paid me, because . . . because I needed the money to help my family. I . . . I . . .'

The man leaned slightly forward over the table, saying quietly now, 'The matter is entirely in your hands, Mr Musgrave. And from the evidence that has been gathered I am afraid I cannot believe your statement when you say you know nothing further of what happened at that particular time. So, as I said, for the time being you will remain in custody.'

'You can't do this. You can't.'

There was a man now on either side of him. Each put a hand on an arm and when they went to turn him about he flung them off, and almost jumping the four steps to the long table, he bent over it and yelled at his interrogator, 'I don't know anything about the jewellery.'

He got no further for the men were now hauling him backwards out of the room and onto the landing again, but they didn't go down the stairs up which he had come but down a narrow stone stairway, so narrow that he was pushed forward and his arms wrenched behind him. They passed through a warren of passages until they came to a broad one which made him think that they were entering bedlam, such was the noise from the cells, then through this

339

to a shorter passage, quieter here, even, you could say, quiet. A heavy door was opened and he was thrust inside, and when the door banged closed he beat on it and yelled until his throat was sore. Then limp, he turned and took stock of where he was: a narrow slit of a room, lit by a grating high up in the wall. The only article of furniture in the place was a pail and what appeared to be some wooden planks attached to the wall to form a bed. There was no bedding of any kind.

The anger had by now seeped from him and what came from his lips sounded like a whimper as he said, 'Oh, Maggie. Maggie.'

13

The pain was tearing at her. She wanted to cry out but she pressed her hands tightly on her stomach, the nails digging into the bare flesh as she waited for the door to open. When, a minute later, it did, Jinny stood aside and let the pockmarked woman, as she thought of Connie, enter the room.

There was no powder on Connie's face today, the pocks furrowed her cheeks as a miniature wind distorted landscape, making her nose, which was bare of signs of the disease, stand forth like a lone hillock; her bonnet shaded her brown hair but not her eyes. Maggie was experiencing an added and strange pain as she looked at the woman and said, 'Thank you for coming.'

Connie sat down on the chair that Jinny placed near the bedside and she thanked her with a muttered, 'Ta;' then she looked towards the hand that was plucking the threads of the eiderdown before raising her eyes to Maggie. 'I didn't know till last night about him,' she said. 'Eeh! it's awful. I was upset. I . . . I wanted to go and see him, but I didn't know if that would make things worse for him or not. I mean, they'd want to know who I was. They shouldn't have done it to him; he's never done anything but help people and be kind . . .'

She stopped talking abruptly and brought out a handkerchief and blew her nose, and now Maggie said simply, 'You *can* help him.'

'I can? I'll do anything . . . well, I mean . . .'

'Listen to me, my dear.' Maggie was speaking to her now as if she were a young girl. 'I can't get out of this bed or else I'd be with him at this moment, but I've done what I can. I've seen to it that he'll be cleared of one accusation. Jinny here is his mother.'

The two women looked at each other now, then nodded, and Maggie went on, 'His brother and Jinny saw him yesterday. He's being accused not only of' – she now closed her eyes for a moment and pressed the hand that was underneath the bedclothes tight into her stomach before going on – 'murdering or knowing who murdered your master, but also of being in possession of what he carried that night to him. They think he has them stored away some place. What did you say?'

Connie's head was bowed now, and what she had muttered was, 'Oh my God!' But when she lifted her head again and looked at Maggie she said nothing further; and Maggie went on, 'Can I ask you, my dear, if you know anything about those stones?'

Connie's lids were blinking rapidly. She looked from Maggie up to Jinny, then back to Maggie again, and she seemed to have to make an effort to speak, for twice her mouth opened then closed before she brought out what could not have been interpreted as either, 'Yea' or 'Nay', but then she said, 'I . . . I'll be able to fix it so as he'll be all right.'

Maggie's hand gripped hers now as she said, 'Thank you. Thank you, my dear. When . . . when will you do this?'

Again Connie seemed to find difficulty in speaking, but eventually she said, 'As . . . as soon as I get back. I'll . . . I'll go to them.'

'To them? Who?'

'Those at the Court House.'

Maggie's head now dropped back into the pillows,

and with her eyes closed she lay quiet for a moment until Jinny said, 'Would you like a drop of your medicine, dear?' and she answered, 'Yes, Jinny. Yes.'

Jinny now measured two teaspoonfuls of a clear liquid from a bottle into a glass and she placed her big hand between Maggie's shoulder blades, then put the glass to her lips. And Maggie's hand covered hers for a moment until she swallowed the bromide. Then, looking at Jinny, she said, 'Would ... would you like to make Miss Wheatley a cup of tea?'

'Aye, yes. Yes of course.'

The moment the door closed on Jinny, Maggie said, 'How will you go about it? Have you got them ... I mean, to hand?'

Connie nodded, then said, 'Yes, they're to hand, and I've never known an easy minute since they first came to hand. Me da would take them. We told him we could never do anything with them. The sovereigns and silver that we picked up was enough to get us going, but he wouldn't listen. I won't be able to tell them that, the authorities, that I've known about them all the time else I'd be for it, wouldn't I? I've got a good little business going and I don't want to lose it in any way. Leave it to me.' She bent forward and patted the eiderdown. 'I'll ... I'll think up something, make up something convincing like about him having them hidden or stored away and he's just told me. Well, I could say, the day before he took the stroke. I could say they had got on his mind, that's what brought it on. Oh, don't worry, I'll say something. There's one thing sure, they'll get nothing out of him now for he's as dumb as a bell without a clanger. And I thank God for it. I've been worn out of late with him. He took to the drink, you know. And when he was like that he split his mouth open ... Eeh!' Her head was moving from side to side now.

343

'I'm sorry to the heart of me about Freddie. Oh dear! I've just thought of something else. It'll have to come out about Miss Belle, won't it?'

'Yes. Yes, I'm afraid so.'

'Eeh! It'll be a nine days' wonder. It'll be in all the papers. Will she be very upset, d'you think?'

'Not as much as her husband will, I fear, for her birth now will have to be brought into the open, otherwise there would be more complications, wouldn't there?'

'Yes, yes indeed. But that part'll be awful for her. I'm sorry for the lass, for she was so nice and bonny. And to think –' She paused. 'You know' – she leant forward now – 'there are nights I can't go to sleep. I just think back to the time when that young lass gave birth. That awful night when he acted like a maniac . . . Mr Gallagher, and I can see him now pushing that tiny scrap of a lad under the bed. It all started from then, didn't it?'

'If . . . if they question you about . . . about how you hid the child, will . . . will you tell them exactly what happened?'

'Oh, aye, aye I will. I've got nothin' to cover up there. I only thought of that bairn; she was so bonny and so full of life and kicking. I can remember the time as if it was yesterday when I knew what he meant to do so I played rough and said, "Give her me here!" And I hauled her up roughly by the little nightgown neck and I said to me da, "Get a shovel." Then I yelled at him, the master, "D'you want to come and see how deep we lay her?" I think now it was only me brazenness that stopped him from comin' with us at first, but come he did. You see I had pushed her into a box, but as soon as I got into the garden I took her out of the box, dropped off me petticoat, wrapped her in it and pushed her in the bushes. And it's as well I did for, not five minutes later there he was. He didn't come close up, but he watched me da digging, then me lifting the box and laying it gently in the bottom of the hole. And he stayed for some minutes until the soil was all pushed back, then he turned about and we heard him get on his horse and gallop off. You know, he often rode half the night. But as soon as he was out of the way I took the bairn and I put her upstairs in that room. Me da wasn't for it, he was scared, because, believe me, the master was a dangerous man, even when he wasn't in one of his turns. Me ma said that he had quite a bit in him that had been in his grandma, that's the one the room was built for. It only showed at times, but when it did, eeh! God, he raised skull and hair through that house. By the way, where is the young lass now?'

'She's on her honeymoon.'

'So she won't know about Mr Musgrave and him being taken to Newcastle?'

'She will now. I sent her an express letter on Sunday. I don't think she'll even bother to write, she'll come straight back.'

'Aye, yes, she would, 'cos she owes him a lot, she does.'

Maggie's hand was again pressing tight on her stomach and her words came out between gasps now as she said, 'You'll . . . you'll do something . . . right away . . . won't you?'

'Aye; yes, I will; and I'll get off now.'

As she stood up she added, 'I'm sorry to see you like this. Are you in much pain?'

'A . . . a little.'

'That's a pity, it surely is. But some folks get off lightly; the doctor said me da's not suffering at all, he's just lying there like a log. Well, I'll go then and do me best, but –' she backed a step from the bed, then she paused before she ended, 'I'm not goin' to say I'm not afraid, 'cos inside I'm all worked up. I know I've got to stick to the first thing I say and I'll get that pat in me mind. So, don't you worry; I'll . . . I'll do what I can. Ta-ra then.'

Maggie inclined her head towards her for she was unable to speak at the moment; but as the door closed on her visitor she thought, Some people get off lightly . . . and that's true. But God or the powers that existed somewhere had a strange way of working things out because if she hadn't been near her end, her end would have been either in jail for life or at the end of a rope, having done what she did this morning.

It was six o'clock the same day. The room where Freddie had been questioned now seemed packed with people. The same man with the accentless voice sat behind the table and on his right was the inspector, but at his other side sat a magistrate. And at the corner of the table sat a clerk, as also did one at the desk further back in the room.

The wooden bench on which Freddie had sat was now occupied by Maggie's Doctor Wright, her solicitor, Connie Wheatley and the doctor who was attending her father.

It was the magistrate who now addressed Doctor Wright. 'You say that the woman Margaret Hewitt is on the point of death and cannot be moved?' he said.

'I do, sir. Your men have already ascertained this.'

'My men are not doctors, they cannot give a medical opinion.'

'One of them was a police doctor.' Doctor Wright's voice was terse, and the magistrate, nodding now, said, 'Oh, yes, yes, of course, yes.' He now leant forward and had a word with the man sitting next to the doctor. 'You maintain, sir, she was in her right mind when she dictated this letter to you?' He patted some paper that lay to his hand on the table.

'I do, sir. She was in great pain but her mind was clear.'

There was further whispered conversation; and then he was addressing Connie. 'You have a very strange tale to tell, Miss Wheatley, and it would be quite unbelievable if it wasn't for the practical evidence you have brought here today.' He now gently lifted up a small chamois leather bag. 'But when your father confessed to having stolen and hidden these jewels three weeks ago why didn't you then inform the authorities?'

'I've told you, sir.' Her voice was weary because she had told the story three times in the last two hours. 'I was frightened. I didn't know what to do with them. If he hadn't had the stroke I would have made him come and own up, at least I would have tried. He . . . he was a very dominating man.' She hung her head as she congratulated herself once again on how she was putting this over. Then she added, 'But when I heard that Mr Musgrave was being charged with stealing them . . .'

'Mr Musgrave was not being charged with stealing them. He was being held pending enquiries concerning them.'

'As you say, sir. But remembering what a good little lad he was and how he was upset when he saw the bairn in that awful room and couldn't bear to leave her there, I knew I just couldn't keep me tongue quiet about them jewels. Anyway' – her voice took on a louder tone – 'what could I have done with them?'

'I'm going to ask you now, Miss Wheatley, why all those years ago when Mr Gallagher's body was found that you didn't come into the open, you and your family, and explain about the child? It could then have been made a Ward of Court and given its rightful position.'

'Well, sir, we felt that nobody would believe us, but . . . but I think I would have done something about it later only that I saw that she was in very good hands and being beautifully looked after at Miss Hewitt's and Miss Hewitt seemed to love her. So we decided to let sleeping dogs lie, sort of, and when Mrs Birkstead took over and brought all her own servants we were turfed out and went to Scotland and started a new life.'

Connie now put her hand out to the back of the bench to steady herself, and this was no acting because she was tired and really sick with fear inside trying to remember to say the same things each time she was questioned.

'You can sit down and continue answering.' The man motioned his hand towards her, and she sat down and when he said, 'Where is the letter now that the young lady's mother wrote explaining the rightful father? . . .'

The man to the magistrate's side leant forward and was once more whispering; and now the magistrate said, 'Oh, yes, yes, as has been said, it is in the possession of the young lady herself and she' – his head wagged in disbelief – 'is now married, you say, to Mr Gallagher's son by his first wife?'

Connie nodded her head. 'Aye, yes sir, she is.'

'Amazing. Amazing.' There was more whispering at the table and after a full minute the man in the middle stood up and said, 'This is but a preliminary hearing but it is enough to allow Mr Musgrave to be

348

freed for the present. This much I must say, his being in possession of information all these years of the said murder will have to be dealt with later. But for today we are finished now, though you will be called back to a full court at another date. You understand?'

They all answered by a motion of the head, and Connie finally ended the meeting by clapping her hand tightly over her mouth and making for the door, assisted now by a policeman . . .

Fifteen minutes later Freddie was brought into the same room and, standing between two policemen, he faced the men at the table and was told briefly of what had transpired and also that he was free to go until a certain date when he would be recalled to answer the charge of withholding information. Did he understand?

He understood.

As he walked through the long corridor, then into the hallway and looked to where his mother and John, Nell and Nancy were waiting, he felt as if he were an old man returning home after years of absence.

He could find no words to say to them as they gathered round him, Jinny saying, 'Oh, lad, lad. Thank God.'

And John saying, 'How are you feelin'?'

Nell said, 'It's over. It's over.'

Only Nancy said nothing but she gripped his arm with one hand and touched his face with the other.

They went into the street in a bunch. The twilight was deepening and Freddie stopped and looked upwards, his eyes travelling past the buildings and up to the sky. Then looking at John, he said in a broken voice, 'I know how you used to feel, lad, down the pit;' and the next moment he gave his head a

349

violent shake because he knew he was on the verge of crying, bursting out like a child, howling. He'd only been in that cell a matter of thirty-six hours but they had been like thirty-six lifetimes. And he had discovered himself in those lifetimes and knew there were great pockets of weakness in him and that he would never be able to stand a prison sentence without losing his mind. How did men ever survive, some of them manacled too? And those people back there who dealt out justice: they were a different kind of human being, their minds worked like machines . . .

It wasn't until they were in the train that he looked from one to the other and realised what an effort it had been for them all to come up to the city to see him; they couldn't have known if he would be released or not. He said, 'It was good of you to make the journey.'

'Don't be daft. It's like a holiday . . . well' – Nell's whole body seemed to wag – 'you know what I mean, at least for me it is in a train. This is only the second time I've been to Newcastle, and I hope it's me last. Aw! lad.' She leant forward and gripped his knee. 'I'm pleased to see you.'

'No more than I'm pleased to see you, Nell.' And now he looked at John and said, 'How did you manage to get off? It must have taken you nearly a day.'

'Oh, I just gave him a sort of ultimatum, either he let me go or I went.'

Freddie smiled weakly; then addressing his mother, he said, 'Who's seeing to Maggie?'

'Oh, I got Mrs Carter. You know, she does nursing. She charges. Oh my! she charges. But she's very good.' Her voice broke, her throat became full and she turned abruptly and looked out of the window;

350

then after a moment she spoke again, saying now, 'Your da said I had to give you . . . his best. He's very cut up. D'you think you could slip along and see him in the mornin'?'

'Yes, I'll do that, Ma.'

They parted at the station, Nell going home with Nancy, for she was staying the night, John making his way down to the sculler ferry, and Jinny and Freddie hurrying now towards the house.

In the hallway, Freddie paused a moment. The lamps were lit, the house had its usual warm comforting, welcome feeling, but in this moment it could have been like a portion of heaven except for one thing, there would be no agonizing pain in heaven. He threw off his coat and hat and went straight to the bedroom.

The sturdy middle-aged woman standing at the side-table said, 'Oh, you've got back then;' then she looked behind him, and when she saw Jinny beckoning her she went towards her, and they left the room together.

Maggie didn't say anything at his approach, but she held out her arms and he went into them, and in spite of the effort he endeavoured to make the tears sprang from his eyes and mingled with those on her cheeks.

'My dear. My dear.' She was stroking his hair and murmuring almost unintelligible words now till he raised himself from her, saying, 'There, there, stop it. Stop it,' and looking into her misted blue eyes he said, 'You shouldn't have done it.'

'What does it matter? They can't make me pay in any way. And you know something? I always meant to do it just in case something might come up. I thought about writing it out years ago; then got a bit fearful. But I thought today it was wicked of me to

351

have put it off because I could have had a stroke, like Miss Wheatley's father, and then wouldn't have been able to say or write anything. That thought has made me sick all day.'

He said now, 'Have you heard from Belle?'

'No; and that's strange. Somehow, I've been expecting her to walk in the door.'

'You sent the letter off on Sunday, didn't you?'

'Yes; she would get it yesterday morning, and if she expressed back I would have got it this morning. But what I'm thinking is perhaps they were out and didn't get back till late and that they're on their way today. Here it is, though, nine o'clock, so she won't be home tonight. I can't understand it.'

'I can, Maggie.' He rose from the side of the bed now. 'He's likely stopped her.'

'Oh, I can't see that. If she thought either of us were in need she would have defied him and come, I feel sure of that.'

'He's her husband, Maggie, and, to me, he's what you would call an unknown quantity. I've never been sure of him; I'm still not. Anyway, how are you feeling really? How's the pain?'

'Not too bad at all, not too bad at all, so don't worry. I've just got to pull a face and your mother pours more laudanum into me. I'll be floating in it next. Aw, Freddie' – she held out her hand – 'I don't care about anything now as long as you're with me.' She did not add: for as long as I've got left, which isn't very long; instead, she said, 'The sight of you has given me a new lease of life. Go on now; Jinny, I know, is making you a meal. I bet you haven't had a decent bite in the past two days. I'm all right. Go on. And you could do with a wash, by the look of you, and a good shave.'

He said nothing, but his eyes lingered on her for a moment longer before he left the room.

He didn't go down to the kitchen, but went into his own room; he didn't grope for the matches on the side table and light the lamp; but he made his way to the bedside basket chair and, dropping into it, he laid his head against the padded cushion attached to the top of it and muttered aloud, 'Don't go. Don't leave me. I'm lost, Maggie.'

14

It was three days later when Belle stood in the sitting-room confronted by Freddie, and for the third time she ground out from between her teeth, 'I've told you and told you! I didn't get the letter Aunt Maggie sent on Sunday. I've never received any such letter. I wrote you both on Sunday. I've told you, haven't I, I knew nothing about it until yesterday when your own letter came.'

'Yes, I know you've told me, and told me you never got it, but what I'm saying is, somebody got it. There are very few letters lost in the post these days. I say again, *somebody* got it.'

'What are you insinuating?'

'Well, you should have an idea by now what I'm insinuating.'

'How dare you! If Marcel heard that he would . . .'

'Yes, he would what?'

'He'd be very angry, to say the least.'

'I wonder.'

'What's got into you, Freddie?' Her voice was now soft, pleading. 'It isn't like you. And do you think for a moment I wouldn't have come straight home if I had got that letter? And don't you think that Marcel would have had us return immediately if he had known anything about the letter?'

He remained silent, but he gazed at her. She was married yet she seemed not to have changed, and she didn't look happy. Well, she wouldn't, would she? with Maggie being in the state she was. But there was something about her. He couldn't lay his finger on it. He said, 'Where is he now?'

Her chin worked up and down before she said, 'He's had to go to Harrogate. His grandmama wanted some business done and she thought it best as I was coming across here and . . . and might stay for the night that he should take the opportunity.'

'How long is he likely to be away?'

'I don't know. A day or two perhaps, perhaps as long as a week. His grandmama says there was some important business had come to light and it might take a little time.'

'Why couldn't you have gone with him?'

Now she almost barked at him: 'What would you have said if I had, instead of coming across here?' She could not say to him that no such invitation had been made and that her new husband had seemed at cross purposes with himself throughout the journey home, and more so this morning because he had scarcely given her a civil goodbye. She had thought that he must have been annoyed with his grandmama for making such a demand upon him at this time and also with herself for stating flatly that she must come across and stay the night, if not two.

His change of manner towards her had upset her and she felt deeply unhappy, and not only because of Maggie. But oh yes! she was unhappy about Maggie, and so she said now, 'Please don't let us quarrel, Freddie, it will upset Aunt Maggie. Tell me truthfully, how much longer do you think . . . she will be with us?'

He turned from her and went towards the fire and, putting his hands on the mantelshelf, he bowed his head towards it as he said, 'I don't know. It could be tonight, tomorrow, or next week, but it will be soon, and the sooner the better. God forgive me for saying

355

it, but she's in dire pain and the laudanum is not touching it now.'

She came swiftly towards him and put her arm around his shoulders as she said softly, 'Oh, Freddie, I'll be heart-broken at the loss of her, but you, oh! you more so, I know, because she meant so much to you and you to her. She might have loved me. Oh yes, she did love me, but the word for the feeling she had for you couldn't be expressed in just love, it went so deep. When she used to speak of you it was as if she herself had created you.'

He did not shrug her arm from his shoulder, he just turned his head away from her. But when she said softer still, 'Freddie, I miss you so,' he almost sprang away from her. And now his shoulders hunched and his head pushed forward, he cried at her, 'You miss me so, you say. What does that mean? You should have thought about that before you married him.'

'Oh! Freddie' – she backed from him – 'I . . . I didn't mean. . . .'

'Well! what did you mean? You know what I could do at this moment, I could take this hand' – he thrust out his hand, his fingers spread and shaking – 'and swipe you from the face of the earth with it, as far away as possible. I'm going to lose Maggie, but I want to lose you an' all. D'you hear?'

When he turned about and stalked from the room she dropped into a chair and, her two hands cupping her face, she whispered to herself, 'Oh, my God! What have I done? What have I done?'

Maggie died at three o'clock the following morning. She did not have any last words of farewell; she did not die in Freddie's arms but she died while looking at him asleep in the chair to the side of her bed. She experienced one great flash of pain which seemed to cleanse her body of every vestige of discomfort and for a space she was aware of utter peace so wide, so deep, so high was the peace she was lying in she had the desire to put her hand out and tell Freddie about it. She wanted to say to him: The disease has gone, I am cured; but he had dropped off to sleep only minutes ago, so she would let him sleep and lie watching him while she rested in this floating peace . . .

The face was that of a young woman, a smiling young woman. It was turned on the pillow and looking at him. There was a loud cry within him but it made no sound. He fell onto his knees by the side of the bed and laid his face on the pillow beside hers and, his voice calm-sounding, he said to her, 'Good-bye my dear, dear Maggie. We'll meet up again and you will be as you look now, young and beautiful. And we'll be of an age to come together. Yes, we will. Oh yes, we will.'

He now gently closed her eyelids, turned her head away, then went from the room to wake his mother and tell her that Maggie needed her for the last time.

15

The funeral took place five days later. It was said for a long time afterwards that most of the town attended Maggie Hewitt's passing: fishermen, longshore men, keelmen, sailors of various nationalities, townsmen, councillors and even some dignitaries from Newcastle. This in spite of her having been denounced as a confessed murderess only a short time earlier.

It had been a story in the newspapers that people said was quite unbelievable and it had all begun with little Freddie Musgrave who used to act as runner when there was a lot of smuggling going on but who was now a highly respected member of the community. He, too, was due to face a charge of having kept the knowledge to himself of Maggie Hewitt's murdering Mr Gallagher. But the common sympathy was with him: he had been but a lad of twelve years old. And as it had said in the papers, Maggie Hewitt had emphasised that the man Gallagher had meant to kill the boy and the child, and herself into the bargain. It hadn't really been murder but self-defence because when she had struck out at him he had toppled into the water and the night was dark and she couldn't get him out. At least that's what the papers said, and she was supposed to have made a written confession to a parson and a doctor.

And then there was the business of this jewellery coming to light that the servant man had pinched it all those years ago, and his daughter just getting to know about it and bringing it to the police.

Oh, you didn't need pamphlets about the murders and the robberies that went on in London and other big cities, they were on your very doorstep. But who would have thought that Maggie Hewitt had carried that secret on her shoulders all these years?

Then, there was that nice kettle of fish wasn't there? That lass could have married her half-brother, couldn't she? But her mother had left a letter to say that his father wasn't her father. Now that was a mix-up, and, as some said, if you ask them that was too convenient to be real. What had happened was the two had fallen for each other and got spliced, then found out their relationship and the rest had been made up. Still, it was done now; they had been on their honeymoon. Anyway, it was nothing new. After all, they would only be half-brother and sister and there were lots of brothers and sisters doing what they didn't ought to do in this town, and lots of fathers and daughters an' all if the truth was known. And it *was* known in some quarters, but people minded their own business, especially mothers who were afraid of ending up in the workhouse. But wasn't it odd when you came to think about it that that young lass's husband, whether he be her half-brother or not, hadn't turned up at the funeral? But the lass was there walking alongside of Freddie Musgrave. And that was a bit of a disgrace too, wasn't it now, for a female to openly attend a funeral? That kind of thing wasn't done: women should know their place in matters like this.

And another thing, only a comparatively few people had been invited back to the house for a meal, not more than a dozen it was said. Of course, it was well known there were always a lot of scroungers after a free tuck-in at a time like this;

they just attended the funerals for what they could get afterwards. But apparently Jinny Musgrave had given them short shrift, and there had only been ale for the pall-bearers, no hard stuff at all. And it was wondered all about who would come into Maggie Hewitt's pile for it was well known she was a very warm woman. It wasn't very likely she would have left it all to Freddie Musgrave. Although he stayed up at the house a lot he was after all only a clerk.

The lawyer finished reading the will and he raised his eyes to look at Freddie where he was sitting next to Belle on the couch in the sitting-room. And he said, 'It was a simple will with no conditions. If Mrs Birkstead had not been married she would have inherited half of the estate, but as she is, and undoubtedly well provided for' – the solicitor smiled in Belle's direction – 'there is no need for commiseration. I would wish that all wills were as simple, and I must congratulate you, Mr Musgrave, on becoming a very rich young man. Well now, that matter completed, I will take my leave, and I must thank you for that enjoyable repast and for your taste in wine.'

Freddie made no reply to this, but he saw the man out. When he returned to the sitting-room Jinny was sitting beside Belle holding her hand, saying, 'There, there, lass. Don't upset yourself so. We'll all miss her. Oh yes, we'll all miss her.' She turned to her son now who had taken a seat to the side of the fireplace and she said quietly, 'I asked you yesterday what you intended to do and you said you wouldn't know until today. So do you know now?'

He looked at her for a moment or two before saying, 'Well, what d'you expect me to do, Ma?'

'I don't know; that's why I asked. You did say a

360

few days ago that you didn't think you could stay here, didn't you?'

'Well, there's one thing sure, Ma, I won't be able to leave the country as I'm due in court again, aren't I?'

'Yes, I'm well aware of that, but nothin' will come of it, it can't. And you're a man of means now and that makes all the difference. Oh, don't shake your head, because yes, it does, money calls the tune.'

'Not when you're facing a judge, Ma.'

'Well, I have me own opinion of that. Anyway, Belle here will have to get across the water before it gets dark. Are you goin' to take her over?'

'There's no need. I can go by myself.'

He got to his feet and, looking down at her now, he said, 'Don't be silly.' Then he asked, 'Have you had word that he's back?'

'No, no, nothing. I would have thought though that he would have come over, had he returned.'

'Get yourself ready. We'll get across while it's light.'

She rose slowly from the couch, looked at him for a moment, then at Jinny, and went out without making further comment. And Jinny, looking at her son, said, 'Now, I don't know what you think, but they've been married barely a week and he goes off on business an' not a scribe of a pen from him. I think it's funny an' that's sayin' the least. If I were you I'd do a bit of questionin' when you get across there. . . .'

'I'll do no such thing, Ma. It isn't my business and I'm not going into that house. I'll set her to the gates and that's as far as I'll go.'

'Oh well, if that's how you feel, that's how you feel. I was only thinkin' that you might find out how the land lay with this granny of his.'

'How the land lies or how it doesn't lie is no concern of mine now. She's a married woman.'

361

She was on her feet now, her fingers stabbing at him: 'You brought her up. Guardian, or brother, whatever name you like to put to yourself, you brought her up. You were the man in her home, in her life, now you're washin' your hands of her. Well, as I see it I don't think that's anythin' to be proud of. She's still a bit of a lass an' that fancy school has left her still wet behind her ears. She hasn't been out in the world an' she knows nothin' about it. She's plunged herself into marriage, an' that, I can tell you, for any woman is a strange sea. My God! it is; and you've got to be tough to swim it.'

'I take your analogy, Ma.'

'Look, don't you come with any of your fancy words with me. Take me meanin', all right? Well, I think you would be wise to think on it an' don't throw her as if to the wolves.'

'I wouldn't think that marrying into The Towers would be classed as being thrown to the wolves.'

'Wouldn't you? Well, in my reckonin' it's equal to it. There was a mad woman there some years ago and her grandson was mad enough to try and murder a child, an' that child is married to that man's son. You might be smart up top, lad, but apparently you don't put two and two together.'

He looked at her in silence and he could have said, 'Right from the beginning, Ma, I've put two and two together, and that's what worries me, has worried me all along.' But what he said was, 'Can you stay here till I get back?'

Her tone softer now, she said, 'Of course I can stay here until you get back. Your da thinks I've been left him for months now, so one more night won't matter. But' – she smiled – 'he seems to get on pretty well without me. Since he made himself that little push-chair he practically runs the house.'

'That's something I want to talk to you about, Ma, the house. We'll go into it later, but I'd like you to move into a decent place.'

She stared at him hard before saying, 'Freddie, that house is as decent as I ever hope to live in; I'm happy in it. I've got good neighbours there, they're good to me and I'm good to them. I don't want to move to any better place where . . . well, let's put it frankly, I'd be looked down on. Oh, oh' – she raised her hand – 'don't say it, nobody's goin' to look down on me, because I can say that, but it doesn't stop people from doing it. No, lad; thanks all the same. I appreciate it. I tell you what you can do though, if you can manage it: I would like to see our John set up in something and, if it's not too late, Nancy to have proper trainin', although she's dead set on this fella. I never thought she'd pick up with a customs bloke; but there, he picked up with her, she didn't have much choice, but she seems to care for him and he for her. But I don't suppose he'd object to her havin' her voice trained. And I know that those fellas, with all their posh uniform and classin' themselves above the rest, their wages won't bear their pockets down.'

'Yes, I'll see to them, Ma, and glad to; and Maggie wanted it that way.'

'She did? Well, I know she wanted it for you, but, you mean she wanted me to have a better place?'

'Yes; she put it into plain words, as plain as what I've said.'

She turned away from him, and after a moment, her voice very small, she said, 'That was nice of her, very nice, 'cos she knew, you know, that I was jealous of her; she couldn't help but. But oh dear God, I wouldn't have minded goin' on bein' jealous of her till she was a hundred-an'-one 'cos I miss her, already I miss her. Still' – the last word was sharp – 'life's got to go on, you've got to go on. Once this business of the court is over what you want to do is to look round and find yourself a nice lass, or let's say a young lady, and. . . .'

'*Ma!*' The word was like a command. 'Stop it! I'll marry when I want to, if ever I want to. Now have you got that?'

She stared at him, her lips working in and out; then she said in a voice that was harsh and firm, 'Yes, Mr Musgrave, your ma's got that,' and she flounced from the room, leaving the door open when she saw Belle approaching from the stairway. And Belle, noticing her expression, entered the room, saying, 'You've upset your mother now. It's getting a habit with you, isn't it, upsetting people? . . . I'm ready.'

He walked past her without a word, took up his knee-length coat from where he had left it earlier over the back of a chair, picked up his tall hat from the hall table and put them both on before opening the front door, saying, 'Well, I'm ready too.'

The small ferry-boat was at the landing-stage when they reached the Low Lights, and when he helped her onto it she sat on the slatted seat, her hands tightly joined in her lap, her back straight, and gazed before her while knowing she was at the centre of attention of the other passengers.

When they landed on the far side he said briefly, 'We'll walk up to the market and take a cab from there.' He was carrying her valise and when, putting out his other hand, he went to take her elbow to help her mount some greasy stone steps she shrugged off his hold, he moved sharply from her side and walked a step ahead of her until they reached the market place. And there, hailing a cab, he did not assist her into it but left her to arrange her skirt, then pull herself up and onto the seat.

He sat next to her in order that he wouldn't have to look at her, but they hadn't gone very far when she turned to him and caught his hand, saying, 'Freddie. Oh please, don't be angry with me. I'm . . . I'm so unhappy at the moment.'

He looked back into her eyes now and asked quietly, 'Why are you unhappy, that is apart from losing Maggie? You broke your neck to get married and now you are married; why are you unhappy?'

'Because it is all so strange, the house and everything. Oh, it is beautiful. Everybody is so nice but it doesn't seem home. I've told myself that I'll get used to it; and it really is my natural home, isn't it? So it should come easy. But, somehow I can't see it. And madam has kept telling me in the short time I've been there that I am mistress of the house, but I'll never be mistress as long as she's alive. Oh, please, you know what I mean, I don't want her to go . . . to die, but everyone looks up to her so much. She reigns in the house like an old queen, and that is the point, she is old, very old I would say, but acts like someone young, her mind is so sharp.'

'You are not married to her, you are married to him, and if you care for him so much, that's all that matters, or should be.'

'Yes' – she nodded – 'or should be. But, Freddie' – she looked into his face again – 'if I could only think I was still welcome across the river as if Aunt Maggie was still there, I . . . I would feel happier inside.'

Of a sudden he gripped both her hands and his voice shook slightly as he said, 'Well, if that's all that's worrying you you're out of trouble because you know there'll always be a welcome there for you. That is still your home, the home I brought you to.

Don't forget that, ever, Belle. It was me that brought you to that house, it was me that ran with you from the house you're returning to now, and into the cart down to the river, and held you tight while Maggie had to commit murder in order to save us both. So, in a way you belong to me. I . . . I've never said this to you before, but that's how I feel about you, you belong to me. So whatever happens in the future, remember I'm there over the river and that it's your home too.'

'Oh, Freddie.' Of a sudden she was in his arms and he was holding her tightly, and they swayed together until the cab, turning a corner, caused her bonnet to fall back from her head, and he put his lips into her hair.

Then they were apart, sitting close, looking at each other; and they seemed to continue to look at each other, saying nothing, until the cab stopped, and the driver, from his box, shouted, 'Is this the place, mister?'

And Freddie, looking out of the window through the open gates, called back, 'Yes. Yes.'

He had intended to go no further than this, but he did not alight and say to the driver, 'Take your passenger to the door of the house and return straightaway; I'll be waiting;' he remained seated.

It was just before the cab stopped again that he said, 'I won't come in.' And she said, 'All right, Freddie. And . . . and I feel better now.'

He alighted and assisted her down to the ground, and stood watching her walk towards the front door before he entered the cab again.

The door was opened by Benedict, and he peered at Belle for a moment before exclaiming, 'Oh! the young madam,' and looked past her beyond the door, saying, 'Have you come alone, madam?'

'No. Mr Musgrave brought me, but he had to return home because of business.'

'Oh, yes, yes. Let me take your coat, madam. I am so glad you have returned. The mistress will be so pleased to see you.'

'Has she retired?'

'Oh yes, madam. She has been in her room these past few days. The weather has been anything but clement. Could I ask Cook to get you a tray, madam, as dinner is over?'

'No, thank you; but I would be glad of a hot drink in my room.'

'Very well, madam. Just leave your valise; I will see that it is taken up.'

She wanted to say, Oh, I can carry it myself, but she knew that was one of the things she would have to learn; as madam had once said, 'Servants are there to be used'. And she realised that if she didn't use them in this way they would consider her odd, perhaps not fitted to her position.

When she reached the room which she knew was hers and Marcel's but which she had not yet slept in, she looked about her. It was still light enough to take in each object in the room and, as she had realised the other day when she first saw it, it was all frills and furbelows, but a replica of his grandmama's. She herself loved pretty things, or perhaps that wasn't the right word to use for her particular taste, rather she loved beautiful things. For instance, she would not have draped the head of the bed with yards of lace to look like a miniature waterfall and to strengthen the impression by its pale blue colour. The bedcover, too, was blue, but made up of heavy quilted padded satin.

The four armchairs in the room were also uphol-stered in blue quilted padded satin, as was the small chaise longue at the foot of the bed. The walls she had noticed were not painted nor papered but were made up of silk panels, these in an oyster colour, and a rose pink carpet covered the entire floor.

Mrs Birkstead had informed her that she was having the room decorated for her in a French style, and it was certainly that, overpoweringly French, she would say. And she wondered how long it would be before she could change what the grand old lady called the décor. But now she would have to go and see her.

She took off her bonnet and coat and as she was placing them on the bed there came a tap on the door. She called, 'Come in!' and a housemaid entered and, bobbing her knee, said, 'Good-evening, madam. I . . . we didn't expect you or we'd have had the hot water up and the bed turned down.'

'It's all right. Thank you. You are?'

'Mary, madam, Mary Chambers. I am the first housemaid.'

'Of course, of course. Well, Mary, I'll be glad of some hot water, thank you; but in the meantime I'll go and pay my respects to Mrs Birkstead.'

'Yes, madam, yes.' She pulled the door wide and dipped her knee again as Belle passed her.

When Belle tapped on Madam Birkstead's door it was opened by her maid who smiled at her, then turned her head and looked back into the room, saying, ''Tis the young madam, mistress.'

There was a considerable pause before the voice said, 'Well, show her in.'

Belle entered the room, and for a moment she hesitated in her step as she approached the bed for the person in it had no connection with the one who took court in her drawing-room. Here was an old lady, a very old lady, wearing a pink night-cap made up entirely of plaited ribbons and bows. It was a high cap but its brim was not broad enough to hide the white streaks of hair that fell about the ears. The face beneath the night-cap was no longer covered with powder and paint but with what looked like grease, and when the mouth opened to smile, as it did, there was a gaping hole where the teeth had been.

Hiding her surprise and not a little shocked at what she thought was a frightful sight, likening the face to that of an animated corpse, Belle said, 'Good-evening, madam. I hope I find you well.'

'Good-evening, child; and you don't find me very well. I'm somewhat changed from the last time you saw me, isn't that so? Oh, I'm not going to wait for your opinion. Sit down' – she pointed – 'and tell me all that has transpired these past few days.'

Belle took the seat Sarah Cummings placed for her while thinking that whatever was changed in the old lady's appearance command of speech certainly wasn't. And now she looked at her as she pointed to Sarah Cummings, saying, 'Leave us now; you can do my massage later.'

The woman gave a slight bend to her knee, then left the room, and Mrs Birkstead said, 'Well, so you've buried her, have you, the woman who murdered my son-in-law?'

'She didn't murder him; it was self-defence and in order to save me . . . and Freddie.'

'Well, that's one version of it; but like all these cases the real truth will never be known, I suppose. But all that jewellery being in the hands of those servants all those years. They're thieves, the lot of them! No matter how long they serve you they'll rob you. Remember that, girl. Although I must say mine are as faithful as dogs. Again though, only because it

369

pays them. But the scandal, and how it was reported in that paper. I don't know how Marcel is going to take this.'

'He was aware of most of it, madam.'

'Oh no, he wasn't. Do you think he would have tolerated that woman for a moment knowing that she had murdered his father? No matter what kind of a man Gallagher was, he was his father. And then, he never thought for a moment that your parentage would be made public.'

'He can be no more embarrassed than I was, madam.'

The old lady now raised her hairless eyebrows, and then said, 'Well, I suppose that's right enough. By the way, what did she leave you, that woman? From what I understand she was very rich.'

'Nothing.'

'*What! Nothing?*'

'No; it's all been left to Freddie . . . Mr Musgrave.'

'*Why?*'

'Because she thought that, being married, I was well provided for.'

'Oh, *did she? Did she?* But . . . but you were her ward, sort of, you should have been the one that inherited, for what was he? Just someone she took under her wing and, as Marcel says, a very common fellow at bottom.'

'He is not a very common fellow.' Belle rose to her feet and stared down into the wrinkled face that was visibly quivering with indignation, but before she could continue in Freddie's defence the cutting voice of the old lady forestalled her: 'Girl! please remember to whom you are speaking. And if Marcel judged him to be a common fellow, then he is a common fellow. And it isn't right that he should have come into that woman's fortune.'

'As I see it, madam, he has every right to her fortune: he has looked after her and been her right hand for years, and loved her and cared for her as he did for me.'

The figure pulled itself up in the bed, the arm came out and the frilled nightdress fell away showing the loose sagging flesh; but it lacked no strength as the hand pointed towards the door and the voice commanded, 'Leave me! girl.'

Belle had no need to be told to leave the room. Her indignation carried her swiftly back to her own bedroom where she asked herself as she stood in the middle of it how she was going to put up with that changeable old lady who apparently allowed no opinion to be voiced, except her own. But it was enlightening to her in this moment that she didn't stand in awe of her. Everyone else in the house seemed to, for her name was mostly uttered in a reverential or revered tone. Oh, why wasn't Marcel here? What was keeping him?

Her night-clothes had been put on the bed and there was a copper jug of steaming hot water on the wash-hand stand in the closet. She opened the wardrobe door and saw that among her own clothes were arranged all the new ones Marcel had bought her on the second day in London. They had spent most of that day shopping, and she recalled that it had taken her mind off things which had disturbed her but which she knew she must get used to, for marriage, she had found immediately, was not exactly what she had imagined it to be.

The bed was high and the bedtick was filled with feathers, which some people would have welcomed, but years spent sleeping on a dormitory bed, then at home on an ordinary flock-filled mattress, had given her no taste for this kind of luxury which she termed 'smothering'.

Having told herself she wouldn't sleep, nevertheless, she did sleep, and she was utterly amazed when she heard a voice saying, 'I have brought your early tea, madam. Have you slept well? It's a beautiful morning.'

She pulled herself up out of the depths of the feathers and blinked at Mary Chambers who was smiling widely at her. And when she said, 'Is it morning?' the maid laughed and said, 'Yes, madam; it is morning and turned eight. I have brought your early tea; breakfast is at nine; and madam sends you her regards and hopes you have slept well.'

This latter brought Belle into a sitting position. Was the maid just being tactful? And then she had the source of the message when Mary said, 'And Miss Cummings said that the mistress would be pleased if you would call on her after breakfast.'

The bed tray which Mary arranged across Belle's knees held a small tea service and a plate of four biscuits on it; and their appearance Mary now explained by saying, 'Mr Marcel always liked biscuits with his early tea. I thought you might like them too.'

'Thank you. Thank you, Mary; but I won't have anything to eat.' She handed the plate back, and the woman seemed a little disappointed but said, 'Is there anything you would like in place, madam, a light scone or toast?'

'Oh, no thanks, Mary; that would ruin my breakfast. No, I'll just have the tea. I'll enjoy that.'

Mary now smiled; then pointing to the bell-pull, she said, 'If you should want any help with your dressing, madam, I'd be pleased to see to it. You just need ring.'

Belle had already glanced at the bell-pull; then she said, 'I . . . I won't need you for that, Mary, but thank you.'

After the maid had taken her leave, it was quite some minutes before Belle poured herself out a cup of tea and then lay back on the pillows against the shower of falling lace while comparing this present life-style with the one she had only recently left. And she knew at the moment which one she preferred . . .

She presented herself at the mistress's bedroom door at half-past nine, and was admitted to see the now transformed old woman, the wig in place, the powder and the paint applied, the silk negligée topped with a frill that covered the sagging flesh below the chin, and the voice too so changed from that of last night that she could hardly believe her ears as the greeting came to her, saying, 'Good-morning, my dear. Have you slept well? You look a little pale. What did you have for breakfast? Come and sit down by me.' She patted the side of the chaise-longue on which she was reclining.

Belle did not fully obey the order and sit on the edge of the chaise-longue, but she sat on a dressing stool nearby and answered the questions one after the other: 'I slept very well, thank you. And for breakfast, I just had toast and orange preserve.'

'Oh, my goodness! That will never do. Breakfast is the main meal on which to start the day. Wasn't there any choice?'

'Oh yes.' She was about to say, Too much of a choice, but deciding to match the old lady's manner with a change in her own, she smiled as she said, 'The smell was most appetising, but I wasn't hungry. I think I'll take a brisk walk this morning and that will give me an appetite for dinner.'

'Oh, you can't go on till dinner-time, my dear, on

an empty stomach. You must have something at eleven o'clock. Cummings, you see to it. Give an order downstairs, young madam will have a light meal around eleven o'clock. That will serve until dinner at three.'

Belle made no protest; she knew it would be a waste of words: this lady reigned in this house and her word was law. But there was one thing: she could order food but she couldn't make her eat. On the other hand though, by twelve o'clock she'd likely be hungry. Back home she could have eaten at any time of the day. Jinny used to laugh and say, 'You make up for the mean years you had at that school, for, from what I hear, hard tack is nothing to what that must have been.' Why was she still thinking of Maggie's house as home, and of Jinny and the warm . . . ?

'When Marcel returns you must ride with him. That will put colour into your cheeks, and you'll eat like the proverbial horse then.'

'When may we expect him, madam?'

'Oh . . . Oh.' The bony hand now dusted an imaginary crumb or some such from the white-laced cover that was spread across the couch and reached to her waist, and she said, 'Well now, it all depends on business. It is very unfortunate that it should happen at this time. I told you about my elder brother, didn't I? But of course, he is no use, it is his own son who is now in charge of the estate and . . . and the business. But . . . but I'm afraid James hasn't got a head on him like Marcel.'

'What is the business, madam?'

'Mm . . . er . . . what is the business?' the old lady repeated. 'I should have said businesses; they are so varied. Now, let me see.' She put her head back, then began to count on her fingers. 'There is first of all the

374

property; then there are the shops. Yes, there are the shops. When I was a girl there were seventeen shops and they were about to spread out further into the villages. But do you know, my dear, it was most difficult to set up shops in villages; they're so clannish, the people in villages. Their little industries have been established for years. Yes, so clannish.' She shook her head now as if she couldn't fathom the reason for the clannishness. 'Then there is the railway. But of course, there's only shares in that. That is quite a separate thing. Oh, my dear, I've forgotten how many businesses there are altogether. And from what he tells me things haven't been going very smoothly. So it could be another week, perhaps a little more, before he returns. But you mustn't worry, my dear; he'll be all the more loving when you meet. And you know' – her voice dropped – 'he does love you, and dearly. And you love him, don't you?'

She felt embarrassed to have to answer this question in front of the maid, but in just as low a voice, she said, 'Yes; yes, I love him.'

'Then everything is all right. Now it's such a lovely day I'm going down into the drawing-room later, when we will have another chat. Perhaps you will bring your embroidery . . . you do embroider?'

'Oh, yes, yes.'

'Do you paint or draw?'

'I like sketching, but mostly I like to embellish book-plates.'

'Oh, that is interesting and unusual. You mean you do the titles and things?'

'Well . . . well . . . yes, and enhance the flyleaves and the capitals.'

'How interesting. Now that is a wonderful hobby. I am so glad you have things that will fill your time.

375

Now you must take that walk which will make you ready for your meal later.'

Dismissed, Belle went out and back to her room where she selected a plain straw hat and a dust-coat. She did not, however, use the main staircase but went down a side one. Marcel had shown her this one because it led out near the corner of the house and right next to the big conservatory.

It was a lovely morning, and she walked through the gardens. She stopped and spoke to a man who was sweeping a grass path on which there were a few leaves: 'It's a lovely morning, isn't it?' she said to him.

'Oh . . . oh yes, madam, 'tis a lovely morning.'

'Are you the head gardener?'

'Oh no, madam!' He gave a deprecating smile. 'Me, I'm the runabout. Well, Mr Victor is the head one and Dan Watson comes next.'

'Oh, I see. Do you like gardening?'

'Yes, madam, I like it very much.'

'I have never done any gardening. I must take it up sometime; I'm sure it's very interesting.'

The young man laughed now as if at a joke and she laughed with him as she said, 'Oh, I mean that.' And still laughing, he said, 'Yes, madam, yes.'

Belle knew as she walked away that the man was still laughing at her statement.

She walked aimlessly for half an hour. She had seen another gardener in the distance but hadn't gone out of her way to have a word with him. Her ambling had brought her to another drive. This wasn't so well kept as the main drive and as she followed its winding way back she found a branching off which led to the stable yard, and from this a path that brought her out opposite the conservatory and the door from which she had emerged to start her walk and to which she now made her way with the intention of returning to her room.

She had almost reached the door when she imagined she heard Marcel's voice. She stopped and stepped back onto the path and looked into the conservatory. There was no one there. But again she heard his voice, and so, excitedly, she entered the conservatory.

The glass-domed L-shaped conservatory was heavy with the scent of plants of all varieties and part of it was almost obliterated with greenery. At the far end was, she knew, the door that led into the drawing-room, and she realised it was from there that the voice was emanating now. Almost at a run she started to move towards the door, only to be halted by the words: 'You should not have come back so early.'

Her eyes widened even further at her husband's reply, for it was undoubtedly Marcel's voice that said, 'I had to. What do you think I am? You don't know how I feel.' Then his grandmama's voice answering, 'Oh my darling, of course I know how you feel; and I feel for you. Haven't I always? But this was unwise, you should have given yourself another week.'

Then his voice again, 'I'm all right . . . I'm perfectly all right. I know I am.'

'How have you got back so soon?'

'I spent the night in the city.'

'Alone?'

'No; Harry stayed with me.'

'Oh, my dear, dear, you must be careful. And this business is bound to have disturbed you.'

'Disturbed me! That's putting it mildly. My God! when I think of the scandal.'

'What had my dear brother to say?'

377

'I didn't bother calling on him because they would inform him soon enough. As for James, I'll knock him flat one of these days.'

'Now, now, you must bear with James.'

'Where is she?'

'Out in the garden. Be gentle with her, Marcel. She is very sweet but somewhat headstrong. But don't try to cope with that all at once.'

Belle now backed down the aisle between the greenery, and immediately she emerged from it she turned and ran towards the door, out of it, then into the other door and up the stairs to her room. It was evident that he had already been there for a small leather portmanteau was on the floor near the couch.

Standing near the window, her hands clasped tightly in front of her, she asked herself if she had heard aright? But what had she heard? Could she make sense of it? The only thing that had come out of it was that for some reason he'd had to go away and it hadn't been for business; and that his grandmama was surprised at his return and worried . . . as she herself was too. Even during those few days in London questions had arisen in her mind, but they had been swept away by his loving kindness, at least during the day, and the constant declaring of his love for her.

She wished she could rush out at this moment, down to the river and take a boat across to home and Freddie, and Jinny, and Nancy, and everybody on that side of the water, because here she was in a foreign land in which the language made her fearful, so fearful that she dare not translate it in her mind.

It was almost twenty minutes later when he came into the room and found her sitting at her dressing-table. In a high voice he exclaimed, 'There you are,

378

my dear. Oh, my dearest dear.' He came behind her and put his arms about her and tilted her head back and looked down into her face, asking softly, 'Have you missed me?'

To this she could answer truthfully, 'Yes. Yes, Marcel, I have missed you.' Then having already made up her mind that she had a part to play until she managed to get to the bottom of why her husband had to take these mysterious visits to Harrogate, she asked, 'Why did you stay away so long? Was business so pressing?'

He released his hold of her and, straightening up, said flatly, 'Yes, very pressing, very boring. But I think I have settled the affairs now for some time.'

She turned on the seat and looked at him fully, and she paused before she said, 'You are pale. Have you been unwell?'

'No, no.' His voice was high again. 'Unwell? No; but harassed; business can be very harassing. . . . But all that is past.' He flung his arms wide; then taking two steps towards her, he pulled her into his embrace and pressed her jerkingly to him, once, twice, three times, until she gasped and said, 'Oh! Marcel, you . . . you are hurting me.'

'Oh, come now, come; you're not such a delicate little thing as to be hurt by a hug. What is it?' He pressed her from him. 'It is you who don't look very well.'

'Perhaps you are not aware that Aunt Maggie died and has been buried in your absence?'

'Yes, yes.' His tone and manner altered now. 'Since you bring it up, I am very well aware that your Aunt Maggie died and has been buried, and I should say it is fortunate for her she died as she did, because, being a confessed murderess, she would have died in any case.'

'Oh no, she wouldn't! She wasn't a murderess.'
Here she was, going again. She must be careful for
his expression was thunderous now and his voice
matched it as he cried, 'She killed my father, and all
this business about one of the servants stealing
those jewels is all poppycock. Your Freddie likely
paid that woman to come up with that tale.'

'Freddie would do no such thing. He would speak
the truth, he always did.'

For a moment she was fearful of what was going to
happen next: she could see that he was making a
great effort to control himself. He turned from her
and walked to the far end of the room and stood
facing the blank door of the wardrobe for a moment
before once again turning around and, his voice now
low and his tone appealing, he said, 'Oh! Belle,
please, please don't let us quarrel. I've . . . I've been
very upset about that report in the paper and all the
fuss. And there's still more to face, because, you
know, people will not really believe that we are in no
way related. But, oh my dear' – he approached her
now, his hands extended – 'don't . . . don't let us
quarrel. I have missed you so much and longed to be
with you. Be . . . be gentle with me, I beg; I need you,
your gentleness.'

She was overcome. Here she was being presented
with two different natures within a matter of
minutes. So, so like his grandmother. Yet she
couldn't resist the appeal in his voice and his countenance, and so, her own voice soft, she said, 'Marcel,
my dear, I don't want to quarrel, but I want to
understand; everything is so strange. You go away
and you don't leave me a word. Why? Can't you tell
me why?'

She watched him close his eyes and jerk his head
backwards as he said, 'I . . . I thought Grandmama

explained everything to you, everything that you need to know. It's . . . it's my business, my dear, it's business, all business, business.' His voice was rising; then again swinging round from her, he said, but in a more subdued tone, 'I just want to forget about it, Harrogate and all in it. Quite candidly' – he was once again facing her – 'I hate Harrogate and everything that drags me there. But look, my dear –' He bounced towards her now in boyish fashion and, catching her hands, he said, 'Today we are going out riding.'

'But I can't ride; I have never been on a horse, Marcel.'

'Today you will be on a horse, my dear; you will have your first lesson. And from now on every day we shall ride, trot, gallop.' His arms now were acting his words and when his legs, too, illustrated a gallop she forced herself to laugh, saying, 'I'll never get to that stage; I'll be on the ground most of the time.'

'Come on!' He pulled her hand. 'Get into your coat and bonnet and winter boots. We must get you a riding habit. Yes, yes, that's what we must do. That's the next thing, we'll go into Newcastle and get you a riding habit. But not today. Today you will be just introduced to your horse, a gentle saunter. Oh, my love! my love!' She was in his arms again. 'You have no idea how I feel when I am with you, when I can hold you, when I know that you love me.'

He was holding her chin tightly with one hand now, his fingers pressing into the side of one cheek, the thumb into the other pushing her mouth out of shape. And there was a plea, yet a demand, in his voice when he now said, 'Tell me that you'll always love me. Tell me. Say it.'

Through her distorted lips she said, 'You're hurting me.'

'Oh! Oh, I'm sorry. I'm sorry. I wouldn't hurt you for the world.' He was stroking her cheeks now with both hands. 'But tell me that you'll always love me. Say it. I want to hear it.'

As she looked into the face that had first fascinated her a few months previously and continued to do so as recently as a fortnight ago, she would have then been able to answer without hesitation, but now she dared to say, 'Always is a long time. We have just begun our life together; it . . . it depends on how we react on each oth . . .'

She was almost thrust on her back. She stumbled and was saved from falling only by the low back of the dressing-table stool. And he was yelling at her now, 'I don't want philosophy! I want love. Do you hear? I want love.'

She watched him throw himself on the chaise-longue, his body bent almost double, his face in his hands, and although she was experiencing fear of him she was, at the same time, filled with compassion; and this drove her to him and, bending above him and putting her arm around his shoulder, she brought his head to her waist, saying, 'You have love, my dear, you have love. What is it? What is the matter?'

He lay against her for some minutes, and when at last he looked up at her he asked softly, 'Bear with me, will you? Please bear with me. I . . . I unfortunately have this quick turn of temper. I must try to control it. I will for your sake.' And his voice still gentle, he said, 'Come, let us get into the fresh air and ride. Yes, and ride, for you'll find the wind rushing through you is the most exhilarating feeling in the world. It clears your mind. It makes you a new being. Although' – he smiled gently now – 'I don't want you ever to be a new being. It is me who must mend my ways. Come, my dear. Get into your things and let us go.'

She did as he bade her and accompanied him downstairs for her first riding lesson.

16

She did tolerably well with her first riding lesson. The following day she had another lesson, in which she did better. He also took her into Newcastle, and she was fitted for a riding habit. And then they called at his other house. It was only a small house, comprising eight rooms altogether and situated at the end of a very nice terrace on the outskirts of Jesmond. And there they found Marcel's friend, Harry Benson. Apparently he was living there. As Marcel explained, he looked after the place and so it only needed one servant, and he a daily man.

Marcel's friend, Belle found, was what she termed a nice man, quiet, slightly aloof. He was a very big man, all of six foot two and broad with it, and that he was not only a friend but also a sort of superior servant she deduced from the fact that he asked Marcel if he would be needing him, did he think, within the next two days? And Marcel assured him that he wouldn't. He seemed to emphasise this. Then as she happened to glance back as they were leaving, she saw Marcel place a small chamois leather coin bag on the corner of the sideboard.

In the street a disturbing thought came into her mind, but she countered it by saying to herself, Well, there are some things that it's best not to know, only to attack this immediately: She should know; he was her husband.

The following morning she did not go down to breakfast, she felt very tired. Love-making, she was finding, was not only tiring, it was disturbing and distressing. She never expected it to be like this and therefore wasn't complying to Marcel's satisfaction. That he was annoyed with her was evident because he hadn't come back to see her after breakfast. It was eleven o'clock when she rose from the bed. She wasn't feeling at all well, and it didn't help matters when Mary Chambers came to the room and said that the mistress would be pleased if she would call in and see her before she went for her morning walk.

Was she expected to go for a morning walk? What she should be doing was go down and see the cook and arrange the meals. Part of her training at school had covered the running of a household and she had bought a book on it and so she knew the procedure. But she also knew she wasn't mistress of this house.

When she entered the old lady's room it was to find her in bed but adorned with wig, and paint, and powder, and wearing a different coloured negligee. Her greeting was rather cool. 'Good-morning, my dear. I understand that you have not been down to breakfast?'

'I did not feel hungry, madam, and I was feeling a little tired.'

'Huh! Tired at your age, girl! You should never use that word. I myself have never used it.'

Belle did not answer, but she thought, No, you've likely never done enough work in your life to feel tired. And for a moment she had a picture of Maggie's daily routine. Oh, she longed for Maggie and Freddie. Oh, yes, Freddie.

'You look surly. Why do you look surly?'

'I wasn't aware that I looked surly. Perhaps slightly bored. I have nothing with which to occupy my time. You can't embroider all day, madam, or take walks. I . . . I understood that I should be seeing to the household.'

She thought for a moment that her words were going to cause the old lady to collapse but her voice gave no indication of this when she barked at her, 'Young madam! let me make the situation quite clear. This is my establishment. I order it. I have always ordered it and I shall go on doing so. Do we understand each other?'

'Yes, madam; I think we understand each other very well. But can you advise me what I am to do with my time?'

'Yes, yes, I can advise you what to do with your time, and that is be a good wife to my grandson. Be his companion; and if you are a wise woman you would be entertaining during the daytime and –' She brought herself up from her pillows, leant forward and said, 'And at other times.' And now her voice was a low hiss: 'A wife's duty is adaptation and sublimation of self. These are the qualities that a wise wife aims at in marriage, and they are necessary for a successful marriage. Do I make myself clear?'

'Perfectly clear, madam, perfectly clear. And do I also make myself clear, madam, when I say I did not enter marriage to become an entertainer, nor a being who practises sublimation of self.'

They were glaring at each other, Belle in pure anger, Mrs Birkstead in sheer amazement and indignation.

'Get out! Leave me, girl! And don't come near me again until I send for you. Do you hear?'

She was half-way across the room when she turned and said, 'I hear, madam, I hear.'

As she pulled open the door Sarah Cummings

nearly fell forward into the room, and the woman's face was stretched, her eyes were wide, her mouth was open. But if Belle had had time to think and describe the expression she would have put the term 'glee' to it.

On the landing she wavered whether to go back to her room or down to the kitchen and say to Mrs Welch, the cook, 'What are we having for dinner today, Mrs Welch?' Then follow it up with, 'I don't like that. Serve it to madam; but we will have so and so, and so and so.'

But she went to her room, and there, going to the window, she beat her fists against the wooden stanchion. Adaptation and sublimation. She knew exactly the meaning of that old woman's words. Well, she couldn't adapt and she wasn't going to submit, not to things that had happened last night. That wasn't love, she was sure of it. She had known what to expect from marriage and had longed for it. Yes, yes, she had longed for it, but not for what was happening. Oh no, no. Oh, if she could only go across and talk to . . . Who could she talk to? She couldn't talk to Freddie about this. No; but she could talk to Jinny. Oh yes, she could talk to Jinny; even more so than she could have talked to Maggie about this: Jinny had been married; Jinny had a large family: she was an understanding woman; she would tell her if she was right or wrong in her attitude towards her husband.

It came to her that she couldn't go across the water because she hadn't any money with her. Maggie made her an allowance all the years she was at school. And from the time she had come home she had given her one pound a month to spend on trifles; and, too, she had only to ask if she wanted more. Nor had she ever had to buy anything for herself in the way of clothes.

387

But now Marcel hadn't even mentioned a dress allowance. She had thought about it yesterday when they were in Newcastle because there were one or two things she had seen in the shops that she would like to have purchased. So she had made up her mind that she was going to put it to him.

She thought it must be miles from here to the ferry, and then she would have to hire a boat to get across the river. But what was she thinking about? Even if she could get over there alone he would certainly follow her and raise a scene; and oh, she didn't want that. She didn't want to have to prove to Freddie that he was right.

She swung round from the window. Had Freddie been right? Had his instincts been more clear than her own reasoning? She must get outside and walk. Not horse-riding. Oh no, she didn't like horse-riding and never would.

She walked for an hour or more, and when she returned to the house he was waiting for her. She was crossing the hall towards the stairs when he appeared and beckoned her imperiously towards him. And she followed him down the corridor and into the library, where he had a desk and did whatever business he might have to do.

He was well into the room when he turned to her and said, 'You have upset Grandmama.'

'Your grandmama upset me.'

'Can't you understand' – he took two steps towards her but halted – 'she is an old lady; and, what is more, she is a grand lady, and she has run her own establishments since before she was your age and is not used to being contradicted and bullied.'

'Nor am I used to being bullied. Her manner towards me was outrageous.'

'Look . . . look, Belle' – his voice had dropped back

into his throat and each word was weighed now –
'she is in a position to be as outrageous as she likes.
You are not. It is a wonder she has received you into
this house at all, let me tell you. It was only my
affection for you and her affection for me that
outweighed her first judgement, so, as long as you
are in this house . . . and you are going to be a long
time in this house, Belle, you will be subservient to
her. *You* understand?'

She understood. Fearfully she understood. But she
cried out against it, saying, 'I shan't! As your wife I
demand my rights.'

'*Demand. Demand.*' His tone was scornful. 'You
can demand nothing. Anyway, what are you? You
are a bastard. You realise that? You are a bastard . . . Oh my God!' He put his hand to his head and
flung round from her. 'You're upsetting me.' As
quickly as he had turned from her he was facing her
again, once more his hands outstretched: 'I'm sorry.
I'm sorry. But you make me say these things; and
you never exasperated me like this before, you were
so docile.'

'I have never been docile. I'm not a docile person.'

'Well, you were different when you were over
there. You have changed.'

'Me! changed? Have you seen yourself?'

A silence came between them; it fell like a heavy
veil over them, and it seemed to emanate from his
face. It was a figure of speech to say a person had a
dark expression, but she saw that her husband's
countenance was definitely dark. Yet there was a
white line circling his mouth. For a moment his face
appeared like that of a dark devil. Then he was gone
from her, the heavy mahogany door crashing behind
him.

She literally groped her way to his desk and

389

dropped into the swivel chair. Then, putting her forearms on the big leather blotting-pad, she was about to drop her face onto her hands when the movement of the chair caused her elbow to slip on the pad and knock against the brass inkstand and cause it to slide an inch or so on the polished surface.

The well must have been freshly filled for some of the ink slopped onto the desk. So, grabbing at a small rocker blotter, she dabbed at the spilt ink; but this wasn't quite enough to sop it all up.

Quickly but carefully now, she lifted a sheet of blotting-paper from the slots in the pad and used one edge to deal with the few remaining drops. This done, she was about to replace it when she noticed that there were at least two more sheets beneath, this to form a softer base on which to write; she did this with her own writing pad. Her hand paused and she put her head to one side as part of a name caught her eye on the lower blotter. It was, naturally, back to front but EVAR stood out in a large scrawling hand, then a squiggle, and the letters GSUM were quite plain.

Marcel had only ever written her one letter and the writing was small and neat. When he signed his name in the register his signature had been small; and the letter he had written to Aunt Maggie had been in a small hand. But of course, you would change your style of writing when you wrote an anonymous letter, wouldn't you?

She stared at the letters; then turning her head sharply, she looked back down the room before she pulled out the blotter, folded it in four, and pushed it into the pocket of her dust-coat. Then, her whole body shivering as if from ague, she made her way back upstairs to her room. But she did not open up the blotter and look at it right away; she hung her coat in the wardrobe, went out of the room again and along the corridor and onto the gallery that over-looked the stable yard. And there he was, mounted, ready for a gallop. Hurrying back to her room again, she now took the blotter from her pocket, smoothed it out, then held it up to the mirror. And there she saw the word 'Musgrave', and before that she could make out the word 'Frederick', although it had other words blotted over it. Further up the blotter she made out the word, 'Information', then what she took to be 'authentic statement'.

Of a sudden she dropped the blotter onto the dressing-table and, turning from it, she began to pace the length of the room. How right Freddie had been. How right Maggie had been. And how mad she had been. What had she done? What kind of a man had she married? One minute like a child, the next like a fiend. And those letters to the police. He had wanted Freddie out of the way. She must get across to Fred-die. She must go home. But she hadn't any money. It seemed impossible, but she hadn't any money. And she had no one to ask. That nice maid, Mary. Yes, yes, that's whom she would ask. She rushed now to the dressing-table, grabbed up the blotter, folded it into a small square, and put it in the bottom of her dressing-case. And her hand was actually on the knob of the door when she heard her husband's voice from the far end of the corridor, calling 'Grant! Grant!'

She was standing at the window looking out when the door opened and immediately his voice came at her, saying, 'You're coming riding.'

She turned slowly and looked at him. 'I am not up to riding. I don't feel at all well. What is more I don't like riding.'

'You're coming riding.' He was striding towards her. 'Do you want me to drag you out?'

'Don't you dare!' She pressed herself back against the stanchion of the window.

'Don't dare what? Tell me what I mustn't dare now. You have two choices: one, to come quietly downstairs and get on the horse, or, I drag you down by the scruff of the neck.'

She watched him straighten himself up, push his shoulders back and say, 'Do you know who I am, or don't you know who I am? I'm somebody who must be obeyed. I am your husband. Now I shall count five, just five, in which time you will make up your mind.'

'Oh dear God! Dear Father in Heaven!' She found she was praying. At school, when she had been forced to attend certain services it had been, 'Dear Father, keep me a good girl. Don't let me hate Miss Rington. Oh, please Father, let me finish school this year. Persuade Aunt Maggie not to send me back.' But now she was beseeching Him: 'Oh, Lord, help me. Help me.'

Slowly she walked past her husband to the wardrobe, and there she took down a coat and a form of bonnet with straps which she could tie under her chin, and with trembling hands put them on. Then, still without looking at him directly, she went before him out of the room, across the landing, down the stairs, through the hall and into the lobby, and so out onto the drive where the breeze cooled the sweat that was running down both sides of her face; in fact, her body was running with sweat bred by her fear.

It was Billy Martin the groom who helped her up into the saddle and put her foot into the stirrup before leading her horse forward until it was level with her husband's mount. Then at a word from him the horses moved forward and they walked down the drive and onto a bridle-path. They walked thus for

392

almost a quarter of an hour, and he hadn't spoken. Now he said, 'Trot!' and when he put his horse into a trot hers followed.

He led the way through a narrow gap in a hedge and there, before them, was a wide hilly field, and perhaps because the horses were used to a routine once in the field they began to gallop.

She didn't cry out, but she hung on for dear life to the front of the saddle and was amazed when they reached the brow of the hill that she was still on the horse's back.

And apparently he was amazed too, for he said, 'See what you can do when you try? Now if you do that every day for the next month you'll be a horsewoman.'

She made no response; and again they were trotting. When the horses went into another gallop she still hung on.

They must have been out almost two hours, and when they returned to the yard she actually fell into the groom's arms when he went to assist her out of the saddle. And she had to lean on his arm for support for a moment before she could make her hips move.

She did not know how she managed the stairs, and her husband offered her no assistance; in fact he went before her and straight into his dressing-room where his man was waiting for him with a hot tub ready as if he had timed his return.

In her own room, she made straight for the bed feeling she must collapse onto it when Mary Chambers appeared at the dressing-room door. Her sleeves were rolled up and she had a large towel over an arm and, her voice different, she said, 'When you were so long out, madam, I . . . we thought you might like a warm tub. It is ready at your pleasure.'

Instead of throwing herself on the bed face forward, she slowly lowered herself down and, holding on to the bottom draped rail, she let out a long slow breath, then said, 'Thank you, Mary. That will be very welcome.'

A few minutes later, when she was partly undressed, Mary said, 'You could sit in with your pantaloons and your camisole, madam, and I could massage your back.'

'That . . . that is very kind of you, Mary, but . . . but I can manage.'

The maid looked at her pityingly for a moment; then turning away, she said, 'I hate horses, smelly things.'

As Belle lowered herself into the long zinc bath she said almost aloud, 'I don't hate horses . . . it isn't horses I hate.'

She had made herself go down to dinner where she hardly touched any plate that was put before her. The first was a clear soup. She took three spoonfuls of it. Next, there followed rolled sole in sauce. She nibbled at this. But when there was placed before her a plate on which a small complete bird with a white frill around its stumped neck sat as if deep in a nest of varied vegetables, she felt she would vomit. She didn't know whether it was pigeon, grouse, pheasant, or wild fowl. She only knew she was disgusted by the sight of it and so pushed her plate away. But she had hardly done so when her husband startled even Benedict, who was pouring him wine, by bawling, 'What is it woman! Not to your taste?'

She glanced from Benedict who was now approaching her, to Linda Everton who was at the sideboard and whose duty it was to help Benedict in the dining-room, and the woman had turned and

394

was looking at her. And when she forced herself to say, 'I am not at all hungry,' Linda hurried to the table and removed the plate, only to hear her master command, 'Put that back!'

The maid put the plate back and retreated to the sideboard. And now Marcel was yelling at Benedict, 'Inform the cook that my wife doesn't like her cooking. It's inferior stuff, not what she's been used to across the water.'

She didn't recognise her own voice for it was loud and harsh as she cried down the table, 'Sir! Please conduct yourself.'

It was hard to say who was the most startled in the room. Then, a most surprising thing happened. She watched her husband slowly rise from the table and as slowly walk down the dining-room and go out.

Benedict was now pouring wine into her glass and in a low voice he said, 'The master is not well at the moment, madam. It will pass. Do try to eat a little. The pudding is light; it's sponge.'

'No thank you, Benedict. I want nothing more; but . . . I will drink a little wine.'

She wasn't fond of wine, but she drained the glass, telling herself she must be fortified in some way to help her through this day, for tomorrow, by whatever means, she would be gone. Oh yes, she was determined on that. As soon as he should leave the house, and a day never passed, she imagined, but he rode his horse, she would go, even if she had to walk all the way to the boat landing and then beg a keelman to take her across. She was sure most of them would know her, for had she not just recently made news in the newspapers.

The meal over, she did not return upstairs because she was afraid to be alone in her room with him; instead, she went to the drawing-room where she took up her embroidery frame and forced herself to sew.

For two hours she sat, and no one came near her, except Benedict who came in to see to the fire. But he himself did not build it up, he called Mary Chambers to bring in more coal and to blaze it with the ornamental blazer.

She had been expecting a summons from the lady of the house but none had come. Supper was to be at seven-thirty, and so, some time before, she went upstairs, washed her hands and face, changed her dress, as was the custom, and returned downstairs to find herself the only one in the dining-room.

The supper consisted of hot broth, followed by a soufflé and a choice of cold meats, cold pie and cheeses.

As Benedict placed the broth before her, he said quietly, 'The master asks to be excused. He is eating with the mistress tonight.'

She inclined her head towards him; then, as much to please him and the cook, she endeavoured to eat some of the meal; and she found it easier, with her husband being absent from the table.

It was half-past eight when she went up to her bedroom. The lamps were lit all over the house. She should have been saying to herself, 'Doesn't it look beautiful,' but the whole place was now appearing to her like a decorated cage from which she knew she must escape, or her reason, too, would become affected. . . .

Was his reason affected, or was his change of character just temper, like that of a spoilt child? And he had been a spoilt child. She knew that now. That old woman must have indulged him from the day he came into her care.

What she did when she reached her bedroom, and

made sure by listening that he was not in his dressing-room, was to put a few of her valuables she had brought with her into the dressing-case. On top of these she placed a dress and some underwear, for that was all the case would hold. But she did not get undressed, for she did not want to take her things off and get into that bed; she would not be able to tolerate a repeat of last night.

So it was that she was still fully dressed at half-past nine when he entered the bedroom from his dressing-room. She had heard him there for the last quarter of an hour or more, and so she had sat near the side table where the lamp was and pretended to read.

He did not speak immediately he entered the room, but he stared at her till she raised her eyes and met his hard gaze.

'You are not undressed.'

'I . . . I don't feel tired.'

'It is time for bed . . . I am ready for bed' – he swept his hand down his dressing-gown – 'so, undress.'

She rose from the chair, slowly laid the book by the side of the lamp, then looking at him and in a quiet, even placating, tone, she said, 'I was unwell this morning; the horse ride did not help. I . . . I would feel obliged if you would allow me to sleep alone tonight. There is the couch in your bedroom . . .'

So quickly did his hand come out and grab the front of her dress that she had no time to step back from him. And now he was actually shaking her as he said, 'You telling me where to sleep! My wife telling me to get out of my own bed! We have scarcely been married a number of days. Get those clothes off, woman!' The last words were uttered as he thrust her back towards the bed, and as she fell onto her elbow she turned and cried at him, 'No! no! I won't.'

What happened next brought a loud cry from her,

for he was actually tearing her dress from the neck downwards, ripping it from her body. It was belted at the waist, and he wrenched the buckle away from the band, and all the while she cried at him, 'Stop it! Don't! Leave me be! Please! Please!'

She was swung round and thrown on her face. And now he was ripping the laces from the back of her corsets, and when she kicked out backwards he brought the side of his hand across the back of her knees and caused her to bury her face into the bedcover as she screamed.

By the time he had her naked she was too exhausted to resist him further, but not too exhausted to cry at him, 'You're a fiend! I am leaving you. I am going home to Freddie tomorrow.'

When his fists caught her one after the other between the eyes she screamed and fell back onto the bed. And then he was gone. She knew he had rushed from the room, but before she could pull herself upwards he was back standing over her, something in his hand, and through her blurred and tear-filled vision, she recognised that he was holding a razor strop. Freddie had one like that; it hung on a hook to the side of the fireplace and there was a little mirror above it. She could see him stropping the razor backwards and forwards; then his name was shouted down into her face, 'Freddie! Freddie! You are going back to Freddie, are you? Not if I know it, madam, you're not. *Never. Never.* Do you hear me? I'll kill you first. You're a slut. That's what you are, a slut.' When the strop caught her across her breast her screams mingled with his yelling: 'Freddie! Freddie! Lusting after you and you throwing yourself at him. Don't want to take your clothes off for your husband? But what did you take off for him?' Again the strop descended; and now she flung herself onto

398

her face and went to crawl over the bed, but one hand came on her neck almost pressing her face into the counterpane so that she could hardly breathe. But when a lash caught her across the shoulders her body jerked and she let out a higher scream and then another and another as the leather strop or the buckle tore at her flesh.

She wasn't aware that the door had opened and that Mary Chambers now stood on the landing, herself yelling, nor was she aware of Benedict and Alan Grant pulling the man from the bed and of Grant shouting, 'Go get Billy and Roy!' Nor was she aware of the struggle that went on on the floor, when Benedict was knocked onto his back and Alan Grant was almost being overpowered, until he took his fist and landed it on his master's jaw.

Commotion followed commotion. At one time the room seemed to be full of people; then of a sudden everything went quiet. . . .

It seemed that everything had been quiet for a long time. She was in bed now, lying on her side, and there were voices about her, murmuring. One said, 'My God! When she comes to she'll be in agony. I've never known him go on like this.'

Another voice said, 'Oh, he went for a stable lad once, nearly did for him, all because the lad hadn't strapped the saddle tight or something. He shouldn't have come back last week. The mistress told him; but at times it's no good talkin' to him. Now she'll be upset again because it won't be just a week or two this time.'

'How long has he ever gone without having to go to Harrogate?'

'Oh, six months, nine months, if he keeps off the drugs.'

'I thought he had to keep takin' the stuff?'

'Yes, the white powder, but it's when he goes on to that brown stuff; that's the stuff that sends him over the hill.'

'Well, why does he take it?'

'Don't ask me. . . . She's groanin', poor lass. Hand me that other bowl of fat.'

'Anyway, the doctor'll have to pump him full of the horse that bit him to get him away this time. It's funny, isn't it, other times he goes on his own when he knows he's got a spasm comin' on. I'm sorry for him in a way.'

'My God! I'm not. I'm not sorry for any man who can do this to a bit lass, and them not married for five minutes. You know what?' The voice dropped to a whisper: 'I blame the mistress. She shouldn't have allowed it to happen. She knows what happens when he gets excited or anyone thwarts him.'

'Shut up, Mary, and keep your tongue quiet. You know what happened to the last one that opened her mouth here, she got short shrift. And it's a good place: we do our work, we mind our own business, and let them get on with their lives, such as they are. Turn her over.'

'How do you feel now, madam?'

She slowly opened her eyes and looked into Mary Chambers's face, but she could give her no answer. How did she feel? What was it like to feel you were in hell and your body was being consumed by flames, that the devil himself had set light to you? She must get away. She must.

'Mary.'

'Yes, madam?'

'Lend . . . lend me some money.'

Mary Chambers looked at Linda Everton and whispered, 'She must be ravin' a bit. She asked if I would lend her some money. Now, isn't that laughable.

400

'All right, madam; I'll lend you some money the morrow. All I've got I'll lend you. Go to sleep now.' Mary turned her head away and whispered again to Linda, 'Should we give her a dose of laudanum?'

'Can't see it would do any harm.'

So they gave Belle a dose of laudanum, and she went into a fitful sleep.

The next morning she woke again in hell. When she couldn't open her eyelids fully and her face was so stiff and painful and her whole body burning as if she were in a white-hot furnace, she knew she must be in hell.

'Will you try to drink this, madam? It's just warm, it's some tea.'

As Mary dribbled the tea between her lips Belle moved them painfully and whimpered, 'My . . . my face?'

'Yes, yes, madam; it's a bit of a mess, but it'll go down. Cook's sending up some steaks.'

'Mary.' She caught hold of the maid's hand. 'Where is . . .?'

'Don't worry, madam, don't worry, he's gone. He went early this morning. You'll be all right now. Don't be frightened any more. It was a spasm he was in. He'll be different when he comes back.'

'Mary.'

'Yes, madam?'

'Will y'you loan me some m'money?'

The maid straightened up from the bed and stared down into the distorted features. Her mistress seemed to mean what she said; she was sounding sensible enough now. 'What d'you mean, madam?' she asked.

'Mary, I . . . I have no money of my own. I . . . I want to engage a cab and to p'pay' – she had to swallow and wait before finishing – 'the ferry. I . . . I'm going home.'

'Yes, madam, yes. But just lie still now.'

Eeh! she had thought she had come round but she hadn't, couldn't have. But she talked to her as though she had: 'Me and Linda's goin' to see to your back again. There's nothin' like goose fat for healing – ' she wouldn't say flagellating or flaying, so she said, 'Sores like.'

A moment later when Linda came into the room, Mary said, 'She's still not right in the head; she asked me again to lend her some money.'

'Well, the state she's in it's not surprisin'. She'll likely be like this for days. The mistress is coming along to see her later, so Miss Cummings said.'

'Now I wonder if she'll be on her high horse, or will she be kindly? You never know with her either. You'd think in a way the master was from her side, wouldn't you?'

'Oh no! Her manner is the same as all the grand ladies. Mr Benedict says it's because she's an autocrat, the same as aristocrats you know. But there, I wouldn't have Miss Cummings's job for a pound a week.'

There was a slight 'huh!' before Mary said, 'I wouldn't like to tempt you, Linda. But there, that's the last of that bowl of fat. Eeh! just look at the sight of her legs. He could have done her in.'

'D'you think the mistress will call the doctor?'

'I doubt it. You know what she's like for hushing things up. What is it, dear?' She was now bending over Belle.

'I . . . I must go home. Will . . . will you get my clothes, please?'

'Oh, madam, you couldn't get into your clothes, you're not well enough yet. And . . . and you are home. Well – ' Mary turned and exchanged glances with Linda, and Linda, now looking down at Belle, said softly, 'You'll be all right now, madam. Things'll be all right now.'

They didn't understand. Belle closed her eyes. They thought she was rambling but her mind was clear, so very, very, painfully clear. This wasn't her home and never would be and things would never be all right. Never again would things be all right; well, not until she got into the shelter of Maggie's home and Freddie's protection. Oh, Freddie, Freddie. If only she could be near Freddie. Why hadn't she valued Freddie? But she had, oh yes, she had, but not in the way she should, not in the way he valued her. And it was clear to her now how he valued her. It was clear to her now, too, why he hadn't married May Harper.

When the sheet was drawn up over her body she wanted to cry out against its contact with her seared flesh. What had he done to her body besides abusing it?

The answer came from a faint voice in the middle of the room. It was saying, 'By! he must have laid into her.'

'Well he did; when you think her screams could be heard in the hall and they caused the mistress to interfere by ringing the bell. But she, of course, would have guessed what had happened.'

The voices faded away, the door closed, and she was alone.

When she tried to raise herself from the pillows she let out a low agonised groan of pain, but she persevered and pulled herself up into a sitting position. If she could only walk.

She attempted to swing her legs from the bed, but the effort on her torn flesh was too much and she lay back gasping.

She'd have to wait. But how long? . . .

She did not know what time in the morning it was when she became aware of the tall, scented and perfumed figure standing by the side of the bed. But when she looked up into the face she saw no sympathy or pity there and there was certainly none in the voice that remarked, 'You brought this on yourself, you know that?'

She made no effort to answer.

'When Marcel is handled properly there's not a kinder or more gentle person. You must have exasperated him in some outrageous way. I've been sadly mistaken in you; you're not a pliable person at all. But you will have to learn.'

It was an effort to move her lips, but move them she did, and her own voice sounded to her like a growl now as she said, 'I have no intention of learning, madam. How can one learn anything from a man who acts like a maniac. I have no intention of remaining his wife either; and you will kindly think on that, madam, and, believe me. . . .'

It gave her some satisfaction now as she watched the effect her words were having on the woman for she was clutching the front of her high-necked gown and her voice had a strangled sound as she said, 'Cummings! Cummings!'

Her maid took her arm now and turned her from the bed. And when the door had closed on them Belle lay back on the pillows gasping for breath: as if she had been running a race, her heart was pumping against her ribs.

Once more she pulled herself up into a sitting position. She knew now that definitely she must get away from this place, and soon, because in a way that old lady was as dangerous as her husband and would find ways and means of keeping her here, even going as far as to lock her in her room. Of a sudden she thought of the padded room in which she had spent her early life and from which Freddie had rescued her, and with the thought she brought her legs over the side of the bed. When her feet touched the floor she felt no pain in them; they at least had escaped the strop.

Clinging now to the side of the bed, she made herself walk to the foot of it; then she guided herself across the bottom by stretching painfully over the chaise-longue to its ornamental back to come within a few steps of the dressing-table. With difficulty she managed to take these, but as she lowered herself onto the seat she let out a smothered groan, only for the groan to die away on a gasp as she looked at her reflection in the mirror. The skin around her right eye was almost as black as her hair, and part of the left, too, was deeply discoloured. Her cheeks were puffed out and her mouth was swollen.

After a moment, she drew herself up from the chair and, her face twisting in agony, she now eased off the lawn nightdress that was stuck to her greased body. Then, seemingly unconscious and unashamed of her nakedness, she shuffled into the dressing-room. But here, she could not find the clothes that she had worn the previous day.

Of course, she now told herself, they would have been removed last night. So, opening one of the press drawers, she took out a clean chemise, two waist petticoats and a pair of grey silk stockings. She did not take out any corsets because she knew she would be unable to wear them.

Slowly and painfully she got into the garments, but when she pulled her garters on and they pressed against the weals behind her knees, she closed her eyes tightly, at the same time opening her mouth wide. But no sound was emitted.

In the bedroom again, she took down from the wardrobe a plain-fronted dress that was easy to get into. And she was sitting on the chaise-longue when the door opened and Mary entered.

The maid stood gasping for a moment before hurrying towards her, saying, 'Oh! madam, madam, you shouldn't. How on earth have you got into your clothes? Oh! madam, you're not well enough to be up. Come on.' And she went to help Belle up from the seat, but Belle caught at her hand, saying, 'Mary, close the door. I want to talk to you.'

Mary ran back to the door, closed it, then returned to her. And once again Belle took her hand, and when she said, 'I want to ask you a great favour. You see I have no money of my own, not even any coppers, would you loan me something, four or five shillings?' Mary's mouth became agape, and she said, 'Eeh! madam, I thought you were . . . well, delirious like. But what do you want the money for, may I ask, madam?'

'I want to hire a cab to the landing stage in Shields, then take a sculler or the ferry across to the north side and home.'

'Oh, madam, madam. Eeh! if madam knew, she would. . . .'

'Please, Mary, don't say anything to madam, I beg of you. And . . . and I will return the money twofold. But in the meantime, I will −' She now pointed: 'Would you please hand me my dressing-case?'

When Mary placed the dressing-case on her knee she opened it and from the bottom she took a small gold fob watch and, pressing it into Mary's hand, she said, 'That is for your kindness to me, in any case, during the short time I have been in this house.'

'Eeh! madam, I . . . I can't. Eeh! where would I say I got it? Eeh! madam. No, madam.'

'Take it, Mary. You may not always be in service. But whatever you lend me I promise you I will return it with interest. Have . . . have you got four or five shillings?'

'Yes, madam, yes. But . . . but there's no way to get a cab out here; you would have to send a servant for it. And we never use cabs. There's the coach and the trap.'

'Well, it is certain that I cannot use either of those without being seen and, as yet, I'm unable to walk as far as Harton from where I might hire a cab.' She lay back slowly now against the frame of the couch, and she stared helplessly through her narrowed vision at Mary. Then Mary, casting her eyes quickly towards the door and back to her again, bent close to her, saying, 'Billy Martin the groom's had to go with Mr Grant to take the master to Harrogate, but there's Roy Yarrow. He's taking the store cart into Shields for fodder and stuff this morning; well, in half an hour or so I should say. But, madam . . . would you ride in a cart?'

Belle was sitting upright again and once more holding Mary's hand as she said, 'Oh, Mary, I'd ride in any vehicle, no matter what it was. But . . . but do you think he will agree? Will it cost him his post?'

'He'll agree, madam; he'll do it for me 'cos we're walking out.'

'Oh, I am pleased for you.'

'I'll slip down now, madam, an' see him. But you won't be able to go from the yard; he'll have to pick you up somewhere down the back drive. D'you think you could walk that far? 'Cos you'll have to go on your own; you see, I can be on call any minute.'

'I'll walk that far, Mary. Oh, yes, I'll walk that far.'

'Well, I'll be back in a minute. In the meantime, madam, if you took to walking up and down the room to get your legs flexed sort of 'cos . . . 'cos they're in a state all round the back and you might find it difficult.'

'Don't worry about that, Mary, only go, please, and try and make the arrangements.' . . .

She walked up and down the room gritting her teeth against the agony each step brought her, and by the time Mary returned she had also donned her coat, put on some comfortable shoes, and chosen a bonnet with a large brim in the hope that it would hide some of her disfigurement.

'I've brought you six shillings, madam. If you wouldn't mind giving Roy a shilling when you leave him, I'd be obliged. And . . . and he says he can take you as far as the market place 'cos the corn and hay chandlers' warehouse is just beyond King Street.'

Clutching the six shillings in her hand, Belle looked at Mary and, her voice trembling on the verge of tears, she said, 'I'll . . . I'll never forget you for this, Mary. And if you are ever in need, you and your . . . fiancé, then you must come to me. Will you remember that?'

'I will madam, and thank you. And may I say it would be a pleasure working for someone like you, it would that. One of the conditions of employment here, you know, is to keep your tongue quiet or else you're out without a reference. But now, madam, I'd be on your way. I'll go first and try to stall anybody that might be wanting to come along the landing. I'll keep them chatting until you've made your way down the side staircase, and it's only a few yards from there to where the back drive starts. Goodbye, madam, and good luck.'

'Goodbye, Mary. And oh, I do thank you so much.'

The maid, herself almost in tears now, hurried out; and Belle, picking up the small dressing-case,

408

followed her slowly, eased open the door, glanced along the corridor, then as quickly as her seared flesh would allow she did a shuffling walk to the staircase. But when she went to descend she felt she was going to topple head first down. It was one thing shuffling on the level, but another when she was forced to bend her knees. But she managed.

She paused by the door at the foot of the stairs and drew in a number of breaths. Then again she looked to right and left before stepping out onto the pathway that led to the drive.

She didn't know how far she had walked down the drive, she only knew she couldn't continue for much longer when she heard the sound of a trotting horse, and, turning, there came into view the high-backed cart.

When it drew up at her side Roy Yarrow jumped down and, taking her gently by the arm, led her to the back of the cart, saying, 'I've put some horse blankets in it, madam; you'd be able to sort of . . . well lie down, if you wanted to.'

'Thank you. Thank you, Roy.'

He had to lift her up onto the back of the cart; and when she was settled on the blankets, he took another from the side and, putting it round her, said, 'There now, madam. I'll go as careful as I can, but the side road's rough until we make the village.'

'That will be all right, Roy. I don't mind. And . . . and thank you so much.'

'That's all right, madam. That's all right. And let me say now what I think, madam, an' that is you're doin' the right thing, yes you are, in gettin' away from there. It's a pity you ever came, it is that. Mary's told me quite a bit about you, madam. Are you comfortable?'

'Oh, yes, yes, thank you.'

409

'Well, we'll get goin' then.' He nodded at her, then jumped down from the back of the cart and mounted the front seat again. And so for the second time in her life, she escaped from The Towers.

The first part of the journey she found excruciating, for her torn body registered every bump in the road. But once they reached the village the much smoother swaying of the cart almost lulled her into sleep.

Before they reached the market Roy descended from his high seat and, going round to the back of the cart, he said, 'You all right, madam?'

She nodded, then said quietly, 'Yes, yes, thank you, Roy.'

'I've just thought, madam: seeing as Mr Martin won't be back from Harrogate the night there's nobody back there to check on me, how long I've been, and so I'm gona take you down to the ferry or where you can get a boat across. Which would you like to travel in, the ferry or the sculler?'

'Whatever comes first, Roy. And thank you so much, that will be a great help.'

Again he took his seat and the cart now rumbled over the cobbled road that led down to the water-front. Here he stopped it, and again hurried round to her, saying quickly, 'We're in luck, madam; the ferry's just come in.'

She now eased herself slowly forward from the blankets to the edge of the cart; and there he put his arms under her oxters and gently lifted her onto her feet. But she swayed and leant against him for a moment, and he said, 'Just hang on there near that rail for a minute, will you, madam, till I tie the horse to the post? Then I'll take you down and see you set.'

When, a moment later, he went to take her arm she put her hand out and pressed two shillings

410

towards him, for she realised now that she would still have more than enough to see her across the river.

'Oh, madam, I don't want that. I haven't done this for money.'

'No, I know you haven't, Roy; but I'm so grateful to you and to Mary. I'll never forget either of you. I've . . . I've told Mary.'

'Mary thinks highly of you, madam. From the moment she saw you. Well now, d'you think you can walk to the ferry?'

'Oh, yes, yes.'

She had said, yes, yes, but she found she was hardly able to put one leg before the other. It wasn't only the pain now, it was a great weakness that seemed to be overpowering her.

Not until she was seated did he leave her; but just before taking his departure he bent down, put his lips close to her ear and said, 'Could I say to you, madam, that you should see your solicitor. You've got a case. It's not right. They should have told you.'

She didn't ask, Tell me what? because she knew; but she was feeling so ill now that she could make no response to him, she could only hold out her hand and touch his.

The movement of the small ferry told her that she was on her way home; even so, she wasn't aware when it stopped until a voice said, 'Well, we're here, missis.'

When she lifted her head and looked at the man who was one of the small crew, he said softly, 'Oh! my, my. Come on, lass,' and he helped her to rise from the seat, calling to another man, 'Give me a hand here, will you? this lady's not well.'

She felt herself being lifted bodily onto the quay; then the man was speaking to her again: 'Anybody to meet you, missis?' he asked.

411

She peered at him, but didn't answer. Then one of the passengers took the man aside, saying, 'That's Maggie Hewitt's girl, the one that married and went across the water to live.'

'My God! so it is. I didn't recognise her. Well, this is a to do. Somebody's busted her up and done the job well. Poor lass.' He turned to her again, saying, 'I think you'd better rest on the quay, missis, and somebody'll go and tell Freddie Musgrave. That's where you're makin' for, isn't it?'

She was swaying slightly as she turned to the man who had been a passenger on the ferry: 'Would . . . would you be so kind as to help me to Miss . . . Miss Hewitt's office on the quay?' she asked him.

'Yes, yes; of course I'll do that.' The man took her arm, and slowly now they made their way past interested spectators along the Low Lights, and then there she was entering Maggie's office.

The sight of her brought Andy Stevens up from his desk and caused George Hooper to drop his pen to the floor.

When the man supporting her said, 'The lady is not well, she needs seeing to,' Andy Stevens came forward and, placing a chair, muttered, 'Sit down. Sit down, miss . . . I mean missis. In the name of God! what's happened to you? I better get Mr Musgrave. You, Hooper, go and see if you can find him. He was to see Skipper Hannan along at the fish quay. If he's not there he'll be at the top of the hill seeing what needs doing to that house. Go on. Go on, man.'

Belle told herself she must not fall asleep. She did not put the name faint to the feeling that was overwhelming her, nor did she say she mustn't become unconscious, but she told herself that she

412

must not fall asleep until Freddie came. And when Freddie came she would be able to rest. Freddie would look after her. Oh, Freddie, Freddie.

'What did you say, Mrs Birkstead?'

She wanted to ask for a drink of water but the words wouldn't come. The men were talking over her head; the voices were low, and they went on and on and on. She felt her body falling forward, and then hands staying her and keeping her upright. But the voices went on, until there was the sound of pounding steps on the wooden pavement that ran along the front of the buildings, and then the door burst open. And there he was. She tried to open her eyes to see him but she could only dimly make out his face.

She spoke his name. Twice she said it: 'Freddie. Freddie.' And when his arms went about her she went to sleep.

17

And this sleep seemed to have taken over her life; for three days she floated in and out of it. At times she was aware of gentle hands on her and the familiar voice of Jinny saying, 'Oh, me pet. Oh, me pet.' And that other voice, that beloved voice, talking gently to her, talking her into the sleep again, telling her that never again would he let her go. Saying words to her that she never imagined he would utter . . . not Freddie.

Then there were other voices that impinged upon the sleep: The doctor's voice. Often she heard his voice. And then another strange voice and a word, 'Horrendous'. She hadn't heard that word before; she had read it, but she hadn't heard it spoken. What was 'horrendous'? There was one time she became afraid, because they brought the police into the room and she had done nothing. She tried to tell them that she had only run away.

She came fully to herself one morning when the dawn was breaking. She had always been able to tell this through the chink in the curtains when they weren't pulled closely enough together. Slowly she moved her head and looked to the side of her. There, seated in a chair close to the bed, was Jinny. Her eyes were closed and she was breathing heavily; but all of a sudden she snorted and sat up with a slight jerk, then exclaimed, 'Ah! pet. Ah! pet. You're awake. You're really awake. D'you want a drink, hinny?'

'Yes, please, Jinny.'

'Oh, you look better, lass.' She was bending over her now, stroking the damp hair from her forehead. 'And your face has gone down. Aw, you'll soon be yourself again. Aw, I'll wake him.'

'Oh, no, no, don't please.'

'Oh, he'd want to know you're back along of us again. He's been sitting up night after night, but he was all in. Now lie there still, pet, and I'll get you some tea. Oh my! am I glad to see you lookin' like that.'

How was she looking? She didn't know.

How was she feeling? At the moment she felt nothing, no searing pain, nothing, her body seemed at rest and free. At least, it was until she attempted to turn on her side; and then she let out a low groan for it was as if her skin had turned to stiff hide and was cracking in various places with her movements.

She was lying fully on her side and gasping slightly when Freddie came in. His hair was wet and he was pushing it back from his forehead. It was as if his head had been immersed under the pump. She watched him grab a towel and dry his hands; then he was kneeling by the bed and his fingers were gently stroking her cheek.

'Hello, my dear.'

'Hello, Freddie.'

She could see his Adam's apple bobbing up and down in his throat. 'Feel better?' he said.

'Yes, Freddie, so much better . . . . How long is it since I came home?'

'Four days.'

'Four days!' She looked away from him for a moment; then softly she said, 'It's a wonder I ever reached this side. I was helped by Mary and her young man.'

She was looking at him again. 'I must do . . . do something for them, Freddie.'

'All right. All right. We'll do something for them. Whoever helped you out of there, oh yes, we'll do something for them. But don't talk now. Ma's bringing you a cup of tea; then I want you to go to sleep again.'

'Freddie.'

'Yes, my dear?'

'You . . . you won't let them take me . . . I mean, I can stay with you, can't I? Freddie, I'll never go . . . go back.'

He slipped his arm gently behind her shoulders and, holding her thus and his face close to hers, he said, 'No. That's one thing you can be certain of, you'll never go back. And another thing you can be certain of, my love, is that I'll never leave you ever again. You are here to stay, always . . . . You understand?'

'Oh, Freddie, Freddie. Why . . . why did I do it? Why?'

'Well, you were a young lass, headstrong. You always were, you know.' He smiled at her. 'And it's my fault: I . . . I should have made myself plain long before now about . . . about how I felt for you.'

'Oh, Freddie, Freddie, I wish you had, because . . . because I've always loved you. But . . . but I didn't know which way until recently. And now it's . . . it's too late.'

'Oh no, my dear, my dear, my dear, it's not too late. You are never going back to that man. The witnesses who have seen the state you're in will bear out that you have a case, and a very, very, strong case, to prove that the marriage is at an end. But now, don't distress yourself. Lie back, that's it, and go to sleep. Ah, what am I talking about? Here's Ma with the tea.'

He did not withdraw his arm from about her shoulders, but he took the cup and saucer from his mother with his free hand and held it while she slowly and thankfully drank the tea. Then when the cup was empty and he handed it back to his mother Belle put her hand out towards Jinny, and when it was clasped she said in a small voice, 'You'll never know, Jinny, how glad I am to see you.'

Jinny, deeply touched, now wagged her head, saying, 'Well, the best thing you can do is to prove it an' get back on your feet an' be a nuisance to me runnin' in and out of that kitchen. D'you hear now?' Then she turned abruptly and left the room. And Freddie, touching Belle's face again with his fingers, said, 'She's been sick with worry over you, and those simple words can explain her feelings; but I'll never find words to explain mine the minute I saw you down at that office. I'll never forget my reaction as long as I live, because in that moment I could have really done murder. Oh yes' – he moved his head slowly up and down – 'that isn't an exaggeration. If on that day I could have found him in the house across the water I would have certainly done murder. It was just as well he was away. And that's another thing we'll talk about. I'm going to be away for a day, maybe two, but you have no need to worry. John will be here all the time.'

'John?'

'Yes, my brother John. I've got him and the family in the empty terraced house at the top of the hill. It was a fine little house, if you remember, and I've never seen a happier man. To be able to go and tell the head gardener to tell his mistress that, all right, he would forfeit the three weeks pay owing to him, made him, as he said, feel like a king. They moved their stuff in yesterday, and now he's working for

417

me. And Ma couldn't be happier about it. So he'll be here night and day the time I'm gone.'

'Where are you going?'

'Go to sleep now; we'll talk about that later.'

'Freddie, please.'

'Shh! Be quiet.' He stared down into her discoloured face; then slowly and gently he lowered his head until his mouth hung over hers, and then for the first time he really kissed her firmly but gently. And when her arms went round his neck he withdrew his lips from hers, saying, 'There now, there now, no tears, no tears, not any more. We're together and nothing can part us, nothing or no one. Not any more.'

'Nothing or no one. Not any more . . . . Freddie, he wrote those letters to the police. I found your name on the blotter; and you'll have to go to court again, won't you?'

'Yes; I guessed he did. But now be quiet and go to sleep. That's it, love, go to sleep.'

18

He arrived in Harrogate at twelve-thirty; quickly found an hotel, then ordered a cab to take him to Wellindean Hall.

It was an hour all but five minutes before he heard the cab driver call to someone to open the gates; and then they were bowling up a long winding drive. The cab came to a halt at the foot of a flight of broad stone steps leading to a wide terrace, the masonry of which was looking the worse for wear, with coping stones off here and there.

Bidding the cab driver wait, he crossed the terrace to the heavy closed door and pulled on the bell. It was some little time before the door was opened by a man-servant who seemed to be almost bent double, so stooped were his shoulders; and so frail was he that he was unable to control two bounding dogs who barked and yelped all round Freddie's legs, but in a quite friendly welcoming way.

'Yes, what?'

'I would like to speak to Mr Fuller, please.'

The hand was cupping the ear and the voice was loud as it repeated, 'What?'

Freddie moved nearer the man and in a louder voice said, 'I would like to have a word with Mr Fuller.'

The back endeavoured to straighten itself and the old butler said, 'Colonel's in bed. See nobody. But Mr James, he's here somewhere.'

'Could I have a word with him then?'

'In the stables likely.' He put out his arm and, his hand held at an angle, he pointed it as if the stables were further along the terrace, then added, 'If not there, down at the farm, West Side.'

Freddie gazed at him in silence for a moment before saying, 'Thank you;' then turned to take the direction the hand had indicated to find, when he rounded the corner of the house, he was in the stable yard. He noticed straightaway that this was in parts overgrown with grass, and there seeming to be no one about, he stood in the middle of the yard and shouted, 'Is anyone there?'

And then a head appeared over a horse box, the head of a lad. 'Aye, yes, what's it you want?' he called back.

'I'm looking for Mr Fuller.'

'Oh.' The head disappeared, and Freddie walked across the yard to the box and saw the lad talking to a man who was attending to a horse; in fact, he was on his hunkers rubbing the animal's back leg. Freddie watched him straighten up, then rub his hands down his corduroy breeches before moving towards the half-door, saying in a voice that belied his attire, 'Yes, what can I do for you?'

The voice and the manner both demanded that the person should be addressed as 'sir', but Freddie said simply, 'I would like to have a word with you.'

'What about? I'm busy.'

'It is rather important. I . . . I am young Mrs Birkstead's guardian.'

He watched the man straighten up further and the chin sag just a little, then snap closed as he said to the young boy, 'Keep rubbing in that liniment, Gerry; I'll be back.' Then he pulled open the half-door and saying, 'You'd better come in,' he walked ahead of Freddie towards the house and a door that

420

led into a long dark kitchen where a woman turned from a stove, saying, 'You ready for a bite, Mr James?' But her voice trailed off when she saw that her master wasn't alone and he answered her, 'Hold it, Peggie; I'll have it later.' Then with a jerk of his head, he addressed Freddie again: 'This way,' he said.

After going through what seemed to be a maze of passages, they passed into a hall that appeared as dark and as untidy and dirty as the kitchen had. But when the man pushed open a door, they entered a smallish room which did show a little comfort, if only in a masculine sort of way. A fire was burning low on an open hearth and there were two leather chairs and a long couch which had presumably been used as a bed, and not too long ago, for there, on it, was a pillow and a blanket.

Pointing to one of the chairs, the man said, 'You may as well sit down.' And Freddie sat down; and the man did so, too, but he didn't speak until after he had reached out and taken a pipe from the rack, knocked the doddle out on to the dirty hearth to the side of him, refilled the pipe with shag and lit it from a spill that he had thrust into the low embers. Even then, he drew on the pipe three times before he said, 'So he beat her up?'

Freddie was slightly taken aback, but he said, 'Yes, if you put it like that, he beat her up.'

'Well, she can't blame anybody but herself in the first place, and you, if you are her guardian, for letting the marriage take place. You must have noticed something odd about him, surely. Even when he's normal, he's odd; always has been since she brought him into this house when he was four years old. He was showing signs of it then. My God! the tantrums. Many a time I was for throwing him out of the top window. I'm talking about my aunt, you understand . . . Mrs Birkstead.'

'Yes, I understand.'

'Well, she's to blame in the first place I suppose.' He now leant forward, took the pipe from his mouth and laid it on a stand; then with his forearms on his knees, he leaned forward and looked from Freddie towards the fireplace before he went on, his tone low now, 'The havoc that woman's caused in so many bloody ways. She's brought this house down, you know. Do you know that? You might think your ward's had the rough end of the stick. You know nothing about it. She's lucky: she can get shot of him now; I've heard what he's done to her. We thought we had got rid of him when Aunt took him to Shields, but when he had his spasms, he'd be back here on the doorstep. He knew when they were coming on.' He nodded to Freddie now. 'Father put his foot down and made her send him to Havensford; but it was too late. She hated parting with her own money. And you know she's rotten rich. Birkstead was rolling in it and she got the lot when he broke his neck out hunting. They hadn't been married five minutes. But do you think she'd part with a penny except what she spends on adorning herself and for her own comfort. You wonder why I'm telling you all this, don't you? Well, I'm just putting you in the picture. You've come here to complain, haven't you?'

'I've come here to find out exactly what is wrong with Marcel Birkstead.'

'Oh, that's easily answered. He's mad. He's a maniac. Must have come from his father, the Gallagher man; and look at Aunt Annette, Annette Birkstead. But she's mostly cunning and possessive.' He leant back in the chair now and, picking up his pipe again, he once more drew on it, having to pull hard to get it going now. Then as if to himself he said, 'That a woman could get an old man to sign away his personal fortune in dribs and drabs. That's what she did. I was in India most of the time. My father's been bedridden for years. He came out of the Army shot to pieces. Do you know, if he lives till next year he'll be a hundred. Imagine that! He's lived for more than thirty years in bed . . . and she even ruled him long before he took to bed. They say she looks like a painted gargoyle. Well, she's well in her eighties, too, and with stamina she too could live to a hundred. Her daughter Ellen ran away and got married you know to Gallagher. She nearly went mad because she had reckoned to take her into the aristocracy. Oh, yes.' He was nodding his head briskly as if Freddie had denied the statement. 'But when Ellen died and Gallagher, being the kind he was, couldn't stand his son . . . well, likely he had already witnessed some of the traits in him, it gave her a new aim in life and she became obsessed with the lad and he with her. Weird. Weird.'

He now rose to his feet, saying, 'Can I offer you a drink?'

'No, thank you.'

Freddie too got to his feet. 'What I want to know is, has he been certified?' he said.

'Certified? No. He only has spasms.' He laughed now. 'That's all he has, spasms. At first they were put down to just fits of temper, until he was round about seventeen or eighteen when he had grandiose ideas; he even started up companies here and there. But she put a stop to that. She got the solicitors on the job to state that she could not be held responsible for any debt he incurred and pointed out that he had no money of his own. He was cute enough to learn that lesson. And then she had him put on drugs.

That's when she first contacted the clever Doctor Villiers at Havensford who's supposed to cure by nature. Nature be damned!'

'Couldn't he be certified?'

'Oh, yes; if anyone could stand up to her and get round the doctor and prove that his actions were abnormal. Oh now' – he was wagging his finger at Freddie – 'you might be the very person. You might have a case. Was she really badly knocked about?'

'Yes, really badly, from head to foot.'

The man sighed now and his tone changed and he said, 'Well, I'm really sorry because I understand she was nothing but a chip of a girl. And look, I'll tell you this much.' He took a step nearer to Freddie and in a low voice he said, 'If you were to take this to court I would bear witness for you. Yes . . . yes, I would, and be glad to. But I must admit it wouldn't be through pure altruism; no, because I would see it as a sort of recompense for what that bitch of a woman has done to this place.' He waved his hand as if encompassing the whole estate. Then he added, 'You know something? He still has the nerve to come here, very often after they let him out. Only a few months ago he stood where you are standing now, and when I told him to clear out and not to come back here again, do you know what he said? Oh, he would come back because when I died he would inherit all the entailed property, and the Birkstead money would restore the place. Do you know, I nearly did for him . . . You're sure you wouldn't like a drink?' He looked towards the corner of the room to a table on which were two decanters and some glasses, and he said, 'That's one good thing we've got left, a few bottles in the cellar.'

Freddie nodded as though agreeing with this statement, but said, 'If you'll excuse me I'll be on my way. I've got to get back to Harrogate before nightfall.'

'Well, all I can say is good luck to you. But don't forget, that was a promise I made: if you ever need a witness you have one.'

'Thank you.' For the first time Freddie smiled at the man, and the man smiled back and surprisingly held out his hand, and Freddie shook it. Then the man once again led the way, but to the front door this time; and after opening it he went out to the steps and remained there while Freddie walked down them to the cab; and before entering, Freddie turned and touched his hat to him, and the man raised a hand in salute.

John was tidying the garden near the gate when Freddie arrived back home the next day, and straightaway he enquired of his brother: 'Well, how did it go?'

'All very enlightening, John. It proved at least one thing for me, that the fellow is mad. But now my job will be to find out if that constitutes what they call grounds for divorce.'

'A divorce?'

'Yes, John, a divorce.'

'Difficult things to get, I should imagine.'

'Yes; but not impossible. . . . How is she?'

'Oh, Ma has her propped up in bed, and she's had some broth and beef jelly.'

He left him and hurried into the house, and the first person he saw was Nancy. Her hand outstretched, she came towards him, saying, 'Freddie?'

'Yes, dear. How are you?'

'I'm . . . I'm fine, Freddie; but Belle . . . her poor face and her back. Ma got me to lay my hands on her back, yesterday, and Belle said she found ease.'

'You've got good hands, Nancy, always have had. Where's Ma now?'

'She's in the bedroom.'

He patted her arm, saying, 'Be seein' you.'

'Freddie.' He stopped. 'I've . . . I've got something to tell you, but later on.'

'Be glad to hear it, dear. Be glad to hear it.' He hurried from her, but when he opened the bedroom door he paused for a second. Belle was propped up in bed. If anything she seemed to look worse than when he had last seen her. Her eyes looked to be great lumps in a puffed mass of yellow flesh.

Jinny turned to him, saying, 'He walks in just like that as if he had been down to the fish market. Had a nice time then?'

'Excellent, marvellous holiday.' He slapped her on the buttocks, and as she cried, 'You look out now, lad!' she was smiling at what she would term a form of endearment; and when he said, 'Ma, you know what I want? The strongest cup of tea you can brew,' she answered, 'Well, I'll think about it.' She now patted the side of the bed, smiled at Belle, then went out. But only when the door closed did he bend down and gently kiss the swollen cheeks and then the lips. And she put her arms around his neck but she said nothing.

Pulling up a chair, he asked gently, 'How are you feeling now?'

She drew in a long gasping breath before she answered, 'If I was to speak the truth, Freddie, worse than I did yesterday. I seem to be coming more aware of every inch of my body. And yet you know something? When Nancy put her hands on my back yesterday the pain eased considerably. Do you think she could be what you call a healer?'

'She could, yes, I suppose so. She's gifted in many

426

ways, is Nancy. But dear, listen; I want to ask you something. I want you to do something for me.'

'Anything, Freddie. I would do anything in the world for you that was possible, except' – she smiled wanly – 'get up at the moment.'

'I don't want you to get up, my dear, not for another week, or for as long as you want to lie there, but this is what I want you to do for me. I want you to allow a photographer to come in and take a picture of all your cuts and bruises.'

'You . . . you mean my body, my back and legs and . . .?'

'Yes. He would do it in sections. You would be partly covered up. You see, it's this way, dear. That man is mad. He is a maniac but he is not certified and if you want free from him you've got to have proof that he's unsafe to live with. Now, by the time you're on your feet and the case comes up in court, there'll only be shadows of the weals and scars on your body, and your face will be completely normal by then. But if we can produce photographs of what he did to you and how your body looks even a week after the incident, then this will go a long, long way to proving his insanity or whatever is wrong with him. For I can tell you, my dear, there'll be a great deal of opposition from his grandmother. Oh yes, she'll fight you tooth and claw. But we have one ally, and that's her nephew. Oh, my dear, there's a story. I'll tell you about it later. But I've been to see this man, a Mr James Fuller of Wellindean Hall near Harrogate. That's the place you said the old lady bragged about. Well, you should see it now. And there's one thing certain, James Fuller detests Marcel and has promised to help by standing as a witness if we ever need him. And we're going to need him, aren't we, dear?'

'Oh yes, Freddie. Yet at the back of my mind I have this fear that he could force me back.'

'Not on your life! No one or nothing will get you back there. Now rest your mind easy on that. You know something? I never wanted Maggie's money, I felt guilty at taking it; at least half of it I felt should be yours, now all of it, every penny, can be used to fight this case. But . . . but about the photographer: You'll allow it?'

'Yes. Oh yes, Freddie, anything, anything you say.'

For a moment he felt a great sadness overwhelming him: 'Anything Freddie,' she had said, 'anything you say.' All the sparkle, all the spunk had gone from her. Never a day had passed for years, as a young child and then whenever she was home from school, when she hadn't teased him, contradicted him, or stood up to him. But now, 'Anything, anything you say, Freddie.'

'Why do you look like that, Freddie?'

He smiled at her now and, gently holding her face between his hands, he said, 'I'll never know real happiness again until I hear you cheek me and tell me to shut up, that I'm too big for me boots, and that I'm devoid of taste in all that really matters.'

'Did I act like that?'

'You did, madam.'

'Oh, I'm sorry, Freddie.' She tried to smile and he said, 'Don't be sorry. Don't you ever say to me you're sorry. Do you hear?'

The door opened and Jinny entered. 'I've left your tea in the kitchen,' she said; 'Nancy wants a word with you. And you'd better prepare yourself.'

'Why?'

'Oh, there's goin' to be another addition to the family.'

When his eyes widened and his mouth fell into a slight gape she yelled at him, 'You've got a bad mind, you! She's goin' to marry that customs fella, at least she wants to, but she doesn't want to upset the lot of us.'

'Why should she upset the lot of us by marrying him?'

'Well, you know yourself.'

'I know no such thing, Ma. Anyway, it'll be a step up for her.'

'You know what, Freddie Musgrave, you're gettin' too big for your boots. Something's turned your head.'

He laughed at her now while looking towards the bed and saying, 'Yes, I know; she'll tell you all about it.' Then he went out.

In the kitchen John and Nancy were sitting having a cup of tea, and it was John who said, 'You know what our Nancy here is just tellin' me? She's thinkin' about movin' up to the aristocracy of the town, the enemy's camp, me da would say.'

'Well, you know what I would say' – he put his hand on Nancy's shoulder – 'you couldn't be in a better or safer camp, nor a more respectable one. But I'm glad I'm not still a nipper, else I would have a bad time of it, wouldn't I, lass?'

She laughed, then stood up and, putting her arms around his neck, she kissed him. 'He wants to come and see you,' she said.

'Why see me? It's Da he's got to see.'

'He said he would rather see you.'

'Well, any time tell him. Any time.'

'You know something? It was he who was on the ferry that day. He didn't tell me till last night. It was he who helped Belle to the office.'

'Was it now? Was it now? Well, Nancy, that'll be in his favour. Oh yes, yes.'

'Oh, by the way, Freddie,' John said, 'I forgot to tell you. A young fella, not from this side, well I mean by the sound of him, he said his name was Yarrow, he came askin' to see you. It was around four o'clock or so. I said I didn't know when you'd be back and he said he'd look in later the night. D'you know anybody called Yarrow?'

'Yarrow?' Freddie shook his head.

'Well, he seemed to know you, or Belle, 'cos he called her Mrs Birkstead. And he said something about one of the maids. He kept mumbling. He seemed upset, sort of.'

'Just a minute.' Freddie now went back to the bedroom again, silencing what was going to be a quip from his mother by raising his hand and saying, 'Just a minute.' He bent over Belle and asked softly, 'What was the name of the young fella who brought you in the cart?'

'Roy . . . Roy Yarrow.'

'Ah, that's it. And . . . and the maid?'

'Oh, I told you that was Mary . . . Mary Chambers. They are . . . I think they are close friends.'

'Well, it appears that he's in trouble of some kind because John tells me he called here just recently; but he's coming back. D'you think they were found out and they've got the push?'

'I . . . I shouldn't be at all surprised. But, Freddie, I . . . I promised Mary that if she ever needed a friend she . . . she had to come to me.'

'Well' – he smiled broadly at her – 'your friends are my friends. And I'll see to them both, never fear. Now what did you want to say, Mrs Musgrave?'

'Nothin' important, Mr Musgrave, only to repeat you're gettin' too big for your boots.'

Belle made a queer sound in her throat and her discoloured eyelids closed as she murmured, 'Oh,

Jinny, don't . . . don't make me laugh. I . . . I don't want to laugh. Don't make me laugh, Jinny. Oh! Oh! Freddie.' As the tears sprang from her eyes he put his arms round her and held her, and as the sobs mounted his mother turned away, saying as she made for the door, 'The best thing for her, better than the medicine. It'll wash it away.'

But as he held Belle's shaking body and listened to her gasping breath as the sobs seemed to tear her apart, he wondered at the strangeness of old women's sayings: this tortured crying, the best thing that could have happened. Wash it all away.

He held her till her crying subsided, and he went on holding her, for that's what he wanted to do, hold her for the rest of his life, but legally.

19

During the following days a number of things happened. Roy Yarrow had called again that particular night and told Freddie that both he and Mary had taken lodgings in Shields after being dismissed on the spot. It would appear that Mrs Birkstead hadn't been apprised of Belle's departure until the following day and that she herself had almost had a seizure when hearing of it. Both Mary and Linda had been summoned before her, and when neither of them would speak she ordered their dismissal. It was then that Mary owned up that she was the one. She did this, she said, because Linda had no one belonging to her, whereas she knew that Roy would stand by her. And Roy did stand by her; and he too was dismissed at a minute's notice with no references. Apparently it wasn't so much the fact that they, like John, had to forgo their wages but that they needed a reference to get another position, and their small savings were now exhausted. That was the important thing. And so the next day Roy brought Mary across to an emotional scene between her and Belle, whereupon Freddie, much to his mother's chagrin, engaged Mary as a maid. As Freddie said, his da was always complaining about his mother never being at home and she was always saying she would really have to cut her time down here; so what was she grumbling about? Anyway, Mary was a nice lass who had started her life in the workhouse; and this alone should endear her to her. Didn't she think so? For answer, Jinny had said that one of these days she would tell him what she really thought, and that would be that.

Nevertheless, Mary was happily installed, and Freddie found Roy temporary work doing necessary repairs on the property, until such time as they would build a stable and have, if not a carriage and pair, a horse and trap.

The second thing that occurred was Freddie's receiving a communication commanding him to appear in court in Newcastle in three weeks' time to answer the charge of withholding information all these years.

Then a photographer had come, commissioned as he put it himself, to take very odd photographs, but nevertheless very interesting. And as he could only take small parts of the body at one time it was a very long session, which Belle found tiring. The doctor had happened to call during the process, and after expressing his surprise had nodded his approval. His words were: a very clever move, one which would likely come in useful.

That it seemed the whole town was whispering again they were all well aware, but nothing had appeared in the newspapers, not even in Probes Column, which ferreted out information and, over the past year, had increased twofold the circulation of one particular local paper. Before, it had been known as merely a political stirrer, and, as most people who were wise knew, politics were best left alone; only people with devious minds went in for such things; and if they didn't trouble the country the country wouldn't trouble them, and things would go on smoothly as they had done for hundreds of years. A war here and there, a famine, a few epidemics, and a bright note now and again with news of the Royal Family and the Queen herself and things like the Great Exhibition, which was still talked about, and, of course, there was Barge Day on Holy Thursday on the river. Now that parade would cheer anybody up, for all the towns on the river were turned topsy-turvy with merriment. . . .

The day Belle came downstairs for the first time she wore only her nightdress, a dressing-gown, and a lace shawl, for as yet she could not bear anything close pressed against her skin.

It was just past noon and the sun was shining, and when Jinny guided her through the door into the sitting-room she stopped for a moment, and looking up into Jinny's face, she said, 'I think it's the most beautiful room in the world.'

'What!' said Jinny. 'You still think that way after being in The Towers?'

'Oh' – Belle gave a little shudder – 'that wasn't a home, Jinny; it was an enormous doll's house.' Yes, she nodded to herself, that's what it was, an enormous doll's house. And that old woman was the big doll.

'Well, there's the couch all ready for you; and you know, when his nibs comes in the first thing he'll do is bawl at me and say, "Why did you let her come downstairs? And then he'll come in here as soft as pie and say, "How are you, dear? You're looking better."'

Jinny's mimicry made Belle laugh. And as she sat on the couch she said to Jinny, 'You know your son, Jinny, inside out.'

And surprisingly Jinny answered flatly, 'Oh, no, I don't, lass. No, I don't. There's things that's always gone on in his mind that I couldn't reach to or fathom. He's been different to the rest from the first, sharper you know, thinks ahead. Aye' – she nodded now – 'too much ahead, and it gets him into trouble. But he's got a daft spot that contradicts all the rest of him, if you know what I mean. Like it was with May: how he let himself be caught and hung onto with that one, God knows, 'cos I don't. Except that for all his bawling and his big head he doesn't like hurtin' people.'

'Well, you know, Jinny, you've given an exact picture of yourself.'

'Go on with you, cheeky face. Exact picture of meself, indeed! Huh!' But as she repeated this apparent summing up of her feelings, her expression showed that she was not a little pleased at the compliment. Nevertheless, having to act like Jinny, she turned away, saying, 'I'd better go and see what that one's doin' in the kitchen.'

She was half-way down the room when she turned and said, 'She might be all right with a duster and a mop but she's got a hand like an iron shovel when it comes to pastry.'

'You'll soon alter that, Jinny, and' – Belle paused – 'be nice to her, please. I'm here now because of her, otherwise I know I'd never have made it from that place. And as Mary says, that very afternoon the mistress ordered her to lock me in. I shiver when I think of it, Jinny. So, be nice to her. And she's never had a mother.'

'Oh! Talk about soft soap, go on with you.'

On this Jinny went out and Belle lay back against the cushions and looked about her. It was indeed a beautiful room because it was homely. She never wanted to leave this house. Suddenly she began to pray that nothing would happen to cause her ever to leave it again, and Freddie. She put her fingers to her face. The swelling had gone down but her eyes were still discoloured and her cheeks a muddy yellow

435

colour. The doctor had assured her only this morning that in a week or so's time her colour would be back to normal.

When a shadow passed the window she started, then let out a slow breath. As she did so she saw John pause, look in on her and wave, and she waved back. Yet the sight of him outside didn't bring her a feeling of security; she wanted someone near her; she had this fear of being left alone. She just stayed her hand from going to the little brass bell on the table and bringing in Mary or Jinny again and asking one of them to stay with her until Freddie came in. It was odd, but once Freddie came into the house this fear would be subdued; it seemed not to matter if he wasn't in the same room with her as long as he was somewhere about. . . .

It was just on two o'clock when Freddie came in, and she had to hide both her relief and her anxiety for she wanted to say, 'Where have you been? What's kept you? You weren't in for dinner,' almost like a nagging wife might. What she said was, 'Hello, my dear. Have you had a busy morning?'

'Busy morning.' He sat down on the edge of the couch, her hand tight in his. 'You wouldn't believe it. It must be almost two hours ago when I left to come home when Hooper came dashing after me. You know the cottage that became vacant on the road out and we had it spruced up ready for the people going in tomorrow? You wouldn't believe it, but some of the scum from the lodging-house settled themselves in there, fourteen of them and it's only got two little bedrooms and a sitting-room and a kitchen and the attic in the roof. Four kids, four women, and six men, thieves and vagabonds the lot of them. Anyway, I didn't want to get the polis at them again as the bairns would have landed up in the workhouse and

436

the rest in the House of Correction, where they'll surely land in any case. I threatened to burn them out if they didn't open up – they had barred the doors inside. Now the people can't move in tomorrow. It'll take another couple of days to get rid of the filth they've left. You wouldn't credit it. Animals are cleaner. Anyway, that's today finished, at least the working part. How are you?'

'Feeling much better; so much better when you're here, but. . . .'

'But what?' He took her other hand. 'What's worrying you?'

'Oh, I can't really explain but I seem to be waiting for them to make some move, because they will make some move won't they, Freddie? I feel any minute that there'll be a visit from her solicitor or one of her influential friends. You know, she was always talking about the influential friends, but for the time I was there, I know it wasn't very long, but there never was one caller. And . . . and Marcel only ever had that one friend, Harry Benson; at least, I thought of him as that, not as a guard. I couldn't have known that.'

'Well, my dear, it doesn't matter; they can do nothing further to you. You're not to think about any of them again. Now that's an order from the boss, as Mrs Musgrave would say, that upstart, big-headed individual who happens to be her son.'

'She's a wonderful woman, your mother, Freddie, and you know, you've been very fortunate, you've had two wonderful women in your life.'

'Yes' – he answered her solemnly – 'you're right there. I've had two wonderful women in my life. And you know, I've still got two wonderful women in my life.'

When she looked at him softly, he said, 'But tell

me, how is the second wonderful woman getting on with the new maid?'

'Oh, I think it will work out. I told her not so long ago that Mary needed a mother . . . needed mothering, and I think that touched the right chord. You know, some women are made to do mothering whether they are married or not. But strangely, Maggie wasn't. She was the auntie, but she could have been the sister. She wasn't a mother to you, was she? What was she really to you, Freddie?'

He bowed his head and looked to the side. He couldn't say to her, she was my first love. It was a love that superseded the natural love for my mother or a man's love such as I have for you. It was a love that we both recognised but daren't put a name to, because we didn't know a name that would fit it. And so, looking at her again, he answered simply, saying, 'I can't put a name to the feeling I had for Maggie because I owe all I am to her.'

There was a tap on the door and Mary entered, pushing a trolley on which were set tea things and, on the lower shelf, a standing meat pie cut into slices, bread and butter, scones, and a ginger cake. And when, looking at Belle, she said, 'Will I pour, madam?' Freddie answered her, 'No, I'll see to it, Mary,' and she replied, 'Very good, sir,' dipped her knee and went out.

'What are you laughing at?' Belle now asked softly, as she watched Freddie pouring the tea. And shaking his head he said, 'Sir, madam, and a bobbing knee, it takes some getting used to. She set my breakfast in the dining-room this morning. I wanted to say to her, "Lass, I always have it in the kitchen. And sit yourself down with me." But somehow I knew that would embarrass her. On the other hand though she wasn't a bit embarrassed to sit down with me ma. But then nobody could be embarrassed with me ma.' . . .

The tea over, they chatted and then Freddie said, 'I'm going upstairs to have a good wash and a shave. Now I can no longer do it in the kitchen, that puts me out a bit, you know.' He pulled a face at her. 'This arrangement has its drawbacks.'

As he was about to turn away, she said, 'You don't speak of what you have yet to face in Newcastle,' and he, pausing a moment, said, 'There's a saying, "Sufficient unto the day is the evil thereof."'

'What if things go against you, Freddie? I wouldn't be able to. . . .'

'I'm not going to stand here and listen to that sort of thinking, madam. Nothing is going to go against me. My life has changed, you're in it, so nothing can go wrong.' He smiled at her, then went out.

Fifteen minutes later, as he was putting on Maggie's last present to him, a smoking-jacket, he heard a scream, followed by another. Before the second one had echoed away he was taking the stairs two at a time. But when he burst through the open door and into the sitting-room it was to come to a skidding stop, for there, standing at the head of the couch, a gun in his hand, was Marcel Birkstead.

Freddie stood as if he had suddenly become embalmed, unable to move or speak for a moment, so great was his fear of that gun pointing at Belle's head. Then Birkstead spoke, or growled out, 'I've come for my wife. If she comes with me she may live, if she stays she'll be dead. It's up to you.'

Freddie had to lever his tongue backwards and forwards over the roof of his mouth before he could say, 'If you shoot her, that'll be murder and you'll die too.'

He had hardly finished the word when Birkstead

said, 'Well, there won't just be two of us there'll be three because I'll see that you go before me. Oh, yes, I'll see to that. There are six bullets in this gun; I can afford to miss three times when dealing with you.'

As if staring at a snake, Freddie's eyes were fixed on the gun. Six bullets. He had heard about a revolver that didn't need reloading. A Colt it was called, first used in America. But he imagined it being only a tall tale, a sailor bragging about the wonders of the New World.

The cry came from Belle now: her head was being pushed into the corner of the couch by Birkstead's other hand. 'I'll go, Freddie, I'll go. Just . . . just let me go.'

'You'll not go, not with this madman who should never have been let out of that asylum. . . .'

It seemed for a moment that the world had exploded in the side of Freddie's head. As he staggered he put his hand up to his ear and his hot blood gushed over it. Mingled with the sounds of the explosion there was Belle's scream, and as his right hand moved out for support against the table to his side his fingers touched the cherub.

The cherub was a foot high lead statuette. The fat arms of the boy were extended upwards to support a shallow dish above his head. He had often wondered why Maggie liked it so much because, to his eye, there was no beauty about it; being made of lead, the colour was a dirty grey. And he had recalled the time she had gone for him when he had used it as a door-stop.

It could be that the movement his body made in throwing it saved him from the next bullet which struck the glass cabinet behind him sending glass and china spraying the corner of the room.

The cherub caught Birkstead on the shoulder, and

as his body swayed and the gun dropped from his hand, Freddie leaped over the distance; and then they were grappling together. The blood was spreading into his mouth and almost choking him, but he aimed to get his hands around Birkstead's throat. Birkstead, however, was a strongly built man and his strength was increased with his madness. One moment Freddie was gripping his neck, the next he himself was almost stunned as he hit the wall to the side of the fireplace. But only for a second, for with his fist he caught Birkstead on the chin. The blow seemed to halt him for a moment. Then Freddie was grappling with him again, but with a difference now, for although Birkstead's arms were about him, there was no response from them. But the dead weight of the man brought them both to the floor by the side of the fireplace. And there they lay perfectly still, both now covered in blood.

Belle was moaning, and it was as she dragged herself from the couch that Mary came scampering up the room, crying, 'Oh! madam. Are you all right? Oh my God!' She looked at the two prone figures on the floor, then said, 'Has he . . . has he killed him?' She did not make it clear who had killed whom, but gabbled on, 'Oh dear! When I first saw him I sent Roy for the polis and Mr John. Oh, miss, you'll fall.'

Belle now pushed Mary away and lowered herself painfully onto her knees at the side of Freddie. He was lying with his shoulders on the rim of the steel fender. His head was hanging slightly to one side and the hand of one outstretched arm was cupping Birkstead's shoulder as if in the act of patting it.

'Freddie! Freddie! Please.' Inwardly squirming as she was at the nearness of Birkstead, she went to put her arms about Freddie when he opened his eyes, blinked twice and made an effort to move. His

441

left hand covering his lacerated ear, he made as if to withdraw his other arm from the twisted position in which it was lying. But at this he let out a low groan, and Mary said, 'He's hurt it, miss, his arm. Let's get him round on the mat.' And it was she who now put her sturdy arms around Freddie and eased him, amid his groans, onto the rug. And there, pulling a cushion from the couch, she put it under his head while saying, 'We'd better do something, madam, to try and stop the bleeding.'

Belle had already thought of that for she had taken off her shoulder shawl and formed it into a soft wool pad. And now she gently pressed it onto the lacerated flesh, yet cringed as she did so. Then turning to Mary, she said, 'The little table cloth, bring it here.'

Mary ripped off the fancy cloth from the side table and then, folding it into four, tied it round Freddie's head in an endeavour to keep the pad in place. Another time he would have looked laughable like a child with the toothache.

'Get Ma . . . and John.'

'It's all right, dear, it's all right. Mary's seen to that. Are you . . . you all right?' She knew it was a silly question to ask because he wasn't all right, there was something wrong with his arm. Thinking that she might ease it back by laying it gently across his stomach, she went to do this, but a cry through his clenched teeth checked her and he said, 'Leave it. Leave it.' Then his eyes wide now he looked at the prostrate figure lying against the end of the fender. The cloak that Birkstead had worn was lying in a crumpled heap to the side of him, and the bottom of his face and his white cravat shirt and jacket were saturated with blood.

Following his gaze, Mary said, 'Will I straighten him, sir?'

'No, no, leave him till they come.'

It then seemed to all three of them that no one came for hours. But John was there within ten minutes, the police within fifteen, and Jinny and the doctor arrived almost at the same time.

It was the policeman who, after looking at the position of Birkstead's head, said, 'Better leave him till the doctor comes.'

A minute later, the doctor raised Birkstead's head from the fender, then felt for the beat of his heart. He looked up first at the policeman, then at Freddie who was now seated at the end of the couch, and he said quietly, 'He's dead.' Then he pointed down to the three spikes that protruded from the steel rim. They were of practical use: the middle one was the largest; it was used for holding the two foot steel tongs in place; the other two supported a steel shovel and a hearth brush. The doctor pointed to the middle spike, saying flatly, 'It seems to have penetrated his jugular vein.'

They all became quiet until the policeman appeared about to question Freddie, only to be interrupted by the doctor, saying, 'I'm afraid you'll have to wait for that, constable. I must get this man to the surgery, or most likely to the hospital if we want to save any part of his ear. And then his arm that's apparently broken in more places than one.' And nodding at Freddie now, he said, 'You're a very lucky man, another fraction and that bullet would have done its job.' He pointed down the room now to the wall, saying to the policeman, 'Don't touch anything there. Nor that.' He was now pointing to the gun on the table. 'A lot of people are going to be interested in that, for more reasons than one.'

'What about the body, sir?' The officer was asking now, and the doctor replied, 'Well, that's up your

443

street, isn't it? It'll have to go to the prison mortuary. But your inspector will have to see it first. Then of course you'll have to inform his people. But you, sir,' he addressed Freddie now; 'do you think you're able to make your way to my carriage?'

At the moment Freddie didn't feel he could make his way any place. He wasn't in any pain, not from his ear or his arm, but a great weakness was enveloping him. He was aware that his mother was standing to the side of him and he had a great desire to lay his head against her waist because life seemed to be draining from him and he wanted her sturdy support. He knew that Belle was on the other side of him, but it wasn't to her he put out his hand, but to Jinny. And when she clasped it she said brokenly, 'Oh, lad; you are an unlucky swine, aren't you?'

When they lifted him to his feet and guided him out of the house and down the path and into the doctor's carriage, the words kept repeating in his mind, 'You are an unlucky swine, aren't you?' And just before he passed out altogether on the doctor's table he asked himself why she had said that because he had always been lucky. He supposed it was because no two people saw the same things in the same way.

20

The first day of the inquest was over, and they returned to the house, each and every one slightly bemused at the happenings in the court.

On both sides of the river it had been prophesied a foregone conclusion. The newspapers, too, had been of that opinion. When the incident happened it made front page reporting for two days; it was also the main topic of conversation in every inn and hotel: There he was again, that Freddie Musgrave in the news. And here and there it was recalled that it was odd but he had always been mixed up in shady business right from the time he had been a runner not the size of two penn'orth of copper. Then of course he had got in with Maggie Hewitt, and you couldn't say that Maggie's business was as straight as a die, now could you? She didn't just exchange money for those foreigners on the boats, there was underhand stuff slipping backwards and forwards there, if you asked them. There was that business, too, not five minutes ago, of his being brought up in court and just saved from standing trial for pinching jewels from that Mr Gallagher, then murdering him. He had been cleared at the last minute, oh yes, but only up to a point for he had known all along that Maggie Hewitt had done it. Hadn't he stood and watched her? That was likely why she had sort of befriended him. He had probably blackmailed her in a sort of way because he was always a sharp young 'un.

And so the discussions went on. But what did they think about the day's do?

And yes, that's what they were saying in the sitting-room, each one of them, What did they think about today's do?

Freddie was sitting between his mother and Belle on the couch, and John asked, 'Could a blow to the jaw kill a man as he said? Do you think it could, Freddie?

'Well –' Freddie let out a long sigh before he answered, 'His jaw was broken and the doctor confirmed a blow to a certain point along there could kill a man.'

'But he had shot you beforehand, fully intending to kill you.' Jinny's voice was loud. 'You've only got one ear, lad; you'll always only have one ear. Your man pointed that out and said if he had gone just the slightest fraction further you wouldn't be here now to tell the tale. He meant to kill you, not once but twice. Look what happened to the second bullet. It seems to me daft, it really does.' Her head wagging now, she looked at John, then towards Nancy who was seated at the opposite side of the fire, then went on, 'If the blow had killed him it was in self-defence; so why couldn't they finish the day?'

Freddie put his hand on her knee and patted it slowly as he said, 'Because it's a case, Ma, and that's how justice works, at least so I'm told. My solicitor man said to me, they've got to put up a front, and' – he gave a derisive laugh – 'he was what was known as a gentleman and that old gizzard of a woman is rich and influential.'

'Eeh! I thought I would die when I saw them helping her into the court. She's like nothing I've ever seen before on this earth.' Jinny now leant forward and looked at Belle. 'Does she do up like that every day?'

'Yes, Jinny. Yes, she does, and at night too.'

'My God! It must take her all her time to put the paint on.'

'She doesn't put it on,' said Belle flatly; 'her maid does, and washes her, and dresses her, and practically feeds her. But she is quite capable of doing all those things for herself. She toddled into court today, but the last time I saw her she marched out of the bedroom like a soldier.'

They all looked at Belle now. Her face was as it had been once: the scars on her body had faded and so she felt no pain except in her mind; Birkstead was dead and yet he haunted her: whenever she looked at the hearth she saw him lying there, his eyes wide, staring at her, and the intervening weeks since that night had not erased his presence from her mind. She doubted if time ever would.

Like everyone else, she too thought that the verdict at the inquest would be a foregone conclusion. And it must be, it must. So why were they going to allow his grandmama to speak tomorrow? What evidence could she give; she hadn't been there. And oh, how that woman hated her. When, with Miss Cummings on one side and Mr Grant on the other, they had helped her into the courtroom she had stopped and glared at her. And everyone in that packed place had noticed it.

Freddie squeezed her hand now, saying, 'Look, let's forget about it until the morning at least. What about a drink, eh Ma? and not tea, or cocoa, or coffee.'

Pulling herself up from the couch, Jinny said, 'I hadn't any of those in mind meself.'

John, now bending forward towards Freddie, asked him, 'Who was the pockmarked woman you were talking to?'

'Oh, that was Connie. She used to be one of

447

Gallagher's servants. I told you about them, you know.'

'Aye, but you didn't say that she looked like that. Poor soul.'

Yes, poor soul, but she was a good poor soul. She had said to him, 'Freddie, if you want me, I'll get up on that stand and tell them of the things that he did when he was four, that was before the old dame took him away. There was the instance with the cat and the curling tongs. We had to put the cat down.' And he had answered her, 'Thanks, Connie. If things get into a tight corner, I don't see how they can, but you never know with that lot, I'll be glad to call on you.' She had patted his arm and said, 'You'll be all right, lad. It's a foregone conclusion.'

That saying, 'It's a foregone conclusion'. Everybody was so sure. And he had been, until he had got on that stand today. My God! How that man twisted things. And his voice had been so soft, so kindly, but so insistent in repeating and repeating a simple question: When he was pushed against the wall by the man in question and he had struck out with his fist, what had happened then? Three times he told him what had happened, at least what he thought had happened. He thought that Birkstead had come at him, but then had seemed to fall on him, and they both went down to the floor. And that's all he remembered for some minutes.

But did he think the man in question had collapsed from the blow he had delivered? Or did he think he was about to attack him again?

He didn't know, it all happened so quickly.

But did he struggle any more with the man in question when he fell against him?

No, not as far as he could remember. They both fell, as he said, to the floor. And it must have been he

448

himself had passed out for a moment when his arm snapped. And what was more, he had then added somewhat angrily, he was losing a great deal of blood which must have made him feel weak. In consequence, things weren't clear in his mind.

He had then been reprimanded by the coroner because he had almost bawled at the old girl's barrister, saying, what was clear in his mind was that the man in question, as he was called, was out to kill him. His first bullet had found its target but hadn't finished him, so then he had tried again. Could anything be more clear than that?

When he was almost yelling the last words the coroner had cried, 'You will kindly answer the questions put to you as briefly as possible. You will have time enough later to give a description of your feelings.'

Whose side were these people on? Birkstead had been out to kill him, wasn't it evident to them all? Why were they keeping on? His solicitor had been against his allowing himself to be questioned, saying that the case against him in the first place was too complicated, being that it was suggesting he had arranged the abduction of his ward, Birkstead's wife. So it could be suggested the shooting was instigated by the act of the abduction. This, of course, was what had to be decided: whether Birkstead had died from the blow inflicted by the perpetrator of the abduction or by accidentally falling on a spike on the end of a steel fender.

So what if it was decided that Birkstead had died from the blow he delivered him, and what if they tried to prove that he had a hand in abducting his ward from her husband? Would they exonerate Birkstead for aiming to kill him?

He could give himself no answer because he had

lost faith in justice. And, as his solicitor had pointed out, he still had to face a charge of being an accessory to the murder of Gallagher, which might have been understandable in the boy that he was when he witnessed the act, but not in the man that had withheld this knowledge.

John and Nancy had left the room with their mother, and now he turned to Belle and, putting his arm about her, drew her head on to his shoulder, saying, 'This time tomorrow night it should be all over.'

'What if it isn't, Freddie? I wasn't fearful this morning for the outcome, but now I am.'

'Well, if it isn't, it isn't. That's all about it. I don't think they can hang me nor put me away for life. I don't think they can put me away at all.' He now looked away from her towards the fire and stopped himself from adding, At least that's what I thought this morning, but, like you, I'm not so sure now.

'Freddie. I love you so and I can't bear the thought of. . . .'

'Now be quiet. There's no thoughts to bear on that point, just let's not think about it. I tell you what, I've decided I need a holiday and you certainly do. So, tomorrow night we will sit here and plan where we are going. But of course,' he lifted her chin up towards him, 'that is after . . . the wedding ceremony.'

She drew herself gently from him, but held on to his hand and in a low voice she said, 'It's the first time you have mentioned marriage. You have said you loved me, oh many times, but you have never said we would be married.'

'Well now I'm saying it. I didn't intend to until after all this business was over and you were really free, and me too. Oh yes, and me too. But now I say,

Miss Belle Hewitt, *would* you *like* to be Freddie Musgrave's wife? But mind' – he smiled – 'just if you'd like to be.'

'Freddie. Oh, Freddie don't joke about it. I dream about being Freddie Musgrave's wife. I long to be Freddie Musgrave's wife. And if I can't be Freddie Musgrave's wife I won't be anyone's wife again. Oh, no, never again. But, Freddie, you . . . you won't be getting the girl that I once was. The girl that just a short while ago used to prance around this house, because I know I will never feel young again. I'm not yet twenty, but youth seems to have left me. I feel old inside myself as if in a matter of weeks I had run the whole gamut of life and it had left me empty except for my love for you. But it's a different love, I must tell you this, quite a different love. It's no longer gay, and joyful. . . .'

When the words seemed to stick in her throat he drew her gently into his arms and said, 'I can promise you one thing and you've got to believe me, this feeling will pass. You'll be young and gay again, I'll see to it, and respected and looked up to, I promise you that too. Oh yes, you will, don't shake your head. Once this is over we'll start a new life, a really new life. Just trust me.'

It was two o'clock the following afternoon when those last words of Freddie's returned to Belle's mind and she said to herself, 'You will be respected and looked up to,' because now the court was all ears listening to that dreadful old woman evading the barrister's questions and gabbling on: 'My grandson had a dreadful time with her. He was so patient. But what will a husband do when another man is flaunted to his face. The night he smacked her was because she deliberately bragged about her affection

451

for the fellow Musgrave. That he smacked her face, yes, he admitted to me, but the flagellation, that is all nonsense. She did that to herself. I ask you, a woman who would allow pictures to be taken of her naked body to expose weals is not a proper person. And if she is capable of doing that she is capable, in the mind of any decent person, of preparing herself for those pictures to be taken. She did this in order to blacken my grandson.'

The barrister was looking downwards, the coroner was looking at his desk, that was until the voice, high-pitched now, almost at a scream, rang through the court and denying the frailty of the stance and looks: 'She's killed my beloved boy! He was all I had in the world. She dares to blacken him and say he's of unsound mind. She's a whore, a whore, consorting from a child with her supposed guardian.'

The coroner called, 'Order! Order!' then motioned to her barrister to get rid of his witness. But the witness was now gripping the front rail of the box and was addressing him pointedly: 'You have got to jail him for life, for life. That blow killed my darling grandson. You must do this. You see, I knew your father, I dined with him a number of times. I recall him very well because he never waited for his port. . . .'

She was being helped forcibly out, but still she went on, 'He had it with his meal. Couldn't wait till after dinner. Very odd. Very odd.'

Freddie's solicitor, sitting on the bench to his left, leaned across and said, 'I should imagine it wasn't only from his paternal side that the mania came, if you ask me.'

Two more people were questioned and both by Freddie's barrister. The first was a Mr James Fuller. He was asked his relationship with Mrs Birkstead and her grandson. He was Mrs Birkstead's nephew and thus her grandson's first cousin once removed.

What did he know of the deceased?

What he knew of the deceased caught the whole attention of the court. He went through his association with him from when, at ten years old, his grandmother took him from the ancestral home to live in The Towers, a house situated on the outskirts of South Shields. Then in later years when it was obvious he was about to have one of his spasms his aunt would call upon him to accompany Birkstead to Havensford, which to his mind was a private asylum. Sometimes he would stay for only a week or two, but other times his stay might go into months.

The barrister now asked him if, to his knowledge, Birkstead was ever certified? And the answer was, No; his grandmother did everything in her power to prevent this. He went on to say that he had for some time now washed his hands of both of them and his aunt had engaged a man of good quality to act as a sort of warder while posing as a friend. They lived together in a small house in the city.

The barrister thanked Mr Fuller; then the next man was called. His name, he said, was Malcolm Villiers.

The barrister now said, 'You call yourself a doctor. Are you a doctor?'

'Not in the medical sense of the word. I deal in herbs and natural medicine.'

'Do you own a house that is run as a private asylum?'

'I own a house,' the man said, 'but it is not run as a private asylum, but for guests suffering from nerves.'

The barrister now asked if he kept a record of the number of times guests visited him to be cured of their nerves; and after hesitating, he said he kept such a record.

Then how many times had Mr Marcel Birkstead been on such visits to his house?

He wasn't quite sure.

'Come come. You were asked to have this information ready. How many times, I repeat, did Mr Birkstead visit you?'

'Thirty-two.'

'Thirty-two visits for nerves! Over what period of time?'

'Eleven years.'

'And during any one of these periods did you have to restrain him?'

The man stared down at the barrister; then after a moment he replied, 'Not restrained, just treatment with herbs.'

'What was the longest period he stayed with you?'

'Nine months.'

The barrister now turned from the box and, looking at the coroner and then the jury, he repeated, 'Nine months for treatment with *herbs*.' He then turned to the man again and, smiling gently, said, 'That will be all.' . . .

Freddie had his eyes now fixed on the coroner. He was summing up and if his last words had been, 'I sentence you to ten years imprisonment,' it couldn't have had a greater effect than when he finished, 'I am recommending to the jury that there is no case to answer here and to return a verdict of death by misadventure. You, Frederick Musgrave, acted entirely in self-defence, therefore you can leave this court without any feeling of guilt.'

He rose, the clerks and the usher rose, the court rose, then the family were around him. But he could make no answer to their relieved greetings, not even to Belle, for he felt he could be violently sick at any moment.

In the hallway he was surrounded by reporters and well-wishers. People he didn't know wanted to shake his hand: was he not famous? or infamous? whichever way you looked at it. By! with the way things had gone in there, with that old girl's barrister, he could have been brought up for murder.

His solicitor and barrister managed to extricate him from the crowd and his family and lead him into a small room. And there his solicitor did not congratulate him on the verdict, but reminded him: 'You know, you'll be appearing in Newcastle again in three days' time; and I don't know if things will run so smoothly then for you, because, let me tell you, there are some disappointed officials in that courtroom. They were hoping this was just the beginning of your case. You were fortunate to get Mr Owen.'

Knowing that his man's bill would be large enough already, Freddie chipped him: 'Well, don't tell me you were one of them,' at which the barrister put his head back and laughed: 'It sounded so, didn't it?' he said.

Freddie looked at the man, this important man, the man who had the power to sway a case one way or the other and at this moment he looked so ordinary and sounded so ordinary, more so than the solicitor, and his voice and words were reassuring when he said, 'Don't worry about the other business. They can't do anything. I've learned of all the ins and outs of the case.' He laughed again now, saying, 'By! you've had some experiences, haven't you? Have you ever thought of trying your hand at writing a book?'

'Writing a book? Me? Huh! That'll be the day. All I want, sir, is to get back home and live a quiet life out of the limelight. Oh, aye, out of the limelight. So if you want to read adventures, sir, there's always Mr Dickens or Wilkie Collins, or men like them.'

'You read them?'

'Yes.'Freddie's voice was flat. 'Them and many more.' Then he smiled at the man, saying, 'And I'll keep it at that. But thank you for what you have done, sir.'

The man now leant towards him and in a stage whisper he said, 'Your note of hand will be all the thanks I need; I never do anything for love.'

Freddie now actually laughed a deep, deep laugh. He was a good fellow, he liked him. He now turned to his solicitor, saying, 'Well, see you on Monday, Mr Roland.'

And then he left to go home and start his new life with Belle, for that's what he wanted, all he had ever dreamed about, all that he craved for, a life with Belle, a life with Belle all down the years that were left to him: Belle by his side in the days and enfolded in his arms at night until at death did they part.

THE END

THE SOLACE OF SIN
by Catherine Cookson

As soon as she saw the house on the wild moorlands near Hexham, Constance Stapleton was attracted to it. With her marriage to Jim on the brink of collapse, she had already decided to sell the large flat they shared. And a further visit convinced her that she could live quite happily at Shekinah Hall, despite its isolation and lack of basic amenities. Connie also sensed that the move would initiate the separation from Jim she knew was inevitable, especially now that her son Peter was old enough to go off to university.

Connie was told she must negotiate with Vincent O'Connor if she wanted to buy the house, although his abrupt manner and insistence that the papers must be signed the following day took her by surprise. She was to discover that mystery was a way of life for Vincent and began to rely on him increasingly as she settled into her new routine. However, when shocking revelations about the man with whom she spent so many years came to light, she realised that her life at Shekinah could be under threat . . .

'Dame Catherine has done it again . . . a rattling good story with a satisfying ending, plenty of gritty dialogue, a tricky affair of the heart, and a strong, honourable heroine'
Val Hennessy, *Daily Mail*

0 552 14583 1

THE UPSTART
by Catherine Cookson

Suddenly risen to power and influence, Samuel
Fairbrother, manufacturer and retailer of boots,
shoes and clogs, decided that his new station in life
deserved a more imposing residence, so when a
thirty-four roomed mansion, situated on the
outskirts of Fellburn, became available, he found
himself the owner of a property he saw as a suitable
reward for his newly gained position in the business
community. And that was not all, for with the house
came the butler, Maitland, who at once made plain
his belief that Samuel, far from being the gentleman his predecessor had been, was no more than an
upstart.

So began a clash of wills between master and man,
at which Samuel Fairbrother discovered that he
was at a distinct disadvantage, for Maitland was
well skilled in the art of maintaining his
indispensability. Fairbrother, for his part, was only
too aware that he dare not dispense with Maitland's
services. And so an uneasy truce was declared
between them.

As the years went by and the century turned,
Samuel Fairbrother saw his children, one by one,
leave the big house to make lives of their own – all
except his eldest daughter Janet who, by means of a
legacy, was enabled to shape the destiny of her
father's scattered family and effect the
reconciliation that he thought was impossible.

0 552 14037 9

THE OBSESSION
by Catherine Cookson

Beatrice Steel had always been over-possessive about her family home, Pine Hurst, but since the death of her mother, she has become insufferably dominating, ruling her father, her sisters and the servants with an iron hand. Of course, she constantly has to remind herself, it is her father who actually owns the house, but it is the thought that he might re-marry, thus making another woman mistress of Pine Hurst, that fills her with dread.

Then, unexpectedly, her father dies and when the family gather for the reading of the will, nothing she hears matches her expectations. It is then she realises that her security is threatened and that she must begin to lay plans to protect her position and allow her to enjoy her most prized possession.

0 552 14157 7

THE DESERT CROP
by Catherine Cookson

Money is tight in the farming community around Fellburn in the 1880s, so when Hector Stewart announces to his children that he is to marry wealthy Moira Conelly, who lives in a 'castle' in Ireland, it is his son Daniel who guesses the real reason for the union.

However, Moira has not been entirely honest about her background or finances. She certainly expects to become wealthy, although that depends on the generosity of an aunt whose money she has been promised. She had also assumed she would be marrying into money, but to her surprise finds the Stewart farm anything but gentrified.

Then, some years later when her aunt dies, to Moira's dismay she is not the one to benefit. The effects of this bombshell spread far and wide throughout the Stewart family, now without the means by which the farm could have prospered. Daniel, deprived of an opportunity to better himself, can see no escape, until a family tragedy opens up the way for him to expand his horizons and find the love and happiness he thought unattainable . . .

0 552 14156 9

THE BONDAGE OF LOVE
by Catherine Cookson

The Baileys, Bill and Fiona, live in the Tyneside town of Fellburn where Bill is a successful building contractor. Years ago he had met and married Fiona, a young widow with her own lovable family, to which they had shortly added by adoption the orphaned Mamie. Then, when one of Fiona's children, Willie, acquired a new friend, the wayward Sammy, it was he and his father Davey Love who, by one means or another, were able to make a special contribution to the lives and fortunes of the Bailey family.

Now with Davey dead there would be new challenges to face. It had been agreed that Sammy would live with them – but would this formidable lad with his colourful language fit in as a fully-fledged member of the Bailey family? As for Fiona, it was she who bore the brunt of the arguments and disagreements that were an inevitable part of life in the Bailey household. Whatever life had in store, however, she knew she could always rely on Bill, that rock of a man with a rough tongue but a heart of gold.

The Bondage of Love concludes the long-running saga of Bill Bailey and his family told in *Bill Bailey, Bill Bailey's Lot* and *Bill Bailey's Daughter.*

0 552 14533 5

THE BRANDED MAN
by Catherine Cookson

Fourteen-year-old Marie Anne Lawson, youngest daughter of a prosperous Northumbrian family, had always run when she might have walked, and it was as she was running away from a sight she would rather not have witnessed that she fell, to be discovered by a local man who, because of a disfigurement, was known thereabouts as The Branded Man.

Her mother, with no love and little sympathy, awaited her recovery from injury with impatience, for she had already planned to send her wayward daughter to London, where her Aunt Martha could encourage the child's natural talent for the piano. But Aunt Martha's frosty reception soon caused Marie Anne to wonder if she had exchanged one domination for another. Only the friendship of her aunt's companion, Sara Foggerty, stopped her from plunging into despair – that and the encouragement she received from her music tutor. Why, then, did his sudden disappearance make it necessary for her to return to Northumberland, this time into the care of her grandfather?

0 552 14348 0

THE LADY ON MY LEFT
by Catherine Cookson

Alison Read, orphaned at the age of two, had for some years lived and worked with Paul Aylmer, her appointed guardian. Paul, an experienced antique dealer whose business thrived in the south-coast town of Sealock, had come to rely on Alison, who had quickly learned the trade.

But when he asked her to value the contents of Beacon Ride, a chain of events was set off that led to the exposure of a secret he had for years managed to conceal. As a result, Alison's relationship with Paul came under threat and she knew that only by confronting the situation head-on would her ambitions be realised.

0 552 14569 6

A SELECTION OF OTHER CATHERINE COOKSON TITLES AVAILABLE FROM CORGI BOOKS

THE PRICES SHOWN BELOW WERE CORRECT AT THE TIME OF GOING TO PRESS. HOWEVER TRANSWORLD PUBLISHERS RESERVE THE RIGHT TO SHOW NEW retail PRICES ON COVERS WHICH MAY DIFFER FROM THOSE PREVIOUSLY ADVERTISED IN THE TEXT OR ELSEWHERE.

All Transworld titles are available by post from:

Book Service By Post, P.O. Box 29, Douglas, Isle of Man IM99 1BQ

Credit cards accepted. Please telephone 01624 675137, fax 01624 670923, Internet http://www.bookpost.co.uk or e-mail: bookshop@enterprise.net for details.

Free postage and packing in the UK. Overseas customers allow £1 per book (paperbacks) and £3 per book (hardbacks).